REAR WINDOW

AND OTHER

MURDEROUS TALES

Other Novels by Cornell Woolrich

Cover Charge (1926)
Children of the Ritz (1927)
Times Square (1929)
A Young Man's Heart (1930)
The Time of Her Life (1931)
Manhattan Love Song (1932)
The Bride Wore Black (1940)
The Black Curtain (1941)
Marihuana (1941, originally as by William Irish)
The Black Alibi (1942)
The Black Angel (1943, based on his 1935 story "Murder in Wax")
The Black Path of Fear (1944)
Deadline at Dawn (1944, originally as by William Irish)
Night Has a Thousand Eyes (1945, originally as by George Hopley)
Waltz into Darkness (1947, originally as by William Irish)
Rendezvous in Black (1948)
I Married a Dead Man (1948, originally as by William Irish)
Savage Bride (1950)
Fright (1950, originally as George Hopley)
You'll Never See Me Again (1951)
Strangler's Serenade (1951, originally as by William Irish)
Hotel Room (1958)
Death is My Dancing Partner (1959)
The Doom Stone (1960, previously serialized in *Argosy* 1939)

Woolrich also published over 200 short stories and various novellas.

Praise for Cornell Woolrich

"Along with Raymond Chandler, Cornell Woolrich practically invented the genre of noir."
—Newsday

"Critical sobriety is out of the question so long as this master of terror-in-the-commonplace exerts his spell."
—Anthony Boucher, *The New York Times Book Review*

"Revered by mystery fans, students of film noir, and lovers of hardboiled crime fiction and detective novels, Cornell Woolrich remains almost unknown to the general reading public. His obscurity persists even though his Hollywood pedigree rivals or exceeds that of Cain, Chandler, and Hammett. What Woolrich lacked in literary prestige he made up for in suspense. Nobody was better at it."
—Richard Dooling, from his Introduction to the Modern Library print edition of *Rendezvous in Black*

"He was the greatest writer of suspense fiction that ever lived."
—Francis M. Nevins, Cornell Woolrich Biographer

REAR WINDOW
AND OTHER MURDEROUS TALES

A COLLECTION OF SHORT FICTION
BY CORNELL WOOLRICH

a Villa Romana Book

Published by Villa Romana Books,
a division of Renaissance Literary & Talent
Beverly Hills, California
www.renaissancemgmt.net

Rear Window

The Corpse Next Door

Morning After Murder

Two Murders, One Crime

Dusk to Dawn

Silent as the Grave
Originally published in *Mystery Book Magazine*
Vol. 2 No. 1, November 1945
Copyright © 1945 William H. Wise & Co
Copyright © 1973 JPMorgan Chase Bank, N.A. as
Trustee of the Claire Woolrich Memorial Scholarship
Fund u/w of Cornell Woolrich

Murder at the Automat
Originally published in *Dime Detective*
Vol. 25 No. 1, August 1937
Copyright © 1937 Popular Publications
Copyright © 1964 Popular Publications

Crazy House
Originally published in *Dime Detective*
Vol. 36 No. 3, June 1941
Copyright © 1941 Popular Publications
Copyright © 1968 Popular Publications

New York Blues
Originally published in *Ellery Queen Mystery Magazine*
Vol. 56 No. 6, December 1970
Copyright © 1970 Davis Publications

ISBN: 978-1-950369-61-4

Cover art: Abigail Larson
www.abigaillarson.com

Contents

INTRODUCTION

Murder. It's one of the most unspeakable acts a human can commit. And yet, we are fascinated by it. What motivates a person to kill another? Was it premeditated, or committed in a fit of rage? What happens after such a gruesome crime? Did the murderer flee the scene? Was the carnage covered up, the body hidden, or was it left in plain sight for some innocent soul to stumble upon? And what about the human element? How is a community affected? How do loved ones cope with the trauma? These questions have inspired storytellers for millennia. Today, they spur endless media content: novels, true crime, films, television series, podcasts. But few have treated the topic with the haunting psychological nuance of Cornell Woolrich.

One of the foremost crime and suspense fiction writers of the 20th century, Woolrich takes his readers deep into the disturbed minds of murderers, evoking the roiling rage, anxiety and fear that go hand in hand with the crime and its aftermath. Some of his best writing explores the stories of those surrounding the crime: detectives, witnesses, amateur sleuths, the falsely accused, the bereaved. *The Bride Wore Black,* published in 1940 as the first of his classic *Black Series* of suspense novels, and perhaps his most revered work, made an enormous splash in the genre. When a woman's fiancé is killed on their wedding day, she embarks on a brutal revenge spree, hunting down and killing each man responsible, sending police scrambling to solve the murders before she strikes again. Woolrich's masterstroke is in getting the reader to sympathize with, even root for, the vengeful bride in her murderous pursuits.

In his short stories, of which there are over 200, Woolrich demonstrates his range, giving readers a 360-degree view into this most gruesome human crime. *Rear Window and Other Murderous Tales* collects nine of his best, and seeks to showcase how a master of the crime and suspense genres deals with the psychology of murder from a variety of different perspectives. Whether committing the act, fleeing from it, reeling from it, or investigating it, murder is the unspeakable crime that drives the characters in these nine stories to desperate ends. Many of these tales take place during the Great Depression. As Woolrich surely witnessed, the economic struggles of that era only exacerbated people's worst impulses. In these pages, Woolrich uses it to exacerbate the worst human impulse of all.

The centerpiece of this collection, and its most famous story, is "Rear Window." Woolrich submitted the story to his editor under the title "Murder from a Fixed Viewpoint," which certainly suggests the cloistered voyeurism of the tale. However, *Dime Detective* published it in February 1942 under the title "It Had to be Murder," a much snappier, and perhaps more fitting, title for a pulp magazine. It was only two years later that the story took on its famous "Rear Window" moniker when it appeared under that name in the 1944 fiction collection *After-Dinner Story,* and that's the name that stuck.

Once the story was adapted by Alfred Hitchcock into the classic 1954 film starring James Stewart and Grace Kelly, it became forever inseparable from that name. The film is a marvelous adaptation of the source material. Woolrich's story is wonderfully sparse and claustrophobic, much of the suspense coming from the turmoil inside our protagonist's head. Jeffries is a man alone, a "blank slate," as Francis Nevins, Woolrich's biographer, puts it.[1] The reader is not meant to know of his job, interests or relationships, only that he is immobile in his apartment and suspects his neighbor across the courtyard of murdering his wife. And that's the magic of it. In a feature length film, however, Hitchcock has more room to play, so he gives Jeffries a fuller, richer life. In the film, the character is a storied reporter/photographer, and thus, a professional observer. He has a girlfriend, Lisa, played by Grace Kelly, and a nurse, Stella, played by Thelma Ritter. Through Jeffries' on-screen interactions with these women, Hitchcock masterfully externalizes the internal conflict Jeffries suffers in Woolrich's original pages.

Lisa and Stella are willing participants in Jeffries' paranoia and investigation, talking through the possible motives and mechanics of the murder with him. They take active roles in uncovering clues while Jeffries is relegated to passive spectator. Best of all, Hitchcock's characters wrestle with the ethics of their voyeurism, and in turn, so must the viewer.

But in translating the story to the screen, a few of its best elements are inevitably lost. Woolrich's story is not just claustrophobic because Jeffries' physical situation is claustrophobic, but because the reader only experiences the events of the plot within his obsessive mind. Jeffries is bound to his wheelchair, and we are bound to his thoughts. While he tries to determine whether, and how, his neighbor Lars Thorwald murdered his wife, we are left to determine whether he is right, or if we're reading the paranoid ravings of a madman. This "did he or didn't he" question is what Francis Nevins calls the "oscillation story," a trope Woolrich uses in infinite permutations throughout his writing.[2]

Most fascinating is what Jeffries calls "delayed action." As he peers into the windows of Thorwald's apartment, he senses something amiss about it, something *wrong* with the space itself, and this 'something wrong' spells murder. As the title suggests, it *had* to be murder. This amorphous suspicion plagues him constantly, but he can't quite put his finger on it:

> For two days a sort of formless uneasiness, a disembodied suspicion...had been flitting and volplaning around in my mind, like an insect looking for a landing place. More than once, just as it had been ready to settle, some slight thing, some slight reassuring thing, such as the raising of the shades after they had been down unnaturally long, had been enough to keep it winging aimlessly, prevent it from staying still long enough for me to recognize it.

As he explains, "the rational part of [his] mind was far behind the instinctive, subconscious part." It's his instincts that tell him foul play is afoot, the tortured instincts we as the reader are trapped within, until his rational mind can catch up and provide tangible proof. Once his rational mind does catch up, however, the answers to his suspicions come together in the most satisfying of ways. Though the story's general plot ends in much the same way as the film, the details of the murder itself, and specifically its aftermath as it relates to Jeffries' "delayed action," are quite different in the story, and unsettling enough that any Hitchcock aficionado can appreciate the singularity of the original text.

One of the only other characters in Woolrich's story is Sam, Jeffries' "houseman," who comes each day to help the immobile protagonist with cooking and cleaning. While his race is never explicitly specified, Woolrich's biographer Francis Nevins assumes him to be Black, most likely based on his dialogue. Sam and Jeffries share a friendly, familiar rapport. They even spent time "bumming around on that cabin-cruiser" some time ago, implying an established relationship. But Hitchcock eliminates Sam from his adaptation entirely. It is Sam who bravely embarks on many of the actions given to Lisa in the film, such as sneaking into Thorwald's apartment. Nevins posits that Sam and Jeffries' exchanges are "on a level of genuine equality like no other interaction between people of different races in the entire Woolrich canon." How film audiences in 1954 might have received such an interaction on screen is, sadly, another story.[3]

Another rift between story and film occurred not on the page or screen, but in the United States Supreme Court. Though the 1990 case *Stewart v. Abend* may be little known to fans of both Hitchcock and Woolrich, the effects swept violently through the literary and entertainment industries. According to the Copyright Act of 1909, a work, such as a short story or book, was given two terms of copyright protection: one for 28 years and, following a copyright renewal, another term of 28 years. Woolrich died in 1968, two years before he could have renewed the copyright on the story. He left his estate to a trust at Columbia University via Chase Manhattan Bank, who renewed the copyright to the story in 1969. Chase later transferred their renewal rights to Sheldon Abend, a literary agent.

When *Rear Window* was broadcast on ABC television in

1971, during this "renewal term," Abend sued the owners of the film, Hitchcock and star James Stewart. Though Hitchcock and Stewart had purchased the motion picture rights to the story from Woolrich in 1953 during the original copyright term, Abend argued that the broadcast, which went ahead without Abend's permission during the renewal term, thus infringed on his copyright. The case worked its way through circuit and appeals courts, eventually reaching the Supreme Court, where it was decided in Abend's favor: because the film was broadcast during the renewal term, and because Hitchcock and Stewart did not get permission from Abend to use the underlying work, they did in fact infringe upon Abend's copyright.[4]

This sent shock waves through the entertainment industry. Many films and television shows based upon books or short stories had been produced during those works' original copyright terms. Owners of the films and shows suddenly found that they no longer owned the film or television rights to their own productions if the books or stories those productions were based upon were now in their renewal term. Chaos ensued. Vast sums of money were paid by studios and production companies to the owners of the underlying works so they could continue broadcasting their own productions. The copyright law eventually changed, and any underlying work published after 1978 enjoyed copyright protection for the duration of the author's life plus fifty years. The law changed again with the Sonny Bono Copyright Term Extension Act, which extended copyright protection for the life of the author plus seventy years. Woolrich could never have known the impact his story would have on the very foundations of the literary and entertainment worlds.

"Rear Window" went on to helm a classic collection published first by Ballantine Books in 1984, *Rear Window and Four Short Novels,* and then by Penguin in 1994, *Rear Window and Other Stories,* alongside four other acclaimed Woolrich stories. It appeared in Penguin's *The Cornell Woolrich Omnibus* in 1998, and Centipede Press' 2012 deluxe hardcover collection *Speak to Me of Death,* but all of these versions have gone out of print. For the first time since these releases, "Rear Window" starts readers on a chilling literary journey of murder and mayhem within this brand new collection. The additional eight stories collected here have been unfairly neglected, gathering dust for decades, or completely forgotten since their original magazine or collection publications almost a century ago.

We'd like to extend a special thank you to Francis Nevins, Cornell Woolrich's official biographer, without whom much of the information about this mysterious writer's life and work would be lost to history.

~Jacklyn Saferstein-Hansen, Editor

Rear Window

I DIDN'T KNOW THEIR names. I'd never heard their voices. I didn't even know them by sight, strictly speaking, for their faces were too small to fill in with identifiable features at that distance. Yet I could have constructed a timetable of their comings and goings, their daily habits and activities. They were the rear-window dwellers around me.

Sure, I suppose it *was* a little bit like prying, could even have been mistaken for the fevered concentration of a Peeping Tom. That wasn't my fault, that wasn't the idea. The idea was, my movements were strictly limited just around this time. I could get from the window to the bed, and from the bed to the window, and that was all. The bay window was about the best feature my rear bedroom had in the warm weather. It was unscreened, so I had to sit with the light out or I would have had every insect in the vicinity in on me. I couldn't sleep, because I was used to getting plenty of exercise. I'd never acquired the habit of reading books to ward off boredom, so I hadn't that to turn to. Well, what should I do, sit there with my eyes tightly shuttered?

Just to pick a few at random: Straight over, and the windows square, there was a young jitter-couple, kids in their teens, only just married. It would have killed them to stay home one night. They were always in such a hurry to go, wherever it was they went, they never remembered to turn out the lights. I don't think it missed once in all the time I was watching. But they never forgot altogether, either. I was to learn to call this delayed action, as you will see. He'd always come skittering madly back in about five minutes, probably from all the way down in the street, and rush around killing the switches. Then fall over something in the dark on his way out. They gave me an inward chuckle, those two.

The next house down, the windows already narrowed a little

with perspective. There was a certain light in that one that always went out each night too. Something about it, it used to make me a little sad. There was a woman living there with her child, a young widow I suppose. I'd see her put the child to bed, and then bend over and kiss her in a wistful sort of way. She'd shade the light off her and sit there painting her eyes and mouth. Then she'd go out. She'd never come back till the night was nearly spent. Once I was still up, and I looked and she was sitting there motionless with her head buried in her arms. Something about it, it used to make me a little sad.

The third one down no longer offered any insight, the windows were just slits like in a medieval battlement, due to foreshortening. That brings us around to the one on the end. In that one, frontal vision came back full-depth again, since it stood at right angles to the rest, my own included, sealing up the inner hollow all these houses backed on. I could see into it, from the rounded projection of my bay window, as freely as into a doll house with its rear wall sliced away. And scaled down to about the same size.

It was a flat building. Unlike all the rest it had been constructed originally as such, not just cut up into furnished rooms. It topped them by two stories and had rear fire escapes, to show for this distinction. But it was old, evidently hadn't shown a profit. It was in the process of being modernized. Instead of clearing the entire building while the work was going on, they were doing it a flat at a time, in order to lose as little rental income as possible. Of the six rearward flats it offered to view, the topmost one had already been completed, but not yet rented. They were working on the fifth-floor one now, disturbing the peace of everyone all up and down the "inside" of the block with their hammering and sawing.

I felt sorry for the couple in the flat below. I used to wonder how they stood it with that bedlam going on above their heads. To make it worse the wife was in chronic poor health, too; I could tell that even at a distance by the listless way she moved about over there, and remained in her bathrobe without dressing.

Sometimes I'd see her sitting by the window, holding her head. I used to wonder why he didn't have a doctor in to look her over, but maybe they couldn't afford it. He seemed to be out of work. Often their bedroom light was on late at night behind the drawn shade, as though she were unwell and he was sitting up with her. And one night in particular he must have had to sit up with her all night, it remained on until nearly daybreak. Not that I sat watching all that time. But the light was still burning at three in the morning, when I finally transferred from chair to bed to see if I could get a little sleep myself. And when I failed to, and hopscotched back again around dawn, it was still peering wanly out behind the tan shade.

Moments later, with the first brightening of day, it suddenly dimmed around the edges of the shade, and then shortly afterward, not that one, but a shade in one of the other rooms—for all of them alike had been down—went up, and I saw him standing there looking out.

He was holding a cigarette in his hand. I couldn't see it, but I could tell it was that by the quick, nervous little jerks with which he kept putting his hand to his mouth, and the haze I saw rising around his head. Worried about her, I guess. I didn't blame him for that. Any husband would have been. She must have only just dropped off to sleep, after night-long suffering. And then in another hour or so, at the most, that sawing of wood and clattering of buckets was going to start in over them again. Well, it wasn't any of my business, I said to myself, but he really ought to get her out of there. If I had an ill wife on my hands. . . .

He was leaning slightly out, maybe an inch past the window frame, carefully scanning the back faces of all the houses abutting on the hollow square that lay before him. You can tell, even at a distance, when a person is looking fixedly. There's something about the way the head is held. And yet his scrutiny wasn't held fixedly to any one point, it was a slow, sweeping one, moving along the houses on the opposite side from me first. When it got to the end of them, I knew it would cross over to my side and come back along there. Before it did, I withdrew several yards inside my room, to let it go safely by. I didn't want him to think I was sitting there prying into his affairs. There was still enough blue night-shade in my room to keep my slight withdrawal from catching his eye.

When I returned to my original position a moment or two later, he was gone. He had raised two more of the shades. The bedroom one was still down. I wondered vaguely why he had given that peculiar, comprehensive, semicircular stare at all the rear windows around him. There wasn't anyone at any of them, at such an hour. It wasn't important, of course. It was just a little oddity, it failed to blend in with his being worried or disturbed about his wife. When you're worried or disturbed, that's an internal preoccupation, you stare vacantly at nothing at all. When you stare around you in a great sweeping arc at windows, that betrays external preoccupation, outward interest. One doesn't quite jibe with the other. To call such a discrepancy trifling is to add to its importance. Only someone like me, stewing in a vacuum of total idleness, would have noticed it at all.

The flat remained lifeless after that, as far as could be judged by its windows. He must have either gone out or gone to bed himself. Three of the shades remained at normal height, the one masking the bedroom remained down. Sam, my day houseman, came in not long after with my eggs and morning paper, and I had that to kill time with for awhile. I stopped thinking about other people's windows and staring at them.

The sun slanted down on one side of the hollow oblong all morning long, then it shifted over to the other side for the afternoon. Then it started to slip off both alike, and it was evening again—another day gone.

The lights started to come on around the quadrangle. Here and there a wall played back, like a sounding board, a snatch of radio program that was coming in too loud. If you listened carefully you could hear an occasional click of dishes mixed in, faint, far off. The chain of little habits that were their lives unreeled themselves. They were all bound in them tighter than the tightest straitjacket any jailer ever devised, though they all thought themselves free. The jitterbugs made their nightly dash for the great open spaces, forgot their lights, he came careening back, thumbed them out, and their place was dark until the early morning hours. The woman put her child to bed, leaned mournfully over its cot, then sat down with heavy despair to redden her mouth.

In the fourth-floor flat at right angles to the long, interior "street" the three shades had remained up, and the fourth shade had remained at full length, all day long. I hadn't been conscious of that because I hadn't particularly been looking at it, or thinking of it, until now. My eyes may have rested on those windows at times, during the day, but my thoughts had been elsewhere. It was only when a light suddenly went up in the end room behind one of the raised shades, which was their kitchen, that I realized that the shades had been untouched like that all day. That also brought something else to my mind that hadn't been in it until now: I hadn't seen the woman all day. I hadn't seen any sign of life within those windows until now.

He'd come in from outside. The entrance was at the opposite side of their kitchen, away from the window. He'd left his hat on, so I knew he'd just come in from the outside.

He didn't remove his hat. As though there was no one there to remove it for any more. Instead, he pushed it farther to the back of his head by pronging a hand to the roots of his hair. That gesture didn't denote removal of perspiration, I knew. To do that a person makes a side-wise sweep—this was up over his forehead. It indicated some sort of harassment or uncertainty. Besides, if he'd been suffering from excess warmth, the first thing he would have done would be to take off his hat altogether.

She didn't come out to greet him. The first link, of the so-strong chain of habits, of custom, that binds us all, had snapped wide open.

She must be so ill she had remained in bed, in the room behind the lowered shade, all day. I watched. He remained where he was, two rooms away from there. Expectancy became surprise, surprise incomprehension. Funny, I thought, that he doesn't go in to her. Or at least go as far as the doorway, look in to see how she is.

Maybe she was asleep, and he didn't want to disturb her. Then immediately: but how can he know for sure that she's asleep, without at least looking in at her? He just came in himself.

He came forward and stood there by the window, as he had at dawn. Sam had carried out my tray quite some time before, and my lights were out. I held my ground, I knew he couldn't see me within the darkness of the bay window. He stood there motionless for several minutes. And now his attitude was the proper one for inner preoccupation. He stood there looking downward at nothing, lost in thought.

He's worried about her, I said to myself, as any man would be. It's the most natural thing in the world. Funny, though, he should leave her in the dark like that, without going near her. If he's worried, then why didn't he at least look in on her on returning? Here was another of those trivial discrepancies, between inward motivation and outward indication. And just as I was thinking that, the original one, that I had noted at daybreak, repeated itself. His head went up with renewed alertness, and I could see it start to give that slow circular sweep of interrogation around the panorama of rearward windows again. True, the light was behind him this time, but there was enough of it falling on him to show me the microscopic but continuous shift of direction his head made in the process. I remained carefully immobile until the distant glance had passed me safely by. Motion attracts.

Why is he so interested in other people's windows, I wondered detachedly. And of course an effective brake to dwell on that thought too lingeringly clamped down almost at once: Look who's talking. What about you yourself?

An important difference escaped me. I wasn't worried about anything. He, presumably, was.

Down came the shades again. The lights stayed on behind their beige opaqueness. But behind the one that had remained down all along, the room remained dark.

Time went by. Hard to say how much—a quarter of an hour,

twenty minutes. A cricket chirped in one of the back yards. Sam came in to see if I wanted anything before he went home for the night. I told him no, I didn't—it was all right, run along. He stood there for a minute, head down. Then I saw him shake it slightly, as if at something he didn't like. "What's the matter?" I asked.

"You know what that means? My old mammy told it to me, and she never told me a lie in her life. I never once seen it to miss, either."

"What, the cricket?"

"Any time you hear one of them things, that's a sign of death—someplace close around."

I swept the back of my hand at him. "Well, it isn't in here, so don't let it worry you."

He went out, muttering stubbornly: "It's somewhere close by, though. Somewhere not very far off. Got to be."

The door closed after him, and I stayed there alone in the dark.

It was a stifling night, much closer than the one before. I could hardly get a breath of air even by the open window at which I sat. I wondered how he—that unknown over there—could stand it behind those drawn shades.

Then suddenly, just as idle speculation about this whole matter was about to alight on some fixed point in my mind, crystallize into something like suspicion, up came the shades again, and off it flitted, as formless as ever and without having had a chance to come to rest on anything.

He was in the middle windows, the living room. He'd taken off his coat and shirt, was bare-armed in his under-shirt. He hadn't been able to stand it himself, I guess—the sultriness.

I couldn't make out what he was doing at first. He seemed to be busy in a perpendicular, up-and-down way rather than lengthwise. He remained in one place, but he kept dipping down out of sight and then straightening up into view again, at irregular intervals. It was almost like some sort of calisthenic exercise, except that the dips and rises weren't evenly timed enough for that. Sometimes he'd stay down a long time, sometimes he'd bob right up again, sometimes he'd go down two or three times in rapid succession. There was some sort of a widespread black V railing him off from the window. Whatever it was, there was just a sliver of it showing above the upward inclination to which the window sill deflected my line of vision. All it did was strike off the bottom of his undershirt, to the extent of a sixteenth of an inch maybe. But I haven't seen it there at other times, and I couldn't tell what it was.

Suddenly he left it for the first time since the shades had gone up, came out around it to the outside, stooped down into another part of the room, and straightened again with an armful of what looked like varicolored pennants at the distance at which I was. He went back behind the V and allowed them to fall across the top of it for a moment, and stay that way. He made one of his dips down out of sight and stayed that way a good while.

The "pennants" slung across the V kept changing color right in front of my eyes. I have very good sight. One moment they were white, the next red, the next blue.

Then I got it. They were a woman's dresses, and he was pulling them down to him one by one, taking the topmost one each time. Suddenly they were all gone, the V was black and bare again, and his torso had reappeared. I knew what it was now, and what he was doing. The dresses had told me. He confirmed it for me. He spread his arms to the ends of the V, I could see him heave and hitch, as if exerting pressure, and suddenly the V had folded up, become a cubed wedge. Then he made rolling motions with his whole upper body, and the wedge disappeared off to one side.

He'd been packing a trunk, packing his wife's things into a large upright trunk.

He reappeared at the kitchen window presently, stood still for a moment. I saw him draw his arm across his forehead, not once but several times, and then whip the end of it off into space. Sure, it was hot work for such a night. Then he reached up along the wall and took something down. Since it was the kitchen he was in, my imagination had to supply a cabinet and a bottle.

I could see the two or three quick passes his hand made to his mouth after that. I said to myself tolerantly: That's what nine men out of ten would do after packing a trunk—take a good stiff drink. And if the tenth didn't, it would only be because he didn't have any liquor at hand.

Then he came closer to the window again, and standing edgewise to the side of it, so that only a thin paring of his head and shoulder showed, peered watchfully out into the dark quadrilateral, along the line of windows, most of them unlighted by now, once more. He always started on the left-hand side, the side opposite mine, and made his circuit of inspection from there on around.

That was the second time in one evening I'd seen him do that. And once at daybreak, made three times altogether. I smiled mentally. You'd almost think he felt guilty about something. It was probably nothing, just an odd little habit, a quirk, that he didn't know he had himself. I had them myself, everyone does.

He withdrew into the room, and it blacked out. His figure passed into the one that was still lighted next to it, the living room. That blacked next. It didn't surprise me that the third room, the bedroom with the drawn shade, didn't light up on his entering there. He wouldn't want to disturb her, of course—particularly if she was going away tomorrow for her health, as his packing of her trunk showed. She needed all the rest she could get, before making the trip. Simple enough for him to slip into bed in the dark.

It did surprise me, though, when a match-flare winked some time later, to have it still come from the darkened living room. He must be lying down in there, trying to sleep on a sofa or something for the night. He hadn't gone near the bedroom at all, was staying out of it altogether. That puzzled me, frankly. That was carrying solicitude almost too far.

Ten minutes or so later, there was another match-wink, still from that same living room window. He couldn't sleep.

The night brooded down on both of us alike, the curiosity-monger in the bay window, the chain-smoker in the fourth-floor flat, without giving any answer. The only sound was that interminable cricket.

I was back at the window again with the first sun of morning. Not because of him. My mattress was like a bed of hot coals. Sam found me there when he came in to get things ready for me. "You're going to be a wreck, Mr. Jeff," was all he said.

First, for awhile, there was no sign of life over there. Then suddenly I saw his head bob up from somewhere down out of sight in the living room, so I knew I'd been right; he'd spent the night on a sofa or easy chair in there. Now, of course, he'd look in at her, to see how she was, find out if she felt any better. That was only common ordinary humanity. He hadn't been near her, so far as I could make out, since two nights before.

He didn't. He dressed, and he went in the opposite direction, into the kitchen, and wolfed something in there, standing up and using both hands. Then he suddenly turned and moved off side, in the direction in which I knew the flat-entrance to be, as if he had just heard some summons, like the doorbell.

Sure enough, in a moment he came back, and there were two men with him in leather aprons. Expressmen. I saw him standing by while they laboriously maneuvered that cubed black wedge out between them, in the direction they'd just come from. He did more than just stand by. He practically hovered over them, kept shifting from side to side, he was so anxious to see that it was done right.

Then he came back alone, and I saw him swipe his arm across his head, as though it was he, not they, who was all heated up from the effort.

So he was forwarding her trunk, to wherever it was she was going. That was all.

He reached up along the wall again and took something down. He was taking another drink. Two. Three. I said to myself, a little at a loss: Yes, but he hasn't just packed a trunk this time. That trunk has been standing packed and ready since last night. Where does the hard work come in? The sweat and the need for a bracer?

Now, at last, after all those hours, he finally did go in to her. I saw his form pass through the living room and go beyond, into the bedroom. Up went the shade, that had been down all this time.

Then he turned his head and looked around behind him. In a certain way, a way that was unmistakable, even from where I was. Not in one certain direction, as one looks at a person. But from side to side, and up and down, and all around, as one looks at—*an empty room.*

He stepped back, bent a little, gave a fling of his arms, and an unoccupied mattress and bedding upended over the foot of a bed, stayed that way, emptily curved. A second one followed a moment later.

She wasn't in there.

They use the expression "delayed action." I found out then what it meant. For two days a sort of formless uneasiness, a disembodied suspicion, I don't know what to call it, had been flitting and volplaning around in my mind, like an insect looking for a landing place. More than once, just as it had been ready to settle, some slight thing, some slight reassuring thing, such as the raising of the shades after they had been down unnaturally long, had been enough to keep it winging aimlessly, prevent it from staying still long enough for me to recognize it. The point of contact had been there all along, waiting to receive it. Now, for some reason, within a split second after he tossed over the empty mattresses, it landed—*zoom!* And the point of contact expanded—or exploded, whatever you care to call it—into a certainty of murder.

In other words, the rational part of my mind was far behind the instinctive, subconscious part. Delayed action. Now the one had caught up to the other. The thought-message that sparked from the synchronization was: He's done something to her!

I looked down and my hand was bunching the goods over my kneecap, it was knotted so tight. I forced it to open. I said to myself, steadyingly: Now wait a minute, be careful, go slow. You've seen nothing. You know nothing. You only have the negative proof that you don't see her any more.

Sam was standing there looking over at me from the pantryway. He said accusingly: "You ain't touched a thing. And your face looks like a sheet."

It felt like one. It had that needling feeling, when the blood has left it involuntarily. It was more to get him out of the way and give myself some elbow room for undisturbed thinking, than anything else, that I said: "Sam, what's the street address of that building down there? Don't stick your head too far out and gape at it."

"Somep'n or other Benedict Avenue." He scratched his neck helpfully.

"I know that. Chase around the corner a minute and get me the exact number on it, will you?"

"Why you want to know that for?" he asked as he turned to go.

"None of your business," I said with the good-natured firmness that was all that was necessary to take care of that once and for all. I called after him just as he was closing the door: "And while you're about it, step into the entrance and see if you can tell from the mailboxes who has the fourth-floor rear. Don't get me the wrong one now. And try not to let anyone catch you at it."

He went out mumbling something that sounded like, "When a man ain't got nothing to do but just sit all day, he sure can think up the blamest things—" The door closed and I settled down to some good constructive thinking.

I said to myself: What are you really building up this monstrous supposition on? Let's see what you've got. Only that there were several little things wrong with the mechanism, the chain-belt, of their recurrent daily habits over there. 1. The lights were on all night the first night. 2. He came in later than usual the second night. 3. He left his hat on. 4. She didn't come out to greet him—she hasn't appeared since the evening before the lights were on all night. 5. He took a drink after he finished packing her trunk. But he took three stiff drinks the next morning, immediately after her trunk went out. 6. He was inwardly disturbed and worried, yet superimposed upon this was an unnatural external concern about the surrounding rear windows that was off-key. 7. He slept in the living room, didn't go near the bedroom, during the night before the departure of the trunk.

Very well. If she had been ill that first night, and he had sent her away for her health, that automatically canceled out points 1, 2, 3, 4. It left points 5 and 6 totally unimportant and unincriminating. But when it came up against 7, I hit a stumbling block.

If she went away immediately after being ill that first night, why didn't he want to sleep in their bedroom *last night?* Sentiment? Hardly. Two perfectly good beds in one room, only a sofa or uncomfortable easy chair in the other. Why should he stay out of there if she was already gone? Just because he missed her, was lonely? A grown man doesn't act that way. All right, then she was still in there.

Sam came back parenthetically at this point and said: "That house is Number 525 Benedict Avenue. The fourth-floor rear, it got the name of Mr. and Mrs. Lars Thorwald up."

"Sh-h," I silenced, and motioned him backhand out of my ken.

"First he wants it, then he don't," he grumbled philosophically, and retired to his duties.

I went ahead digging at it. But if she was still in there, in that bedroom last night, then she couldn't have gone away to the country, because I never saw her leave today. She could have left without my seeing her in the early hours of yesterday morning. I'd missed a few hours, been asleep. But this morning I had been up before he was himself, I only saw his head rear up from the sofa after I'd been at the window for some time.

To go at all she would have had to go yesterday morning. Then why had he left the bedroom shade down, left the mattresses undisturbed, until today? Above all, why had he stayed out of that room last night? That was evidence that she hadn't gone, was still in there. Then today, immediately after the trunk had been dispatched, he went in, pulled up the shade, tossed over the mattresses, and showed that she hadn't been in there. The thing was like a crazy spiral.

No, it wasn't either. *Immediately after the trunk had been dispatched——*

The trunk.

That did it.

I looked around to make sure the door was safely closed between Sam and me. My hand hovered uncertainly over the telephone dial a minute. Boyne, he'd be the one to tell about it. He was on Homicide. He had been, anyway, when I'd last seen him. I didn't want to get a flock of strange dicks and cops into my hair. I didn't want to be involved any more than I had to. Or at all, if possible.

They switched my call to the right place after a couple of wrong tries, and I got him finally.

"Look, Boyne? This is Hal Jeffries——"

"Well, where've you been the last sixty-two years?" he started to enthuse.

"We can take that up later. What I want you to do now is take down a name and address. Ready? Lars Thorwald. Five twenty-five Benedict Avenue. Fourth-floor rear. Got it?"

"Fourth-floor rear. Got it. What's it for?"

"Investigation. I've got a firm belief you'll uncover a murder there if you start digging at it. Don't call on me for anything more than that—just a conviction. There's been a man and wife living there until now. Now there's just the man. Her trunk went out early this morning. If you can find someone who saw *her* leave herself——"

Marshaled aloud like that and conveyed to somebody else, a lieutenant of detectives above all, it did sound flimsy, even to me. He said hesitantly, "Well, but——" Then he accepted it as was. Because I was the source. I even left my window out of it completely. I could do that with him and get away with it because he'd known me years, he didn't question my reliability. I didn't want my room all cluttered up with dicks and cops taking turns nosing out of the window in this hot weather. Let them tackle it from the front.

"Well, we'll see what we see," he said. "I'll keep you posted."

I hung up and sat back to watch and wait events. I had a grandstand seat. Or rather a grandstand seat in reverse. I could only see from behind the scenes, but not from the front. I couldn't watch Boyne go to work. I could only see the results, when and if there were any.

Nothing happened for the next few hours. The police work that I knew must be going on was as invisible as police work should be. The figure in the fourth-floor windows over there remained in sight, alone and undisturbed. He didn't go out. He was restless, roamed from room to room without staying in one place very long, but he stayed in. Once I saw him eating again—sitting down this time—and once he shaved, and once he even tried to read the paper, but he didn't stay with it long.

Little unseen wheels were in motion around him. Small and harmless as yet, preliminaries. If he knew, I wondered to myself, would he remain there quiescent like that, or would he try to bolt out and flee? That mightn't depend so much upon his guilt as upon his sense of immunity, his feeling that he could outwit them. Of his guilt I myself was already convinced, or I wouldn't have taken the step I had.

At three my phone rang. Boyne calling back. "Jeffries? Well, I don't know. Can't you give me a little more than just a bald statement like that?"

"Why?" I fenced. "Why do I have to?"

"I've had a man over there making inquiries. I've just had his report. The building superintendent and several of the neighbors all agree she left for the country, to try and regain her health, early yesterday morning."

"Wait a minute. Did any of them *see* her leave, according to your man?"

"No."

"Then all you've gotten is a second-hand version of an unsupported statement by him. Not an eyewitness account."

"He was met returning from the depot, after he'd bought her ticket and seen her off on the train."

"That's still an unsupported statement, once removed."

"I've sent a man down there to the station to try and check with the ticket agent if possible. After all, he should have been fairly conspicuous at that early hour. And we're keeping him under observation, of course, in the meantime, watching all his movements. The first chance we get we're going to jump in and search the place."

I had a feeling that they wouldn't find anything, even if they did.

"Don't expect anything more from me. I've dropped it in your lap. I've given you all I have to give. A name, an address, and an opinion."

"Yes, and I've always valued your opinion highly before now, Jeff—"

"But now you don't, that it?"

"Not at all. The thing is, we haven't turned up anything that seems to bear out your impression so far."

"You haven't gotten very far along, so far."

He went back to his previous cliché. "Well, we'll see what we see. Let you know later."

Another hour or so went by, and sunset came on. I saw him start to get ready to go out, over there. He put on his hat, put his hand in his pocket and stood still looking at it for a minute. Counting change, I guess. It gave me a peculiar sense of suppressed excitement, knowing they were going to come in the minute he left. I thought grimly, as I saw him take a last look around: If you've got anything to hide, brother, now's the time to hide it.

He left. A breath-holding interval of misleading emptiness descended on the flat. A three-alarm fire couldn't have pulled my eyes off those windows. Suddenly the door by which he had just left parted slightly and two men insinuated themselves, one behind the other. There they were now. They closed it behind them, separated at once, and got busy. One took the bedroom, one the kitchen, and they started to work their way toward one another again from those extremes of the flat. They were thorough. I could see them going over everything from top to bottom. They took the living room together. One cased one side, the other man the other.

They'd already finished before the warning caught them. I

could tell that by the way they straightened up and stood facing one another frustratedly for a minute. Then both their heads turned sharply, as at a tip-off by doorbell that he was coming back. They got out fast.

I wasn't unduly disheartened, I'd expected that. My own feeling all along had been that they wouldn't find anything incriminating around. The trunk had gone.

He came in with a mountainous brown-paper bag sitting in the curve of one arm. I watched him closely to see if he'd discover that someone had been there in his absence. Apparently he didn't. They'd been adroit about it.

He stayed in the rest of the night. Sat tight, safe and sound. He did some desultory drinking, I could see him sitting there by the window and his hand would hoist every once in awhile, but not to excess. Apparently everything was under control, the tension had eased, now that—the trunk was out.

Watching him across the night, I speculated: Why doesn't he get out? If I'm right about him, and I am, why does he stick around—after it? That brought its own answer: Because he doesn't know anyone's on to him yet. He doesn't think there's any hurry. To go too soon, right after she has, would be more dangerous than to stay awhile.

The night wore on. I sat there waiting for Boyne's call. It came later than I thought it would. I picked the phone up in the dark. He was getting ready to go to bed, over there, now. He'd risen from where he'd been sitting drinking in the kitchen, and put the light out. He went into the living room, lit that. He started to pull his shirttail up out of his belt. Boyne's voice was in my ear as my eyes were on him, over there. Three-cornered arrangement.

"Hello, Jeff? Listen, absolutely nothing. We searched the place while he was out——"

I nearly said, "I know you did, I saw it," but checked myself in time.

"—and didn't turn up a thing. But——"He stopped as though this was going to be important. I waited impatiently for him to go ahead.

"Downstairs in his letter box we found a post card waiting for him. We fished it up out of the slot with bent pins——"

"And?"

"And it was from his wife, written only yesterday from some farm up-country. Here's the message we copied: 'Arrived O. K. Already feeling a little better. Love, Anna.'"

I said, faintly but stubbornly: "You say, written only yesterday. Have you proof of that? What was the postmark-date on it?"

He made a disgusted sound down in his tonsils. At me, not it. "The postmark was blurred. A comer of it got wet, and the ink smudged."

"All of it blurred?"

"The year-date," he admitted. "The hour and the month came out O. K. August. And seven thirty P.M., it was mailed at."

This time I made the disgusted sound, in my larynx. "August, seven thirty P.M.—1937 or 1939 or 1942. You have no proof how it got into that mail box, whether it came from a letter carrier's pouch or from the back of some bureau drawer!"

"Give up, Jeff," he said. "There's such a thing as going too far."

I don't know what I would have said. That is, if I hadn't happened to have my eyes on the Thorwald flat living room windows just then. Probably very little. The post card *had* shaken me, whether I admitted it or not. But I was looking over there. The light had gone out as soon as he'd taken his shirt off. But the bedroom didn't light up. A match-flare winked from the living room, low down, as from an easy chair or sofa. With two unused beds in the bedroom, he was *still staying out of there.*

"Boyne," I said in a glassy voice, "I don't care what post cards from the other world you've turned up, I say that man has done away with his wife! Trace that trunk he shipped out. Open it up when you've located it—and I think you'll find her!"

And I hung up without waiting to hear what he was going to do about it. He didn't ring back, so I suspected he was going to give my suggestion a spin after all, in spite of his loudly proclaimed skepticism.

I stayed there by the window all night, keeping a sort of death-watch. There were two more match-flares after the first, at about half-hour intervals. Nothing more after that. So possibly he was asleep over there. Possibly not. I had to sleep some myself, and I finally succumbed in the flaming light of the early sun. Anything that he was going to do, he would have done under cover of darkness and not waited for broad daylight. There wouldn't be anything much to watch, for a while now. And what was there that he needed to do any more, anyway? Nothing, just sit tight and let a little disarming time slip by.

It seemed like five minutes later that Sam came over and touched me, but it was already high noon. I said irritably: "Didn't you lamp that note I pinned up, for you to let me sleep?"

He said: "Yeah, but it's your old friend Inspector Boyne. I figured you'd sure want to——"

It was a personal visit this time. Boyne came into the room behind him without waiting, and without much cordiality.

I said to get rid of Sam: "Go inside and smack a couple of eggs together."

Boyne began in a galvanized-iron voice: "Jeff, what do you mean by doing anything like this to me? I've made a fool out of myself thanks to you. Sending my men out right and left on wild-goose chases. Thank God, I didn't put my foot in it any worse than I did, and have this guy picked up and brought in for questioning."

"Oh, then you don't think that's necessary?" I suggested, dryly.

The look he gave me took care of that. "I'm not alone in the department, you know. There are men over me I'm accountable to for my actions. That looks great, don't it, sending one of my fellows one-half-a-day's train ride up into the sticks to some God-forsaken whistle-stop or other at departmental expense——"

"Then you located the trunk?"

"We traced it through the express agency," he said flintily.

"And you opened it?"

"We did better than that. We got in touch with the various farmhouses in the immediate locality, and Mrs. Thorwald came down to the junction in a produce truck from one of them and opened it for him herself, with her own keys!"

Very few men have ever gotten a look from an old friend such as I got from him. At the door he said, stiff as a rifle barrel: "Just let's forget all about it, shall we? That's about the kindest thing either one of us can do for the other. You're not yourself, and I'm out a little of my own pocket money, time and temper. Let's let it go at that. If you want to telephone me in future I'll be glad to give you my home number."

The door went *whopp!* behind him.

For about ten minutes after he stormed out my numbed mind was in a sort of straitjacket. Then it started to wriggle its way free. The hell with the police. I can't prove it to them, maybe, but I can prove it to myself, one way or the other, once and for all. Either I'm wrong or I'm right. He's got his armor on against them. But his back is naked and unprotected against me.

I called Sam in. "Whatever became of that spyglass we used to have, when we were bumming around on that cabin-cruiser that season?"

He found it some place downstairs and came in with it, blowing on it and rubbing it along his sleeve. I let it lie idle in my lap first. I took a piece of paper and a pencil and wrote six words on it: *What have you done with her?*

I sealed it in an envelope and left the envelope blank. I said to Sam: "Now here's what I want you to do, and I want you to be slick about it. You take this, go in that building 525, climb the stairs to the fourth-floor rear, and ease it under the door. You're fast, at least you used to be. Let's see if you're fast enough to keep from being caught at it. Then when you get safely down again, give the outside doorbell a little poke, to attract attention."

His mouth started to open.

"And don't ask me any questions, you understand? I'm not fooling."

He went, and I got the spyglass ready.

I got him in the right focus after a minute or two. A face leaped up, and I was really seeing him for the first time. Dark-haired, but unmistakable Scandinavian ancestry. Looked like a sinewy customer, although he didn't run to much bulk.

About five minutes went by. His head turned sharply, profilewards. That was the bell-poke, right there. The note must be in already.

He gave me the back of his head as he went back toward the flat-door. The lens could follow him all the way to the rear, where my unaided eyes hadn't been able to before.

He opened the door first, missed seeing it, looked out on a level. He closed it. Then dipped, straightened up. He had it. I could see him turning it this way and that.

He shifted in, away from the door, nearer the window. He thought danger lay near the door, safety away from it. He didn't know it was the other way around, the deeper into his own rooms he retreated the greater the danger.

He'd torn it open, he was reading it. God, how I watched his expression. My eyes clung to it like leeches. There was a sudden widening, a pulling—the whole skin of his face seemed to stretch back behind the ears, narrowing his eyes to Mongoloids. Shock. Panic. His hand pushed out and found the wall, and he braced himself with it. Then he went back toward the door again slowly. I could see him creeping up on it, stalking it as though it were something alive. He opened it so slenderly you couldn't see it at all, peered fearfully through the crack. Then he closed it, and he came back, zigzag, off balance from sheer reflex dismay. He toppled into a chair and snatched up a drink. Out of the bottle neck itself this time. And even while he was holding it to his lips, his head was turned looking over his shoulder at the door that had suddenly thrown his secret in his face.

I put the glass down.

Guilty! Guilty as all hell, and the police be damned!

My hand started toward the phone, came back again. What was the use? They wouldn't listen now any more than they had before. "You should have seen his face, etc." And I could hear

Boyne's answer: "Anyone gets a jolt from an anonymous letter, true or false. You would yourself." They had a real live Mrs. Thorwald to show me—or thought they had. I'd have to show them the dead one, to prove that they both weren't one and the same. I, from my window, had to show them a body.

Well, he'd have to show me first.

It took hours before I got it. I kept pegging away at it, pegging away at it, while the afternoon wore away. Meanwhile he was pacing back and forth there like a caged panther. Two minds with but one thought, turned inside-out in my case. How to keep it hidden, how to see that it wasn't kept hidden.

I was afraid he might try to light out, but if he intended doing that he was going to wait until after dark, apparently, so I had a little time yet. Possibly he didn't want to himself, unless he was driven to it—still felt that it was more dangerous than to stay.

The customary sights and sounds around me went on unnoticed, while the main stream of my thoughts pounded like a torrent against that one obstacle stubbornly damming them up: how to get him to give the location away to me, so that I could give it away in turn to the police.

I was dimly conscious, I remember, of the landlord or somebody bringing in a prospective tenant to look at the sixth-floor apartment, the one that had already been finished. This was two over Thorwald's; they were still at work on the in-between one. At one point an odd little bit of synchronization, completely accidental of course, cropped up. Landlord and tenant both happened to be near the living room windows on the sixth at the same moment that Thorwald was near those on the fourth. Both parties moved onward simultaneously into the kitchen from there, and, passing the blind spot of the wall, appeared next at the kitchen windows. It was uncanny, they were almost like precision-strollers or puppets manipulated on one and the same string. It probably wouldn't have happened again just like that in another fifty years. Immediately afterwards they digressed, never to repeat themselves like that again.

The thing was, something about it had disturbed me. There

had been some slight flaw or hitch to mar its smoothness. I tried for a moment or two to figure out what it had been, and couldn't. The landlord and tenant had gone now, and only Thorwald was in sight. My unaided memory wasn't enough to recapture it for me. My eyesight might have if it had been repeated, but it wasn't.

It sank into my subconscious, to ferment there like yeast, while I went back to the main problem at hand.

I got it finally. It was well after dark, but I finally hit on a way. It mightn't work, it was cumbersome and roundabout, but it was the only way I could think of. An alarmed turn of the head, a quick precautionary step in one certain direction, was all I needed. And to get this brief, flickering, transitory give-away, I needed two phone calls and an absence of about half an hour on his part between them.

I leafed a directory by matchlight until I'd found what I wanted: *Thorwald, Lars. 525 Bndct. . . . SWansea 5-2114.*

I blew out the match, picked up the phone in the dark. It was like television. I could see to the other end of my call, only not along the wire but by a direct channel of vision from window to window.

He said "Hullo?" gruffly.

I thought: How strange this is. I've been accusing him of murder for three days straight, and only now I'm hearing his voice for the first time.

I didn't try to disguise my own voice. After all, he'd never see me and I'd never see him. I said: "You got my note?"

He said guardedly: "Who is this?"

"Just somebody who happens to know."

He said craftily: "Know what?"

"Know what you know. You and I, we're the only ones."

He controlled himself well. I didn't hear a sound. But he didn't know he was open another way too. I had the glass balanced there at proper height on two large books on the sill. Through the window I saw him pull open the collar of his shirt as though its stricture was intolerable. Then he backed his hand over his eyes like you do when there's a light blinding you.

His voice came back firmly. "I don't know what you're talking about."

"Business, that's what I'm talking about. It should be worth something to me, shouldn't it? To keep it from going any further." I wanted to keep him from catching on that it was the windows. I still needed them, I needed them now more than ever. "You weren't very careful about your door the other night. Or maybe the draft swung it open a little."

That hit him where he lived. Even the stomach-heave reached me over the wire. "You didn't see anything. There wasn't anything to see."

"That's up to you. Why should I go to the police?" I coughed a little. "If it would pay me not to."

"Oh," he said. And there was relief of a sort in it. "D'you want to—see me? Is that it?"

"That would be the best way, wouldn't it? How much can you bring with you for now?"

"I've only got about seventy dollars around here."

"All right, then we can arrange the rest for later. Do you know where Lakeside Park is? I'm near there now. Suppose we make it there." That was about thirty minutes away. Fifteen there and fifteen back. "There's a little pavilion as you go in."

"How many of you are there?" he asked cautiously.

"Just me. It pays to keep things to yourself. That way you don't have to divvy up."

He seemed to like that too. "I'll take a run out," he said, "just to see what it's all about."

I watched him more closely than ever, after he'd hung up. He flitted straight through to the end room, the bedroom, that he didn't go near any more. He disappeared into a clothes-closet in there, stayed a minute, came out again. He must have taken something out of a hidden cranny or niche in there that even the dicks had missed. I could tell by the piston-like motion of his hand, just before it disappeared inside his coat, what it was. A gun.

It's a good thing, I thought, I'm not out there in Lakeside Park waiting for my seventy dollars.

The place blacked and he was on his way.

I called Sam in. "I want you to do something for me that's a little risky. In fact, damn risky. You might break a leg, or you might get shot, or you might even get pinched. We've been together ten years, and I wouldn't ask you anything like that if I could do it myself. But I can't, and it's got to be done." Then I told him. "Go out the back way, cross the back yard fences, and see if you can get into that fourth-floor flat up the fire escape. He's left one of the windows down a little from the top."

"What do you want me to look for?"

"Nothing." The police had been there already, so what was the good of that? "There are three rooms over there. I want you to disturb everything just a little bit, in all three, to show someone's been in there. Turn up the edge of each rug a little, shift every chair and table around a little, leave the closet doors standing out. Don't pass up a thing. Here, keep your eyes on this." I took off my own wrist watch, strapped it on him. "You've got twenty-five minutes, starting from now. If you stay within those twenty-five minutes, nothing will happen to you. When you see they're up, don't wait any longer, get out and get out fast."

"Climb back down?"

"No." He wouldn't remember, in his excitement, if he'd left the windows up or not. And I didn't want him to connect danger with the back of his place, but with the front. I wanted to keep my own window out of it. "Latch the window down tight, let yourself out the door, and beat it out of the building the front way, for your life!"

"I'm just an easy mark for you," he said ruefully, but he went.

He came out through our own basement door below me, and scrambled over the fences. If anyone had challenged him from one of the surrounding windows, I was going to backstop for him, explain I'd sent him down to look for something. But no one did. He made it pretty good for anyone his age. He isn't so young any more. Even the fire escape backing the flat, which was drawn up short, he managed to contact by standing up on something. He got in, lit the light, looked over at me. I motioned him to go ahead, not weaken.

I watched him at it. There wasn't any way I could protect him, now that he was in there. Even Thorwald would be within his rights in shooting him down—this was break and entry. I had to stay in back behind the scenes, like I had been all along. I couldn't get out in front of him as a lookout and shield him. Even the dicks had had a lookout posted.

He must have been tense, doing it. I was twice as tense, watching him do it. The twenty-five minutes took fifty to go by. Finally he came over to the window, latched it fast. The lights went, and he was out. He'd made it. I blew out a bellyful of breath that was twenty-five minutes old.

I heard him keying the street door, and when he came up I said warningly: "Leave the light out in here. Go and build yourself a great big two-story whisky punch; you're as close to white as you'll ever be."

Thorwald came back twenty-nine minutes after he'd left for Lakeside Park. A pretty slim margin to hang a man's life on. So now for the finale of the long-winded business, and here was hoping. I got my second phone call in before he had time to notice anything amiss. It was tricky timing but I'd been sitting there with the receiver ready in my hand, dialing the number over and over, then killing it each time. He came in on the 2 of 5-2114, and I saved that much time. The ring started before his hand came away from the light switch.

This was the one that was going to tell the story.

"You were supposed to bring money, not a gun; that's why I didn't show up." I saw the jolt that threw him. The window still had to stay out of it. "I saw you tap the inside of your coat, where you had it, as you came out on the street." Maybe he hadn't, but he wouldn't remember by now whether he had or not. You usually do when you're packing a gun and aren't an habitual carrier.

"Too bad you had your trip out and back for nothing. I didn't waste my time while you were gone, though. I know more now than I knew before." This was the important part. I had the glass up and I was practically fluoroscoping him. "I've found out where—it is. You know what I mean. I know now where you've got—it. I was there while you were out."

Not a word. Just quick breathing.

"Don't you believe me? Look around. Put the receiver down and take a look for yourself. I found it."

He put it down, moved as far as the living room entrance, and touched off the lights. He just looked around him once, in a sweeping, all-embracing stare, that didn't come to a head on any one fixed point, didn't center at all.

He was smiling grimly when he came back to the phone. All he said, softly and with malignant satisfaction, was: "You're a liar."

Then I saw him lay the receiver down and take his hand off it. I hung up at my end.

The test had failed. And yet it hadn't. He hadn't given the location away as I'd hoped he would. And yet that "You're a liar" was a tacit admission that it was there to be found, somewhere around him, somewhere on those premises. In such a good place that he didn't have to worry about it, didn't even have to look to make sure.

So there was a kind of sterile victory in my defeat. But it wasn't worth a damn to me.

He was standing there with his back to me, and I couldn't see what he was doing. I knew the phone was somewhere in front of him, but I thought he was just standing there pensive behind it. His head was slightly lowered, that was all. I'd hung up at my end. I didn't even see his elbow move. And if his index finger did, I couldn't see it.

He stood like that a moment or two, then finally he moved aside. The lights went out over there; I lost him. He was careful not even to strike matches, like he sometimes did in the dark.

My mind no longer distracted by having him to look at, I turned to trying to recapture something else—that troublesome little hitch in synchronization that had occurred this afternoon, when the renting agent and he both moved simultaneously from one window to the next. The closest I could get was this: it was like when you're looking at someone through a pane of imperfect glass, and a flaw in the glass distorts the symmetry of the reflected image for a second, until it has gone on past that point. Yet that wouldn't do, that was not it. The windows had been open and there had been no glass between. And I hadn't been using the lens at the time.

My phone rang. Boyne, I supposed. It wouldn't be anyone else at this hour. Maybe, after reflecting on the way he'd jumped all over me— I said "Hello" unguardedly, in my own normal voice.

There wasn't any answer.

I said: "Hello? Hello? Hello?" I kept giving away samples of my voice.

There wasn't a sound from first to last.

I hung up finally. It was still dark over there, I noticed.

Sam looked in to check out. He was a bit thick-tongued from his restorative drink. He said something about "Awri' if I go now?" I half heard him. I was trying to figure out another way of trapping *him* over there into giving away the right spot. I motioned my consent absently.

He went a little unsteadily down the stairs to the ground floor and after a delaying moment or two I heard the street door close after him. Poor Sam, he wasn't much used to liquor.

I was left alone in the house, one chair the limit of my freedom of movement.

Suddenly a light went on over there again, just momentarily, to go right out again afterwards. He must have needed it for something, to locate something that he had already been looking for and found he wasn't able to put his hands on readily without it. He found it, whatever it was, almost immediately, and moved back at once to put the lights out again. As he turned to do so, I saw him give a glance out the window. He didn't come to the window to do it, he just shot it out in passing.

Something about it struck me as different from any of the others I'd seen him give in all the time I'd been watching him. If you can qualify such an elusive thing as a glance, I would have termed it a glance with a purpose. It was certainly anything but vacant or random, it had a bright spark of fixity in it. It wasn't one of those precautionary sweeps I'd seen him give, either. It hadn't started over on the other side and worked its way around to my side, the right. It had hit dead-center at my bay window, for just a split second while it lasted, and then was gone again. And the lights were gone, and he was gone.

Sometimes your senses take things in without your mind translating them into their proper meaning. My eyes saw that look. My mind refused to smelter it properly. "It was meaningless," I thought. "An unintentional bull's-eye, that just happened to hit square over here, as he went toward the lights on his way out."

Delayed action. A wordless ring of the phone. To test a voice? A period of bated darkness following that, in which two could have played at the same game—stalking one another's window-squares, unseen. A last-moment flicker of the lights, that was bad strategy but unavoidable. A parting glance, radioactive with malignant intention. All these things sank in without fusing. My eyes did their job, it was my mind that didn't—or at least took its time about it.

Seconds went by in packages of sixty. It was very still around the familiar quadrangle formed by the back of the houses. Sort of a breathless stillness. And then a sound came into it, starting up from nowhere, nothing. The unmistakable, spaced clicking a cricket makes in the silence of the night. I thought of Sam's superstition about them, that he claimed had never failed to fulfill itself yet. If that was the case, it looked bad for somebody in one of these slumbering houses around here—

Sam had been gone only about ten minutes. And now he was back again, he must have forgotten something. That drink was responsible. Maybe his hat, or maybe even the key to his own quarters uptown. He knew I couldn't come down and let him in, and he was trying to be quiet about it, thinking perhaps I'd dozed off. All I could hear was this faint jiggling down at the lock of the front door. It was one of those old-fashioned stoop houses, with an outer pair of storm doors that were allowed to swing free all night, and then a small vestibule, and then the inner door, worked by a simple iron key. The liquor had made his hand a little unreliable, although he'd had this difficulty once or twice before, even without it. A match would have helped him find the keyhole quicker, but then, Sam doesn't smoke. I knew he wasn't likely to have one on him.

The sound bad stopped now. He must have given up, gone away again, decided to let whatever it was go until tomorrow. He hadn't gotten in, because I knew his noisy way of letting doors coast shut by themselves too well, and there hadn't been any sound of that sort, that loose slap he always made.

Then suddenly it exploded. Why at this particular moment, I don't know. That was some mystery of the inner workings of my own mind. It flashed like waiting gunpowder which a spark has finally reached along a slow train. Drove all thoughts of Sam, and the front door, and this and that completely out of my head. It had been waiting there since midafternoon today, and only now— More of that delayed action. Damn that delayed action.

The renting agent and Thorwald had both started even from the living room window. An intervening gap of blind wall, and both had reappeared at the kitchen window, still one above the other. But some sort of a hitch or flaw or jump had taken place, right there, that bothered me. The eye is a reliable surveyor. There wasn't anything the matter with their timing, it was with their parallel-ness, or whatever the word is. The hitch had been vertical, not horizontal. There had been an upward "jump."

Now I had it, now I knew. And it couldn't wait. It was too good. They wanted a body? Now I had one for them.

Sore or not, Boyne would *have* to listen to me now. I didn't waste any time, I dialed his precinct-house then and there in the dark, working the slots in my lap by memory alone. They didn't make much noise going around, just a light click. Not even as distinct as that cricket out there—

"He went home long ago," the desk sergeant said.

This couldn't wait. "All right, give me his home phone number."

He took a minute, came back again. "Trafalgar," he said. Then nothing more.

"Well? Trafalgar what?" Not a sound.

"Hello? Hello?" I tapped it. "Operator, I've been cut off. Give me that party again." I couldn't get her either.

I hadn't been cut off. My wire had been cut. That had been too sudden, right in the middle of— And to be cut like that it would have to be done somewhere right here inside the house with me. Outside it went underground.

Delayed action. This time final, fatal, altogether too late. A voiceless ring of the phone. A direction-finder of a look from over there. "Sam" seemingly trying to get back in a while ago.

Suddenly, death was somewhere inside the house here with me. And I couldn't move, I couldn't get up out of this chair. Even if I had gotten through to Boyne just now, that would have been too late. There wasn't time enough now for one of those camera-finishes in this. I could have shouted out the window to that gallery of sleeping rear-window neighbors around me, I supposed. It would have brought them to the windows. It couldn't have brought them over here in time. By the time they had even figured which particular house it was coming from, it would stop again, be over with. I didn't open my mouth. Not because I was brave, but because it was so obviously useless.

He'd be up in a minute. He must be on the stairs now, although I couldn't hear him. Not even a creak. A creak would have been a relief, would have placed him. This was like being shut up in the dark with the silence of a gliding, coiling cobra somewhere around you.

There wasn't a weapon in the place with me. There were books there on the wall, in the dark, within reach. Me, who never read. The former owner's books. There was a bust of Rousseau or Montesquieu, I'd never been able to decide which, one of those gents with flowing manes, topping them. It was a monstrosity, bisque clay, but it too dated from before my occupancy.

I arched my middle upward from the chair seat and clawed desperately up at it. Twice my fingertips slipped off it, then at the third raking I got it to teeter, and the fourth brought it down into my lap, pushing me down into the chair. There was a steamer rug under me. I didn't need it around me in this weather, I'd been using it to soften the seat of the chair. I tugged it out from under and mantled it around me like an Indian brave's blanket. Then I squirmed far down in the chair, let my head and one shoulder dangle out over the arm, on the side next to the wall. I hoisted the bust to my other, upward shoulder, balanced it there precariously for a second head, blanket tucked around its ears. From the back, in the dark, it would look—I hoped——

I proceeded to breathe adenoidally, like someone in heavy upright sleep. It wasn't hard. My own breath was coming nearly that labored anyway, from tension.

He was good with knobs and hinges and things. I never heard the door open, and this one, unlike the one downstairs, was right behind me. A little eddy of air puffed through the dark at me. I could feel it because my scalp, the real one, was all wet at the roots of the hair right then.

If it was going to be a knife or head-blow, the dodge might give me a second chance, that was the most I could hope for, I knew. My arms and shoulders are hefty. I'd bring him down on me in a bear-hug after the first slash or drive, and break his neck or collarbone against me. If it was going to be a gun, he'd get me anyway in the end. A difference of a few seconds. He had a gun, I knew, that he was going to use on me in the open, over at Lakeside Park. I was hoping that here, indoors, in order to make his own escape more practicable—

Time was up.

The flash of the shot lit up the room for a second, it was so dark. Or at least the corners of it, like flickering, weak lightning. The bust bounced on my shoulder and disintegrated into chunks.

I thought he was jumping up and down on the floor for a minute with frustrated rage. Then when I saw him dart by me and lean over the window sill to look for a way out, the sound transferred itself rearwards and downwards, became a pummeling with hoof and hip at the street door. The camera-finish after all. But he still could have killed me five times.

I flung my body down into the narrow crevice between chair arm and wall, but my legs were still up, and so was my head and that one shoulder.

He whirled, fired at me so close that it was like looking at sunrise in the face. I didn't feel it, so—it hadn't hit.

"You—" I heard him grunt to himself. I think it was the last thing he said. The rest of his life was all action, not verbal.

He flung over the sill on one arm and dropped into the yard. Two-story drop. He made it because he missed the cement, landed on the sod-strip in the middle. I jacked myself up over the chair arm and flung myself bodily forward at the window, neatly hitting it chin first.

He went all right. When life depends on it, you go. He took the first fence, rolled over that bellywards. He went over the second like a cat, hands and feet pointed together in a spring. Then he was back in the rear yard of his own building. He got up on something, just about like Sam had— The rest was all footwork, with quick little corkscrew twists at each landing stage. Sam had latched his windows down when he was over there, but he'd reopened one of them for ventilation on his return. His whole life depended now on that casual, unthinking little act—

Second, third. He was up to his own windows. He'd made it. Something went wrong. He veered out away from them in another pretzel-twist, flashed up toward the fifth, the one above. Something sparked in the darkness of one of his own windows where he'd been just now, and a shot thudded heavily out around the-quadrangle-enclosure like a big bass drum.

He passed the fifth, the sixth, got to the roof. He'd made it a second time. Gee, he loved life! The guys in his own windows couldn't get him, he was over them in a straight line and there was too much fire escape interlacing in the way.

I was too busy watching him to watch what was going on around me. Suddenly Boyne was next to me, sighting. I heard him mutter: "I almost hate to do this, he's got to fall so far."

He was balanced on the roof parapet up there, with a star right over his head. An unlucky star. He stayed a minute too long, trying to kill before he was killed. Or maybe he was killed, and knew it.

A shot cracked, high up against the sky, the window pane flew apart all over the two of us, and one of the books snapped right behind me.

Boyne didn't say anything more about hating to do it. My face was pressing outward against his arm. The recoil of his elbow jarred my teeth. I blew a clearing through the smoke to watch him go.

It was pretty horrible. He took a minute to show anything, standing up there on the parapet. Then he let his gun go, as if to say: "I won't need this any more." Then he went after it. He missed the fire escape entirely, came all the way down on the outside. He landed so far out he hit one of the projecting planks, down there out of sight. It bounced his body up, like a springboard. Then it landed again—for good. And that was all.

I said to Boyne: "I got it. I got it finally. The fifth-floor flat, the one over his, that they're still working on. The cement kitchen floor, raised above the level of the other rooms. They wanted to comply with the fire laws and also obtain a dropped living room effect, as cheaply as possible. Dig it up—"

He went right over then and there, down through the basement and over the fences, to save time. The electricity wasn't turned on yet in that one, they had to use their torches. It didn't take them long at that, once they'd got started. In about half an hour he came to the window and wigwagged over for my benefit. It meant yes.

He didn't come over until nearly eight in the morning; after they'd tidied up and taken them away. Both away, the hot dead and the cold dead. He said: "Jeff, I take it all back. That damn fool that I sent up there about the trunk—well, it wasn't his fault, in a way. I'm to blame. He didn't have orders to check on the woman's description, only on the contents of the trunk. He came back and touched on it in a general way. I go home and I'm in bed already, and suddenly pop! into my brain—one of the tenants I questioned two whole days ago had given us a few details and they didn't tally with his on several important points. Talk about being slow to catch on!"

"I've had that all the way through this damn thing," I admitted ruefully. "I called it delayed action. It nearly killed me."

"I'm a police officer and you're not."

"That how you happened to shine at the right time?"

"Sure. We came over to pick him up for questioning. I left them planted there when we saw he wasn't in, and came on over here by myself to square it up with you while we were waiting. How did you happen to hit on that cement floor?"

I told him about the freak synchronization. "The renting agent showed up taller at the kitchen window in proportion to Thorwald, than he had been a moment before when both were at the living room windows together. It was no secret that they were putting in cement floors, topped by a cork composition, and raising them considerably. But it took on new meaning. Since the top floor one has been finished for some time, it had to be the fifth. Here's the way I have it lined up, just in theory. She's been in ill health for years, and he's been out of work, and he got sick of that and of her both. Met this other—"

"She'll be here later today, they're bringing her down under arrest."

"He probably insured her for all he could get, and then started to poison her slowly, trying not to leave any trace. I imagine—and remember, this is pure conjecture—she caught him at it that night the light was on all night. Caught on in some way, or caught him in the act. He lost his head, and did the very thing he had wanted all along to avoid doing. Killed her by violence—strangulation or a blow. The rest had to be hastily improvised. He got a better break than he deserved at that. He thought of the apartment upstairs, went up and looked around. They'd just finished laying the floor, the cement hadn't hardened yet, and the materials were still around. He gouged a trough out of it just wide enough to take her body, put her in it, mixed fresh cement and recemented over her, possibly raising the general level of the floor an inch or two so that she'd be safely covered. A permanent, odorless coffin. Next day the workmen came back, laid down the cork surfacing on top of it without noticing anything, I suppose he'd used one of their own trowels to smooth it. Then he sent his accessory upstate fast, near where his wife had been several summers before, but to a different farmhouse where she wouldn't be recognized, along with the trunk keys. Sent the trunk up after her, and dropped himself an already used post card into his mailbox, with the year-date blurred. In a week or two she would have probably committed 'suicide' up there as Mrs. Anna Thorwald. Despondency due to ill health. Written him a farewell note and left her clothes beside some body of deep water. It was risky, but they might have succeeded in collecting the insurance at that."

By nine Boyne and the rest had gone. I was still sitting there in the chair, too keyed up to sleep. Sam came in and said: "Here's Doc Preston."

He showed up rubbing his hands, in that way he has. "Guess we can take that cast off your leg now. You must be tired of sitting there all day doing nothing."

THE CORPSE NEXT DOOR

"The Corpse Next Door" is a clear homage to "The Tell-Tale Heart" by Edgar Allan Poe, the master of macabre. First published at the height of the Depression in *Detective Fiction Weekly* in January 1937, the characters' pitiful situation perfectly evokes the poverty and desperation of the time. Woolrich lays bare a murderer's excruciating anxiety after committing his crime in a fit of rage. What is he to do but hide the body in the empty apartment next door and hope it goes unnoticed? This story appeared in Francis Nevins' wonderful *Nightwebs* collection of 1971, and again in Centipede Press' 2012 hardcover collection *Speak to Me of Death*, which is now out of print. It is resurrected here as a murderous tale not to be forgotten.

HARLAN'S WIFE TURNED AWAY quickly, trying to hide the can-opener in her hand. "What's the idea?" he asked. She hadn't expected him to look across the top of his morning paper just then. The can of evaporated milk she had been holding in her other hand slipped from her grasp in her excitement, hit the floor with a dull whack, and rolled over. She stooped quickly, snatched it up, but he had seen it.

"Looks like somebody swiped the milk from our door again last night," she said with a nervous little laugh. Harlan had a vicious temper. She hadn't wanted to tell him, but there had not been time to run out to the store and get another bottle.

"That's the fifth time in two weeks!" He rolled the paper into a tube and smacked it viciously against the table-leg. She could see him starting to work himself up, getting whiter by the minute even under his shaving talcum. "It's somebody right in the house!" he roared. "No outsider could get in past that locked street-door after twelve!" He bared his teeth in a deceptive grin. "I'd like to get my hands on the fellow!"

"I've notified the milkman and I've complained to the superintendent, but there doesn't seem to be any way of stopping it," Mrs. Harlan sighed. She punched a hole in the top of the can tilted it over his cup.

He pushed it aside disgustedly and stood up. "Oh, yes, there is," he gritted, "and I'm going to stop it!" A suburban commuters' train whistled thinly in the distance. "Just lemme get hold of whoever—!" he muttered a second time with suppressed savagery as he grabbed his hat, bolted for the door. Mrs. Harlan shook her head with worried foreboding as it slammed behind him.

He came back at six bringing something in a paper-bag, which he stood on the kitchen-shelf. Mrs. Harlan looked in it and saw a quart of milk.

"We don't need that. I ordered a bottle this afternoon from the grocer," she told him.

"That's not for our use," he answered grimly. "It's a decoy."

At eleven, in bathrobe and slippers, she saw him carry it out to the front door and set it down. He looked up and down the hall, squatted down beside it, tied something invisible around its neck below the cardboard cap. Then he strewed something across the sill and closed the door.

"What on earth—?" said Mrs. Harlan apprehensively.

He held up his index-finger. A coil of strong black sewing-thread was plaited around it. It stood out clearly against the skin of his finger, but trailed off invisibly into space and under the door to connect with the bottle. "Get it?" he gloated vindictively. "You've got to look twice to see this stuff once, especially in a shadowy doorway. But it cuts the skin if it's pulled tight. See? One tug should be enough to wake me up, and if I can only get out there in time—"

He left the rest of it unfinished. He didn't have to finish it, his wife knew just what he meant. She was beginning to wish he hadn't found out about the thefted milk. There'd only be a brawl outside their door in the middle of the night, with the neighbors looking on—

He paid out the thread across their living-room floor into the bedroom beyond, got into bed, and left the hand it was attached to outside the covers. Putting out the lights after him, she was tempted to clip the thread then and there, as the safest way out, even picked up a pair of scissors and tried to locate it in the dark. She knew if she did, he'd be sure to notice it in the morning and raise cain.

"Don't walk around in there so much," he called warningly. "You'll snarl it up."

Her courage failed her. She put the scissors down and went to bed. The menacing thread, like a powder-train leading to a high explosive, remained intact.

In the morning it was still there, and there were two bottles of milk at the door instead of one, the usual delivery and the decoy. Mrs. Harlan sighed with relief. It would have been very short-sighted of the guilty person to repeat the stunt two nights in succession; it had been happening at the rate of every third night so far. Maybe by the time it happened again, Harlan would cool down.

But Harlan was slow at cooling down. The very fact that the stunt wasn't repeated immediately only made him boil all the more. He wanted his satisfaction out of it. He caught himself thinking about it on the train riding to and from the city. Even at the office, when he should have been attending to his work. It started to fester and rankle. He was in a fair way to becoming hipped on the subject, when at last the thread paid off one night about four.

He was asleep when the warning tug came. Mrs. Harlan slept soundly in the adjoining bed. He knew right away what had awakened him, jumped soundlessly out of bed with a bound, and tore through the darkened flat toward the front door.

He reached it with a pattering rush of bare feet and tore it open. It was sweet. It was perfect. He couldn't have asked for it any better! Harlan caught him red-handed, in the very act. The bottle of milk cradled in his arm, he froze there petrified and stared guiltily at the opening door. He'd evidently missed feeling the tug of the thread altogether—which wasn't surprising, because at his end the bottle had received it and not himself. And to make it even better than perfect, pluperfect, he was someone that by the looks of him Harlan could handle without much trouble. Not that he would have hung back even if he'd found himself outclassed. He was white-hot with thirty-six hours' pent-up combustion, and physical cowardice wasn't one of his failings, whatever else was.

He just stood there for a split second, motionless, to rub it in. "Nice work, buddy!" he hissed.

The hijacker cringed, bent lopsidedly to put the bottle on the floor without taking his terrified eyes off Harlan. He was a reedy sort of fellow in trousers and undershirt, a misleading tangle of hair showing on his chest.

"Gee, I've been so broke," he faltered apologetically. "Doctor-bills, an'—an' I'm outa work. I needed this stuff awfully bad, I ain't well—"

"You're in the pink of condish compared to what you're gonna be in just about a minute more!" rumbled Harlan. The fellow could have gotten down on his knees, paid for the milk ten times over, but it wouldn't have cut any ice with Harlan. He was going to get his satisfaction out of this the way he wanted it. That was the kind Harlan was.

He waited until the culprit straightened up again, then breathed a name at him fiercely and swung his arm like a shot-putter.

Harlan's fist smashed the lighter man square in the mouth. He went over like a paper cut-out and lay just as flat as one. The empty hallway throbbed with his fall. He lay there and miraculously still showed life. Rolling his head dazedly from side to side, he reached up vaguely to find out where his mouth had gone. Those slight movements were like waving a red flag at a bull. Harlan snorted and flung himself down on the man. Knee to chest, he grabbed the fellow by the hair of the head, pulled it upward and crashed his skull down against the flagged floor.

When the dancing embers of his rage began to thin out so that he was able to see straight once more, the man wasn't rolling his head dazedly any more. He wasn't moving in the slightest. A thread of blood was trickling out of each ear-hollow, as though something had shattered inside.

Harlan stiff-armed himself against the floor and got up slowly like something leaving its kill. "All right, you brought it on yourself!" he growled. There was an undertone of fear in his voice. He prodded the silent form reluctantly. "Take the lousy milk," he said. "Only next time ask for it first!" He got up on his haunches, squatting there ape-like. "Hey! Hey, you!" He shook him again. "Matter with you? Going to lie there all night? I said you could take the—"

The hand trying to rouse the man stopped suddenly over his heart. It came away slowly, very slowly. The color drained out of Harlan's face. He sucked in a deep breath that quivered his lips. It stayed cold all the way down like menthol.

"Gone!" The hoarsely-muttered word jerked him to his feet. He started backing, backing a step at a time, toward the door he'd come out of. He could not take his eyes off the huddled, shrunken form lying there close beside the wall.

"Gee, I better get in!" was the first inchoate thought that came to him. He found the opening with his back, even retreated a step or two through it, before he realized the folly of what he was doing. Couldn't leave him lying there like that right outside his own door. They'd know right away who had—and they weren't going to if he could help it.

He glanced behind him into the darkened flat. His wife's peaceful, rhythmic breathing was clearly audible in the intense stillness. She'd slept through the whole thing. He stepped into the hall again, looked up and down. If she hadn't heard, with the door standing wide open, then surely nobody else had with theirs closed.

But one door was not closed! The next one down the line was open a crack, just about an inch, showing a thin line of white inner-frame. Harlan went cold all over for a minute, then sighed with relief. Why that was where the milk-thief came from. Sure, obviously. He'd been heading back in that direction when Harlan came out and caught him. It was the last door down that way. The hall, it was true, took a right-angle turn when it got past there, and there were still other flats around the other side, out of sight. That must be the place. Who else would leave their door off the latch like that at four in the morning, except this guy who had come out to prowl in the hallway?

This was one time when Mrs. Harlan would have come in handy. She would have known for sure whether the guy lived in there or not, or just where he did belong. He himself wasn't interested in their neighbors, didn't know one from the other, much less which flats they hung out in. But it was a cinch he wasn't going to wake her and drag her out here to look at a dead man, just to find out where to park him. One screech from her would put him behind the eight-ball before he knew it.

Then while he was hesitating, sudden, urgent danger made up his mind for him. A faint whirring sound started somewhere in the bowels of the building. Along with it the faceted glass knob beside the automatic elevator panel burned brightly red. Somebody was coming up!

He jumped for the prostrate form, got an under-arm grip on it, and started hauling it hastily toward that unlatched door. Legs splayed out behind it, the heels of the shoes ticked over the cracks between the flagstones like train-wheels on a track.

The elevator beat him to it, slow-moving though it was. He had the guy at the door, still in full view, when the triangular porthole in the elevator door-panel bloomed yellow with its arrival. He whirled, crouching defiantly over the body, like something at bay. He would be caught with the goods, just as he himself had caught this guy, if the party got out at this floor. But they didn't. The porthole darkened again as the car went on up.

He let out a long, whistling breath like a deflating tire, pushed the door carefully open. It gave a single rebellious click as the latch cleared the socket altogether. He listened, heart pounding. Might be sixteen kids in there for all he knew, a guy that stole milk like that.

"I'll drop him just inside," Harlan thought grimly. "Let them figure it out in the morning!"

He tugged the fellow across the sill with an unavoidable wooden thump of the heels, let him down, tensed, listened again, silhouetted there against the orange light from the hall —if anyone was inside looking out. But there was an absence of breathing-sounds from within. It seemed too good to be true. He felt his way forward, peering into the dark, ready to jump back and bolt for it at the first alarm.

Once he got past the closed-in foyer, the late moon cast

enough light through the windows to show him that there was no one living in the place but the guy himself. It was a one-room flat and the bed, which was one of those that come down out of a closet, showed white and vacant.

"Swell!" said Harlan. "No one's gonna miss you right away!"

He hauled him in, put him on the bed, turned to soft-shoe out again when he got a better idea. Why not make it really tough to find him while he was about it? This way, the first person that stuck his head in was bound to spot the man. He tugged the sheet clear of the body lying on it and pulled it over him like a shroud. He tucked it in on both sides, so that it held him in a mild sort of grip.

He gripped the foot of the bed. It was hard to lift, but once he got it started the mechanism itself came to his aid. It began swinging upward of its own accord. He held onto it to keep it from banging. It went into the closet neatly enough but wouldn't stay put. The impediment between it and the wall pushed it down each time. But the door would probably hold it. He heard a rustle as something shifted, slipped further down in back of the bed. He didn't have to be told what that was.

He pushed the bed with one arm and caught the door with the other. Each time he took the supporting arm away, the bed tipped out and blocked the door. Finally at the sixth try he got it to stand still and swiftly slapped the door in place over it. That held it like glue and he had nothing further to worry about. It would have been even better if there'd been a key to lock it, take out, and throw away. There wasn't. This was good enough, this would hold—twenty-four hours, forty-eight, a week even, until the guy's rent came due and they searched the place. And by that time he could pull a quick change of address, back a van up to the door, and get out of the building. Wouldn't look so hot, of course, but who wanted to stay where there was a permanent corpse next door? They'd never be able to pin it on him anyway, never in a million years. Not a living soul, not a single human eye, had seen it happen. He was sure of that.

Harlan gave the closet door a swipe with the loose end of his pajama jacket, just for luck, up where his hand had pushed against it. He hadn't touched either knob.

He reconnoitered, stepped out, closed the flat up after him. The tumbler fell in the lock. It couldn't be opened from the outside now except by the super's passkey. Back where it had happened, he picked up the lethal bottle of milk and took it into his own flat. He went back a second time, got down close on hands and knees and gave the floor a careful inspection. There were just two spots of blood, the size of two-bit pieces, that must have dripped from the guy's ears before he picked him up. He looked down at his pajama coat. There were more than two spots on that, but that didn't worry him any.

He went into his bathroom, stripped off the jacket, soaked a handful of it under the hot water and slipped into the hall with it. The spots came up off the satiny flagstones at a touch without leaving a trace. He hurried down the corridor, opened a door, and stepped into a hot, steamy little whitewashed alcove provided with an incinerator chute. He balled the coat up, pulled down the flap of the chute, shoved the bundle in like a letter in a mail box and then sent the trousers down after it too, just to make sure. That way he wouldn't be stuck with any odd pair of trousers without their matching jacket. Who could swear there had ever been such a pair of pajamas now? A strong cindery odor came up the chute. The fire was going in the basement right now. He wouldn't even have to worry about the articles staying intact down there until morning. Talk about your quick service!

He slipped back to his own door the way he was without a stitch on him. He realized it would have been a bum joke if somebody had seen him like that, after the care he'd taken about all those little details. But they hadn't. So what?

He shut the door of his apartment, and put on another pair of pajamas. Slipping quietly into the bed next to the peacefully-slumbering Missis, he lit a cigarette. Then the let-down came. Not that he got jittery, but he saw that he wasn't going to sleep any more that night. Rather than lie there tossing and turning, he dressed and went out of the house to take a walk.

He would have liked a drink, but it was nearly five, way past closing-time for all the bars, so he had to be satisfied with a cup of coffee at the counter lunch. He tried to put it to his mouth a couple times, finally had to call the waiter back.

"Bring me a black one," he said. "Leave the milk out!" That way it went down easy enough.

The sun was already up when he got back, and he felt like he'd been pulled through a wringer. He found Mrs. Harlan in the kitchen, getting things started for his breakfast.

"Skip that," he told her irritably. "I don't want any—and shove that damn bottle out of sight, will you?"

He took time off during his lunch-hour to look at a flat in the city and paid a deposit for it. When he got home that night he told Mrs. Harlan abruptly, "Better get packed up, we're getting out of here the first thing in the morning."

"Wha-at?" she squawked. "Why we can't do that. We've got a lease! What's come over you?"

"Lease or no lease," he barked. "I can't stand it here any more. We're getting out after tonight, I tell you!"

They were in the living-room and his eyes flicked toward the wall that partitioned them off from the flat next door. He didn't want to do that, but he couldn't help himself. She didn't notice, but obediently started to pack. He called up a moving-van company.

In the middle of the night he woke up from a bad dream and ran smack into something even worse. He got up and went into the living-room. He didn't exactly know why. The moon was even brighter than the night before and washed that dividing wall with almost a luminous calsomine. Right in the middle of the wall there was a hideous black, blurred outline, like an X-ray showing through from the other side. Right about where that bed would be. Stiff and skinny the hazy figure was with legs and arms and even a sort of head on it. He pitched the back of his arm to his mouth just in time to douse the yell struggling to come out, went wet all over as though he were under a shower-bath. He managed to turn finally and saw the peculiar shape of one of Mrs. Harlan's modernistic lamps standing in the path of the moon, throwing its shadow upon the wall. He pulled down the shade and tottered back inside. He took his coffee black again next morning, looked terrible.

She rang him at the office just before closing-time. "You at the new place?" he asked eagerly.

"No," she said, "they wouldn't let me take the stuff out. I had a terrible time with the renting-agent. Ed, we'll just have to make the best of it. He warned me that if we go, they're going to garnished your salary and get a judgment against you for the whole two-years' rent. Ed, we can't afford to keep two places going at once and your firm will fire you the minute they find out. They won't stand for anything like that. You told me so yourself. He told me any justified complaint we have will be attended to, but we can't just walk out on our lease. You'd better think twice about it. I don't know what's wrong with the flat anyway."

He did, but he could not tell her. He saw that they had him by the short hairs. If he went, it meant loss of his job, destitution; even if he got another, they'd attach the wages of that too. Attracting this much attention wasn't the best thing in the world, either. When he got home, the agent came up to find out what was the trouble, what his reasons were, he didn't know what to answer, couldn't think of a legitimate kick he had coming. He was afraid now even to bring up about the chiseling of the milk. It would have sounded picayune at that.

"I don't have to give you my reasons!" he said surlily. "I'm sick o' the place, and that's that!"

Which he saw right away was a tactical error, not only because it might sow suspicion later, but because it antagonized the agent now. "You can go just as soon as you've settled for the balance of your lease. I'm not trying to hold you!" he fumed. "If you try moving your things out without that, I'll call the police!"

Harlan slammed the door after him like a six-gun salute. He had a hunch the agent wouldn't be strictly within his legal rights in going quite that far, but he was in no position to force a showdown and find out for sure. No cops, thanks.

He realized that his own blundering had raised such a stink that it really didn't matter now any more whether he stayed or went. They'd make it their business to trace his forwarding address, and they'd have that on tap when disclosure came. So the whole object of moving out would be defeated. The lesser of two evils now was to stay, lie very low, hope the whole incident would be half-forgotten by the time the real excitement broke. It may have been lesser, but it was still plenty evil. He didn't see how he was going to stand it. Yet he had to.

He went out and came back with a bottle of rye, told his wife he felt a cold coming on. That was so he wouldn't run into any more hallucinations during the night like that phantom X-ray on the wall. When he went to bed the bottle was empty. He was still stony sober, but at least it put him through the night somehow.

On his way across the hall toward the elevator that morning, his head turned automatically to look up at that other door. He couldn't seem to control it. When he came back that evening the same thing happened. It was locked, just as it had been for the past two nights and two days now. He thought, "I've got to quit that. Somebody's liable to catch me at it and put two and two together."

In those two days and two nights he changed almost beyond recognition. He lost all his color; was losing weight almost by the hour; shelves under his eyes you could have stacked books on; appetite shot to smithereens. A backfire on the street made him leave his shoes without unlacing them, and his office-work was starting to go haywire. Hooch was putting him to sleep each night, but he had to keep stepping it up. He was getting afraid one of these times he'd spill the whole thing to his wife while he was tanked without knowing it. She was beginning to notice there was something the matter and mentioned his seeing a doctor about himself once or twice. He snapped at her and shut her up.

The third night, which was the thirty-first of the month, they were sitting there in the living-room. She was sewing. He stared glassy-eyed through the paper, pretending to read, whisky-tumbler at his elbow, sweat all over his ashen forehead, when she started sniffling.

"Got a cold?" he asked tonelessly.

"No," she said, "there's a peculiar musty odor in here, don't you get it? Sickly-sweet. I've been noticing it off and on all day, it's stronger in this room than in—"

"Shut up!" he rasped. The tumbler shook in his hand as he downed its contents, refilled it. He got up, opened the windows as far as they would go. He came back, killed the second shot, lit a cigarette unsteadily, deliberately blew the first thickly fragrant puff all around her head. "No, I don't notice anything," he said in an artificially steady voice. His face was almost green in the lamplight.

"I don't see how you can miss it," she said innocently. "It's getting worse every minute. I wonder if there's something wrong with the drains in this building?"

He didn't hear the rest of it. He was thinking: "It'll pay off, one way or the other, pretty soon—thank goodness for that! Tomorrow's the first, they'll be showing up for his rent, that'll be the finale."

He almost didn't care now which way it worked out—anything so long as it was over with, anything but this ghastly suspense. He couldn't hold out much longer. Let them suspect him even, if they wanted to; the complete lack of proof still held good. Any lawyer worth his fee could get him out of it with one hand tied behind his back.

But then when he snapped out of it and caught sight of her over at the inter-house phone, realized what she was about, he backed water in a hurry. All the bravado went out of him. "What're you doing?" he croaked.

"I'm going to ask the superintendent what that is, have him come up here and—"

"Get away from there!" he bellowed. She hung up as though she'd been bitten, turned to stare.

A second later he realized what a swell out that would have been to have the first report of the nuisance come from them themselves; he wished he had let her go ahead. It should have come from them. They were closest to the death-flat. If it came from somebody else further away—and they seemed not to have noticed it—that would be one more chip stacked up against him.

"All right, notify him if you want to," he countermanded.

"No, no, not if you don't want me to." She was frightened now. He had her all rattled. She moved away from the phone.

To bridge the awkward silence he said the one thing he didn't want to, the one thing of all he'd intended not to say. As though possessed of perverse demons, it came out before he could stop it: "Maybe it's from next-door." Then his eyes hopelessly rolled around in their sockets.

"How could it be?" she contradicted mildly. "That flat's been vacant for the past month or more—"

A clock they had in there in the room with them ticked on hollowly, resoundingly, eight, nine, ten times. Clack, clack, clack, as though it were hooked up to a loudspeaker. What a racket it was making! Couldn't hear yourself think.

"No one living in there, you say?" he said in a hoarse whisper after what seemed an hour ticked by.

"No, I thought you knew that. I forgot, you don't take much interest in the neighbors—"

Then who was he? Where had he come from? Not from the street, because he had been in his undershirt. "I dragged the guy back into the wrong apartment!" thought Harlan. He was lucky it was vacant! It gave him the shivers, even now, to think what might have happened if there had been somebody else in there that night! The more he puzzled over it, the cloudier the mystery got. That particular door had been ajar, the bed down out of the closet, and the guy had been pussyfooting back toward there. Then where did he belong, if not in there? He was obviously a lone wolf, or he would have been missed by now. Those living with him would have sent out an alarm the very next morning after it had happened. Harlan had been keeping close tab on the police calls on his radio and there hadn't been anything of the kind. And even if he had lived alone in one of the other flats, the unlatched door left waiting for his return would have attracted attention from the hall by now.

What was the difference where he came from anyway; it was where he was now that mattered! All he could get out of it was this: there would be no pay-off tomorrow after all. The agony would be prolonged now indefinitely—until prospective tenants were shown the place and sudden discovery resulted. He groaned aloud, took his next swig direct from the bottle without any tumbler for a go-between.

In the morning he could tell breakdown was already setting in. Between the nightly sousing, the unending mental strain, the lack of food, he was a doddering wreck when he got out of bed and staggered into his clothes. Mrs. Harlan said, "I don't think you'd better go to the office today. If you could see yourself—!" But he had to, anything was better than staying around here!

He opened the living-room door (he'd closed it on the two of them the night before) and the fetid air from inside seemed to hit him in the face, it was so strong. He reeled there in that corrupt, acrid draft, not because it was so difficult to breathe but because it was so difficult for *him* to breathe, knowing what he did about it. He stood there gagging, hand to throat; his wife had to come up behind him and support him with one arm for a minute, until he pulled himself together. He couldn't, of course, eat anything. He grabbed his hat and made for the elevator in a blind hurry that was almost panic. His head jerked toward that other door as he crossed the hall; it hadn't missed doing that once for three days and nights.

This time there was a difference. He swung back again in time to meet the superintendent's stare. The latter had just that moment come out of the elevator with a wad of rent receipts in his hand. You couldn't say that Harlan paled at the involuntary betrayal he had just committed because he hadn't been the color of living protoplasm in thirty-six hours now.

The super had caught the gesture, put his own implication on it. "That bothering you folks too?" he said. "I've had complaints from everyone else on this floor about it so far. I'm going in there right now and invest—"

The hallway went spinning around Harlan like a cyclorama. The superintendent reached out, steadied him by the elbow. "See that, it's got you dizzy already! Must be some kind of sewer-gas." He fumbled for a passkey. "That why you folks wanted to move earlier in the week?"

Harlan still had enough presence of mind left, just enough, to nod. "Why didn't you say so?" the super went on. Harlan didn't have enough left to answer that one. What difference did it make. In about a minute more it would be all over but the shouting. He groped desperately to get himself a minute more time.

"I guess you want the rent," he said with screwy matter-of-factness. "I got it right here with me. Better let me give it to you now. I'm going in to town—"

He paid him the fifty bucks, counted them three times, purposely let one drop, purposely fumbled picking it up. But the passkey still stayed ready in the super's hand. He leaned against the wall, scribbled a receipt, and handed it to Harlan. "Thanks, Mr. Harlan." He turned, started down the hall toward that door. That damnable doorway to hell!

Harlan was thinking: "I'm not going to leave him now. I'm going to stick with him when he goes in there. He's going to make the discovery, but it's never gonna get past him! I can't let it. He saw me look at that door just now. He'll read it all over my face. I haven't got the juice left to bluff it out. I'm going to kill him in there—with my bare hands." He let the rent receipt fall out of his hand, went slowly after the man like somebody walking in his sleep.

The passkey clicked, the super pushed the door open, light came out into the dimmer hallway from it, and he passed from sight. Harlan slunk through the doorframe after him and pushed the door back the other way, partly closing it after the two of them. It was only then that Harlan made an incomprehensible discovery. The air was actually clearer in here than in his own place—clearer even than out in the hall! Stale and dust-laden from being shut up for days, it was true, but odorless, the way air should be!

"Can't be in here, after all," the super was saying, a few paces ahead.

Harlan took up a position to one side of the bedcloset, murmuring to himself: "He lives—until he opens that!"

The super had gone into the bath. Harlan heard him raise and slap down the wooden bowl cover in there, fiddle with the washbasin stopper. "Nope, nothing in here!" he called out. He came out again, went into the postage-stamp kitchen, sniffed around in there, examining the sink, the gas-stove. "It *seemed* to come from in here," he said, showing up again, "I can't make head or tail out of it!"

Neither could Harlan. The only thing he could think of was: the bedding and the mattress, which were on *this* side of what was causing it, must have acted as a barricade, stuffing up the closet-door, and must have kept that odor from coming out into this room, sending it through the thin porous wall in the other direction instead, into his own place and from there out into the hall.

The super's eye roved speculatively on past him and came to rest on the closet door. "Maybe it's something behind that bed," he said.

Harlan didn't bat an eyelash, jerky as he had been before out in the hall. "You just killed yourself then, Mister," was his unheard remark. "This is it. Now!" He gripped the floor-boards with the soles of his feet through the shoe-leather, tensed, crouched imperceptibly for the spring.

The super stepped over, so did Harlan, diagonally, toward him. The super reached down for the knob, touched it, got ready to twist his wrist—

The house-phone in the entry-way buzzed like an angry hornet. Harlan went up off his heels, coming down again on them spasmodically. "Paging me, I guess. I told them I was coming in here," said the super, turning to go out there and answer it. "Okay, Molly," he said, "I'll be right down." He held the front door ready to show Harlan he wanted to leave and lock up again. "Somebody wants to see an apartment," he explained. The door clicked shut, the odors of decay swirled around them once more on the outside of it, and they rode down together in the car.

Something was dying in Harlan by inches—his reason maybe. "I can never go through that again," he moaned. The sweat did not start coming through his paralyzed pores until after he was seated in the train, riding in. Everything looked misshapen and out of focus.

He came back at twilight. In addition to the dusky amber hall lights, there was a fan of bright yellow spilling out of the death-door. Open again, and voices in there. Lined up along the wall outside the door were a radio cabinet, a bridge lamp, a pair of chairs compacted together seat to seat. An expressman in a dirty blue blouse came out, picked them up effortlessly with one arm, and slung them inside after him.

Harlan sort of collapsed against his own door. He scratched blindly for admittance, forgetting he had a key, too shell-shocked to use it even if he had taken it out.

Mrs. Harlan let him in, too simmering with the news she had to tell to notice his appearance or actions. "We've got new neighbors," she said almost before she had the door closed. "Nice young couple, they just started to move in before you got here—"

He was groping desperately for the bottle on the shelf, knocked down a glass and broke it. Then they hadn't found out yet; they hadn't taken down the bed yet! It kept going through his battered brain like a demoniac rhythm. He nearly gagged on the amount of whisky he was swallowing from the neck of the bottle all at one time. When room had been cleared for his voice, he panted: "What about that odor? You mean they took that place the way it—?"

"I guess they were in a hurry, couldn't be choosy. He sent his wife up to squirt deodorant around in the hall before they got here. What does he care, once he gets them signed up? Dirty trick, if you ask me."

He had one more question to ask. "Of course you sized up every stick of stuff they have. Did they—did they bring their own bed with them?"

"No, I guess they're going to use the one in there—"

Any minute now! His brain was fifty per cent blind unreasoning panic, unable to get the thing in the right perspective any more. That discovery itself wasn't necessarily fatal, but his own possible implication in it no longer seemed to register with him. He was confusing one with the other, unable to differentiate between them any more. Discovery had to be prevented, discovery had to be forestalled! Why? Because his own corrosive guilty conscience knew the full explanation of the mystery. He was forgetting that they didn't—unless he gave it to them himself.

Still sucking at the bottle, he edged back to the front door, turned sidewise to it, put his ear up against it.

"T'anks very much, buddy," he heard the moving man say gruffly, and the elevator-slide closed.

He opened the door, peered out. The last of the furniture had gone inside, the hall was clear now. The fumes of the disinfectant the super's wife had used were combating that other odor, but it was still struggling through—to his acute senses, at least. They had left their door open. Their voices were clearly audible as he edged further out. Two living people unsuspectingly getting settled in a room with an unseen corpse!

"Move that over a little further," he heard the woman say. "The bed has to come down there at nights. Oh, that reminds me! He couldn't get it open when he wanted to show it to me today. The door must be jammed. He promised to come back, but I guess he forgot—"

"Let's see what I can do with it," the husband's voice answered.

Harlan, like something drawn irresistibly toward its own destruction, was slinking nearer and nearer, edgewise along the corridor-wall. A tom-tom he carried with him was his heart.

A sound of bare hands pounding wood came through the

bright-yellow gap in the wall ahead. Then a couple of heavier impacts, kicks with the point of a shoe.

"It's not locked, is it?"

"No, when I turn the knob I can see the catch slip back under the lock. Something's holding it jammed in there. The bed must be out of true or somebody closed it too hard the last time."

"What're we going to sleep on?" the woman wailed.

"If I can hit it hard enough, maybe the vibration'll snap it back. Run down a minute and borrow a hammer from the super, like a good girl."

Harlan turned and vanished back where he had come from. Through the crack of the door he saw the woman come out into the hall, stand waiting for the car, go down in it. He said to his wife, "Where's that hammer we used to have?" He found it in a drawer and went out with it.

He was no longer quite sane when he knocked politely alongside that open door down the hall. He knew what he was doing, but the motivation was all shot. The man, standing there in the middle of the lighted room staring helplessly at the fast closet-door, turned his head. He was just an ordinary man, coat off, tie off, suspenders showing; Harlan had never set eyes on him before, their paths were just now crossing for the first time. But discovery had to be prevented, discovery had to be prevented!

Harlan, smiling sleepily, said, "Excuse me. I couldn't help overhearing you ask your wife for a hammer. I'm your next-door neighbor. Having trouble with that bed-closet, I see. Here, I brought you mine."

The other man reached out, took it shaft-first the way Harlan was holding it. "Thanks, that's real swell of you," he grinned appreciatively. "Let's see what luck I have with it this time."

Harlan got in real close. The tips of his fingers kept feeling the goods of his suit. The other man started tapping lightly all up and down the joint of the door. "Tricky things, these beds," he commented.

"Yeah, tricky," agreed Harlan with that same sleepy, watchful smile. He came in a little closer. Something suddenly gave a muffled "Zing!" behind the door, like a misplaced spring or joint jumping back in place.

"That does it!" said the man cheerfully. "Now let's see how she goes. Better stand back a little," he warned. "It'll catch you coming out." He turned the knob with one hand and the door started opening. He passed the hammer back to Harlan, to free the other. Harlan moved around to the same side he was on until he was right at his neighbor's elbow. The door swung flat against the wall. The bed started to come down. The man's two arms went out and up to ease it, so it wouldn't fall too swiftly.

Just as the top-side of it got down to eye-level the hammer rose in Harlan's fist, described a swift arc, fell, crashed into the base of the other man's skull. He went down so instantaneously that the blow seemed not to have been interrupted, to have continued all the way to the floor in one swing. Again the red motes of anger, call them self-preservation this time—

A dull boom came through them first—the bed hitting the floor. They swirled thicker than ever; then screams and angry, frightened voices pierced them. They began to dissipate. He found himself kneeling there alongside the bed, gory hammer poised in his hand, facing them across it. There must have been other blows.

A woman lay slumped there by the door, moaning "My husband, my husband!" They were picking her up to carry her out. Another woman further in the background was staring in, all eyes. Wait, he knew her—his wife. Someone out in the hall was saying, "Hurry up, hurry up! This way! In here!" and two figures in dark-blue flashed in, moving so swiftly that before he knew it they were behind him holding his arms. They took the hammer away. Nothing but voices, a welter of voices, heard through cotton-batting.

"This man is dead!"

"He didn't even know him. They just moved in. Went crazy, I guess."

He was being shaken back and forth from behind, like a terrier. "What'd you do it for? What'd you do it for?"

Harlan pointed at the bed. "So he wouldn't find out—"

"Find out what?" He was being shaken some more. "Find out what? Explain what you mean!"

Didn't they understand, with it staring them right in the face? His eyes came to rest on it. The bed was empty.

"God, I think I understand!" There was such sheer horror in the voice that even Harlan turned to see where it had come from. It was the superintendent. "There was a down-and-outer, a friend of mine. He didn't have a roof over his head—I know I had no right to, but I let him hang out in here nights the past couple weeks, while the apartment was vacant. Just common, ordinary charity. Then people started complaining about losing their milk, and I saw I'd get in trouble, so I told him to get out. He disappeared three days ago, I figured he'd taken me at my word, and then this morning I found out he was in the hospital with a slight head-concussion. I even dropped in for a few minutes to see how he was getting along. He wouldn't tell me how it happened, but I think I get it now. *He* must have done it to him, thought he'd killed him, hidden him there in that folding-bed. My friend got such a fright that he lammed out the minute he came to—"

Harlan was mumbling idiotically, "Then I didn't kill anyone?"

"You went to town on this one, all right," one of the men in blue said. He turned to the second one, scornfully. "To cover up a justified assault-and-battery, he pulls a murder!"

When another man, in mufti, took him out in the hall at the end of two or three short steel links, he recoiled from the putrid odor still clinging out there. "I thought they said he wasn't dead—"

Somewhere behind him he heard the super explaining to one of them: "Aw, that's just some sloppy people on the floor below cooking corned-beef and cabbage alla time, we gave 'em a dispossess for creating a nuisance in the building! He musta thought it was—"

Morning After Murder

"Morning After Murder" portrays murder from a detective's point of view. Another one of Woolrich's oscillation stories, the twist here is how exactly the detective is involved in the murder – whether just as investigator, or as something more sinister. His agonizing self-suspicion takes readers on a wild ride of "did he or didn't he." This story is the rewritten and improved version of the original, "Murder on My Mind," published in *Detective Fiction Weekly* in 1936. This updated version appeared as "Morning After Murder" in the 1952 collection *Bluebeard's Seventh Wife* and again in the 2005 collection *Tonight, Somewhere in New York,* both of which are out of print, and appears here for the first time since those publications.

THE ALARM SMASHED ME wide open, like a hand grenade exploding against my solar plexus. I was already into my shoes and pants before my eyes were even open. Funny, I thought dazedly, when I looked down and saw them on me, how you do things like that automatically, without knowing anything about it, just from long force of habit.

The tin clock went into another tantrum, so I chopped my arm at it and clicked it off. "All right, so I'm up!" I groaned. "What more do you want?" I went into the bathroom and shaved. I looked like the morning after a hard night, eyes all bleary and with ridges under them, and I couldn't understand it. Eight hours' sleep ought to be enough for anyone, and I'd gone to bed at eleven. The mattress must be no good, I decided, and I'd better tackle the landlady for a new one. Or maybe I'd been working too hard; I ought to ask the captain for a leave of absence. Of the two of them, I would have much rather tackled him than her.

She was going off like a Roman candle, at Ephie, the colored maid, when I stepped out of my room into the hall. "Wide open!" she was complaining. "I tell you it was standing wide open, anyone could have walked in! You better count the silverware right away, Ephie—and ask the roomers if any of them are missing anything from their rooms. We could have all been murdered in our beds!" Then she saw me and added with a sniff, "Even though there *is* a detective lodging on the ground floor!"

"I'm off-duty when I come back here at nights," I let her know. I took a look on both sides of the lock of the front door, which was what was causing all the commotion. "It hasn't been jimmied or tampered with in any way. Somebody in the house came in or went out, and forgot to close it tight behind them; the draft blew it open again."

"It's probably that no-account little showgirl who has the third-floor-back, traipsing in all hours of the morning!" she decided instantly. "Just let me get my hands on her!"

I took a deep breath to get my courage up, and made the plunge. "Wonder if you could change my mattress. It must be lumpy or something; I don't seem to be getting my right rest."

This time she went into vocal pyrotechnics that would have put a Fourth of July at Palisades Park to shame. It was the newest mattress in her house; she'd bought it only two years ago last fall; nobody else in the house seemed to find anything wrong with their mattresses; funny that a husky young man like me should. She didn't like single young men in her house, anyway, never had; she'd only made an exception in my case. ("It's not my fault if I'm not married," I protested mildly. "Girls have something to say about that, too.") She liked detectives even less; always cleaning their guns in their rooms. ("I don't clean my gun in my room," I contradicted a little more heatedly, "I clean it down at headquarters.")

She was still going strong by the time I was all the way down at the corner, flagging the bus for headquarters. I had sort of waived my request, so to speak, by withdrawing under fire.

A call came in only about an hour after I got in, sent in by a cop on the beat. The captain sent Beecher and me over. "Man found dead under suspicious circumstances. Go to 25 Donnelly Avenue, you two. Second floor, front."

Riding over in the car Beecher remarked, "You look like hell, Mark. Losing your grip?"

I said, "I feel like I've been dragged through a knothole. I'm going to ask the Old Man for a leave of absence. Know what's been happening to me lately? I go home and I dream about this stuff. It must be starting to get me. You ever have dreams like that?"

"No," he said. "It's like a faucet with me, I turn it off and forget about it till the next day. You used to be that way too. Remember when we were both second-graders, the night that messy Scallopini case finally broke, how we both went to see a

Donald Duck flicker, and you fell off your seat into the aisle just from laughing so hard? That's the only way to be in this racket. It's just a job like any other, look at it that way. Why don't you slow up a little, take it easy? No use punishing yourself too hard."

I nodded and opened the door as we swerved in to the curb. "Just as soon as we find out what this thing is."

Number 25 Donnelly Avenue was a cheap yellow-brick flat. The patrolman at the door said, "Now, get away from here, you people. Move on. There's nothing to see." There wasn't, either. Not from down there. "Them are the windows, up there," he said to us. Beecher went straight in without bothering. I hung back a minute and looked up at them. Just two milky-glass panes that needed washing pretty badly.

Then I turned and looked across at the opposite side of the street, without exactly knowing why. There was a gimcrack one-story taxpayer on the whole block-front over there, that looked as if it had been put up within the last year or so, much newer than this flat.

"Coming?" Beecher was waiting for me in the automatic elevator. "What were you staring at out there?"

"Search me," I shrugged. I'd expected to see a row of old-fashioned brownstone houses with high stoops, and then when I turned I saw a cheap row of modern shops instead. But I couldn't have told him why. I didn't know why myself. Maybe the neighborhood seemed to call for them; there were so many other rows of brownstone fronts scattered about here and there. Just some sort of optical illusion on my part, I guess. Or rather, to be more exact, some sort of illusory optical expectancy that had been disappointed. There was almost a sense of *loss* derived from that particular facade, as though it had flattened to one-story height, cheated me of extra height (as I had turned to glance).

A second patrolman outside the flat-door let us in. The first room was a living room. Nothing in it seemed to have been disturbed. Yesterday evening's paper was spread out on the sofa, where somebody had last been reading it; yesterday evening's headline was as dead as the reader who had bought it. Beyond was the bedroom. A man lay dead on the bed, in the most grotesque position imaginable.

He was half-in and half-out of it. He died either getting into it or getting out of it. I looked at the pillow; that answered it for me. He'd died getting out of it. The indentation made by his head overlapped a little on one side. Therefore he'd reared his head, been struck, and his head had fallen back again onto the pillow; but not exactly into the same indentation it had been lying in before.

One whole leg was still under the covers, the other was touching the floor, toes stuck into a bedroom-slipper. The covers had been pitched triangularly off him, up at the right shoulder and side; that was the side the leg was out of bed on. The leg that had never carried him again, never walked again. The window was open about an inch from the bottom, and the shade was down half way.

Apart from the fact that he was half-in, half-out of bed (and that did not constitute a sign of struggle, but only of interruption) there were no noticeable signs of a struggle whatever, in here any more than in the outer room.

The man's clothes were draped neatly across a chair, and his shoes were standing under it side by side. There were three one-dollar bills and a palmful of change standing untouched on the dresser, the way most men leave their money when they empty their pockets just before retiring at night. I say "untouched" because the three bills were consecutively atop one another, and the change was atop the topmost one of them in turn, to hold them down as a weight. And although the continuing presence of money does not always obviate a robbery-motive (it may be too small an amount to interest the killer) the presence of money in that formalized position did proclaim it to be untouched; no intruder would have taken the trouble to replace the coins atop the bills, after having dislodged them to examine the small fund.

I'd worked on Homicide five years to be able to tell small things like that. Only, in murder cases, there are no small things. There are only things.

We were in the bedroom one minute and fifty seconds, by my watch, the first time. We would be in there again, and longer, of course; but that was all, the first time. We'd gotten this from it: It was just like a room with somebody sleeping in it, apart from the distorted position of the dead man's right leg and the scowlingly violent look on his face.

The examiner showed up several minutes after we had got there, and while he was busy in the bedroom we questioned the superintendent and a couple of the neighbors in the outside room. The dead man's name was Fairbanks, he clerked in a United Cigar store, and he was a hardworking respectable man as far as they knew, never drank, never chased women, never played the horses. He had a wife and a little girl in the country, and while they were away for a two-weeks' rest he'd kept his nose to the grindstone, had gone ahead batching it here in the flat.

The couple in the flat across the hall had known him and his wife, and while she was away they'd been neighborly enough to have him in for coffee with them each morning, so he wouldn't have to stop for it on his way to work. In the evenings, of course, he shifted for himself.

They were the ones had first found him dead. The woman had sent her husband over to knock on Fairbanks's door and find out why he hadn't shown up for his morning's coffee yet; they knew he opened his store at seven and it was nearly that already. Her husband rang the bell and pounded for fully five minutes and couldn't get an answer. He tried the door and it was locked on the inside. He got worried, and went down and got the superintendent, and the latter opened it up with his passkey. And there he was, just as he was now.

Beecher said, "When was the last time you saw him?"

"Last night," the neighbor said. "We all went to the movies together. We came back at eleven, and we left him outside of his door. He went in, and we went in our own place."

I said, "Sure he didn't go out again afterwards?"

"Pretty sure. We didn't hear his door open anymore, at least not while we were still awake, and that was until after twelve.

And it started teeming not long after we got in. I don't think he'd have gone out in that downpour."

I went in the other room and picked up the shoes and looked closely at them. "No," I said when I came back, "he didn't go out, the soles of his shoes are powder-dry with dust. I blew on them and a haze came off." I looked in the hall-closet and he didn't own a pair of rubbers. "If he was murdered—and we'll know for sure in a few minutes—somebody came in here after you people left him outside his door. The position of the body shows he didn't get up to let them in, they got in without his knowledge."

And they hadn't forced their way in, either. The flat-door hadn't been tampered with in any way, the living-room window was latched on the inside, the bedroom window was only open an inch and there was a safety-lock on it—besides there was no fire-escape nor ledge outside of it. A quick survey, quick but not sketchy, had been enough to establish all these points.

"Maybe a master-key was used," Beecher suggested.

I asked the superintendent, "How many keys do you give your tenants, just one or a pair of duplicates?"

"Only one to a flat," he said. "We used to hand out two where there was more than one person to a family, but so many of them moved away without returning them that we quit that."

"Then Fairbanks and his wife only had one, is that right?" I went in and looked; I finally found it. It was in a key case, along with the keys to his store. And this key case was still in his clothing, from the night before. Just to make sure we tried the key on the door, and it was the right key. So he hadn't lost it or mislaid it, and it hadn't been picked up by anybody and made unwarranted use of.

The examiner came out, about now, and we shipped our witnesses outside for the present. "Compound fracture of the skull," he said. "He was hit a terrific blow with some blunt object or instrument. Sometime between midnight and morning. He had an unusually thin skull, and a fragment of it must have pierced his brain, because hardly any blood was shed. A little in each ear, and a slight matting of the hair, that's all."

"Die right away?"

"Not more than a minute or two after. Goodbye."

I called the captain. "All right, you're both on it," he said. "Stay with it."

A minute later the phone rang and it was Fairbanks's company, wanting to know why he hadn't opened his branch store on time.

That saved me the trouble of calling them. "This is Police; he's dead," I said. I asked about his record with them.

"Excellent. He's been working for us the past seven years. He is—I mean he was—a good man."

I asked if any report had ever reached them on his having trouble with anyone, customers or co-workers.

Never, the man on the wire said. Not once. He was well liked by everyone. As a matter of fact he was known by name to a great many customers of that particular store. A couple of years ago they had shifted him to another location, and got so many inquiries for him afterward, that they'd put him right back again where he'd been. "Sounds funny in a chain-store business, but everybody missed him, they wanted him back."

I hung up and turned to Beecher. "Can you get a motive out of this?"

"About as little as you can. No money taken—in fact no money *to* take—no enemies, no bad habits."

"Mistaken identity?"

"Mistaken for who?" he said disgustedly. "Somebody else with no money, no enemies, no bad habits?"

"Don't ask me questions on my questions," I pleaded abjectly. "We have to start somewhere. What do you suppose happened to the blunt instrument Doc mentioned?"

"Carried it out with him, I guess."

Fairbanks had been carried out, meanwhile. I'd seen so many of them go, I didn't even turn my head. After all, where they ended, we began. The fingerprint men had powdered everything they could, which wasn't much, and packed up to go, too. I said,

"Wait a minute!" and motioned them back in. I pointed to the ceiling.

"You don't want us to go up *there*, do you?" they jeered.

"The lights are lit, aren't they?" I said. "And they have been ever since it happened. I've established that. And the switch is over by the door, and he was killed with only one leg out of his bed. Now tell me you took prints on that little mother-of-pearl push-button over there."

Their faces told they hadn't, only too plainly. "We'll change jobs with you," one of them offered lamely.

"Not until you know how to do your own right," I said, unnecessarily cuttingly.

They left in silent offense.

We continued working. My back ached from that damned mattress at the rooming-house, and my eyelids felt as if they were lined with lead.

"I've got something," Beecher called to me finally. I went out to him. "What time did it rain last night? It ought to be in here." He picked up the morning paper, the one outside the door that Fairbanks had never lived to read. What we wanted took finding. We found it finally by indirection, in connection with something else. "Started at eleven forty-five and continued until after two." He spanked the item with his fingernail. "Whoever it was, came in here between two-thirty and dawn."

"Why not right during the rain?"

"For Pete's sake, use your eyes, Mark! Don't you see the little dab of dried mud here on the carpet? Came off his shoes, of course. Well, do you see any blurs from drops of water around it? No. This nap is a cross between felt and cheap velour; it would show them up in a minute. His clothes were dry; just his soles had mud on them, probably under the arches. So he came in after the rain, but before the ground had fully dried."

"I've got some more mud," I said finally, crouching down chin to my knees. It was right beside the bed, showing where he'd stood when he struck Fairbanks. The pillows were still in position, even though Fairbanks was gone, one showing a little rusty-brown swirl. Much like a knothole in wood-grain. I stood over the tiny dirt-streak on the floor, and swung my arm stiffly in an arc, down on top of the pillow. It landed too far out, made no allowance for the weapon. No matter how stubby that had been, it would have hit him down near the shoulder instead of on top of the head. Then I remembered that he hadn't been flat on his back but had already struggled up to a sitting position, feeling for his slippers with one foot, when he'd been hit.

I kept my eye on an imaginary point where his head would have been, sitting up, and then swung—and there was a space of about only two or three inches left between my clenched fist and the imaginary point. That space stood for the implement that had been used. What, I wondered, could be that short and still do such damage?

I heard Beecher whistling up for me from down below the windows and chased down. "I've got a print, a whole print!" he yelled jubilantly. "A honey. Perfect from heel to toe! Just look at it! I can't swear yet it was made by the same guy that went into the flat, but I'm certainly not passing it up." I phoned in for him and told them to send somebody over with paraffin and take it, while he carefully covered it over with his own pocket-handkerchief to protect it from harm. Then we stood around it guarding it.

It was a peach, all right. There was a cement sidewalk along the whole length of the flat, but between it and the building-line there was a strip of unpaved earth about three yards wide, for decorative purposes originally, although now it didn't even bear grass. The sidewalk bridged this sod across to the front door, and it was in one of the two right-angles thus formed that the footprint was set obliquely, pointed in toward the building.

"He came along the sidewalk," Beecher reconstructed, somewhat obviously, "and turned in toward the door, but instead of staying on the cement he cut the corner short, and one whole foot landed on the soggy ground. Left foot. It wasn't made by any milkman, either; this man was making a half-turn around to go in, a milkman would have come up straight from the curb. I'd like to bet this is for us!"

"I'm with you," I nodded.

"It's got everything but the guy's initials. Rubber heel worn down in a semicircle at the back, steel cleat across the toe."

We hung around until they'd greased it and filled it with paraffin, and we were sure we had it. They also took microscopic specimens of the dried mud from the room upstairs, and some of the soil down here around the print, for the laboratory to work over.

"Tall guy and pretty husky, too," Beecher decided. "It's a ten-and-a-half." He rolled up the tape-measure. "And pushed down good and hard by his weight, even though the ground *was* wet."

"About my height and build, then," I suggested. "I take a ten-and-a-half myself." I started to lift my foot off the cement, to match it against the impression, but he'd gone in without waiting, and there was a straggling line of onlookers strung along the opposite side of the street taking it all in, so I turned and went in after him. After all, I didn't have to make sure at this late day what size shoe I wore.

"Well, we've got a little something, anyway," he said sanguinely on the way back upstairs. "We've got it narrowed to a guy approximately six-one or over and between one-eighty and two-twenty. At least we can skip all shrimps and skinny guys. As soon as the mold's hardened enough to get a cast from it, we can start tracking down those shoes to some repair-shop."

"And then like in the story-books," I said morbidly, "they got their man."

"I don't think you're eating right," he grinned.

I told him about the arm-measurement I'd taken beside the head of the bed. I repeated it for him; he couldn't try it for himself because his arms weren't long enough. "With just two, three inches to spare, what else could it have been but the butt of a gun? Held right up close to the handle."

"Let's go over the place; we haven't half-started yet." He began yanking open drawers in the dresser; I went out into the other room again, suddenly turned off to one side and went toward the steam-radiator. I put my whole arm down between it and the wall and pulled up a wrench.

"Here it is," I called. "You can stop looking."

He came in and saw what it was, and, by my stance, where it had come from. He took it and looked at it. We could both see the tiny tuft of hair imbedded between its tightly clamped jaws, the bone splinters—or were they minute particles of scalp?—adhering to the rough edge of it.

"You're right, Mark, this is it," he said in a low voice. Suddenly he wasn't looking at it anymore but at me. "How did you know it was there? You couldn't have seen it through the radiator. You went straight toward it; I didn't hear your step stop a minute."

I just stared at him helplessly. "I don't know," I said. "I wasn't thinking what I was doing. I just, I just went over to the radiator unconsciously and put down my arm behind it—and there it was."

It slipped out of my hand, the wrench, and hit the carpet with a dull thud. I passed the back of my hand across my forehead, dazedly. "I don't know," I mumbled half to myself.

"Mark, you're all in. For pete's sake, why don't you ask to be relieved of duty, go home, and catch some sleep. The hell with how you happened to find it, you found it, that's all that matters!"

"I've been put on here," I said groggily, "and I stay on here until it's over."

The superintendent unhesitatingly identified the wrench as his own. He had a straightforward enough story to tell, as far as that went. He'd been in here with it one day tinkering with the radiator—that had been months ago, in the spring, before they turned the heat off—and had evidently left it behind and forgotten about it.

"Does that make it look bad for me, gents?" he wanted to know anxiously. When they're scared, they always call you "gents"; I don't know why.

"It could," Beecher said gruffly, "but we're not going to let it." The superintendent was a scrawny little fellow, weighed about a hundred-thirty. Small feet. "Don't worry about it." Beecher jerked his thumb at the door for him to go.

"Wait a minute," I said, stopping him, "I'd like to ask you a question—that has nothing to do with this." I took him over by the window with me and squinted out. "Didn't there used to be a row of old-fashioned brownstone houses with high stoops across the way from here?"

"Yeah, sure, that's right!" he nodded, delighted at the harmless turn the questioning had taken. "They pulled them down about a year ago and put up that taxpayer. You remembered them?"

"No," I said slowly, very slowly. I kept shaking my head from side to side, staring sightlessly out. I could sense, rather than see, Beecher's eyes fastened anxiously on the back of my head. I brushed my hand across my forehead again. "I don't know what made me ask you that," I said sort of helplessly, "How could I remember them, if I never saw them be—?" I broke off suddenly and turned to him. "Was this place, this street out here, always called Donnelly Avenue?"

"No," he said, "you're right about that, too. It used to be Kingsberry Road; they changed the name about five years ago; why I don't know."

The name clicked, burst inside my head like a star-shell, lighting everything up. I hit myself on the crown with my open hand, turned to Beecher across the superintendent's shoulder, let out my breath in relief. "No wonder! I used to live here, right in this same building, right in this same flat—25 Kingsberry Road. Ten years ago, when my mother and dad were still alive, rest their souls, when I was going to training school. It's been bothering me ever since we got out of the car an hour ago. I knew there was something familiar about the place, and yet I couldn't put my finger on it—what with their changing the street-name and tearing down those landmarks across the way."

"They remodeled this building some, too," the superintendent put in sagely. "Took down the outside fire-escapes and modernized the front of it. It don't look the same like it used to."

Beecher didn't act particularly interested in all this side-talk; it had nothing to do with what had brought us here today. He shifted a little to close the subject, and then said, "I suppose this thing's spoiled as far as prints go," indicating the wrench. "You wrapped your hand around it when you hauled it up."

"Yes, but I grabbed it down at the end, not all the way up near the head the way he held it. He must have held it up there, foreshortened; the mud shows where he stood."

"We'll send it over to them anyway. Peculiar coincidence. Fairbanks must have come across it behind there and taken it out, then left it lying around, out in the open intending to return it to our friend here. Then this intruder comes in, whacks him with it, and on his way out drops it right back where it had been originally. Funny place to drop it."

"Funny thing to do altogether," I said. "Walk into a place, strike a man dead, turn around and walk out again without touching a thing. Absolutely no motive that I can make out."

"I'm going to run this wrench over to the print-men," he said. "Come on, there's nothing more we can do around here right now."

In the car he noticed the dismal face I was putting on. "Don't let it get you," he said. "We're coming along beautifully. Like a timetable, almost. Got a complete, intact print. Now the weapon. And it's not even twelve hours yet."

"Also got a headache," I said under my breath, wincing.

"We might get something out of his wife; she'll be in from the country this evening. Everyone I've spoken to so far has praised her to the skies, but there might be some man in the background had his eye on her. That's always an angle. Depends how pretty she is; I'll be able to tell you better after I get a look at her."

"I don't agree," I said. "If it were a triangle motive, the man would have tried to cloak it with a fake robbery motive, anything at all, to throw us off the track. He'd know that leaving it blank this way would point twice as quickly—" I broke off short. "What's the idea?"

We'd pulled up in front of my rooming house.

"Go on, get out and get in there," he said gruffly, unlatching the door and giving me a push. "You've been dead on your feet all day! Grab a half-hour's sleep, and then maybe we'll be able to get someplace on this case. I'll start in on the shoeprint-mold, meanwhile. See you over at headquarters later."

"Won't that look great when the captain hears about it!" I protested. "Going home to sleep right in the middle of a job."

"The case'll still be there, I'm not swiping it from you behind your back. This way you're just holding the two of us up. They'll probably have the prints and the mud-analysis ready for us by the time you come down; we can start out from there."

He drove off and cut my halfhearted arguments short. I turned and went up to the door, fumbled for my key, stuck it wearily in the lock—and the door wouldn't open. I jiggled it and wiggled it and prodded it, and no use, it wouldn't work. "What'd the old girl do," I wondered resentfully, "change the lock without telling anybody, because she found it standing open this morning?" I had to ring the bell, and I knew that meant a run-in with her.

It did. The scene darkened and there was her face in the open doorway. "Well, Mr. Marquis! What did you do, lose your door-key? I haven't got a thing to do, you know, except chase up and down stairs all day opening the door for people when they have perfectly good latchkeys to use!"

"Aw, pipe down," I said irritably. "You went and changed the lock."

"I did no such thing!"

"Well, you try this, then, if you think it's perfectly good."

She did and got the same result I had. Then she took it out, looked at it. Then she glared at me, banged it down into my palm. "*This* isn't the key I gave you! How do you expect to open the door when you're not using the right key at all? I don't know where you got this from, but it's not one of the keys to my house. They're all brand-new, shiny; look how tarnished this is."

I looked at it more closely, and I saw that she was right. If I hadn't been half-asleep just now, I would have noticed the difference myself in the first place.

I started going through my pockets then and there, under her watchful eye, feeling—and looking—very foolish. The right one turned up in one of my vest-pockets. I stuck it in the door and it worked.

My landlady, however, wasn't one to let an advantage like this pass without making the most of it. Not that she needed much encouragement at any time. She closed the front door and trailed me into the hall, while I was still wondering where the devil that strange key had come from. "And—ahem—I believe you had a complaint to make about your mattress this morning. Well, I have one to make to you, young man, that's far more important!"

"What is it?" I asked.

She parked a defiant elbow akimbo. "Is it absolutely necessary for you to go to bed with your shoes on? Especially after you've been walking around out in the mud! I'm trying to keep my laundry bills down, and Ephie tells me the bottom sheet on your bed was a sight this morning, all streaked with dried mud! If it happens again, Mr. Marquis, I'm going to charge you for it. And then you wonder why you don't sleep well! If you'd only take the trouble of undressing the way people are supposed to—"

"She's crazy!" I said hotly. "I never in my life—What are you trying to tell me, I'm not housebroken or something?"

Her reaction, of course, was instantaneous—and loud. "Ephie!" she squalled up the stairs. "Ephie! Would you mind bringing down that soiled sheet you took off Mr. Marquis's bed this morning? I'd like to show it to him. It hasn't gone out yet, has it?"

"No, ma'm," came back from upstairs.

I kept giving her the oddest kind of look while we stood there waiting. I could tell from her own expression, she couldn't make out what it was. No wonder she couldn't. It was the kind of look you give a person when you're floundering around out of your depth, and you want them to give you a helping hand, and yet you know somehow they can't. You want *them* to give *you* a word of explanation, instead of your giving it to them. You need it badly, even if it's just a single word.

I distinctly recalled pulling off my shoes the night before when I was turning in. I remembered sitting on the edge of the bed, dog-tired and grunting, and doing it. Remembered how a momentarily formed knot in the lace of one had held me up, remembered how I'd struggled with it, remembered how I'd sworn at it while I was struggling (aloud, yet, and extremely bitterly); and then how I'd finally eradicated it, and given the freed shoe a violent fling off my foot. Remembered how the impetus had thrown it a short distance away and it had fallen over on its side and I'd left it there. All that had been real, not imaginary; all that had happened; all that came back clear as a snapshot.

That peculiar feeling I'd had all morning over at Fairbanks's flat returned to me, redoubled. As though there were some kind of knowledge hidden just around the corner from me, waiting to be exposed. And yet I couldn't seem to turn that corner. It kept pivoting out of reach. Or like a revolving door that keeps taking you past the point where you should step out and you miss it each time. Buildings that suddenly flattened from second to first-story level. Monkey wrenches that come up to meet your hand from behind a radiator. Shoes that find their way back onto your feet without your hand touching them, like magic, like with wings, like in a Disney cartoon. Tired nerves, blurred reflexes, a sick detective trying to catch a healthy murderer.

Ephie and the old girl spread out the sheet foursquare between them, as if they were going to catch someone jumping down from upstairs. "Just look at that!" she declaimed. "That was a clean sheet, put on fresh yesterday morning! I suppose you'll stand there and try to tell me—"

I didn't try to tell her anything. What was there to tell her? There were the sidewise-prints of muddied shoes all over it, like elongated horseshoes, and that was that. But I wasn't listening, anyway. I'd just remembered something else, that had nothing to do with this sheet business. Something that hit me sickeningly like that wrench must have hit poor Fairbanks.

I had a flash of myself the previous Sunday night, that was the night before last, rummaging through an old valise for something, finding a lot of junk that had accumulated in my possession for years, discarding most of it, but saving a tarnished door-key, because I couldn't remember where or what it was from, and therefore I figured I'd better hang onto it. I'd slipped it into my vest-pocket, because I'd had that on me at the time, unbuttoned and without any coat over it.

They must have seen my face get deathly white; I could see a little of the fright reflected in both of theirs, like in a couple of mirrors. Or like when you point a pocket-light at a wall, and it gives you back a pale cast of the original.

"I'll be right back," I said, and left the house abruptly, left the street door standing wide open behind me. I sliced my arm at the first cab that came along and got in.

He took me back to 25 Donnelly Avenue. It was still light out, light enough to see by. I got out and went slowly across the sidewalk, as slowly and rigidly as a man walking to his own doom. I stopped there by that footprint Beecher had found. It was pretty well effaced as far as details went, but the proportions were still there, the length and width of it if nothing else. I raised my left foot slowly from the cement and brought it down on top of it.

It matched like a print can only match the foot that originally made it. After a while I turned the bottom of my own foot up toward me and studied it dazedly. The cleat across the toe, the rubber-heel worn down in a semicircle at the back.

The driver must have thought I was going to topple, the way I stood there rocking, and then the way I put out my hand gropingly and tried to find the doorway for support. He made a move to get out and come over to me, but saw that I'd steadied and was starting to go in the house.

I went upstairs to the locked Fairbanks flat and took out the key that I'd found in my valise two nights ago that I'd mistakenly used on the rooming house door a little while ago. It opened the flat; the door fell back without a squeak in front of me.

"Pop's key," came to me then, sadly, "or maybe Mom's from the long ago and far away." I pulled the door toward me, closing it again, without going in. And as it came back close against my eyes, the door's shiny green coat dimmed off it and it became an old-fashioned walnut dye. "This used to be my door," I said to myself. "I used to come in here. On the other side of it was where I came—when I came home." I let my forehead lean against it, and I felt sort of sick all over. Fright-sick, if there is such a thing.

After a while I went downstairs again, still without having gone into the flat. I phoned Beecher from a pay station, on the outside. "Come over to my place," I said, and I hung up again. Just those few words.

"I should never have been a detective," I said out loud, without noticing I was back within earshot of the cabman again.

"What, are you a detective?" he said immediately. "You look awful sick right now. You guys get sick too? I didn't think you ever did."

"Do we," I moaned expressively.

I was waiting for Beecher in my room when he showed up. I had the muddied sheet in there with me (evidence; detective to the bitter end). He found me sitting there staring at the wall, as though I saw things on it. "Was that you?" he said incredulously. "You sounded like the chief mourner at somebody's funer—"

"Beecher," I said hollowly, "I know who killed that guy Fairbanks. It was me."

He nearly yelped with fright. "I knew this was coming! You've finally cracked from overwork, you've gone haywire. I'm going out and get a doctor!"

I showed him the sheet. I told him about the key, about measuring the footprint. My teeth started chattering. "I woke up half-dead this morning and couldn't remember putting my pants on. And they were all wrinkled. I know now that *I'd been sleeping in them.* The street-door here in this house was found standing wide open first thing this morning before anyone was up yet. It was me went out, came in again, in the early hours.

"I used to live in that same flat he did. I went back there last night. Didn't you notice how I found that wrench, went straight toward it without knowing why myself, this morning?" I ducked my face down, away from him. "Poor devil. With a wife and kid. He's never harmed me. I'd never even seen him before. I told you I've been dreaming lately about the cases we've worked on. And this dream *got up and walked.*

"I must have found my way there in my sleep, with crime and criminals on my mind, all because I used to live there long ago. Put on the light in what I thought was my own room, found him there, mistook him for an intruder, and slugged him with a monkey-wrench right in his own bed—all without waking up." I shivered. "I'm the guy we've both been looking for all day. I'm the guy—and I didn't even know it!" I couldn't stop shaking. "I've been chasing myself. I've been on both ends of the case at once!" I covered up my eyes. "I think I'm going crazy."

I had a small-sized bottle there. It was a Christmas gift; I don't use the stuff worth mentioning. He broke the seal and poured me a short drink. He put it away again without taking one himself. On duty, I suppose. He opened the door and looked out into the hall, to see if anyone was around. No one was; he closed it and came back in again.

"Mark," he said gloomily, "I'm not going to tell you to forget it, that you're crazy, that you're talking through your hat. I wish I could; I'd give my eye-teeth if I could. But from me, you're entitled to it straight from the shoulder."

And then he made a face, like every word he was about to say tasted rotten, tasted moldy, ahead of time.

"You did. I think you did. I think you must have."

I didn't answer. I already knew that myself, was sure of it; he wasn't telling *me* anything.

"Here are the findings, as of now. The only prints that would come off the wrench were yours—yours and Fairbanks's. (And he obviously didn't swing it at himself. His were on the mid-section of the stem, where he lifted it from a horizontal position behind the radiator, when he first found it back there.) The ones near the head of the wrench, where by your own calculations the killer actually held it, matched the ones down at the opposite end of the handle. Both yours. From the light push-button, they got one entire thumbprint. Yours. And those lights were already on when we first arrived this morning, I was a witness to that myself.

"Finally, I've already located the shoe repair-shop which did the cleat job matching up with the mold. It wasn't hard; there aren't many people use them; there are even fewer use them on that particular size shoe." He said this slowly, like he hated to have to, "It wasn't hard to find. It was the first shop I walked into, *right on the corner below headquarters*. I didn't expect to find out anything there. I only went in to get an opinion from him. He recognized it at sight. He said, 'That's *my* job.' He said he'd only done one job like that in the past six months. He said, 'I did that for your buddy, you know the one you call Mark, from headquarters.' He even remembered how you had to sit waiting in one of the little stalls in your socks, because you told him you only own one pair of shoes at a time.

"Until I came over here just now, and you told me what you just did, none of this added up. I even cursed you out a little at first, I remember, because I thought you'd simply fouled up the job *after* we got over there this morning, being half-awake like you were all day. Left the footprint *then*, smudged up the wrench and pushbutton *then*. In spite of the fact that with my own eyes I saw that the lights were already on, that your fingers didn't go near the handle of the wrench, that the ground was too hard and dry to take a footprint anymore by the time we got here."

I held myself by my own throat. "You see how your side of it fits with my side. You see how it must be, *has to be*, the only possible thing that could have happened. You see how we've solved it between us, the way we're paid to, the way we're trained to, and come out with the right answer. I don't remember it even yet, but I have proof now that I did. I walked over there and back in my sleep—with my eyes wide open. What am I going to do?"

"I'll tell you what you're going to do," he suggested in a rough-edged undertone, leaning over toward me and putting his hand down on my shoulder. "You're going to shut up and forget the whole thing. Forget every word you've said to me in here. Get me? I don't know anything, and you haven't told me anything. Case unsolved."

I shifted away from him. "That's what you're trying to talk me into doing because I'm your partner and because it's *me*. Now tell me what you'd do if it was *you*."

He sighed. Then he smiled halfheartedly, and turned away, and gave up trying. "Just about what you're going to do anyway, yourself, so why ask?"

He stood there looking out the window of my room at nothing, brooding, feeling bad. I sat there looking down at the floor, hands pressed to my face, feeling worse.

Finally I got up quietly and put on my hat. "Coming?" I said.

"I'll ride over with you," he agreed. "I've got to go back anyway."

In the car he said, "It's not the first man you've killed"; hesitantly, as though realizing it was a rough thing to say to me, especially right then.

"Yes, but they were criminals, and they were trying to kill me at the time. This man wasn't. He had the law on his side. I killed him in his bed."

"It'll be all right. The Old Man'll know what to do. An inquiry. Sick-leave, maybe, for a while."

"That won't bring him back. I have to sleep with this for the rest of life."

"Nothing lasts that long. The very mayor of New York himself once—Memory wears out. Sound sleep comes back, one night. A year from now you'll be chasing assignments in the car with me again, and looking at mud and looking at light-switches."

I knew somehow, deep in my heart, that he was right. But that didn't make tonight any easier on me. Tonight was tonight, and a year from now was a year from now, and never the two could meet. It's the year between you have to pay for, each time, and I was ready to do my paying.

He didn't offer to shake hands with me, when he left me outside the Old Man's door, that would have been too theatrical. Just—

"I'll see you, Mark."

"I'll see you, Beecher."

It must be hell not to have a partner, no matter what your job is.

I opened the door and went in. I didn't say anything; I went all the way over to his desk and just stood there.

The captain looked up finally. He said, "Well, Marquis?"

I said, "I've brought the man who killed Fairbanks in to you, Captain."

He looked around, on this side of me and on that, and there was no one standing there but me.

TWO MURDERS, ONE CRIME

In a clear echo of the twisted relationship between Jean Valjean and Javert in Victor Hugo's *Les Misérables*, **"Two Murders, One Crime"** explores the lengths one self-righteous cop is willing to go to haunt a murderer who walked free. This gem of a noir cop story is painfully relevant to our societal circumstances today, for it lays bare how the actions of lazy, corrupt and vindictive policemen result in consequences that ripple violently through multiple people's lives. Originally published as "Three Kills for One" in *Black Mask* in 1942, the story featured in the 1945 collection *If I Should Die Before I Wake* and the 2004 collection *Night & Fear*.

KNEW THAT NIGHT, just like on all the other nights before it, around a quarter to twelve Gary Severn took his hat off the hook nearest the door, turned and said to his pretty, docile little wife in the room behind him: "Guess I'll go down to the corner a minute, bring in the midnight edition."

"All right, dear," she nodded, just like on all the other nights before this.

He opened the door, but then he stood there undecidedly on the threshold. "I feel kind of tired," he yawned, backing a hand to his mouth. "Maybe I ought to skip it. It wouldn't kill me to do without it one night. I usually fall asleep before I can turn to page two, anyway."

"Then don't bother getting it, dear, let it go if you feel that way," she acquiesced. "Why put yourself out? After all, it's not that important."

"No it isn't, is it?" he admitted. For a moment he seemed about to step inside again and close the door after him. Then he shrugged. "Oh well," he said, "I may as well go now that I've got my hat on. I'll be back in a couple of minutes." He closed the door from the outside.

Who knows what is important, what isn't important? Who is to recognize the turning-point that turns out to be a trifle, the trifle that turns out to be a turning-point?

A pause at the door, a yawn, a two-cent midnight paper that he wouldn't have remained awake long enough to finish anyway.

He came out on the street. Just a man on his way to the corner for a newspaper, and then back again. It was the 181st day of the year, and on 180 other nights before this one he had come out at this same hour, for this same thing. No, one night there'd been a blizzard and he hadn't. 179 nights, then.

He walked down to the corner, and turned it, and went one block over the long way, to where the concession was located. It was just a wooden trestle set up on the sidewalk, with the papers stacked on it. The tabs were always the first ones out, and they were on it already. But his was a standard size, and it came out the last of all of them, possibly due to complexities of make-up.

The man who kept the stand knew him by his paper, although he didn't know his name or anything else about him. "Not up yet," he greeted him. "Any minute now."

Why is it, when a man has read one particular paper for any length of time, he will refuse to buy another in place of it, even though the same news is in both? Another trifle?

Gary Severn said, "I'll take a turn around the block. It'll probably be here by the time I get back."

The delivery trucks left the plant downtown at 11:30, but the paper never hit the stands this far up much before twelve, due to a number of variables such as traffic-lights and weather which were never the same twice. It had often been a little delayed, just as it was tonight.

He went up the next street, the one behind his own, rounded the upper corner of that, then over, and back into his own again. He swung one hand, kept his other pocketed. He whistled a few inaccurate bars of *Elmer's Tune*. Then a few even more inaccurate bars of *Rose O'Day*. Then he quit whistling. It had just been an expression of the untroubled vacancy of his mind, anyway. His thoughts went something like this: "Swell night. Wonder what star that is up there, that one just hitting the roof? Never did know much about them. That Colonna sure was funny on the air tonight." With a grin of reminiscent appreciation. "Gee I'm sleepy. Wish I hadn't come out just now." Things like that.

He'd arrived back at his own doorway from the opposite direction by now. He slackened a little, hesitated, on the point of going in and letting the paper go hang. Then he went on anyway. "I'm out now. It'll just take a minute longer. There and back." Trifle.

The delivery truck had just arrived. He saw the bale being

pitched off the back to the asphalt, for the dealer to pick up, as he rounded the corner once more. By the time he'd arrived at the stand the dealer had hauled it onto the sidewalk, cut the binding, and stacked the papers for sale on his board. A handful of other customers who had been waiting around closed in. The dealer was kept busy handing them out and making change.

Gary Severn wormed his way in through the little cluster of customers, reached for a copy from the pile, and found that somebody else had taken hold of it at the same time. The slight tug from two different directions brought their eyes around toward one another. Probably neither would have seen the other, that is to look at squarely, if it hadn't been for that. Trifle.

It was nothing. Gary Severn said pleasantly, "Go ahead, help yourself," and relinquished that particular copy for the next one below it.

"Must think he knows me," passed through his inattentive mind. The other's glance had come back a second time, whereas his own hadn't. He paid no further heed. He handed the dealer his nickel, got back two cents, turned and went off, reading the headlines as he went by the aid of the fairly adequate shop-lights there were along there.

He was dimly aware, as he did so, of numbers of other footsteps coming along the same way he was. People who had just now bought their papers as he had, and had this same direction to follow. He turned the corner and diverged up into his own street. All but one pair of footsteps went on off the long way, along the avenue, died out. One pair turned off and came up this way, as he had, but he took no notice.

He couldn't read en route any more, because he'd left the lights behind. The paper turned blue and blurred. He folded it and postponed the rest until he should get inside.

The other tread was still coming along, a few yards back. He didn't look around. Why should he? The streets were free to everyone. Others lived along this street as well as he. Footsteps behind him had no connection with him. He didn't have that kind of a mind, he hadn't led that kind of a life.

He reached his own doorway. As he turned aside he started to drag up his key. The other footsteps would go on past now, naturally. Not that his mind was occupied with them. Simply the membranes of his ears. He'd pulled out the building street-door, had one foot already through to the other side. The footsteps had come abreast —

A hand came down on his shoulder.

"Just a minute."

He turned. The man who had been buying a paper; the one who had reached for the same one he had. Was he going to pick a quarrel about such a petty—?

"Identify yourself."

"Why?"

"I said identify yourself." He did something with his free hand, almost too quick for Gary Severn to take in its significance. Some sort of a high-sign backed with metal.

"What's that for?"

"That's so you'll identify yourself."

"I'm Gary Severn. I live in here."

"All right. You'd better come with me." The hand on his shoulder had shifted further down his arm now, tightened.

Severn answered with a sort of peaceable doggedness, "Oh no, I won't go with you unless you tell me what you want with me. You can't come up to me like this outside my house and— "

"You're not resisting arrest, are you?" the other man suggested. "I wouldn't."

"Arrest?" Severn said blankly. "Is this arrest? Arrest for what?"

A note of laughter sounded from the other, without his grim lips curving in accompaniment to it. "I don't have to tell you that, do I? Arrest for murder. For the worst kind of murder there is. Murder of a police offer. In the course of the attempted robbery. On Farragut Street." He spaced each clipped phrase. "Now do you remember?"

Arrest for murder.

He said it over to himself. It didn't even frighten him. It had no meaning. It was like being mistaken for Dutch Schultz or — some sort of a freak mix-up. The thing was, he wouldn't get to bed until all hours now probably, and that might make him late in the morning. And just when he was so tired too.

All he could find to say was a very foolish little thing. "Can't I go inside first and leave my paper? My wife's waiting in there, and I'd like to let her know I may be gone for half an hour or so — "

The man nodded permission, said: "Sure, I'll go inside with you a minute, while you tell your wife and leave your paper."

A life ends, and the note it ends on is: "Can I go inside first and leave my paper?"

On the wall was a typical optician's sight-chart, beginning with a big beetling jumbo capital at the top and tapering down to a line of fingernail-size type at the bottom. The detectives had been occupied in trying themselves out on it while they were waiting. Most, from a distance of across the room, had had to stop at the fourth line below the bottom. Normal eyesight. One man had been able to get down as far as the third, but he'd missed two of the ten letters in that one. No one had been able to get down below that.

The door on the opposite side opened and the Novak woman was brought in. She'd brought her knitting.

"Sit down there. We'd like to try you out on this chart, first."

Mrs. Novak tipped her shoulders. "Glasses you're giving out?"

"How far down can you read?"

"All the way."

"Can you read the bottom line?"

Again Mrs. Novak tipped her shoulders. "Who couldn't?"

"Nine out of ten people couldn't," one of the detectives murmured to the man next to him.

She rattled it off like someone reading a scare-head. "p, t, b, k, j, h, i, y, q, a."

Somebody whistled. "Far-sighted."

She dropped her eyes complacently to her needles again. "This I don't know about. I only hope you'll gentlemen'll going to be through soon. While you got me coming in and out of here, my business ain't getting my whole attention."

The door opened and Gary Severn had come in. Flanked. His whole life was flanked now.

The rest of it went quick. The way death does.

She looked up. She held it. She nodded. "That's him. That's the man I saw running away right after the shots."

Gary Severn didn't say anything.

One of the detectives present, his name was Eric Rogers, he didn't say anything either. He was just there, a witness to it.

The other chief witness' name was Storm. He was a certified accountant, he dealt in figures. He was, as witnesses go, a man of good will. He made the second line from the bottom on the chart, better than any of the detectives had, even if not as good as Mrs. Novak. But then he was wearing glasses. But then — once more — he'd also been wearing them at the time the fleeing murderer had bowled him over on the sidewalk, only a few doors away from the actual crime, and snapped a shot at him which miraculously missed. He'd promptly lain inert and feigned death, to avoid a possible second and better-aimed shot.

"You realize how important this is?"

"I realize. That's why I'm holding back. That's why I don't like to say I'm 100% sure. I'd say I'm 75% sure it's him. I got 25% doubts."

"What you'd *like* to say," he was cautioned, "has nothing to do with it. Either you are sure or you aren't. Sureness has no percentages. Either it's one hundred or it's zero. Keep emotion out of this. Forget that it's a man. You're an accountant. It's a column of figures to you. There's only one right answer. Give us that answer. Now we're going to try you again."

Gary Severn came in again.

Storm moved his figures up. "90% sure," he said privately to the lieutenant standing behind him. "I still got 10% doubt left."

"*Yes* or *no?*"

"I can't say no, when I got 90% on the yes-side and only — "

"YES or NO!"

It came slow, but it came. It came low, but it came. "Yes."

Gary Severn didn't make a sound. He'd stopped saying anything long ago. Just the sound of one's own voice, unheard, unanswered, what good is that?

The detective named Rogers, he was there in the background again. He just took it in like the rest. There was nothing he felt called on to say.

The news-dealer, his name was Mike Mosconi, set in jackknife position in the chair and moved his hat uneasily around in his hands while he told them: "No, I don't know his name and I'm not even sure which house he lives in, but I know him by sight as good as you can know anybody, and he's telling the truth about that. He hasn't missed buying a paper off me, I don't think more than once or twice in the whole year."

"But he did stay away once or twice," the lieutenant said. "And what about this twenty-second of June, is that one of those once or twices he stayed away?"

The news-dealer said unhappily, "I'm out there on the street every night in the year, gents. It's hard for me to pick out a certain night by the date and say for sure that that was the one out of all of 'em – But if you get me the weather for that night, I can do better for you."

"Get him the weather for that night," the lieutenant consented.

The weather came back. "It was clear and bright on the twenty-second of June."

"Then he bought his paper from me that night," Mike Mosconi said inflexibly. "It's the God's honest truth; I'm sure of it and you can be too. The only one or two times he didn't show up was when — "

"How long did it take him to buy his paper each time?" the lieutenant continued remorselessly.

Mike Mosconi looked down reluctantly. "How long does it

take to buy a paper? You drop three cents, you pick it up, you walk away—"

"But there's something else you haven't told us. At what time each night did he do this quick little buying of the paper? Was it the same time always, or did it vary, or what time was it?"

Mike Mosconi looked up in innocent surprise. "It was the same time always. It never varied. How could it? He always gets the midnight edition of the Herald-Times, it never hits my stand until quarter to twelve, he never came out until then. He knew it wouldn't be there if he did — "

"The twenty-second of June — ?"

"Any night, I don't care which it was. If he came at all, he came between quarter of and twelve o'clock."

"You can go, Mosconi."

Mosconi went. The lieutenant turned to Severn.

"The murder was at ten o'clock. What kind of an alibi was that?"

Severn said in quiet resignation, "The only one I had."

Gates didn't look like a criminal. But then there is no typical criminal look, the public at large only thinks there is. He was a big husky blackhaired man, who gave a misleading impression of slow-moving genial good-nature totally unwarranted by the known facts of his career. He also had an air of calm self-assurance, that most likely came more from a lack of imagination than anything else.

He said, "So what do you expect me to say? If I say no, this ain't the guy, that means *I* was there but with someone else. If I say yes, it is him, that means the same thing. Don't worry, Mr. Strassburger, my counsel, wised me up about the kind of trick questions you guys like to ask. Like when they want to know 'Have you quit beating your wife?' "

He looked them over self-possessedly. "All I'm saying is I wasn't there myself. So if I wasn't there myself, how can there be a right guy or a wrong guy that was there with me? *I'm* the wrong guy, more than anybody else." He tapped himself on the breast-bone with emphatic conviction. "Get the right guy in my place first, and then he'll give you the right second guy."

He smiled a little at them. Very little. "All I'm saying, now and at any other time, is I never saw this guy before in my life. If you want it that way, you can have it."

The lieutenant smiled back at him. Also very little. "And you weren't on Farragut Street that night? And you didn't take part in the murder of Sergeant O'Neill?"

"That," said Gates with steely confidence, "goes with it."

Gates got up, but not fast or jerkily, with the same slowness that had always characterized him. He wiped the sweat off his palms by running them lightly down his sides. As though he were going to shake hands with somebody.

He was. He was going to shake hands with death.

He wasn't particularly frightened. Not that he was particularly brave. It was just that he didn't have very much imagination. Rationalizing, he knew that he wasn't going to be alive any more ten minutes from now. Yet he wasn't used to casting his imagination ten minutes ahead of him, he'd always kept it by him in the present. So he couldn't visualize it. So he wasn't as unnerved by it as the average man would have been.

Yet he was troubled by something else. The ridges in his forehead showed that.

"Are you ready, my son?"

"I'm ready."

"Lean on me."

"I don't have to, Father. My legs'll hold up. It ain't far." It was made as a simple statement of fact, without sarcasm or rebuke intended.

They left the death cell.

"Listen, that Severn kid," Gates said in a quiet voice, looking straight ahead. "He's following me in in five minutes. I admit I did it. I held out until now, to see if I'd get a reprieve or not. I didn't get the reprieve, so it don't matter now any more. All right, I killed O'Neill, I admit it. But the other guy, the guy with me that helped me kill him, it wasn't Severn. Are you listening? Can you hear me? It was a guy named Donny Blake. I never saw Severn before in my life until they arrested him. For ——'s sake, tell them that, Father! All right, I'm sorry for swearing at such at time. But tell them that, Father! You've got to tell them that! There's only five minutes left."

"Why did you wait so long, my son?"

"I told you, the reprieve — I been telling the warden since last night. I think he believes me, but I don't think he can get them to do anything about it, the others, over him — Listen, *you* tell him, Father! You believe me, don't you? The dead don't lie!"

His voice rose, echoed hollowly in the short passage. "Tell them not to touch that kid! He's not the guy that was with me—"

And he said probably the strangest thing that was ever said by a condemned man on the way to execution. "Father, don't walk any further with me! Leave me now, don't waste time. Go to the warden, tell him—!"

"Pray, my son. Pray for yourself. You are my charge —"

"But I don't need you, Father. Can't you take this off my mind? Don't let them bring that kid in here after me — !"

Something cold touched the crown of his head. The priest's arm slowly drew away, receded into life.

"Don't forget what you promised me, Father. Don't let — "

The hood, falling over his face, cut the rest of it short.

The current waned, then waxed, then waned again—

He said in a tired voice, "Helen, I love you. I — "

The hood, falling over his face, cut the rest of it short.

The current waned, then waxed, then waned again —

They didn't have the chart on the wall any more. It had done them poor service. The door opened and Mrs. Novak was ushered in. She had her knitting with her again. Only she was making a different article, of a different color, this time. She nodded restrainedly to several of them, as one does to distant acquaintances encountered before.

She sat down, bent her head, the needles began to flicker busily.

Somebody came in, or went out. She didn't bother looking.

The toecaps of a pair of shoes came to a halt just within the radius of vision of her downcast eyes. They remained motionless there on the floor, as though silently importuning her attention. There wasn't a sound in the room.

Mrs. Novak became aware of the shoes at last. She raised her eyes indifferently, dropped them. Then they shot up again. The knitting sidled from her lap as the lap itself dissolved into a straight line. The ball of yarn rolled across the floor unnoticed. She was clutching at her own throat with both hands.

There wasn't a sound in the room.

She pointed with one trembling finger. It was a question; a plea that she be mistaken, but more than anything else a terrified statement of fact.

"It's him — the man that ran past by my store — from where the police-officer — !"

"But the last time you said — "

She rolled her eyes, struck her own forehead. "I know," she said brokenly. "He looked *like* him. But only he looked *like* him, you understand? This one, it *is* him!" Her voice railed out at them accusingly. "Why you haf to bring me here that other time? If you don't, I don't make such a mistake!"

"There were others made the same mistake," the lieutenant tried to soothe her. "You were only one of five or six witnesses. Every one of them—"

She wouldn't listen. Her face crinkled into an ugly mask. Suddenly, with no further ado, tears were working their way down its seams. Somebody took her by the arm to help her out. One of the detectives had to pick up the fallen knitting, hand it back to her, otherwise she would have left without it. And anything that could make her do that —

"I killed him," she mourned.

"It wasn't you alone," the lieutenant acknowledged bitterly as she was led from the room. "We all did."

They seated Donny Blake in a chair, after she had gone, and one of them stood directly behind it like a mentor. They handed this man a newspaper and he opened it and held it spread out before Blake's face, as though he were holding it up for him to read.

The door opened and closed, and Storm, the chartered accountant, was sitting there across the room, in the exact place the Novak woman had been just now.

He looked around at them questioningly, still unsure of just why he had been summoned here. All he saw was a group of detectives, one of them buried behind a newspaper.

"Keep looking where that newspaper is," the lieutenant instructed quietly.

Storm looked puzzled, but he did.

The detective behind the chair slowly began to raise it, like a curtain. Blake's chin peered below first. Then his mouth. Then nose, eyes, forehead. At last his whole face was revealed.

Storm's own face whitened. His reaction was quieter than the woman's had been, but just as dramatic. He began to tremble right as he sat there in the chair; they could see it by his hands mostly. "Oh my God," he mouthed in a sickened undertone.

"Have you anything to say?" the lieutenant urged. "Don't be afraid to say it."

He stroked his mouth as though the words tasted rotten even before they'd come out. "That's — that's the face of the man I collided with — on Farragut Street."

"You're sure?"

His figures came back to him, but you could tell they gave him no comfort any longer. "One hundred percent!" he said dismally, leaning way over his own lap as though he had a cramp.

"They're not altogether to blame," the lieutenant commented to a couple of his men after the room had been cleared. "It's very hard, when a guy looks a good deal like another, not to bridge the remaining gap with your own imagination and supply the rest.

Another thing, the mere fact that we were already holding Severn in custody would unconsciously influence them in identifying him. We thought he was the guy, and we ought to know, so if we thought he was, he probably was. I don't mean they consciously thought of it in that way, but without their realizing it, that would be the effect it would have on their minds."

A cop looked in, said: "They've got Blake ready for you, lieutenant."

"And I'm ready for him," the lieutenant answered grimly, turning and leading the way out.

The doctor came forward, tipped up one of Blake's eyelids. Sightless white showed. He took out a stethoscope and applied it to the region of the heart.

In the silence their panting breaths reverberated hollowly against the basement walls.

The doctor straightened up, removed the stethoscope. "Not very much more," he warned in a guarded undertone. "Still okay, but he's wearing down. This is just a faint. You want him back?"

"Yeah," one of the men said. "We wouldn't mind."

The doctor extracted a small vial from his kit, extended it toward the outsize, discolored mass that was Blake's nose. He passed it back and forth in a straight line a couple of times.

Blake's eyelids flickered up. Then he twitched his head away uncomfortably.

There was a concerted forward shift on the part of all of them, like a pack of dogs closing in on a bone.

"Wait'll the doc gets out of the room," the lieutenant checked them. "This is our own business."

Donny Blake began to weep. "No, I can't stand any more. Doc," he called out frantically, "Doc! Don't leave me in here with 'em! They're killing me — !"

The doctor had scant sympathy for him. "Then why don't you tell 'em what they want to know?" he grunted. "Why waste everyone's time?" He closed the door after him.

Maybe because the suggestion came from an outsider, at least someone distinct from his tormentors. Or maybe because this was the time for it anyway.

Suddenly he said, "Yeah, it was me. I did. I was with Gates and the two of us killed this guy O'Neill. He horned in on us in the middle of this uncut diamond job we were pulling. He didn't see me. I came up behind him while he was holding Gates at the point of his gun. I pinned him to the wall there in the entrance and we took his gun away from him. Then Gates said, 'He's seen us now,' and he'd shot him down before I could stop him. I said, 'He's still alive, he'll tell anyway,' and I finished him off with one into the head."

He covered his face with palsied hands. "Now I've given it to you. Don't hurt me any more. Lemme alone."

"See who that is," the lieutenant said.

A cop was on the other side of the door when it had been opened. "The D.A.'s Office is on the phone for you, lieutenant. Upstairs in your own office."

"Get the stenographer," the lieutenant said, "I'll be right back."

He was gone a considerable time, but he must have used up most of it on the slow, lifeless way he came back. Dawdling along. He came in with a funny look on his face, as though he didn't see any of them any more. Or rather, did, but hated to have to look at them.

"Take him out," he said curtly.

No one said anything until the prisoner was gone. Then they all looked at the lieutenant curiously, waiting for him to speak. He didn't.

"Aren't you going to have it taken down, lieutenant, while it's still flowing free and easy?"

"No," the lieutenant said, tight-lipped.

"But he'll seal up again, if we give him time to rest — "

"We're not going to have a chance to use it, so there's no need getting it out of him." He sank deflatedly onto the chair the prisoner had just been propped in. "He's not going to be brought to trial. Those are the orders I just got. The D.A.'s Office says to turn him loose."

He let the commotion eddy unheard above his head for a while.

Finally someone asked bitterly, "What is it, politics?"

"No. Not altogether, anyway. It's true it's an election year, and they may play a part, but there's a lot more involved than just that. Here's how they lined it up to me. Severn has been executed for that crime. There's no way of bringing him back again. The mistake's been made, and it's irretrievable. To bring this guy to trial now will unleash a scandal that will affect not only the D.A.'s Office, but the whole Police Department. It's not only their own skins, or ours, they're thinking of. It's the confidence of the public. It'll get a shock that it won't recover from for years to come. I guess they feel they would rather have one guilty criminal walk out scot-free than bring about a condition where, for the next few years, every time the law tries to execute a criminal in this State, there'll be a hue and cry raised that it's another miscarriage of justice like the Severn case. They won't be able to get any convictions in our courts. All a smart defense lawyer will have to do is mention the name of Severn, and the jury will automatically acquit the defendant, rather than take a chance. It's a case of letting one criminal go now, or losing dozens of others in the future." He got up with a sigh. "I've got to go up now and get him to sign a waiver."

The handful of men stood around for a minute or two longer. Each one reacted to it according to his own individual temperament. One, of a practical turn of mind, shrugged it off, said: "Well, it's not up to us — Only I wish they'd told us before we put in all that hard work on him. Coming, Joe?"

Another, of a legalistic turn of mind, began to point out just why the D.A.'s Office had all the wrong dope. Another, of a clannish turn of mind, admitted openly: "I wouldn't have felt so sore, if only it hadn't happened to be a police sergeant."

One by one they drifted out. Until there was just one left behind. The detective named Rogers. He stayed on down there alone after all the rest had gone. Hands cupped in pockets, staring down at the floor, while he stood motionless.

His turn of mind? That of a zealot who has just seen his cause betrayed. That of a true believer who has just seen his scripture made a mockery of.

They met in the main corridor at Headquarters a few hours later, the detective and the murderer who was already a free man, immune, on his way back to the outer world.

Rogers just stood there against the wall as he went by. His head slowly turned, pacing the other's passage as their paths crossed. Not a word was exchanged between them. Blake had a strip of plaster alongside his nose, another dab of it under his lip. But Gary Severn was dead in the ground. And so was Police Sergeant O'Neill.

And the little things about him hurt even worse. The untrammelled swing of his arms. The fastidious pinch he was giving his necktie-knot. He was back in life again, full-blast, and the knot of his necktie mattered again.

He met the detective's eyes arrogantly, turning his own head to maintain the stare between them unbroken. Then he gave a derisive chuckle deep in his throat. It was more eloquent, more insulting than any number of words could have been. "Hagh!" It meant "The police — hagh! Their laws and regulations — hagh! Murder — hagh!"

It was like a blow in the face. It smarted. It stang. It hurt Rogers where his beliefs lay. His sense of right and wrong. His sense of justice. All those things that people — some of them anyway — have, and don't let on they have.

Roger's face got white. Not all over. Just around the mouth and chin. The other man went on. Along the short remainder of the corridor, and out through the glass doors, and down the steps out of sight. Rogers stood there without moving, and his eyes followed him to the bitter end, until he was gone, there wasn't anything left to look at any more.

He'd never be back here again. He'd never be brought back to answer for that one particular crime.

Rogers turned and went swiftly down the other way. He came to a door, his lieutenant's door, and he pushed it open without knocking and went in. He put his hand down flat on the desk, then he took it away again.

The lieutenant looked down at the badge left lying there, then up at him.

"My written registration will follow later. I'm quitting the force." He turned and went back to the door again.

"Rogers, come back here. Now wait a minute — You must be crazy."

"Maybe I am a little, at that," Rogers admitted.

"Come back here, will you? Where you going?"

"Wherever Blake is, that's where I'll be from now on. Wherever he goes, that's where you'll find me." The door ebbed closed, and he was gone.

"Which way'd he go?" he said to a cop out on the front steps.

"He walked down a ways, and then he got in a cab, down there by the corner. There it is, you can still see it up ahead there, waiting for that light to change —"

Rogers hoisted his arm to bring over another, and got in.

"Where to, cap?"

"See that cab, crossing the intersection up there ahead? Just go which ever way that goes, from now on."

Blake left the blonde at the desk and came slowly and purposefully across the lobby toward the overstuffed chair into which Rogers had just sunk down. He stopped squarely in front of him, legs slightly astraddle. "Why don't you get wise to yourself? Was the show good? Was the rest'runt good? Maybe you think I don't know your face from that rat-incubator downtown. Maybe you think I haven't seen you all night long, everyplace where I was."

Rogers answered quietly, looking up at him. "What makes you think I've been trying for you not to see me?"

Blake was at a loss for a minute. He opened his mouth, closed it again, swallowed. "You can't get me on that O'Neill thing. You guys wouldn't have let me go in the first place, if you could have held me on it, and you know it! It's finished, water under the bridge."

Rogers said as quietly, as readily as ever, "I know I can't. I agree with you there. What makes you think I'm trying to?"

Again Blake opened and closed his mouth abortively. The best answer he could find was, "I don't know what you're up to, but you won't get anywhere."

"What makes you think I'm trying to get anywhere?"

Blake blinked and looked at a loss. After an awkward moment, having been balked of the opposition he'd expected to meet, he turned on his heel and went back to the desk.

He conferred with the blonde for a few minutes. She began to draw away from him. Finally she shrugged off the importuning hand he tried to lay on her arm. Her voice rose. "Not if you're being shadowed — count me out! I ain't going to get mixed up with you. You should have told me sooner. You better find somebody else to go around with!" She turned around and flounced indignantly out.

Blake gave Rogers the venomous look of a beady-eyed cobra. Then he strode ragingly off in the opposite direction, entered the waiting elevator."

Rogers motioned languidly to the operator to wait for him, straightened up from his chair, ambled leisurely over, and stepped in in turn. The car started up with the two of them in it. Blake's face was livid with rage. A pulse at his temple kept beating a tattoo.

"Keep it up," he said in a strangled undertone behind the operator's back.

"Keep what up?" answered Rogers impassively.

The car stopped at the sixth and Blake flung himself off. The door closed behind him. He made a turn of the carpeted corridor, stopped, put his key into a door. Then he whirled savagely as a second padded tread came down the corridor in the wake of his own.

"What d'ye think you're going to do," he shrilled

exasperatedly, "come right inside my room with me?"

"No," Rogers said evenly, putting a key to the door directly opposite, "I'm going into my own room."

The two doors closed one after the other.

That was at midnight, on the sixth floor of the Congress Hotel. When Blake opened the door of his room at ten the next morning, all freshly combed and shaven, to go down to breakfast, it was on the tenth floor of the Hotel Colton. He'd changed abodes in the middle of the night. As he came out he was smiling to himself behind the hand he traced lightly over the lower part of his face to test the efficacy of his recent shave.

He closed the door and moved down the corridor toward the elevator.

The second door down from his own, on the same side, opened a moment or two after he'd gone by, before he'd quite reached the turn of the hall. Something made him glance back. Some lack of completion, maybe the fact that it hadn't immediately closed again on the occupant's departure as it should have.

Rogers was standing sidewise in it, back to door-frame, looking out after him while he unhurriedly completed hitching on his coat.

"Hold the car for me a sec, will you?" he said matter-of-factly. "I'm on my way down to breakfast myself."

On the third try he managed to bring the cup up to its highest level yet, within an inch of his lips, but he still couldn't seem to manage that remaining inch. The cup started to vibrate with the uncontrollable vibration of the wrist that supported it, slosh over at the sides. Finally it sank heavily down again, with a crack that nearly broke the saucer under it, as though it were too heavy for him to hold. Its contents splashed up.

Rogers, sitting facing him from a distance of two tables away, but in a straight line, went ahead enjoyably and calmly mangling a large dish of bacon and eggs. He grinned through a full mouth, while his jaws continued inexorably to move with a sort of traction movement.

Blake's wrists continued to tremble, even without the cup to support. "I can't stand it," he muttered, shading his eyes for a minute. "Does that man have to – ?" Then he checked the remark.

The waiter, mopping up the place before him, let his eye travel around the room without understanding. "Is there something in here that bothers you, sir?"

"Yes," Blake said in a choked voice, "there is."

"Would you care to sit this way, sir?"

Blake got up and moved around to the opposite side of the table, with his back to Rogers. The waiter refilled his cup.

He started to lift it again, using both hands this time to make sure of keeping it steady.

The peculiar crackling, grating sound caused by a person chomping on dry toast reached him from the direction in which he had last seen Rogers. It continued incessantly after that, without a pause, as though the consumer had no sooner completed one mouthful of the highly audible stuff than he filled up another and went to work on that.

The cup sank down heavily, as if it weighed too much to support even in his double grasp. This time it overturned, a tan puddle overspread the table. Blake leaped to his feet, flung his napkin down, elbowed the solicitous waiter aside.

"Lemme out of here," he panted. "I can still feel him, every move I make, watching me, watching me from behind — !"

The waiter looked around, perplexed. To his eyes there was no one in sight but a quiet, inoffensive man a couple of tables off, minding his own business, strictly attending to what was on the plate before him, not doing anything to disturb anyone.

"Gee, you better see a doctor, mister," he suggested worriedly. "You haven't been able to sit through a meal in days now."

Blake floundered out of the dining room, across the lobby, and into the drugstore on the opposite side. He drew up short at the fountain, leaned helplessly against it with a haggard look on his face.

"Gimme an aspirin!" His voice frayed. "Two of them, three of them!"

"Century Limited, 'Ca-a-awgo, Track Twenty-five!" boomed dismally through the vaulted rotunda. It filtered in, thinned a little through the crack in the telephone-booth panel that Blake was holding fractionally ajar, both for purposes of ventilation and to be able to hear the despatch when it came.

Even now that he had come, he stayed in the booth and the phone stayed on the hook. He'd picked the booth for its strategic location. It not only commanded the clock out there, more important still it commanded the wicket leading down to that particular track that he was to use, and above all, the prospective passengers who filed through it.

He was going to be the last one on that train. The last possible one, and he was going to know just who had preceded him aboard, before he committed himself to it himself.

It was impossible, with all the precautions he had taken, that that devil in human form should sense the distance he was about to put between them once and for all, come after him this time. If he did, then he was a mind-reader, pure and simple; there would be no other way to explain it.

It had been troublesome and expensive, but if it succeeded, it would be worth it. The several unsuccessful attempts he had made to change hotels had shown him the futility of that type of disappearance. This time he hadn't made the mistake of asking for his final bill, packing his belongings, or anything like that. His clothes, such as they were, were still in the closet; his baggage was still empty. He'd paid his bill for a week in advance, and this was only the second day of that week. He'd given no notice of departure. Then he'd strolled casually forth as on any other day, sauntered into a movie, left immediately by another entrance, come over here, picked up the reservation they'd been holding for him under another name, and closed himself up in this phone-booth. He'd been in it for the past three-quarters of an hour now.

And his nemesis, meanwhile, was either loitering around

outside that theatre waiting for him to come out again, or sitting back there at the hotel waiting for him to return.

He scanned them as they filed through in driblets; now one, now two or three at once, now one more again, now a brief let-up.

The minute-hand was beginning to hit train-time. The guard was getting ready to close the gate again. Nobody else was passing through any more now.

He opened the booth-flap, took a tight tug on his hat-brim, and poised himself for a sudden dash across the marble floor.

He waited until the latticed gate was stretched all the way across, ready to be latched onto the opposite side of the gateway. Then he flashed from the booth and streaked over toward it. "Hold it!" he barked, and the guard widened it again just enough for him to squeeze through sidewise.

He showed him his ticket on the inside, after it was already made fast. He looked watchfully out and around through it, in the minute or two this took, and there was no sign of anyone starting up from any hidden position around the waiting rooms or any place near-by and starting after him.

He wasn't here; he'd lost him, given him the slip.

"Better make it fast, mister," the guard suggested.

He didn't have to tell him that; the train didn't exist that could get away from him now, even if he had to run halfway through the tunnel after it.

He went tearing down the ramp, wig-wagging a line of returning redcaps out of his way.

He got on only by virtue of a conductor's outstretched arm, a door left aslant to receive him, and a last-minute flourish of tricky footwork. He got on, and that was all that mattered.

"That's it," he heaved gratifiedly. "Now close it up and throw the key away! There's nobody else, after me."

"They'd have to be homing pigeons riding a tail-wind, if there was," the conductor admitted.

He'd taken a compartment, to make sure of remaining unseen during the trip. It was two cars up, and after he'd reached it and checked it with the conductor, he locked himself in and pulled down the shade to the bottom, even though they were still in the tunnel under the city.

Then he sank back on the upholstered seat with a long sigh. Finally! A complete break at last. "He'll never catch up with me again now as long as I live," he murmured bitterly. "I'll see to that."

Time and trackage ticked off.

They stopped for a minute at the uptown station. There was very little hazard attached to that, he felt. If he'd guessed his intentions at all, he would have been right at his heels down at the main station, he wouldn't take the risk of boarding the train later up here. There wouldn't be time enough to investigate thoroughly, and he might get on the wrong train and be carried all the way to the Mid-West without his quarry.

Still, there was nothing like being sure, so after they were well under way again, he rang for the conductor, opened the door a half-inch, and asked him through it: "I'm expecting to meet somebody. Did anyone get on just now, uptown?"

"Just a lady and a little boy, that who — ?"

"No," said Blake, smiling serenely, "that wasn't who." And he locked the door again. All set now.

Sure, he'd come out there after him maybe, but all he, Blake, needed was this momentary head-start; he'd never be able to close in on him again, he'd keep it between them from now on, stay always a step ahead.

They stopped again at Harmon to change to a coal-powered engine. That didn't bother him, that wasn't a passenger-stop.

There was a knock on the compartment-door, opposite West Point, and dread came back again for a moment. He leaped over and put his ear to it, and when it came again, called out tensely, making a shell of his two hands to alter his voice: "Who is it?"

A stewardess' voice came back, "Care for a pillow, sir?"

He opened it narrowly, let her hand it in to him more to get rid of her than because he wanted one. Then he locked up again, relaxed.

He wasn't disturbed any more after that. At Albany they turned west. Somewhere in Pennsylvania, or maybe it was already Ohio, he rang for a tray and had it put down outside the locked door. Then he took it in himself and locked up again. When he was through, he put it down outside again, and locked up once more. That was so he wouldn't have to go out to the buffet-car. But these were just fancy trimmings, little extra added precautions, that he himself knew to be no longer necessary. The train was obviously sterile of danger. It had been from the moment of departure.

Toward midnight, way out in Indiana, he had to let the porter in to make up the two seats into a bed for him. He couldn't do that for himself.

"I guess you the las' one up on the whole train," the man said cheerfully.

"They all turned in?"

"Hours ago. Ain't nobody stirring no mo', from front to back."

That decided him. He figured he may as well step outside for a minute and stretch his legs, while the man was busy in there. There wasn't room enough in it for two of them at once. He made his way back through sleeping aisles of green berth-hangings. Even the observation-car was empty and unlighted now, with just one small dim lamp standing guard in the corner.

The whole living cargo of humanity was fast asleep.

He opened the door and went out on the observation platform to get a breath of air. He stretched himself there by the rail and drank it in. "Gee," he thought, "it feels good to be free!" It was the first real taste of freedom he'd had since he'd walked out of Head—

A voice in one of the gloom-obscured basket-shaped chairs off-side to him said mildly, "That you, Blake? Been wondering when you'd show up. How can you stand it, cooped up for hours in that stuffy two-by-four?" And a cigar-butt that was all that could be seen of the speaker glowed red with comfortable tranquillity.

Blake had to hang onto the rail as he swirled, to keep from going over. "When did you get on?" he groaned against the wind.

"I was the first one on," Rogers' voice said from the dark. "I got myself admitted before the gates were even opened, while they were still making the train up." He chuckled appreciatively. "I thought sure *you* were going to miss it."

He knew what this was that was coming next. It had been bound to come sooner or later, and this was about the time for it now. Any number of things were there to tell him; minor variations in the pattern of the adversary's behavior. Not for nothing had he been a detective for years. He knew human nature. He was already familiar with his adversary's pattern of behavior. The danger-signals studding it tonight were, to his practised eye, as plainly to be read as lighted buoys flashing out above dark, treacherous waters.

Blake hadn't sought one of his usual tinselled, boisterous resorts tonight. He'd found his way instead to a dingy out-of-the-way rat-hole over on the South Side, where the very atmosphere had a furtive cast to it. The detective could meet "trap" a mile away as he pushed inside after him. Blake was sitting alone, not expansively lording it over a cluster of girls as was his wont. He even discouraged the one or two that attempted to attach themselves to him. And finally, the very way in which he drank told the detective there was something coming up. He wasn't drinking to get happy, or to forget. He was drinking to get nerve. The detective could read what was on his mind by the very hoists of his arm; they were too jerky and unevenly spaced, they vibrated with nervous tension.

He himself sat there across the room, fooling around with a beer, not taking any chances on letting it past his gums, in case it had been drugged. He had a gun on him, but that was only because he always carried one; he had absolutely no intention of using it, not even in self-defense. Because what was coming up now was a test, and it had to be met, to keep the dominance of the situation on his side. If he flinched from it, the dominance of the situation shifted over to Blake's side. And mastery didn't lie in any use of a gun, either, because that was a mastery that lasted only as long as your finger, rested on the trigger. What he was after was a long-term mastery.

Blake was primed now. The liquor had done all it could for him; embalmed his nerves like novocaine. Rogers saw him get up slowly from the table. He braced himself at it a moment, then started on his way out. The very way he walked, the stiff-legged, interlocking gait, showed that this was the come-on, that if he followed him now, there was death at the end of it.

And he knew by the silence that hung over the place, the sudden lull that descended, in which no one moved, no one spoke, yet no one looked at either of the two principals, that everyone there was in on it to a greater or a lesser extent.

He kept himself relaxed. That was important, that was half the battle; otherwise it wouldn't work. He let him get as far as the door, and then he slowly got to his feet in turn. In his technique there was no attempt to dissimulate, to give the impression he was *not* following Blake, patterning his movements on the other's. He threw down money for his beer and he put out his cigar with painstaking thoroughness.

The door had closed behind the other. Now he moved toward it in turn. No one in the place was looking at him, and yet he knew that in the becalmed silence everyone was listening to his slow, measured tread across the floor. From busboy to tawdry hostess, from waiter to dubious patron, no one stirred. The place was bewitched with the approach of murder. And they were all on Donny Blake's side.

The man at the piano sat with his fingers resting lightly on the keyboard, careful not to bear down yet, ready for the signal to begin the death-music. The man at the percussion-instrument held his drumstick poised, the trumpeter had his lips to the mouth-piece of his instrument, waiting like the Angel Gabriel. It was going to happen right outside somewhere, close by.

He came out, and Blake had remained in sight, to continue the come-on. As soon as he saw Rogers, and above all was sure

Rogers had marked him, he drifted down an alley there at that end of the building that led back to the garage. That was where it was going to happen. And then into a sack, and into one of the cars, and into Lake Mich.

Rogers turned without a moment's hesitation and went down that way and turned the corner.

Blake had lit the garage up, to show him the way. They'd gotten rid of the attendant for him. He went deeper inside, but he remained visible down the lane of cars. He stopped there, near the back wall, and turned to face him, and stood and waited.

Rogers came on down the alley, toward the garage-entrance. If he was going to get him from a distance, then Rogers knew he would probably have to die. But if he let him come in close —

He made no move, so he wasn't going to try to get him from a distance. Probably afraid of missing him.

The time-limit that must have been arranged expired as he crossed the threshold into the garage. There was suddenly a blare of the three-piece band, from within the main building, so loud it seemed to split the seams of the place. That was the cover-up.

Rogers pulled the corrugated tin slide-door across after him, closing the two of them up. "That how you want it, Blake?" he said. Then he came away from the entrance, still deeper into the garage, to where Blake was standing waiting for him.

Blake had the gun out by now. Above it was a face that could only have been worn by a man who has been hounded unendurably for weeks on end. It was past hatred. It was maniacal.

Rogers came on until he was three or four yards from him. Then he stopped, empty-handed. "Well?" he said. He rested one hand on the fender of a car pointed toward him.

A flux of uncertainty wavered over Blake, was gone again.

All Rogers said, after that, was one thing more: "Go ahead, you fool. This is as good a way as any other, as far as we're concerned. As long as it hands you over to us, I'm willing. This is just what we've been looking for all along, what's the difference if it's me or somebody else?"

"You won't know about it," Blake said hoarsely. "They'll never find you."

"They don't have to. All they've got to do is find you without me." He heeled his palms toward him. "Well, what're you waiting for, I'm empty-handed."

The flux of uncertainty came back again, it rinsed all the starch out of him, softened him all up. It bent the gun down uselessly floorward in his very grasp. He backed and filled helplessly. "So you're a plant — so they want me to do this to you – I mighta known you was too open about it – "

For a moment or two he was in awful shape. He backed his hand to his forehead and stood there bandy-legged against the wall, his mind fuming like a seidlitz-powder.

He'd found out long ago he couldn't escape from his tormentor. And now he was finding out he couldn't even kill his tormentor. He had to live with him.

Rogers rested his elbow in his other hand and stroked the lower part of his face, contemplating him thoughtfully. He'd met the test and licked it. Dominance still rested with him.

The door swung back, and one of the gorillas from the club came in. "How about it, Donny, is it over? Want me to give you a hand —"

Rogers turned and glanced at him with detached curiosity.

The newcomer took in the situation at a glance. "What're ya, afraid?" he shrilled. "All right, I'll do it for you!" He drew a gun of his own.

Blake gave a whinny of unadulterated terror, as though he himself were the target. He jumped between them, protecting Rogers with his own body. "Don't you jerk! They *want* me to pull something like that, they're *waiting* for it, that's how they're trying to get me! It didn't dawn on me until just now, in the nick of time! Don't you see how he's not afraid at all? Don't you notice how he keeps his hands empty?" He closed in on the other, started to push him bodily back out of the garage, as though it were his own life he was protecting. It was, in a way. "Get out of here, get out of here! If you plug him it's me you kill, not him!"

The gun went off abortively into the garage-roof, deflected by Blake's grip on his wrist. Blake forced him back over the threshold, stood there blocking his way. The gorilla had a moment or two of uncertainty of his own. Blake's panic was catching. And he wasn't used to missing on the first shot, because he was used to shooting down his victims without warning.

"I've drawn on him now, they can get me for that myself!" he muttered. "I'm gonna get out of here —!" He suddenly turned and went scurrying up the alley whence he'd come.

The two men were left alone there together, the hunter and the hunted. Blake was breathing hard, all unmanned by two close shaves within a minute and a half. Rogers was as calm as though nothing had happened. He stood there without moving.

"Let him go," he said stonily. "I don't want him, I just want you."

Rogers sat there on the edge of his bed, in the dark, in his room. He was in trousers, undershirt, and with his shoes off. He was sitting the night through like that, keeping the death-watch. This was the same night as the spiked show-down in the garage, or what there was left of it. It was still dark, but it wouldn't be much longer.

He'd left his room door open two inches, and he was sitting in a line with it, patiently watching and waiting. The pattern of human behavior, immutable, told him what to be on the look-out for next.

The door-opening let a slender bar of yellow in from the hall. First it lay flat across the floor, then it climbed up the bed he was on, then it slanted off across his upper arm, just like a chevron. He felt he was entitled to a chevron by now.

He sat there, looking patiently out through the door-slit, waiting. For the inevitable next step, the step that was bound to come. He'd been sitting there like that watching ever since he'd first come in. He was willing to sit up all night, he was so sure it was coming.

He'd seen the bellboy go in the first time, with the first pint and the cracked ice, stay a minute or two, come out again tossing up a quarter.

Now suddenly here he was back again, with a second pint and more cracked ice. The green of his uniform showed in the door-slit. He stood there with his back to Rogers and knocked lightly on the door across the way.

Two pints, about, would do it. Rogers didn't move, though.

The door opened and the boy went it. He came out again in a moment, closed it after him.

Then Rogers did move. He left the bed in his stocking feet, widened his own door, went "Psst!", and the boy turned and came over to him.

"How much did he give you this time?"

The boy's eyes shone. "The whole change that was left! He cleaned himself out!"

Rogers nodded, as if in confirmation of something or other to himself. "How drunk is he?"

"He's having a hard time getting there, but he's getting there."

Rogers nodded again, for his own private benefit. "Lemme have your passkey," he said.

The boy hesitated.

"It's all right, I have the house-dick's authorization. You can check on it with him, if you want. Only, hand it over, I'm going to need it, and there won't be much time."

The boy tendered it to him, then showed an inclination to hang around and watch.

"You don't need to wait, I'll take care of everything."

He didn't go back into his own room again. He stayed there outside that other door, just as he was, in undershirt and stocking feet, in a position of half-crouched intentness, passkey ready at hand.

The transom was imperfectly closed, and he could hear him moving around in there, occasionally striking against some piece of furniture. He could hear it every time the bottle told off against the rim of the glass. Almost he was able to detect the constantly-ascending angle at which it was tilted, as its contents became less.

Pretty soon now. And in between, footsteps faltering back and forth, weaving aimlessly around, like those of someone trying to find his way out of a trap.

Suddenly the bottle hit the carpet with a discarded thud. No more in it.

Any minute now.

A rambling, disconnected phrase or two became audible, as the tempo of the trapped footsteps accelerated, this way and that, and all around, in blundering search of a way out. "I'll fool him! I'll show him! There's one place he can't — come after me —"

There was the sound of a window going up.

Now!

Rogers plunged the passkey in, swept the door aside, and dove across the room.

He had both feet up on the windowsill already, ready to go out and over and down. All the day down to the bottom. The only thing still keeping him there was he had to lower his head and shoulders first, to get them clear of the upper pane. That gave Rogers time enough to get across to him.

His arms scissored open for him, closed again, like a pair of pliers. He caught him around the waist, pulled him back, and the two of them fell to the floor together in a mingled heap.

He extricated himself and regained his feet before the other had. He went over, closed and securely latched-down the window, drew the shade. Then he went back to where the other still lay soddenly inert, stood over him.

"Get up!" he ordered roughly.

Blake had his downward-turned face buried in the crook of one arm. Rogers gave him a nudge with his foot that was just short of a kick.

Blake drew himself slowly together, crawled back to his feet by ascending stages, using the seat of a chair, then the top of a table next to it, until finally he was erect.

They faced one another.

"You won't let me live, and you won't even let me die!" Blake's voice rose almost to a full-pitched scream. "Then whaddya *after?* Whaddya *want?*"

"Nothing." Rogers' low-keyed response was almost inaudible coming after the other's strident hysteria. "I told you that many times, didn't I? Is there any harm in going around where you go, being around where you are? There's plenty of room for two, isn't there?" He pushed him back on the bed, and Blake lay there sprawled full-length, without attempting to rise again. Rogers took a towel and drenched it in cold water, then wound it around itself into a rope. He laced it across his face a couple of times, with a heavy, sluggish swing of the arm, trailing a fine curtain of spray through the air after it. Then he flung it down.

When he spoke again his voice had slowed still further, to a sluggard drawl. "Take it easy. What's there to get all worked up about? Here, look this over."

He reached into his rear trouser-pocket, took out a billfold, extracted a worn letter and spread it open, holding it reversed for the other to see. It was old, he'd been carrying it around with him for months. It was an acknowledgment, on a Police Department letterhead, of his resignation. He held it a long time, to let it sink in. Then he finally put it away again.

Blake quit snivelling after awhile, and was carried off on the tide of alcohol in him into oblivion.

Rogers made no move to leave the room. He gave the latched window a glance. Then he scuffed over a chair and sat down beside the bed. He lit a cigarette, and just sat there watching him. Like a male nurse on duty at the bedside of a patient.

He wanted him alive and he wanted him in his right mind.

Hatred cannot remain at white heat indefinitely. Neither can fear. The human system would not be able to support them at that pitch, without burning itself out. But nature is great at providing safety-valves. What happens next is one of two things: either the conditions creating that hatred or fear are removed, thus doing away with them automatically. Or else custom, familiarity, creeps in, by unnoticeable degrees, tempering them, blurring them. Pretty soon the hatred is just a dull red glow. Then it is gone entirely. The subject has become *used* to the object that once aroused hatred or fear; it can't do so any more. You can lock a man up in a room even with such a thing as a king cobra, and, always provided he isn't struck dead in the meantime, at the end of a week he would probably be moving about unhampered, with just the elementary precaution of watching where he puts his feet.

Only the lower-voltage, slower-burning elements, like perseverance, patience, dedication to a cause, can be maintained unchanged for months and years.

One night, at the same Chicago hotel, there was a knock at the door of Rogers' room around six o'clock. He opened it and Blake was standing there. He was in trousers, suspenders, and collarless shirt, and smelling strongly of shaving tonic. His own door, across the way, stood open behind him.

"Hey," he said, "you got a collar-button to spare, in here with you? I lost the only one I had just now. I got a dinner-date with a scorchy blonde and I don't want to keep her waiting. By the time I send down for one —"

"Yeah," Rogers said matter-of-factly, "I've got one."

He brought it back, dropped it in Blake's cupped hand.

"Much obliged."

They stood looking at one another a minute. A tentative grin flickered around the edges of Blake's mouth. Rogers answered it in kind.

That was all. Blake turned away. Rogers closed his door. With its closing his grin sliced off as at the cut of a knife.

A knock at the door. A collar-button. A trifle? A turning-point? The beginning of acceptance, of habit. The beginning of the end.

"This guy's a dick," Blake confided jovially to the redhead on his left. "Or at least he used to be at one time. I never told you that, did I?" He said it loud enough for Rogers to hear it, and at the same time dropped an eyelid at him over her shoulder, to show him there was no offense intended, it was all in fun.

"A dick?" she squealed with mock alarm. "Then what's he

doing around you? Aren't you scared?"

Blake threw back his head and laughed with hearty enjoyment at the quaintness of such a notion. "I used to be in the beginning. I'd have a hard time working up a scare about him now, I'm so used to him. I'd probably catch cold without him being around me these days."

Rogers swivelled his hand deprecatingly at the girl. "Don't let him kid you. I resigned long ago. He's talking about two years back, ancient history."

"What made you resign?" the other girl, the brunette, began. Then she checked herself. Blake must have stepped warningly on her toe under the table. "Let it lie," he cautioned in an undertone, this time not meant for Rogers to hear. "He don't like to talk about it. Probably — " And he made the secretive gesture that has always stood for graft; swinging his thumb in and out over his palm. "Good guy, though," he concluded. Rogers was looking off the other way. He smiled to himself at something out on the dance-floor just then. Or maybe it wasn't out on the dance-floor.

"Let's break it up," Blake suggested, as one co-host to another. "This place is going stale."

The waiter came up with the check, and Blake cased his own billfold, down low at his side. "I'm short again," he admitted ruefully.

"Let's have it, I'll pay it for you," Rogers, who had once been a detective, said to the man he considered a murderer. "We can straighten it out between us some other time."

Rogers, paring a corn with a razor-blade, looked up as the familiar knock came on his door. "That you, Donny?" he called out.

"Yeah. You doing anything, Rodge?"

They were Donny and Rodge to each other now.

"No, come on in," Rogers answered, giving the razor-blade a final deft fillip that did the trick.

The door opened and Blake leaned in at an angle, from the waist up. "Fellow I used to know, guy named Bill Harkness, just dropped in to the room. Haven't seen him in years. We been chewing the rag and now we're fresh out of gab. Thought maybe you'd like to come on over and join us in a little three-handed game, what d'ya say?"

"Only for half-an-hour or so," Rogers answered, shuffling on the sock he had discarded. "I'm turning in early tonight."

Blake withdrew, leaving the door ajar to speed Rogers on his way in to them. He left his own that way too, opposite it.

Rogers put out his light and got ready to go over to them. Then he stopped there on the threshold, half in, half out, yawned undecidedly, like someone else once had, one night a long time ago, on his way out to get a midnight edition of the paper.

He didn't have to be right at his elbow every night, did he? He could let it ride for one night, couldn't he, out of so many hundreds of them? He'd be right across the hall from them, he could leave his door slightly ajar — He was tired, and that bed looked awfully good. He was a human being, not a machine. He had his moments of let-down, and this was one of them. Nothing was ever going to happen. All he'd managed to accomplish was play the parole-officer to Blake, keep him straight. And that wasn't what he'd been after.

He was about to change his mind, go back inside again.

But they'd seen him from where they were, and Blake waved him on. "Coming, Rodge? What're you standing there thinking about?"

That swung the balance. He closed his own door, crossed over, and went in there with them.

They were sitting there at the table waiting for him to join them. This Harkness struck him as being engaged in some shady line of business. But then that was an easy guess, anyone on Blake's acquaintance-list was bound to be from the other side of the fence anyway.

"Pleased to meet you."

"Likewise."

He shook hands with him without demur. That was a thing he'd learned to do since he'd been around Blake, shake hands with all manner of crooks.

Blake, to put them at their ease together, trotted out that same worn theme he was so fond of harping on. "Harkness don't wanna believe you used to be a dick. Tell him yourself." He told it to everyone he knew, at every opportunity. He seemed to take a perverse pride in it, as though it reflected a sort of distinction on him. A detective had once been after him, and he'd tamed him into harmlessness.

"Don't you ever get tired of that?" was all Rogers grunted, disgustedly. He took up his cards, shot a covert glance at Blake's friend. "No folding money, only nickels and dimes."

Blake took it in good part. "Ain't that some guy for you?"

The game wore on desultorily. The night wore on desultorily along with it. Just three people at a table, killing time.

Harkness seemed to have a fidgety habit of continually worrying at the cuff of his coatsleeve.

"I thought they quit hiding them up there years ago," Blake finally remarked with a grin. "We're not playing for stakes, anyway."

"No, you don't get it, there's a busted button on my sleeve, and it keeps hooking onto everything every time I reach my arm out."

Only half of it was left, adhering to the thread, sharp-pointed and annoying as only such trivial things are apt to be. He tried to wrench it off bodily and it defeated him because there wasn't enough of it left to get a good grip on. All he succeeded in doing was lacerating the edges of his fingers. He swore softly and licked at them.

"Why don't you take the blame coat off altogether? You don't need it," Blake suggested, without evincing any real interest.

Harkness did, and draped it over the back of his chair.

The game wore on again. The night wore on. Rogers' original half-hour was gone long ago. It had quadrupled itself by now. Finally the game wore out, seemed to quit of its own momentum.

They sat there, half-comatose, around the table a moment or two longer. Rogers' head was actually beginning to nod.

Harkness was the first one to speak. "Look at it, one o'clock. Guess I'll shove off." He stood up and got back into his coat. Then he felt at the mangled thatch the game had left in its wake. "Got a comb I can borry before I go."

Blake, mechanically continuing to shuffle cards without dealing them any more, said: "In that top drawer over there," without looking around. "And wipe it off after you use it, I'm particular."

The drawer slid out. There was a moment of silence, then they heard Harkness remark, "Old Faithful."

Rogers opened his heavy-lidded eyes and Blake turned his head. He'd found Blake's gun in the drawer, had taken it out and was looking it over. "Ain't you afraid of him knowing you've got this?" he grinned at Blake.

"Aw, he's known I've had it for years. He knows I'm licensed for it, too." Then he added sharply, "Quit monkeying around with it, put it back where it belongs."

"Okay, okay," Harkness consented urbanely. He laid it down on the bureau-scarf, reached for the comb instead.

Blake turned back again to his repetitious card-shuffling. Rogers, who was facing that way, suddenly split his eyes back to full-size at something he saw. The blurred sleepiness left his voice. "Hey, that busted button of yours is tangled in the fringe of the scarf, I can see it from here, and the gun's right on the edge. Move it over, you're going to —"

The warning had precisely a reverse effect. It brought on what he'd been trying to avoid instead of averting it. Harkness jerked up his forearm, to look and see for himself; anyone's instinctive reflex in the same situation. The scarf gave a hitch along its entire length, and the gun slid off into space.

Harkness made a quick stabbing dive for it, to try to catch it before it hit the floor. He made it. His mind was quick enough, and so was his muscular coordination. He got it on the drop, in mid-air, in the relatively short distance between bureau-top and floor. But he got it the wrong way, caught at it in the wrong place.

A spark jumped out of his hand and there was a heavy-throated boom.

Then for a minute more nothing happened. None of them moved, not even he. He remained bent over like that, frozen just as he'd grabbed for it. Rogers remained seated at the table, staring across it. Blake continued to clutch the cards he'd been shuffling, while his head slowly came around. Rogers, at least, had been a witness to what had happened; Blake had even missed seeing that much.

Harkness was moving again. He folded slowly over, until his face was resting on the floor, while he remained arched upward in the middle like a croquet-wicket. Then he flattened out along there too, and made just a straight line, and lay quiet, as though he was tired.

Rogers jumped up and over to him, got down by him, turned him over. "Help me carry him over onto the bed," he said, "It musta hit him —" Then he stopped again.

Blake was still stupidly clutching the deck of cards.

"He's gone," Rogers said, in an oddly-blank voice. "It musta got him instantly." He straightened up, still puzzled by the suddenness with which the thing had occurred. "I never saw such a freaky —" Then he saw the gun. He stooped for it. "What did you leave it lying around like that for?" he demanded irritably. "Here, take it!" He thrust it at its owner, and the latter's hand closed around it almost unconsciously.

Blake was finally starting to get it. "A fine mess!" he lamented. He went over to the door, listened. Then he even opened it cautiously, looked out into the hall. The shot apparently hadn't been heard through the thick walls and doors of the venerable place they were in. He closed it, came back again. He was starting to perspire profusely. Then, as another thought struck him belatedly, he took out a handkerchief and began to mop at himself with something akin to relief. "Hey, it's a good thing you were right in here with the two of us, saw it for yourself. Otherwise you might have thought —"

Rogers kept staring down at the still figure, he couldn't seem to come out of his preoccupation.

Blake came over and touched him in anxious supplication on the arm, to attract his attention. "Hey, Rodge, maybe you better be the one to report it. It'll look better coming from you, you used to be on the force yourself —"

"All right, I'll handle it," Rogers said with sudden new-found incisiveness. "Let's have the gun." He lined his hand with a folded handkerchief before closing it on it.

Blake relinquished it only too willingly, went ahead mopping his face, like someone who has just had the narrowest of narrow escapes.

Rogers had asked for his old precinct number. "Give me Lieutenant Colton." There was a moment's wait. He balanced the instrument on one shoulder, delved into his pockets, rid himself of all the paper currency he had on him. He discarded this by flinging it at the table, for some reason best known to himself.

In the moment's wait, Blake said again, mostly for his own benefit: "Boy, it's the luckiest thing I ever did to ask you in here with us to —"

Rogers straightened slightly. Three years rolled off him. "Eric Rogers reporting back, lieutenant, after an extended leave of absence without pay. I'm in room Seven-ten at the Hotel Lancaster, here in the city. I've just been a witness to a murder. Donny Blake has shot to death, with his own gun, a man named William Harkness. Under my own eyes, that's right. Orders, lieutenant? Very well, I'll hold him until you get here, sir." He hung up.

Blake's face was a white bubble. It swelled and swelled with dismay, until it had exploded into all the abysmal fright there is in the world. "I wasn't near him! I wasn't touching it! I wasn't even *looking!* I was turned the other way, with my back to — You know that! Rogers, you know it!"

Rogers kept holding his own gun on him, with the handkerchief around it. "Sure, I know it," he agreed readily. "I know it and you know it, we both know it. You hear me say it to you now, freely, for the last time, while we're still alone here together. And after this once, neither God nor man will ever hear me say it again. I've waited three years, seven months, and eighteen days for this, and now it's here. You found a loophole once. Now I've found a loophole this time. Your loophole was to get out. My loophole is to get you back in again.

"Listen to me so you'll understand what I'm doing, Blake. You're going to be arrested in a few more minutes for murder. You're going to. be tried for murder. You're going to be — if there's any virtue left in the laws of this State — executed for murder. They're going to call that murder by the name of this man, Harkness. That's the only name that'll be mentioned throughout the proceedings. But the murder you're really about to be arrested, tried, and electrocuted for will be that of a man whose name won't appear in it once, from first to last, from beginning to end — Police Sergeant O'Neill. *That's* the murder you're going to die for now!

"We couldn't get you for the one you did commit. So we'll try you for another you didn't commit and get you for that instead."

DUSK TO DAWN

In **"Dusk to Dawn,"** a poor man falsely accused of murder runs for his life through the streets of New York. He takes on various disguises in his flight, assuming the identity of others, but the most surprising identity he assumes is murderer. When he's forced to kill those blocking his path to freedom, he finds he has a taste for the act and the wild power it instills in him. This story is not only a look at the desperation of the poor during the Depression, but a fascinating psychological picture of how committing murder can completely transform a person. Originally published in *Black Mask* in 1937, it made an appearance in 1971's *Nightwebs* and Centipede Press' 2012 collection *Speak to Me of Death*, and has not appeared since.

IT WAS JUST BEGINNING TO grow dark when Lew Stahl went in to the Odeon picture theater where his roommate Tom Lee worked as an usher. It was exactly 6:15.

Lew Stahl was twenty-five, out of work, dead broke and dead honest. He'd never killed anyone. He'd never held a deadly weapon in his hand. He'd never even seen anyone lying dead. All he wanted to do was see a show, and he didn't have the necessary thirty cents on him.

The man on door duty gave him a disapproving look while Lew was standing out there in the lobby waiting for Tom to slip him in free. Up and down, and up again the doorman walked like "You gotta nerve!" But Stahl stayed pat. What's the use having a pal as an usher in a movie house if you can't cadge an admission now and then?

Tom stuck his head through the doors and flagged him in. "Friend of mine, Duke," he pacified the doorman.

"Are you liable to get called down for this?" Stahl asked as he followed him in.

Tom said, "It's O.K. as long as the manager don't see me. It's between shows anyway; everyone's home at supper. The place is so empty you could stalk deer up in the balcony. Come on up, you can smoke up there."

Stahl trailed him upstairs, across a mezzanine, and out into the darkness of the sloping balcony. Tom gave the aisle his torch so his guest could see. On the screen below a woman's head was wavering, two or three times larger than life. A metallic voice clanged out, echoing sepulchrally all over the house, like a modern Delphic Oracle. "Go back, go back!" she said. "This is no place for you!"

Her big luminous eyes seemed to be looking right at Lew

131

Stahl as she spoke. Her finger came out and pointed, and it seemed to aim straight at him and him alone. It was weird; he almost stopped in his tracks, then went on again. He hadn't eaten all day; he figured he must be woozy, to think things like that.

Tom had been right; there was only one other guy in the whole balcony. Kids went up there, mostly, during the matinees, and they'd all gone home by now, and the evening crowd hadn't come in yet.

Stahl picked the second row, sat down in the exact middle of it. Tom left him, saying, "I'll be back when my five-minute relief comes up."

Stahl had thought the show would take his mind off his troubles. Later, thinking back over this part of the evening, he was willing to admit he hadn't known what real trouble was yet. But all he could think of was he hadn't eaten all day, and how hungry he was; his empty stomach kept his mind off the canned story going on on the screen.

He was beginning to feel weak and chilly, and he didn't even have a nickel for a cup of hot coffee. He couldn't ask Tom for any more money, not even that nickel. Tom had been tiding him over for weeks now, carrying his share of the room rent, and all he earned himself was a pittance. Lew Stahl was too decent, too fair-minded a young fellow, to ask him for another penny, not even if he dropped in his tracks from malnutrition. He couldn't get work. He couldn't beg on the street corner; he hadn't reached that point yet. He'd rather starve first. Well, he was starving already.

He pulled his belt over a notch to make his stomach seem tighter, and shaded his hand to his eyes for a minute.

That lone man sitting back there taking in the show had looked prosperous, well fed. Stahl wondered if he'd turn him down, if he went back to him and confidentially asked him for a dime. He'd probably think it was strange that Stahl should be in a movie house if he were down and out, but that couldn't be helped. Two factors emboldened him in this maiden attempt at panhandling. One was it was easier to do in here in the dark than out on the open street. The second was there was no one around to be a witness to his humiliation if the man bawled him out. If he was going to tackle him at all, he'd better not sit thinking about it any longer, he'd better do it before the house started to fill up, or he knew he'd never have the nerve. You'd be surprised how difficult it is to ask alms of a stranger when you've never done it before, what a psychological barrier separates the honest man from the panhandler.

Lew Stahl turned his head and glanced back at the man, to try and measure his chances ahead of time. Then he saw to his surprise that the man had dozed off in his seat; his eyes were closed. And suddenly it was no longer a matter of asking him for money, it was a matter of taking it, helping himself while the man slept. Tom had gone back to the main floor, and there was no one else up there but the two of them. Before he knew it he had changed seats, was in the one next to the sleeper.

"A dollar," he kept thinking, "that's all I'll take, just a dollar, if he has a wallet. Just enough to buy a big thick steak and . . ."

His stomach contracted into a painful knot at the very thought, and salt water came up into his mouth, and his hunger was so great that his hand spaded out almost of its own accord and was groping toward the inner pocket of the man's coat.

The coat was loosely buttoned and bulged conveniently open the way the man was sitting, and Stahl's downward dipping fingers found the stiff grained edge of a billfold without much trouble. It came up between his two fingers, those were all he'd dared insert in the pocket, and it was promisingly fat and heavy.

A second later the billfold was down between Lew's own legs and he was slitting it edgewise. The man must have been sweating, the leather was sort of sticky and damp on one side only, the side that had been next to his body. Some of the stickiness adhered to Stahl's own fingertips.

It was crammed with bills, the man must have been carrying between seventy and eighty dollars around with him. Stahl didn't count them, or even take the whole batch out. True to his word, he peeled off only the top one, a single, tucked it into the palm of his hand, started the wallet back where he'd found it.

It was done now; he'd been guilty of his first criminal offense.

He slipped it in past the mouth of the pocket, released it, started to draw his arm carefully back. The whole revere on that side of the man's coat started to come with Lew's arm, as though the two had become glued together. He froze, held his arm where it was, stiffly motionless across the man's chest. The slightest move, and the sleeper might awake. The outside button on Lew's cuff had freakishly caught in the man's lapel button hole, twisted around in some way. And it was a defective, jagged-edged button, he remembered that now well; it had teeth to hang on by.

He tried to slip his other hand in between the lapel and his arm and free them. There wasn't enough room for leverage. He tried to hold the man's lapel down and pull his own sleeve free, insulating the tug so it wouldn't penetrate the sleeper's consciousness. The button held on, the thread was too strong to break that way.

It was the most excruciating form of mental agony. Any minute he expected the sleeper's eyes to pop open and fasten on him accusingly. Lew had a disreputable penknife in his pocket. He fumbled desperately for it with one hand, to cut the damnable button free. He was as in a strait-jacket; he got it out of his right-hand pocket with his left hand, crossing one arm over the other to do so. At the same time he had to hold his prisoned arm rigid, and the circulation was already leaving it.

He got the tarnished blade open with his thumbnail, jockeyed the knife around in his hand. He was sweating profusely. He started sawing away at the triple-ply button-thread that had fastened them together. The knife blade was none too keen, but it finally severed. Then something happened; not the thing he'd dreaded, not the accusation of suddenly opened eyes. Something worse. The sleeper started sagging slowly forward in his seat. The slight vibration of the hacking knife must have been transmitted to him, dislodged him. He was beginning to slop over like a sandbag. And people don't sleep like that, bending over at the floor.

Stahl threw a panicky glance behind him. And now accusing eyes did meet him, from four or five rows back. A woman had come in and taken a seat some time during the past minute or two. She must have seen the jockeying of a knife blade down there, she must have wondered what was going on. She was definitely not looking at the screen, but at the two of them.

All presence of mind gone, Lew tried to edge his crumpled seat-mate back upright, for appearances' sake. Pretend to her they were friends sitting side by side; anything, as long as she didn't suspect he had just picked his pocket. But there was something wrong—the flabbiness of muscle, the lack of heavy breathing to go with a sleep so deep it didn't break no matter how the sleeper's body fell. That told him all he needed to know; he'd been sitting quietly for the past five minutes next to a man who was either comatose or already a corpse. Someone who must have dropped dead during the show, without even falling out of his seat.

He jumped out into the aisle past the dead man, gave him a startled look, then started excitedly toward the back to tip off Tom or whomever he could find. But he couldn't resist looking back a second time as he went chasing off. The woman's eyes strayed accusingly after him as he flashed by.

Tom was imitating a statue against the wall of the lounge, beside the stairs.

"Come back there where I was sitting!" Lew panted. "There's a guy next to me out cold, slopping all over!"

"Don't start any disturbance," Tom warned in an undertone.

He went back with Lew and flashed his torch quickly on and off, and the face it high-lighted wasn't the color of anything living; it was like putty.

"Help me carry him back to the restroom," Tom said under his breath, and picked him up by the shoulders. Lew took him by the legs, and they stumbled back up the dark aisle with the corpse.

The woman who had watched all this was feverishly gathering up innumerable belongings, with a determination that almost approached hysteria, as if about to depart forthwith on a mission of vital importance.

Lew and Tom didn't really see it until they got him in the restroom and stretched him out on a divan up against the wall—the knife-hilt jammed into his back. It didn't stick out much, was in at an angle, nearly flat up against him. Sidewise from right to left, but evidently deep enough to touch the heart; they could tell by looking at him he was gone.

Tom babbled, "I'll get the manager! Stay here with him a second. Don't let anyone in!" He grabbed up a "No Admittance" sign on his way out, slapped it over the outside door-knob, then beat it.

Lew had never seen a dead man before. He just stood there, and looked and looked. Then he went a step closer, and looked some more. "So that's what it's like!" he murmured inaudibly. Finally Lew reached out slowly and touched him on the face, and cringed as he met the clammy feel of it, pulled his hand back and whipped it down, as though to get something off it. The flesh was still warm and Lew knew suddenly he had no time alibi.

He threw something over that face and that got rid of the awful feeling of being watched by something from the other world. After that Lew wasn't afraid to go near him; he just looked like a bundle of old clothes. The dead man was on his side, and Lew fiddled with the knife-hilt, trying to get it out. It was caught fast, so he let it alone after grabbing it with his fingers from a couple of different directions.

Next he went through his pockets, thinking he'd be helping to identify him.

The man was Luther Kemp, forty-two, and he lived on 79th Street. But none of that was really true any more, Lew thought, mystified; he'd left it all behind. His clothes and his home and his name and his body and the show he'd paid to see were here. But where the hell had he gone to, anyway? Again that weird feeling came over Lew momentarily, but he brushed it aside. It was just that one of the commonest things in life—death—was still strange to him. But after strangeness comes familiarity, after familiarity, contempt.

The door flew open, and Tom bolted in again, still by himself and panting as though he'd run all the way up from the floor below. His face looked white, too.

"C'mere!" he said in a funny, jerky way. "Get outside, hurry up!"

Before Lew knew what it was all about, they were both outside, and Tom had propelled him all the way across the dimly lighted lounge to the other side of the house, where there was another branch of the staircase going down. His grip on Lew's arm was as if something were skewered through the middle of it.

"What's the idea?" Lew managed to get out.

Tom jerked his head backward. "You didn't really do that, did you? To that guy."

Lew nearly dropped through the floor. His answer was just a welter of words.

Tom telescoped it into "No," rushed on breathlessly, "Well then all the more reason for you to get out of here quick! Come on down on this side, before they get up here! I'll tell you about it down below."

Half-way down, on the landing, Tom stopped a second time, motioned Lew to listen. Outside in the street some place the faint, eerie wail of a patrol-car siren sounded, rushed to a crescendo as it drew nearer, then stopped abruptly, right in front of the theater itself.

"Get that? Here they are now!" Tom said ominously, and rushed Lew down the remaining half-flight, around a turn to the back, and through a door stenciled "Employees Only."

A flight of steps led down to a sub-basement. He pushed Lew ahead of him the rest of the way down, but Tom stayed where he was. He pitched something that flashed, and Lew caught it adroitly before he even knew what it was. A key.

"Open twelve, and switch to my blue suit," Tom said. "Leave that gray of yours in the locker."

Lew took a step back toward him, swung his arm back. "I haven't done anything! What's the matter with you? You trying to get me in a jam?"

"You're in one already, I'm trying to get you out of it!" Tom snapped. "There's a dame out there hanging onto the manager's neck with both arms, swears she saw you do it. Hallucinations, you know the kind! Says he started falling asleep on you, and you gave him a shove, one word led to another, then you knifed him. Robbed him, too. She's just hysterical enough to believe what she's saying herself."

Lew's knees gave a dip. "But holy smoke! Can't you tell 'em I was the first one told you about it myself? I even helped you carry him back to the rest-room! Does that look like I—"

"It took me long enough to get this job," Tom said sourly. "If the manager finds out I passed you in free—what with this giving his house a bad name and all—I can kiss my job good-by! Think of my end of it, too. Why do they have to know anything about you? You didn't do it, so all right. Then why be a chump and spend the night in a station-house basement? By tomorrow they'll probably have the right guy and it'll be all over with."

Lew thought of that dollar he had in his pocket. If he went back and let them question him, they'd want to know why he hadn't paid his way in, if he had a buck on him. That would tell them where the buck came from. He hated to pony up that buck now that he had it. And he remembered how he'd tampered with the knife-hilt, and vaguely knew there was something called fingerprints by which they had a way of telling who had handled it. And then the thought of bucking that woman—from what he remembered of the look on her face—took more nerve than he had. Tom was right, why not light out and steer clear of the whole mess, as long as he had the chance? And finally this argument presented itself: If they once got hold of him and believed he'd done it, that might satisfy them, they mightn't even try to look any further, and then where would he be? A clear conscience doesn't always make for courage, sometimes it's just the other way around. The mystic words "circumstantial evidence" danced in front of his eyes, paralyzing him.

"Peel!" Tom said. "The show breaks in another couple minutes. When you hear the bugles bringing on the newsreel, slip out of here and mingle with the rest of them going out. She's tagged you wearing a gray suit, so it ought to be easy enough to make it in my blue. They won't think of busting open the lockers to look. Wait for me at our place." Then Tom ducked out and the passageway-door closed noiselessly after him.

Lew didn't give himself time to think. He jumped into the blue suit as Tom had told him to, put on his hat and bent the brim down over his eyes with fingers that were shaking like ribbons in a breeze. He was afraid any minute that someone, one of the other ushers, would walk in and catch him. What was he going to say he was doing in there?

He banged the locker closed on his own clothes, just as a muffled *ta-da* came from the screen outside. In another minute there were feet shuffling by outside the door and the hum of subdued voices. He edged the door open, and pressed it shut behind him with his elbow. The few movie goers who were leaving were all around him, and he let them carry him along with them. They didn't seem to be aware, down below here, of what had happened up above so short a time ago. Lew didn't hear any mention of it.

It was like running the gauntlet. There were two sets of doors and a brightly lighted lobby in between. One of the detectives was standing beside the doorman at the first set of doors. The watchful way he scanned all faces told Lew what he was. There was a second one outside the street doors. He kept looking so long at each person coming out—that told what he was.

Lew saw them both before he got up to them, through the clear glass of the inner doors. The lights were on their side, Lew was in the dark, with the show still going on in back of him. His courage froze, he wanted to stay in there where he was. But if he was going to get out at all, now was the time, with the majority of the crowd, not later on when he'd be more conspicuous.

One thing in his favor was the color of his suit. He saw the detectives stopping all the men in gray and motioning them aside; he counted six being sidetracked before he even got out into the lobby. They weren't interfering with anyone else.

But that ticket-taker was a bigger risk than either of the plainclothes-men. So was the doorman. Before he'd gone in he'd been standing right under both their eyes a full five minutes waiting for Tom to come down. He'd gone in without paying, and that had burned the ticket-taker up. But going past them, Lew had to walk slow, as slowly as everyone else was walking, or he'd give himself away twice as quick. He couldn't turn around now and go back any more, either; he was too close to the detectives and they'd notice the maneuver.

A clod-hopper in front of him came to his rescue just when he thought he was a goner. The clod-hopper stepped backward unexpectedly to take a look at something, and his whole hoof landed like a stone-cutter's mallet across Lew's toes. Lew's face screwed up uncontrollably with pain, and before he straightened it out again, the deadly doorman's gaze had swept harmlessly over it without recognition, and Lew was past him and all he could see was the back of Lew's head.

Lew held his breath. Nothing happened. Right foot forward, left foot forward, right foot forward. . . . The lobby seemed to go on for miles. Someone's hand touched him, and the mercury went all the way down his spine to the bottom, but it was only a woman close behind him putting on her gloves.

After what seemed like an eternity of slow motion, he was flush with the street-doors at last. Only that second detective out there to buck now, and he didn't worry him much. He drifted through with all the others, passed close enough to the detective to touch him, and he wasn't even looking at Lew. His eyes were on the slap-slap of the doors as they kept swinging to and fro with each new egress.

Lew moved from under the revealing glare of the marquee lights into the sheltering darkness. He didn't look back, and presently the hellish place was just a blob of light far behind him. Then it wasn't even that any more.

He kept dabbing his face, and he felt limp in the legs for a long time afterwards. He'd made it, but whew! what an experience; he said to himself that he'd undergone all the emotions of a hunted criminal, without having committed a crime.

Tom and Lew had a cheap furnished room in a tenement about half an hour's walk away. Lew walked there unhesitatingly now, in a straight line from the theater. As far as he could see, it was all over, there wasn't anything to worry about now any more. He was out of the place, and that was all that mattered. They'd have the right guy in custody, maybe before the night was over, anyway by tomorrow at the latest.

He let himself into the front hallway with the key, climbed the stairs without meeting anyone, and closed the room door behind him. He snapped on the fly-blown bulb hanging from the ceiling, and sat down to wait for Tom.

Finally the clock rotated to 11 P.M. The last show broke at 11:30, and when Tom got here it would be about twelve.

About the time Tom should have been showing up, a newspaper delivery truck came rumbling by, distributing the midnight edition. Lew saw it stop by a stand down at the corner and dump out a bale of papers. On an impulse he got up and went down there to get one, wondering if it would have the story in it yet, and whether they'd caught the guy yet. He didn't open it until he'd got back.

It hadn't made a scare-head, but it had made a column on the front page. "Man stabbed in movie house; woman sees crime committed." Lew got sort of a vicarious thrill out of it for a minute, until he read further along. They were *still* looking for a guy just his height and build, wearing a gray suit, who had bummed his way in free. The motive—probably caught by the victim in the act of picking his pocket while he slept. In panic, Lew doused the light.

From then on it was a case of standing watching from behind the drawn shade and standing listening behind the door, and wearing down the flooring in between the two places like a caged bear. He knew he was crazy to stay there, and yet he didn't know where else to go. It would be even crazier, he thought, to roam around in the streets, he'd be sure to be picked up before morning. The sweat came out of every pore hot, and then froze cold. And yet never once did the idea of walking back there of his own accord, and saying to them, "Well, here I am; I didn't do it," occur to him. It looked too bad now, the way he'd changed clothes and run out. He cursed Tom for putting him up to it, and himself for losing his head and listening to him. It was too late now. There's a finality about print, especially to a novice; because that paper said they were looking for him, it seemed to kill Lew's last chance of clearing himself once and for all.

He didn't see Tom coming, although he was glancing out through a corner of the window the whole time; Tom must have slunk along close to the building line below. There was a sudden scurry of quick steps on the stairs, and Tom was trying the door-knob like fury. Lew had locked it on the inside when he'd put the light out.

"Hurry up, lemme in!" Tom panted. And then when Lew had unlocked the door: "Leave that light out, you fool!"

"I thought you'd never get here!" Lew groaned. "What'd they do, give a midnight matinee?"

"Down at Headquarters, they did!" Tom said resentfully. "Hauled me down there and been holding me there ever since! I'm surprised they let me go when they did. I didn't think they were gonna." He threw the door open. "You gotta get out of here!"

"Where'm I gonna go?" Lew wailed. "You're a fine louse of a friend!"

"Suppose a cop shows up here all of a sudden and finds you here, how's that gonna make it look for me? How do I know I wasn't followed coming back here? Maybe that's why they let me go!"

Tom kept trying to shoulder Lew out in the hall, and Lew kept trying to hang onto the door-frame and stay in; in a minute more they would have been at it hot and heavy, but suddenly there was a pounding at the street-door three floors below. They both froze.

"I knew it!" Tom hissed. "Right at my heels!"

The pounding kept up. "Coming! Wait a minute, can't you?" a woman's voice said from the back, and bedroom-slippers went slapping across the oilcloth. Lew was out on the landing now of his own accord, scuttling around it like a mouse trying to find a hole.

Tom jerked his thumb at the stairs going up. "The roof!" he whispered. "Maybe you can get down through the house next door." But Lew could see all he cared about was that he was out of the room.

Tom closed the door silently but definitely. The one below opened at the same instant, to the accompaniment of loud beefs from the landlady, that effectively covered the creaking of the stairs under Lew's flying feet.

"The idea, getting people out of their beds at this hour! Don't you tell me to pipe down, detective or no detective! This is a respectable hou—"

Lew was up past the top floor by that time. The last section was not inclined stairs any more but a vertical iron ladder, ending just under a flat, lead skylight, latched on the underside. He flicked the latch open, climbed up a rung further and lowered his head out of the way, with the thing pressing across his shoulders like Atlas supporting the world. He had to stay there like that till he got in out of the stair-well; he figured the cop would hear the thing creak and groan otherwise. It didn't have hinges, had to be displaced bodily.

There was a sudden commanding knock at Tom's door on the third, and an "Open up here!" that left no room for argument. Tom opened it instantly, with a whining, "What do you want this time?" Then it closed again, luckily for Lew, and the detective was in there with Tom.

Lew heaved upward with all his might, and felt as if he were lifting the roof bodily off the house. His head and shoulders pushed through into the open night. He caught the two lower corners of the thing backhanded so it wouldn't slam down again as he slipped out from under it, and eased it down gently on its frame. Before the opening had quite closed, though, he had a view down through it all the way to the bottom of the stair-well, and half-way along this, at the third floor, a face was sticking out over the banister, staring up at him. The landlady, who had stayed out there eavesdropping. She had the same bird's-eye view of him that he had of her.

He let go the skylight cover and pounded across the graveled tar toward the next roof for all he was worth. The detective would be up here after him in a minute now.

The dividing line between the two roofs was only a knee-high brick parapet easy enough to clear, but after that there was only one other roof, instead of a whole block-length of them. Beyond the next house was a drop of six stories to a vacant lot. The line of roofs, of varying but accessible heights, lay behind him in the other direction; he'd turned the wrong way in the dark. But it didn't matter, he thought, as long as he could get in through the twin to the skylight he'd come out of.

He couldn't. He found it by stubbing his toe against it and falling across it, rather than with the help of his eyes. Then when he knelt there clawing and tugging at it, it wouldn't come up. Latched underneath like the first one had been!

There wasn't any time to go back the other way now. Yellow light showed on the roof behind him as the detective lifted the trap. First a warning thread of it, then a big gash, and the dick was scrambling out on the roof-top. Lew thought he saw a gun in his hand, but he didn't wait to find out. There was a three-foot brick chimney a little ways behind Lew. He darted behind it while his pursuer's head was still turned up the other way. But the gravel under him gave a treacherous little rattle as he carried out the maneuver.

There was silence for a long time. He was afraid to stick his head out and look. Then there was another of those little giveaway rustles, not his this time, coming from this same roof, from the other side of the chimney.

Then with a suddenness that made him jump, a new kind of planet joined the stars just over his head, blazed out and spotted him from head to foot. A pocket-torch. Lew just pressed his body inward, helpless against the brick work.

"Come on, get up," the detective's voice said without any emotion, somewhere just behind the glare. To Lew it was like the headlight of a locomotive; he couldn't see a thing for a minute. He straightened up, blinking; even thought he was going to be calm and resigned for a minute. "I didn't do it," he said. "Honest, I didn't do it! Gimme a break, will you?"

The detective said mockingly that he would, sure he would, using an expression that doesn't bear repetition. He collared Lew with one hand, by both sides of his coat at once, pulling the reveres together close up under Lew's chin. Then he balanced the lighted torch on the lip of the chimney-stack, so that it stayed pointed at Lew and drenched him all over. Then he frisked him with that hand.

"I tell you I was just sitting next to him! I didn't touch him, I didn't put a finger on him!"

"And that's why you're hiding out on the roof, is it? Changed your suit, too, didn't you? I'll beat the truth out of you, when I get you where we're going!"

It was that, and the sudden sight of the handcuffs twinkling in the rays of the torch, that made Lew lose his head. He jerked backwards in the detective's grip, trying to get away from him. His back brushed the brick work. The flashlight went out suddenly, and went rattling all the way down inside the chimney. Lew was wedged in there between the detective and the stack. He raised the point of his knee suddenly, jabbed it upward between them like a piston. The detective let go Lew's collar, the manacles fell with a clink, and he collapsed at Lew's feet, writhing and groaning. Agonized as he was, his hand sort of flailed helplessly around, groping for something; Lew saw that even in the dark. Lew beat him to it, tore the gun out of his pocket, and pitched it overhand and backwards. It landed way off somewhere behind Lew, but stayed on the roof.

The detective had sort of doubled up in the meantime, like a helpless beetle on its back, drawing his legs up toward his body. They offered a handle to grab him by. Lew was too frightened to run away and leave him, too frightened that he'd come after him and the whole thing would start over. It was really an excess of fright that made him do it; there is such a thing. He grabbed the man around the ankles with both hands, started dragging him on his back across the gravel toward the edge of the roof, puffing, "You're not gonna get *me!* You're not gonna get *me!* You're not taking *me* with ya while I know it!"

Toward the side edge of the building he dragged the detective. He didn't bother looking to see what was below; just let go the legs, spun the detective around on his behind, so that the loose gravel shot out from under him in all directions, grabbed him by the shoulders, and pushed him over head-first. The dick didn't make a sound. Lew didn't know if he was still conscious or had fainted by now from the blow in the groin Lew had given him. Then he was snatched from sight as if a powerful magnet had suddenly pulled him down.

Then Lew did a funny thing. The instant after the detective was gone, Lew stretched out his arms involuntarily toward where he'd been, as if to grab him, catch him in time to save him. As though he hadn't really realized until then the actual meaning of what he was doing. Or maybe it was his last inhibition showing itself, before it left him altogether. A brake that would no longer work was trying to stop him after it was too late. The next minute he was feeling strangely light-headed, dizzy. But not dizzy from remorse, dizzy like someone who's been bound fast and is suddenly free.

Lew didn't look down toward where the man had gone, he looked up instead—at the stars that must have seen many another sight like the one just now, without blinking.

"Gosh, it's easy!" he marveled, openmouthed. "I never knew before how easy it is to kill anyone! Twenty years to grow 'em, and all it takes is one little push!"

He was suddenly drunk with some new kind of power, undiscovered until this minute. The power of life and death over his fellowmen! Everyone had it, everyone strong enough to raise a violent arm, but they were afraid to use it. Well, he wasn't! And here he'd been going around for weeks living from hand to mouth, without any money, without enough food, when everything he wanted lay within his reach all the while! He *had* been green all right, and no mistake about it!

Death had become familiar. At seven it had been the most mysterious thing in the world to him, by midnight it was already an old story.

"Now let 'em come after me!" he thought vindictively, as he swayed back across the roof toward the skylight of the other house. "Now I've given 'em a real reason for trying to nab me!" And he added grimly, "If they can!"

Something flat kicked away from under his foot, and he stopped and picked up the gun that he'd tossed out of reach. He looked it over after he was through the skylight and there was light to examine it by. He'd never held one in his hand before. He knew enough not to squint down the bore, and that was about all he knew.

The stair-well was empty; the landlady must have retreated temporarily to her quarters below to rouse her husband, so he wouldn't miss the excitement of the capture and towing away. Lew passed Tom's closed door and was going by it without stopping, going straight down to the street and the new career that awaited him in the slumbering city, when Tom opened it himself and looked out. He must have heard a creak and thought it was the detective returning, thought Lew, and figured a little bootlicking wouldn't hurt any.

"Did you get him—?" Tom started to say. Then he saw who it was, and saw what Lew was holding in his hand.

Lew turned around and went back to him. "No, he didn't get me," he said, ominously quiet, "I got him." He went in and closed the door of the room after him. He kept looking at Tom, who backed away a little.

"Now you've finished yourself!" Tom breathed, appalled.

"You mean I'm just beginning," Lew said.

"I'm going to get out of here!" Tom said, in a sudden flurry of panic, and tried to circle around Lew and get to the door.

Lew waved him back with the gun. "No, you're not, you're going to stay right where you are! What'd you double-cross me for?"

Tom got behind a chair and hung onto it with both hands—as though that was any good! Then almost hysterically, as he read Lew's face: "What's the matter, ya gone crazy? Not *me*, Lew! Not *me!*"

"Yes, you!" Lew said. "You got me into it. You knew they'd follow you. You led 'em to me. But they still don't know what I look like—but you do! That one went up there after me can't tell now what I look like, but you still can! They can get me on sight, while you're still around."

Tom was holding both palms flat out toward Lew, as though Lew thought they could stop or turn aside a bullet! Tom had time to get just one more thing out: "You're not human at all!"

Then Lew pulled the trigger and the whole room seemed to lift with a roar, as though blasting were going on under it. The gun bucked Lew back half a step; he hadn't known those things had a kick to them. When he looked through the smoke, Tom's face and shoulders were gone from behind the chair, but his forearms were still hanging across the top of it, palms turned downward now, and all the fingers wiggling at once. Then they fell off it, went down to join the rest of him on the floor.

Lew watched him for a second, what he could see of him. Tom didn't move any more. Lew shook his head slowly from side to side. "It sure is easy all right!" he said to himself. And this had been even less dramatic than the one up above on the roof.

Familiarity with death had already bred contempt for it.

He turned, pitched the door open, and went jogging down the stairs double-quick. Doors were opening on every landing as he whisked by, but not a move was made to stop him—which was just as well for them. He kept the gun out in his hand the whole time and cleared the bottom steps with a short jump at the bottom of each flight. Bang! and then around to the next.

The landlady had got herself into a bad position. She was

caught between him and the closed street-door as he cleared the last flight and came down into the front hall. If she'd stayed where she belonged, Lew said to himself, she could have ducked back into her own quarters at the rear when he came down. But now her escape was cut off. When she saw it was Lew, and not the detective, she tried to get out the front way. She couldn't get the door open in time, so then she tried to turn back again. She dodged to one side to get out of Lew's way, and he went to that side too. Then they both went to the other side together and blocked each other again. It was like a game of puss-in-the-corner, with appalled faces peering tensely down the stair-well at them.

She was heaving like a sick cat in a sand-box, and Lew decided she was too ludicrous to shoot. New as he was at the game of killing, he had to have dignity in his murders. He walloped her back-handed aside like a gnat, and stepped over her suddenly upthrust legs. She could only give a garbled description of him any way.

The door wasn't really hard to open, if you weren't frightened, like Lew wasn't now. Just a twist of the knob and a wrench. A voice shrieked down inanely from one of the upper floors, "Get the cops! He's killed a fellow up here!" Then Lew was out in the street, and looking both ways at once.

A passerby who must have heard the shot out there had stopped dead in his tracks, directly opposite the doorway on the other side of the street, and was gawking over. He saw Lew and called over nosily: "What happened? Something wrong in there?"

It would have been easy enough to hand him some stall or other, pretend Lew was himself looking for a cop. But Lew had this new contempt of death hot all over him.

"Yeah!" he snarled viciously. "I just shot a guy! And if you stand there looking at me like that, you're gonna be the next!"

He didn't know if the passerby saw the gun or not in the dark, probably not. The man didn't wait to make sure, took him at his word. He bolted for the nearest corner. *Scrunch*, and he was gone!

"There," Lew said to himself tersely, "is a sensible guy!"

Black window squares here and there were turning orange as the neighborhood began belatedly to wake up. A lot of interior yelling and tramping was coming from the house Tom and Lew had lived in. He made for the corner opposite from the one his late questioner had fled around, turned it, and slowed to a quick walk. He put the gun away; it stuck too far out of the shallow side-pocket of Tom's suit, so he changed it to the inner breast-pocket, which was deeper. A cop's whistle sounded thinly behind him, at the upper end of the street he'd just left.

A taxi was coming toward him, and he jumped off the sidewalk and ran toward it diagonally. The driver tried to swerve without stopping, so he jumped up on the running-board and wrenched the wheel with his free hand. He had the other spaded into his pocket over the gun again. "Turn around, you're going downtown with me!" he said. A girl's voice bleated in the back. "I've got two passengers in there already!" the driver said, but he was turning with a lurch that nearly threw Lew off.

"I'll take care of that for you!" he yanked the back door open and got in with them. "Out you go, that side!" he ordered. The fellow jumped first, as etiquette prescribed, but the girl clung to the door-strap, too terrified to move, so Lew gave her a push to help her make up her mind. "Be a shame to separate the two of you!" he called after her. She turned her ankle, and went down kerplunk and lay there, with her escort bending over her in the middle of the street.

"Wh-where you want me to g-go with you, buddy?" chattered the driver.

"Out of this neighborhood fast," Lew said grimly.

He sped along for a while, then whined: "I got a wife and kids buddy—"

"You're a very careless guy," Lew said to that.

He knew they'd pick up his trail any minute, what with those two left stranded in the middle of the street to direct them, so he made for the concealing labyrinth of the park, the least policed part of the city.

"Step it down a little," he ordered, once they were in the park. "Take off your shoes and throw them back here." The driver's presence was a handicap, and Lew had decided to get rid of him, too. Driving zig-zag along the lane with one hand, the cabbie threw back his shoes. One of them hit Lew on the knee as it was pitched through the open slide, and for a minute Lew nearly changed his mind and shot him instead, as the easiest way out after all. The cabbie was half dead with fright by this time, anyway. Lew made him take off his pants, too, and then told him to brake and get out.

Lew got in at the wheel. The driver stood there on the asphalt in his socks and shirt-tails, pleading, "Gee, don't leave me in the middle of the park like this, buddy, without my pants and shoes, it'll take me all night to get out!"

"That's the main idea," Lew agreed vindictively, and added: "You don't know how lucky you are! You're up against Death's right-hand man. Scram, before I change my mind!"

The cabbie went loping away into the dark, like a bow-legged scarecrow and Lew sat at the wheel belly-laughing after him. Then he took the cab away at top speed, and came out the other end about quarter of an hour later.

He was hungry, and decided the best time to eat was right then, before daylight added to the risk and a general alarm had time to circulate. The ability to pay, of course, was no longer a problem in this exciting new existence that had begun for him tonight. He picked the most expensive place open at that hour, an all-night delicatessen, where they charged a dollar for a sandwich and named it after a celebrity. A few high-hats were sitting around having bacon and eggs in the dim, artificial blue light that made them look like ghosts.

He left the cab right at the door and sat down where he could watch it. A waiter came over who didn't think much of him because he didn't have a boiled shirt. He ran his finger down the list and picked a five-dollar one.

"What's a Jimmy Cagney? Gimme one of them."

151

"Hard-boiled egg with lots of paprika." The waiter started away.

Lew picked up a glass of water and sloshed it across the back of his neck. "You come back here! Do that over, and say sir!" he snarled.

"Hard-boiled egg with lots of paprika, sir," the waiter stuttered, squirming to get the water off his backbone.

When he was through, Lew leaned back in his chair and thumbed him over. "How much do you take in here a night?"

"Oh, around five hundred when it's slow like this." He took out a pad and scribbled "5.00" at the bottom, tore it off and handed it to Lew.

"Lend me your pencil," Lew said. He wrote "Pay me" in front of it, and rubbed out the decimal point. "I'll take this over to the cashier myself," he told the waiter.

Then as he saw the waiter's glance sweep the bare table-top disappointedly, "Don't worry, you'll get your tip; I'm not forgetting you."

Lew found the tricky blue lighting was a big help. It made everyone's face look ghastly to begin with and you couldn't tell when anyone suddenly got paler. Like the cashier, when he looked up from reading the bill Lew presented and found the bore of the gun peering out from Lew's shirt at him like some kind of a bulky tie pin.

He opened the drawer and started counting bills out. "Quit making your hands shake so," Lew warned him out of the corner of his mouth, "and keep your eyes down on what you're doing, or you're liable to short-change me!"

Lew liked doing it that way, adding to the risk by standing there letting the cashier count out the exact amount, instead of just cleaning the till and lamming. What was so hectic about a hold-up, he asked himself. Every crime seemed so simple, once you got the hang of it. He was beginning to like this life, it was swell!

There were thirty or so bucks left in the drawer when the cashier got through. But meanwhile the manager had got curious about the length of time Lew had been standing up there and started over toward them. Lew could tell by his face he didn't suspect even yet, only wanted to see if there was some difficulty. At the same time Lew caught sight of the waiter slinking along the far side of the room, toward the door in back of him. He hadn't been able to get over to the manager in time, and was going to be a hero on his own, and go out and get a cop.

So Lew took him first. The waiter was too close to the door already for there to be any choice in the matter. Lew didn't even aim, just fired what he'd heard called a snap-shot. The waiter went right down across the doorsill, like some new kind of a lumpy mat. Lew didn't even feel the thing buck as much as when he'd shot Tom. The cashier dropped too, as though the same shot had felled him. His voice came up from the bottom of the enclosure, "There's your money, don't shoot me, don't shoot me!" Too much night-work isn't good for a guy's guts, Lew mused.

There was a doorman outside on the sidewalk. Lew got him through the open doorway just as he got to the curb, in the act of raising his whistle to his lips. He stumbled, grabbed one of the chromium stanchions supporting the entrance canopy, and went slipping down like a fireman sliding down a pole. The manager ducked behind a table, and everyone else in the place went down to floor-level with him, as suddenly as though they were all puppets jerked by strings. Lew couldn't see a face left in the room; just a lot of screaming coming from behind empty chairs.

Lew grabbed up the five hundred and sprinted for the door. He had to hurdle the waiter's body and he moved a little as Lew did so, so he wasn't dead. Then Lew stopped just long enough to peel off a ten and drop it down on him. "There's your tip, chiseler!" Lew hollered at him, and beat it.

Lew couldn't get to the cab in time, so he had to let it go, and take it on foot. There was a car parked a few yards in back of it, and another a length ahead, that might have blocked his getting it out at the first try, and this was no time for lengthy extrications. A shot came his way from the corner, about half a block up, and he dashed around the next one. Two more came from that, just as he got to the corner ahead, and he fired back at the sound of them, just on general principle. He had no aim to speak of, had never held one of the things in his hand until that night.

He turned and sprinted down the side street, leaving the smoke of his shot hanging there disembodiedly behind him like a baby cloud above the sidewalk. There were two cops by now, but the original one was in the lead and he was a good runner. He quit shooting and concentrated on taking Lew the hard way, at arms' length. Lew turned his head in time to see him tear through the smoke up there at the corner and knock it invisible. He was a tall limber guy, must have been good in the heats at police games, and he came hurtling straight toward Death. Tick, tick, tick, his feet went, like a very quick clock.

A fifth shot boomed out in that instant, from ahead of Lew this time, down at the lower corner. Somebody had joined in from that direction, right where Lew was going toward. They had him sewn up now between them, on this narrow sidestreet. One in front, two behind him—and to duck in anywhere was curtains.

Something happened, with that shot, that happens once in a million years. The three of them were in a straight line—Lew in the middle, the sprinter behind him, the one who had just fired coming up the other way. Something spit past Lew's ear and the tick, tick behind him scattered into a scraping, thumping fall— *plump*!—and stopped. The runner had been hit by his own man, up front.

He didn't look, his ears had seen the thing for him. He dove into a doorway between the two of them. Only a miracle could save him, and it had no more than sixty seconds in which to happen, to be any good.

His star, beaming overtime, made it an open street door, indicative of poverty. The street was between Second and Third Avenues, and poverty was rampant along it, the same kind of poverty that had turned Lew into a ghoul, snatching a dollar from a dead man's pocket, at six-thirty this night. He punched three bell-buttons as he flashed by.

"If they come in here after me," he sobbed hotly, "there's going to be shooting like there never was before!" And they would, of course. The header-offer down at Second, who had shot his own man, must have seen which entrance he'd dived for. Even if he hadn't, they'd dragnet all of them.

Lew reached in his pocket as he took the stairs, brought out a fistful of the money and not the gun for once. At least a hundred's worth came up in his paw. One of the bills escaped, fluttered down the steps behind him like a green leaf. What's ten, or even twenty, when you've got sixty seconds to buy your life?

"In there!" One of the winded, surviving cops' voices rang out clearly, penetrated the hall from the sidewalk. The screech of a prowl car chimed in.

He was holding the handful of green dough up in front of him, like the olive branch of the ancients, when the first of the three doors opened before him, second-floor front. A man with a curleycue mustache was blinking out as he raced at him.

"A hundred bucks!" Lew hissed. "They're after me! Here, hundred bucks if you lemme get in your door!"

"Whassa mat'?" he wanted to know, startled wide awake.

"Cops! Hundred bucks!" The space between them had been used up, Lew's whole body hit the door like a projectile. The man was holding onto it on the inside, so it wouldn't give. The impact swung Lew around sideways, he clawed at it with one hand, shoved the bouquet of money into the man's face with the other. "Two hundred bucks!"

"Go 'way!" the man cried, tried to close Lew out. Lew had decided to shoot him out of the way if he couldn't buy his way in.

A deep bass voice came rumbling up behind him. "*Che cosa, Mario?*"

"Two hundred bucks," Lew strangled, reaching for the gun with his left hand.

"*Due cento dollari!*" The door was torn away from him, opened wide. An enormous, mustached, garlicky Italian woman stood there. "Issa good? Issa rill?" Lew jammed them down her huge bosom as the quickest way of proving their authenticity. Maybe Mario Jr. had had a run-in with cops about breaking a window or swiping fruit from a pushcart; maybe it was just the poverty. She slapped one hand on her chest to hold the money there, grabbed Lew's arm with the other. "*Si! Vene presto!*" and spat a warning "*Silenzio! La porta!*" at her reluctant old man.

She pounded down the long inner hall, towing Lew after her. The door closed behind them as the stairway outside was started vibrating with ascending feet—flat feet.

The bedroom was pitch black. She let go of him, gave him a push sideways and down, and he went sprawling across an enormous room-filling bed. A cat snatched itself out of the way and jumped down. He hoisted his legs up after him, clawed, pulled a garlicky quilt up to his chin. He began to undress hectically under it, lying on his side. She snapped a light on and was standing there counting the money. "*Falta cento—*" she growled aggressively.

"You get the other hundred after they go 'way." He stuck his hand out under the cover, showed it to her. He took the gun out and showed her that too. "If you or your old man give me away—!"

Pounding had already begun at their door. Her husband was standing there by it, not making a sound. She shoved the money down under the same mattress Lew was on. He got rid of his coat, trousers and shoes, pitched them out on the other side of him, just as she snapped out the light once more. He kept the gun and money with him, under his body.

The next thing he knew, the whole bed structure quivered under him, wobbled, all but sank flat. She'd got in alongside of him! The clothes billowed like sails in a storm, subsided. She went, "Ssst!" like a steam radiator, and the sound carried out into the hall. Lew heard the man pick up his feet two or three times, plank them down again, right where he was standing, to simulate trudging toward the door. Then he opened it, and they were in. Lew closed his eyes, spaded one hand under him and kept it on the gun.

"Took you long enough!" a voice said at the end of the hall. "Anyone come in here?"

"Nome-body."

"Well, we'll take a look for ourselves! Give it the lights!"

The lining of Lew's eyelids turned vermilion, but he kept them down. The mountain next to him stirred, gyrated. *"Che cosa, Mario?"*

"Polizia, non capisco."

Kids were waking up all over the place, in adjoining rooms, adding to the anvil chorus. It would have looked phony to go on sleeping any longer in that racket. Lew squirmed, stretched, blinked, yawned, popped his eyes in innocent surprise. There were two cops in the room, one of them standing still, looking at him, the other sticking his head into a closet.

Lew had black hair and was sallow from undernourishment, but he didn't know a word of Italian.

"Who's this guy?" the cop asked.

"Il mio fratello." Her brother. The volume of noise she and Mario and the kids were making covered him.

The first cop went out. The second one came closer, pulled the corner of the covers off Lew. All he saw was a skinny torso in an undershirt. Lew's outside shirt was rolled in a ball down by his feet. His thumb found and went into the hollow before the trigger underneath him. If he said "Get up outa there," those would be the last words he ever said.

He said, "Three in a bed?" disgustedly. "Sure y'ain't got your grandfather in there, too? These guineas!" He threw the covers back at Lew and went stalking out.

Lew could hear him through the open door tramp up the stairs after the others to the floor above. A minute later their heavy footsteps sounded on the ceiling right above his head.

A little runty ten-year-old girl peered in at him from the doorway. He said, "Put that light out! Keep them kids outa here! Leave the door open until they go! Tell your old man to stand there rubber-necking out, like all the others are doing!"

They quit searching in about fifteen minutes, and Lew heard

them all go trooping down again, out into the street, and then he could hear their voices from the sidewalk right under the windows.

"Anything doing?" somebody asked.

"Naw, he musta got out through the back yard and the next street over."

"O'Keefe hurt bad?"

"Nicked him in the dome, stunned him, that was all." So the cop wasn't dead.

When Mario came out the front door at eight-thirty on his way to the barber shop where he worked, his "brother-in-law" was with him, as close to him as sticking plaster. Lew had on an old felt hat of Mario's and a baggy red sweater that hid the coat of Tom's blue suit. It would have looked too good to come walking out of a building like that on the way to work. That red sweater had cost Lew another fifty. The street looked normal one wouldn't have known it for the shooting gallery it had been at four that morning. They walked side by side up toward Second, past the place where O'Keefe had led with his chin, past the corner where the smoke of Lew's shot had hung so ghostily in the lamplight. There was a newsstand open there now, and Lew bought a paper. Then he and Mario stood waiting for the bus.

It drew up and Lew pushed Mario on alone, and jerked his thumb at the driver. It went sailing off again, before Mario had time to say or do anything, if he'd wanted to. It had sounded to Lew, without knowing Italian, as though the old lady had been coaching Mario to get a stranglehold on the rest of Lew's money. Lew snickered aloud, ran his hand lightly over the pocket where the original five-hundred was intact once more. It had been too good to miss, the chance she'd given him of sneaking it out of the mattress she'd cached it under and putting it back in his pocket again, while her back was turned. They'd had all their trouble and risk for nothing.

Lew made tracks away from there, went west as far as Third and then started down that. He stayed with the sweater and hat, because they didn't look out of character on Third. The cops had seen him in the blue suit when they chased him from Rubin's; they hadn't seen him in this outfit. And no matter how the *signora* would blaze when she found out how Lew had gypped them, she couldn't exactly report it to the police, and tell them what he was wearing, without implicating herself and her old man.

But there was one thing had to be attended to right off, and that was the matter of ammunition. To the best of Lew's calculations (and so much had happened, that they were already pretty hazy) he had fired four shots out of the gun from the time he had taken it over from the dick on the roof. One at Tom, two in Rubin's, and one on the street when they'd been after him. There ought to be two left in it, and if the immediate future was going to be like the immediate past, he was going to need a lot more than that. He not only didn't know where any could be bought, he didn't even know how to break the thing and find out how many it packed.

He decided a pawnshop would be about the best bet, not up here in the mid-town district, but down around the lower East Side or on the Bowery somewhere. And if they didn't want to sell him any, he'd just blast and help himself.

He took a street car down as far as Chatham Square. He had a feeling that he'd be safer on one of them than on the El or the subway; he could jump off in a hurry without waiting for it to stop, if he had to. Also, he could see where he was going through the windows and not have to do too much roaming around on foot once he alighted. He was a little dubious about hailing a cab, dressed the way he now was. Besides, he couldn't exactly tell a hackman, "Take me to a pawnshop." You may ride in a taxi coming out of one, you hardly ride in a taxi going to one.

He went all the way to the rear end and opened the newspaper. He didn't have to hunt it up. This time it *had* made a scare-head. "One-Man Crime Wave!" And then underneath, "Mad dog gunman still at large somewhere in city." Lew looked up at the oblivious backs of the heads up forward, riding on the same car with Lew. Not one of them had given him a second glance when he'd walked down the aisle in the middle of all of them just now. And yet more than one must be reading that very thing he was at the moment; he could see the papers in their hands. That was he, right in the same trolley they were, and they didn't even know it! His contempt for death was beginning to expand dangerously toward the living as well, and the logical step beyond that would be well past the confines of sanity—a superman complex.

Fortunately, he never quite got to it. Something within this same paper itself checked it, before it got well started. Two things that threw cold water over it, as it were. They occurred within a paragraph of each other, and had the effect of deflating his ego almost to the point at which it had been last night, before he'd touched that dead man's face in the theater restroom. The first paragraph read: "The police, hoping that young Tom Lee might unknowingly provide a clue to the suspect's whereabouts, arranged to have him released at Headquarters shortly after midnight. Detective Walter Daly was detailed to follow him. Daly trapped Stahl on the roof of a tenement, only to lose his balance and fall six stories during the scuffle that ensued. He was discovered unconscious but still alive sometime after the young desperado had made good his second escape, lying with both legs broken on an ash-heap in a vacant lot adjoining the building."

That was the first shock. Still alive, eh? And he'd lost his balance, huh? A line or two farther on came the second jolt:

"Stahl, with the detective's gun in his possession, had meanwhile made his way down the stairs and brutally shot Lee in his room. The latter was rushed to the hospital with a bullet wound in his neck; although his condition is critical, he has a good chance to survive. . . . "

Lew let the thing fall to the floor and just sat there, stunned. Tom wasn't dead either! He wasn't quite as deadly as he'd thought he was; death wasn't so easy to dish out, not with the aim he seemed to have. A little of his former respect for death came back. Step one on the road to recovery. He remembered that waiter at Rubin's, flopping flat across the doorway; when he'd jumped over him, he'd definitely cringed—so he hadn't finished him either. About all he'd really managed to accomplish, he said to himself, was successfully hold up a restaurant, separate a cab driver from his pants and his machine, and outsmart the cops three times—at the theater, on the roof, and in the Italians' flat. Plenty for one guy, but not enough to turn him into a Manhattan Dillinger by a long shot.

A lot of his self-confidence had evaporated and he couldn't seem to get it back. There was a sudden, sharp increase of nervousness that had been almost totally lacking the night before.

He said to himself, "I need some bullets to put into this gun! Once I get them, I'll be all right, that'll take away the chills, turn on the heat again!"

He spotted a likely looking hockshop, and hopped off the car.

He hurried in through the swinging doors of the pawnshop and got a lungful of camphor balls. The proprietor came up to him on the other side of the counter. He leaned sideways on his elbow, tried to stop the shaking that had set in, and said: "Can you gimme something to fit this?" He reached for the pocket he'd put the gun in.

The proprietor's face was like a mirror. Expectancy, waiting to see what it was; then surprise, at how white his customer was getting; then astonishment, at why Lew should grip the counter like that, to keep from falling.

It was gone, it wasn't there any more. The frisking of the rest of his pockets was just reflex action; the emptiness of the first one told the whole story. He thought he'd outsmarted that Italian she-devil; well, she'd outsmarted him instead! Lifted the gun from him while she was busy seeming to straighten this old red sweater of her husband's on him. And the motive was easy to guess: So that Mario wouldn't be running any risk when he tried to blackmail Lew out on the street for the rest of the five hundred, like she'd told him to. Lew had walked a whole block with him, ridden all the way down here, and never even missed it until now! A fine killer he was!

He could feel what was left of his confidence crumbling away inside him, as though this had been the finishing touch it needed.

Panic was coming on. He got a grip on himself; after all, he had five hundred in his pocket. It was just a matter of buying another gun and ammunition, now.

"I wanna buy a revolver. Show me what you've got."

"Show me your license," the man countered.

"Now, listen," he was breathing hard, "just skip that part of it. I'll pay you double." He brought out the money.

"Yeah, skip it," the proprietor scoffed. "And then what happens to me, when they find out where you got it? I got myself to think of."

Lew knew he had some guns; the very way he spoke showed he did. He sort of broke. "For the love of Gawd, lemme have a gun!" he wailed.

"You're snowed up, mac," he said. "G'wan, get out of here."

Lew clenched his teeth. "You lemme have a gun, or else—" And he made a threatening gesture toward the inside of his coat. But he had nothing to threaten with; his hand dropped limply back again. He felt trapped, helpless. The crumbling away kept on inside him. He whined, pleaded, begged.

The proprietor took a step in the direction of the door. "Get out of here now, or I'll call the police! You think I want my license taken away?" And then with sudden rage, "Where's a cop?"

Police. Cops. Lew turned and powdered out like a streak.

And Lew knew then what makes a killer; not the man himself, just the piece of metal in his hand, fashioned by men far cleverer than he. Without that, just a snarling cur, no match even for a paunchy hockshop owner.

Lew lost track of what happened immediately after that. Headlong, incessant flight—from nothing, to nothing. He didn't actually run, but kept going, going, like a car without a driver, a ship without a rudder.

It was not long after that he saw the newspaper. Its headline screamed across the top of the stand where it was being peddled. "Movie Murderer Confesses." Lew picked it up, shaking all over.

The manager of Tom's theater. Weeks, his name was.

Somebody'd noticed that he'd been wearing a different suit during the afternoon show than the one he'd had on earlier. The seat behind Kemp's, the dead man's, had had chewing gum on it. They'd got hold of the suit Weeks had left at the dry-cleaner's, and that had chewing gum on the seat of the trousers, too. He'd come in in a hurry around six, changed from one to the other right in the shop, the tailor told them. He'd had one there, waiting to be called for. He admitted it now, claimed the man had been breaking up his home.

Lew dropped the paper and the sheets separated, fell across his shoes.

It stuck to his shoe and Lew was like someone trudging through snow. "Movie Murderer Confesses—Murderer Confesses—Confesses. . . . "

Subconsciously he must have known where he was going, but he wasn't aware of it, was in a sort of fog in the broad daylight. The little blue and white plaque on the lamp-post said "Center Street." He went slowly down it. He walked inside between the two green lamps at the police station entrance and went up to the guy at the desk and said, "I guess you people are looking for me. I'm Lew Stahl."

Somehow, Lew knew it would be better if they put him away for a long while, the longer the better. He had learned too much that one night, got too used to death. Murder might be a habit that, once formed, would be awfully hard to break. Lew didn't want to be a murderer.

Silent as the Grave

Woolrich delivers an oscillation story dripping with paranoia and the economic desperation of the Depression in **"Silent as the Grave."** A man confesses to his wife that he killed someone in the past, and she promises to keep his secret. But when his ex-boss is found murdered, she torments herself with the question of whether her husband is responsible until a fateful decision sends her spiraling even further into doubt. With a climax as tortured as the rest of the story, it's a fascinating look at what murder puts innocent spouses through. In addition to an appearance in the 2018 collection *Literary Noir: A Series of Suspense* Volume 1, this story has not seen print since publication in *Mystery Book Magazine* in 1945 and in the 1946 collection *The Dancing Detective.*

IT WAS A NIGHT LIKE any other night. The moon was out; and there were stars.

A man and a girl strolling in the dark; the oldest story in the world. The music, mournful, nostalgic on the night air, ebbed away behind them, and the lights of the pavilion went with it. She was glad they were gone; just being with him was entertainment enough. She had her music and her dancing in the sound of his voice, the touch of his hand in hers.

Presently they came to a bench and, without a word, sat down. She knew why they had come out here. She knew what he was going to ask her. She wanted him to ask her. She had her answer ready, before he asked her, and it was "Yes."

His head went back, to look up at the stars. She looked at the turn of his chin, at the gnarled hitch in his throat, those were, for her, the stars. The starlight traced a thin silver line, like frost, along the upturned edge of his profile. That was proportionately all she knew of him, she reflected, that thin, argent, contour line; and the rest was still all in darkness, unknown, unguessed, like a planet already there but not yet emerged.

Her mother said it was risky to love anyone as much as she did him, so soon after meeting him, and knowing so little about him. Her mother said with dark head shakes, "Now don't be in too much of a hurry, young lady!" and "Just be careful what you're doing!" and other things like that your mother says to you. What did her mother know? Her mother's time for love was past.

Three weeks, two days, twelve hours. Yes, it was a short time. Very short for a lifetime.

Mitchell. Kenneth Mitchell. She said it over softly in her mind. Mitchell. Mrs. Frances Mitchell. No, Mrs. Kenneth

Mitchell. That was better. She wanted everything to belong to him, even her first name.

"Frances—" His arm slipped around her.

This was it. Here it came now. She nestled closer. "Yes, Ken?"

"I'm in love with you. Would you—you wouldn't marry me, would you?"

"Yes, Ken," she sighed. "I would." She seemed to blend into his arms, almost to lose her own identity, as if she were a part of him, his other self. They didn't stir for awhile, just stayed like that, blindly contented, without need for anything else. All the traffic of courtship—caresses, kisses, words of love—were superfluous. Their oneness was their sole caress.

Then suddenly his arm was gone. She was alone again, there was space between them on the bench.

"I had no right—I didn't mean to ask you that."

"But it's all right, Ken. Can't you tell it's all right?"

"There's something I have to tell you first. Something you've got to know."

Something about some other girl, of course. What else could it be? What else did a man have to tell a girl at a time like this, what else ever mattered between man and girl? All the rest belonged in the man's world, a sphere apart that the girl never entered, that didn't conflict with her.

"But Ken, it doesn't matter. I don't want to know."

"You have to know this. This is something you have to. Before I ask you. Before you answer me."

She edged closer, by way of mute consent. She waited.

"Frances, I killed a man once."

For a minute it was meaningless. All she could feel was a sense of relief. It was almost anticlimax. The threatened impediment had dissolved. She had been afraid of some entanglement barring her way, some undissolved marriage or unsevered amorous connection. But this was from that other sphere, that other plane, the man's world; this had nothing to do with her, this didn't conflict with her in any way. This wasn't anything that could affect their love.

This was almost as if a small boy were to come to you and say, "I threw a rock through somebody's window and broke it." He shouldn't have, it was wrong of him, the policeman down on the corner mightn't approve—but that didn't lessen your own affection for him in any way; how could it?

She breathed deeply, in lightened tension. "I thought it was—that there was somebody else." Then almost in parenthesis, "What was it, an accident?"

He shook his head doggedly. "It was no accident. It was what they call—murder. I went looking for him, and I found him, and—I did it."

Their oneness persisted; the thing had no power to divide them, every pore in her body was conscious of that fact. "What did they do to you, Ken?"

He said it lower than before. "They never found out it was me. They don't know to this day. I never gave myself up, because—well, he had it coming to him, he deserved it. He'd done me an injury. And I never forgive an injury."

An old rancor came up in him. She could feel the stiffening, the anger, from somewhere out of his past.

"It happened in St. Louis, long ago. Ten years ago. His name was Joseph Bailey, and he—"

Her hand flew up against his mouth, sealing it. "No more. I don't want to know any more."

They sat like that for a few minutes. Then, finally, her hand dropped. She had made her decision.

"Ask me what you were going to," she whispered. "Ask me. Nothing makes any difference. Nothing could change the way I feel about you. Nothing you could tell me."

His eyes kept pleading with her in the starlight. "But maybe later you won't feel the same. That's what I'm afraid of. Promise me you won't change. Promise me you won't throw it up to me, some day, if we should quarrel, like people do. I couldn't stand that, Frances. Promise me you'll never mention it, never remind me, in days to come."

She tilted her face to look up into his eyes. "I'll do more than promise. I swear it to you. I take a sacred vow, here and now. You'll never hear me speak of it again. It'll be just as though you never told me. It'll never pass my lips. *I'll be as silent as the grave, dear heart. As silent as the grave, forever."*

He made a sudden little move, and her arms, outstretched to poise protestingly against his shoulders, seemed to cave in across the little dimpled hollows opposite their elbows, and the span between the two of them had vanished, they were together again for good.

It was a night like any other night. The moon was out; and there were stars.

That this state of chronic happiness could keep on like that for three years after was no surprise to her, for she had expected it to. She had known it would, she had been sure it would, but still she could not have explained why it should. How was it that it lasted with them, when others seemed to lose it so slowly but nevertheless so surely? Was she different from others? Was he?

She knew they weren't. She knew it wasn't that. They were as hemmed-into a tiny cubicle of two rooms and bath, ceilings low over their heads, as any other city dwellers. They were stripped of all artifices, all privacy, all mystery, before one another. There would be nothing, soon, that they could say to one another they had not said before; nothing they could do they had not seen one another do already. Almost, nothing they could think, the other did not guess that they were thinking.

He came home as pinched and chilled in the winter, as frayed and tired in the summer, as any other man, as all other men. His feet sometimes would hurt and he would take his shoes off. On Sundays he didn't shave, and the rim of his jaw would look shadowed and soiled. Her hair could grow as dank hovering over the torrid steaming stewpans, of a blazing July evening, as any other woman's; her nose could grow as blue and she could sniffle just as inelegantly through it, on arising before him at the crack of a bitter winter dawn to close the windows and turn the heat valves, as any other woman's.

And still, whatever this magic was that filled their hearts with content, it survived all that. It survived without a necktie at the table, without cosmetics at the night table, without the utterance of any startlingly original remark any longer, without the belated revelation of any new quality, any unguessed facet to the personality, kept hidden until now.

Why was this? No one could know. If they could not know themselves, how could anyone else know?

It wasn't one of these gusty, flaring things that quickly exhausts itself and dies out again, leaving an ash of bitterness and cold. It reminded her of the pilot light on the gas stove in her kitchen. Not very bright, not very noticeable, but always there, burning steady, burning low, at the center of its little world.

A doctor once, whom they had gone to consult about some minor matter—a boil on Ken's neck that required lancing—came as close, perhaps, to putting his finger on it as anyone could have, though even his interpretation may have veered too closely to the clinical. Looking them over in shrewd appraisal, as they sat there before him side by side after the trivial operation, he asked with kindly interest, "About how long are you two married, six months or so?"

"Three years last May," she answered, with a smile that had in it both vainglory and humility.

It apparently startled him somewhat. She saw him shake his head slightly, in admiring approval. "You seem to be very well-mated," he murmured thoughtfully. Then added, "Both mentally and physically."

She looked down at the floor for a moment, and could feel her face grow warm. It was a little bit like—being disrobed for an examination. Neither she nor Ken referred to it between themselves afterward, on leaving.

They were so content, so at peace with one another and hence with the world, they didn't even want much more than they had in a material way. Ambition is a plant that sprouts best in the loam of discontent. Certainly they didn't crave great wealth. For what purpose? Clothes? In the darkness of the picture theater they went to once a week, who could tell whether she had on a fifty-dollar or a five-dollar dress? Better furniture, a roomier apartment? They'd have that some day, maybe in a year, or two, or three; it wasn't urgent. What difference did your surroundings make, when all you saw, all you cared about, all you were aware of, was that other face before you? When it wasn't there, the walls were barren; when it was, they were lighted, radiant, warm. A car? They could have that, too, in a little while; only a very small down payment was required. But what real need was there for one, when the subway kiosk was only down at the next corner?

Even children—She didn't really miss them, and when her mother, once or twice, slyly asked her if she were avoiding having any, her answer was: "No, but it's just as well we haven't had any. It's Ken I love; I haven't room for anything else."

The job he had, fit him like a comfortable pair of old shoes. He'd grown into it. He'd already had it for two years before their marriage, five in all now. It had become a part of the very warp and woof of his existence, as closely knitted to him as she was. It was not a job, that designation was incorrect, not just an offhand way of earning a living. It was that part of his life that was spent away from her, from morning until early evening each day, and just as cherished, just as dear to him in another way, as the part spent with her.

The man over him was lenient, friendly, understanding. Hallett was his name, and he had made an invisible third at the table with them so many nights that she felt she knew him well, though she had never met him.

He'd say, "Hallett came back from his vacation today, and you wouldn't know him. He's put on fifteen pounds in the two weeks."

"I'm glad he picked up a little, he was looking all in before he went away," she would say, although she'd never seen him. But Ken had said he was.

Or, "Hallett's kid is coming out with a new tooth. I wish you could have seen him. He was sitting there proud as a peacock all day."

"My, but it's forward!" she'd marvel. "That's the second one, already, in no time at all."

Nearly every night he sat there with them at the table like that, an invisible but welcome third.

Once, around the time the dying decade was merging unnoticeably into the strange new times ahead, Ken received an offer of another job, at better pay.

"Did you tell Hallett about it?" she asked him.

"Sure. I wouldn't do anything behind his back. He's been too regular to me."

"What did he say?"

"He said much as he'd hate to see me go, he didn't want to stand in my way. He gave it to me fair and square. He said he couldn't give me any more than I'm getting now. He said the bottom's starting to drop out of everything; what happened in Wall Street is starting to spread around now, and it'll take a good six months, maybe more, before it wears off again. But on the other hand, he told me, as long as he's with the outfit, I haven't got a thing to worry about, he'll see that I'm treated fair and square. I can consider myself set for life."

And in a day or two, when she asked him, "Have you decided what you'll do about that?"

"I've turned the offer down; I'm staying with Hallett."

She'd known he would. She was glad he had. She wanted him happy. Or rather, she wanted the two of them to be happy; his happiness was hers.

And then suddenly there was no Hallett any more. He was gone overnight, and a stranger had taken his place at their supper table. It was almost like a personal bereavement to the two of them, that first night when he came home and told her. Her face even paled for a moment or two, as his must have when he'd first learned it earlier in the day. He couldn't eat very much.

"What's he like, this new man, this Parker?"

"I can't tell yet, I only saw him today for the first time." He tried to be fair to him. "I suppose he's all right. He's sort of lost, hasn't got the hang of things yet." He turned his fork over a few times, without lifting it from the table.

"You'll get used to him," she tried to console him. And then with an odd little burst of commiseration, "That poor woman! Hallett's wife. Just think what she must be going through tonight!"

She had a rather strongly developed fellow-feeling for other women, not a very commonly met with trait.

"He doesn't like me," he blurted out one night a few weeks later.

"Maybe you just imagine that." She wondered, privately, how anyone could possibly not like Ken.

"I can tell. He knows I'm one of Hallett's old men, of course, and he's got it in for me. I can tell by the way he looks at me."

"Well, don't give him an opening, don't give him a chance to show it."

"I'm not. I'm minding my own business, and doing my job, like I've always done."

They were selling apples and tangerines on the street corners now. That is to say, peddling them out of sheer destitution, in a city that had never known emergency beggary before, only the professional kind. These vendors were men in their prime, able-bodied. Then abruptly within a month or two, the phenomenon had vanished again, as if already the proportion of those reduced to such straits, as over against those remaining still above it, had increased too greatly to permit any further profit to be derived from it. The ratio of the needy to the prospering had reversed itself.

Parker cut his wages in half. His bitterness, brought home to smoulder there in worried sight of her, was not due so much to that in itself as to the fact that others, there a shorter time than he, had not been similarly reduced. "Parker's own men," as he expressed it.

"But are you sure?"

"I asked a couple of them. They wouldn't admit it, but I could tell by the look on their faces when they heard it that they hadn't been cut themselves."

"But that's not fair."

His mouth twisted into an ugly shape. "You bet it isn't. I'm taking the cut, so that some of his men don't have to be let out."

"Maybe if you went to him and—"

"That's just what he'd like me to do, so that he could chuck me out altogether. You should have seen his face when I stepped away from the cashier's window and opened my envelope. I caught him looking at me with a smirking expression all over his face."

"But why, Ken? You haven't done anything to him."

"He's got it in for me, that's all. And that's something you can't buck. You can't buck that on any job, when the guy over you has it in for you. He's got you, and you know it, and he knows it."

"Maybe things'll begin to clear up, and you can go somewhere else. The President says by next spring—"

"Does he work at my job?" he said glumly. Then after a while he added, "I'm only hanging on because I have to. I've got to get out of there, the minute I can. It's gotten so that just looking at the guy does something to me, inside. Every time he even passes in back of me while I'm busy at my layouts, I can feel something—"

She could sense that tightening-up again come over him that she had noticed one night long ago. Long ago, on a bench, beneath the stars.

"I don't hate easy, Frances," he muttered, "but once I start in, I don't quit easy either. I never forget an injury."

She dropped her eyelids for a moment, raised them again. A forbidding memory had crossed her mind just then. "Sh!" she urged, "Sh-h-h," and pressed her hand soothingly to his forehead, as if to cool it.

It was a night like any other night. There was no moon, but there were stars.

She was already badly frightened by then, it was so late and she had stood so long watching for him from the window. Then when she finally saw his figure approaching below in the dark, she knew by his walk something was the matter. He didn't even remember the right door, went on past their own house entrance almost to the next one down, then just as she was about to fling up the window and call out to him, he turned abruptly, retraced his steps, and came in where he belonged.

She left the window, and in the moment or two it took her to reach their flat door, wrung her hands close before her face in flurried, unseen appeal, to whom or what she did not know herself.

He came up the stairs quietly and slowly, to where she was waiting. His face was white with spent emotion, but composed. There was a big rent in his shirt, up near the collar, and two of the buttons on his coat were gone. Then when he'd gone in past her, wordlessly, and raised his hands to remove his hat, she saw that his hair was disordered, and there was a faint trace of orange across his knuckles that must have been left there by shed blood.

He sat down heavily and blew breath between his cupped hands, as though to warm them, although it wasn't cold out.

She drew up a kitchen chair and sat down across the table from him. He didn't seem to want to say anything, and she was afraid to for awhile. Presently she reached over toward him timidly, as if afraid of being rebuffed, and drew the knot of his necktie out from under his rumpled collar, where it had become wedged, and around toward the front where it belonged.

"Parker, Ken?" she asked finally.

He began to speak as though his silence had been an oversight, he had simply been waiting to have it called to his attention. His voice was husky from recent stress. "They took me to the police station, that's why I got back so late."

She started using the tips of her fingers for the teeth of a comb, raking his hair back with them, very softly, very persuasively. She didn't say anything.

He smiled at nothing she could see there on the floor. "I hit him *good*," he said with grim satisfaction. "Boy, what a slam I gave him! That one sock alone was worth everything I've had to take from him all these months. He went all the way back across his own desk and then down to the floor on the other side of it, and all the stuff he had on it went down on top of him. Just like you see in the pictures."

They were just like little boys, she thought. Only, the consequences of their acts could be so much graver when their bodies had become those of men.

"If they hadn't grabbed me and held me back, I think while I was at it I would have—"

She tried to ward the word off by quickly shuttering her eyes. He didn't say it anyway.

"So then he called in a cop. You know—trying to throw a scare into me. They held me over there for awhile. Finally he phoned in that he didn't intend lodging any complaint, they could let me go if they wanted to. Bighearted." He almost spat the word. "So I'm through there," he said finally.

"Never mind, maybe it's better so. I'm glad it's over. It was starting to get you, Ken. I could see it more and more every day."

"I'll get another job," he said. "Watch me."

She waited a moment or two. Then she asked timidly, "But what about references, Ken? They'll want them everywhere, no matter where you go; these days especially, when there are a dozen and one applicants for every job. And as long as he's down there in charge, even if someone just phones in to ask anything about you, he'd be just mean enough to—"

He didn't answer for some time, as though that had only now occurred to him—for the first time. Then finally he said, "If I ever find that out—" And didn't finish it.

Their money came to an end on a crisp fall morning in the third year of the bad new times, the Election Year, that was. They went together to the bank to draw it out, although the account was in his name alone. The way a couple feel obliged to attend some solemn formal occasion together, a deathbed or a funeral, when the presence of one without the other would be unthinkable.

"This closes the account," the teller reminded them gratuitously.

It was only a matter of four-dollars-fifty-cents, that was all that was left by then; but somehow when the leaves of the passbook had been perforated to form the letters "Closed" and it had been returned to them worthless, it did make a difference, a vast difference. She could feel it herself; a psychological difference. There was a horrid nightmare-feeling to it of going down over their heads into black, bottomless depths of water, never to rise again.

He walked out of the bank dazed, staring down at the little booklet, frittering its pages back and forth under his thumb endlessly. She had to guide him, unnoticeably, with her arm under his to keep him from jostling into people. Outside on the sidewalk he came to a halt, as though not knowing which way to go. "There goes—security," he said finally. "There go—three years of our lives."

"Don't, Ken," she pleaded. "Don't take it like that." She freed the booklet gently from his hands and shied it into a refuse can. "Come on. Come on home now."

He only said one thing more, very quietly, almost stonily. But she didn't like the sound of it. "I have Garrett Parker to thank for this."

He got something to do several weeks later, but it wasn't a job any more. He was paid by the hour, twenty-five cents an hour. Demonstrating in a drugstore window. Some impulse made her follow him there later in the day; he had told her where it was.

She saw this small crowd collected in front of the place, and she crept up behind them, rose on tiptoes, looked fearfully over their shoulders. He was within the lighted showcase, stripped to his undershirt and trousers. He had always had powerful shoulders and biceps, they showed up well. He was holding up a small patent-medicine, pointing to it, then flexing his arms so that his muscles swelled, striking himself on the chest like Tarzan in the movies. At twenty-five cents an hour. For anyone who came along the street to stand and gape at.

She would have died rather than let him see her looking at him; his crucifixion was complete enough without that. She turned and fled all the way home, her arms protectively clasped around her own form as though she had been suddenly stripped naked. She couldn't forget that telltale pulsing she had noted at his temple, that betrayed how he had been steeling himself.

She didn't say anything when he came home at last, only tried not to look at the seventy-five cents he put down on the edge of the table. She didn't tell him that she'd seen him, that she knew what it was for.

He toppled into a chair and hung his head.

"I'm ashamed," he breathed stifledly. "Frances, I'm so ashamed."

"Don't go back there again, Ken," she said. "I won't let you."

His attitude of humiliation, of self-reproach, was much harder to bear than the conditions that had brought them to this pass. "I shouldn't have met you, married you. I'm not even able to give you food for your mouth, I'm no good."

She dropped to her knees beside him. "I don't know what words to say, to tell you what you mean to me. I'm as proud of you now as if you had all kinds of money, and were on top of the world. I don't know how not to be proud of you."

From his hidden face and concave middle, arched over the table-top, came those peculiar, wrenching guttural sounds of male grief she had never heard before and never wanted to hear again. And through the subsiding sobs, at last, a still, cold voice filtered. "One man did this to me. One man."

Then a ray of brightness, when night was at its darkest. A beam of hope. He went to look up Hallett in his despair; his former boss, the one before.

"Oh, Ken! Can he do something for you—?"

He couldn't bring it out coherently at first. But the mere fact that he wanted to so bad, was so pitifully anxious to tell it, showed her in a flash that it must be good. "Wait'll you hear—My own line of work, France! He's going to talk to them right tomorrow. I'm to go down there. He's not in the business himself any more, but he knows these people, and he thinks he can swing it for me. He says with my previous experience there shouldn't be any reason—And what do you think he tried to do? I caught him trying to slip something into my pocket when I wasn't looking. A five-dollar bill. Didn't want to hurt my feelings by asking me openly if I—"

His face was a poem of gratitude. He said with husky, feigned censure that was meant for the deepest admiration, "The old son-of-a-gun. What can you do with a guy like that?"

He couldn't sleep all night, that night. But there was a difference. He didn't lie there growling surreptitiously deep inside his throat, hissing maledictions through his clenched teeth. He lay there wide-eyed, breathlessly hopeful. She knew, because she couldn't sleep either. They both got up much earlier than they needed to, red-eyed, haggard, supremely happy. She walked with him as far as the corner to see him off. She wished him luck. Long after he had disappeared from sight she stood there looking after him. Praying.

But when he came back there was something wrong. Her own face dimmed to the lacklustre of his.

"Ken, didn't they—? Did Hallett forget to talk to them?"

"References," he said tersely. He swallowed before he could bring himself to pronounce the name. "Parker."

She just looked at him, caught her underlip with her teeth in foreboding.

"He was my last boss, after Hallett. Hallett's recommendation wasn't enough by itself."

He dropped heavily into a chair, shaded his eyes. "They'll let me know tomorrow. It's still this way." He seesawed his hand uncertainly, to show her. "I think I still have a chance."

She knew what he was thinking, though. "Don't be afraid. No one could be that inhuman. What can he truthfully say against your ability? Nothing. Only that you lost your temper once and went for him."

She could see his cigarette all night in the dark, glowing and then dimming again, over there by the window. Like a pulsing ember of frustration.

When he was leaving the next day, she said: "Ken, I know it's extravagant, but would you phone me as soon as you find out? I'll wait downstairs in the candy store, right by their phone. Just so I'll—I'll know sooner."

He didn't say anything, but he kissed her affirmatively.

She waited there from ten on. She sat perched on one of the high stools before the soft-drink counter. She chatted with the proprietor's wife. She sat on, waiting, long after they'd stopped chatting for lack of anything further to talk about. She was glad when three o'clock came, and the woman changed places with her high-school-age daughter, and was no longer there to be a witness to her misery.

Four o'clock came, and five, and the new place would be closing soon. All business places closed around five or so.

She stood up abruptly, and put a nickel in the phone, and called it herself; he'd given her its name.

Timidly she asked, "Has there—has there been a new man taken on today?"

The girl said, "Yes, I believe there has."

Her heart soared, and all the wait was nothing. "Could you—would you give me his name, please?"

The girl looked it up, or got it from someone.

"Howard Ellson," she said.

She felt her way along the soft-drink counter, and out the door, and upstairs to their flat. He was sitting there, with the lights unlit. He must have come back long ago, hours ago, while she stayed on waiting in the candy store below.

He just looked up at her, then looked down again. She would have read that look anyway, even if she hadn't already known. She didn't go to him and put her hands on him. His grief needed elbowroom.

"He did it," he said after a long time.

He took a long breath, seemed to draw air slowly into his lungs, for a whole minute or two, and never let it out again. "I ought to kill him," he said almost inaudibly.

"Ken," she moaned. "Ken."

"It was my one chance, and it won't come again. I had it, and

I lost it—thanks to him. Someone else has the job now, and people hang onto their jobs these days. I can't asked Hallett to go around acting as an employment agent for me. Months more of misery now for the two of us. On *his* account. Maybe years. Do you know what that means?" He pulled his shirt open and ground his fist against his bared chest. "Do you know what it does to you, in *here*, when you can blame that all on one man? Not Fate, not Conditions, not Bad Luck or Coincidence—but one man, walking around on the very same streets you are, not very far from where you are."

"Ken, don't. Think of me. I can't stand it when I hear you talk like that."

And then he said again, more softly than the first time, almost in a baleful whisper, "I'd like to kill him." And she saw his hands close up and freeze.

She got him to eat a little, after awhile. She thought the worst of it was over by then. And then later, he was sitting there in the kitchen, directly behind her, while she washed the dishes.

There wasn't a sound from him. She turned her head suddenly and looked, and the chair was empty. The wet plate dropped and shattered into the spokes of a wheel, and she ran to the door and looked out.

Hours later she was waiting down on the corner for him, when he finally came along. He was drunk, she could tell by his walk. But that didn't matter, nothing mattered; only that he came along. She ran to him and put her arm about his waist, and they went wavering back toward the house together.

"Ken, why did you do this to me, why did you frighten me this way? You left without a word, without saying goodbye. Ken, I thought such awful things."

He knew what she was saying, could understand. "Poor France," he said. "I'm drunk. It didn't do any good. I didn't forget once, the whole time I was doing it."

They went up the inside stairs slowly, side by side, reeling as though they were both drunk and not just one of them. "I'm drunk, France. You never saw me that way before, did you? You don't want to kiss me now, do you? But I still want to kiss you. More than ever."

"I do. Look. I do."

When they got inside their own flat, he toppled heavily into a chair, almost pulling her down with him.

"Shall I help you off with your shoes?"

He shook his head, smiled wanly. "I'm not that drunk." His hands went up.

"Let me see your face. Why are you covering your face like that?"

"What is there to see?"

There was nothing. It was just his face, as it had always been. His hands, released, went up to it again and covered it once more.

Just before their evening meal, something happened to change him. She couldn't tell exactly what it was, at first. He'd still seemed all right when he came in with the paper and sat down to read it. Then by the time she'd called him to eat, there was already something different about him, some alteration had taken place. It had none of the symptoms she was so familiar with by now. She couldn't tell what it was. She could discern something utterly new in it, constraint, furtiveness; and could only ascribe it to remorse for last night's drunkenness. But if he was ashamed, why so belatedly ashamed, at the end of the day? Why not immediately on getting up and facing her this morning? He hadn't been then.

She saw him looking at her closely several times, as if wondering how to forestall some discovery she was bound to make eventually herself. Abruptly, he said, "Did you see that, in the paper?"

"What?" she asked.

"Turn toward the back. No, the page after that."

Parker had been found dead on the street near his house. The details didn't matter. Scarcely any were given, anyway. Only that he had met death by violence at somebody's hands. "Some person unknown," the paper said.

She peered at him through the mist of stupefaction that the

item had created in her mind. She saw him drop his eyes, then raise them again with an effort, to meet hers.

"Why didn't you tell me right away? As soon as you first read it?"

"I felt funny about it," he admitted with a defensive shrug.

At first she couldn't understand what he meant by that. "But why, Ken? Why should you feel funny about it?"

He looked away, sidewise, down at the floor. "Because I've been talking about him like I have; knocking him so."

It sounded lame, it didn't ring true somehow. She felt his real reason went deeper than that. But for once her understanding of him failed her, she couldn't imagine what it was.

Presently, as they sat there discussing the event, she murmured, with that characteristic compassion of hers toward other women: "I feel sorry for his poor wife. What she must have felt, when he didn't come home, and then finally a stranger rang the doorbell to tell her—"

"It was a good job!" he blurted out savagely. "He had it coming to him, if anyone ever did!"

She sat in stunned silence after that. Not because of what he'd just said, but because of a discovery that what he had just said had brought about. The discovery was this: his recent self-consciousness about the item being in the paper was not due to the way he had reviled Parker, as he had said it was. It could not be. For here he was doing it again. He'd contradicted himself, without realizing it.

It must have been due to something else.

It only came to her that night, in a flash, as she lay awake in the dark, thinking. A flash that seemed to light up the whole room, with a horrid ruddy glow. She had been thinking: It may be better, for Ken's sake, that this has happened to Parker, that he's out of the way now. It's like a load off my mind. Because I've been dreading for weeks and months past now, that this very thing *might* happen some day. Only it would be Ken who—

And then the flash came.

Why should he be self-conscious in front of me when he first read it tonight?

Why should be take such a long time to show it to me? Why not instantly?

He told me once he never forgives an injury.

He's done it once already, *there*, before we were married.

Even to herself she never said "St. Louis."

She propped herself up on her elbow, turned toward him. She stretched out her hand to touch him, but something seemed to hold it back, she couldn't make it go all the way. "Ken," she whispered fearfully.

He was either fast asleep or he didn't hear the faint breathing of his name.

No, I'd better not ask him, she thought. How can I ask him? To ask him about this would be like reproaching him for that other time. I've made my vow, and I must keep it. Never to speak of it, never.

She forced herself to lie back again. She pressed her hand tightly to her mouth, held it that way, as if to smother the horrid question that kept trying to force its way out.

"It isn't so," she said to herself over and over again. "It can't be. He was out drinking that night. Only out drinking."

And then an insidious afterthought, as if malignantly hovering about waiting its opportunity, forced its way in.

"But *where* was he out drinking that night? Where did he go?"

The next night he was sitting there in the room with her reading the paper.

She spoke at last. For five whole minutes she'd been trying to. "Ken. Where—what bar did you go to, that night you—came home like that?"

He took a minute's time. "I don't remember," he said, through the newspaper like a screen.

"Quinn's, down by the corner?"

"No," he said. "Further away. Some bar or other. I don't remember." He gave the newspaper a shake, as if to say: Stop this.

She daren't go any farther. Why should he go farther away than Quinn's? In Quinn's they'd trust him for a drink or two. Elsewhere they wouldn't. And he must have had quite a few that night.

"Did they get him yet?" she asked presently.

"Who?"

"Whoever did that. You know, Parker." She turned to look at him as she asked it, drying a dish with its rim held pressed into her midriff. She could only see the top of his forehead, the paper hid his face from there down.

"No," he said tonelessly. "Not as far as I see."

"They will in a day or two, I suppose?" she suggested. "They always do."

"Not always," he said curtly. Neither forehead nor paper moved. He must have stopped reading, or the one would have slowly climbed above the other as his eyes went down the page.

She turned away again, put the dried plate down atop the others. They didn't once, she agreed silently. In St. Louis.

He roamed restlessly about for awhile, stood here, stood there. Finally he said, "Think I'll take a little walk, get some air."

"You'd better cover up good," she warned. "It's ice-cold out. Your coat is like tissue paper. Put your sweater on underneath."

But when he'd done so, he complained, "I can't wear both things. Too bulky." And he took the coat off, and left just the sweater on. He went out, and it stayed there where he'd flung it, carelessly rumpled on a chair.

She got a clothesbrush, and drew the coat across her lap, and started to dust it off a little. She turned the linings of the pockets out, to rid them of the debris, the tobacco grains and clotted bits of wool that she knew by experience were likely to adhere along their seams. A crumpled scrap of pale-green paper clung to one of them even after it had been reversed, and she plucked it off. It was nothing, only a trolley-car ticket.

Her clothesbrush halted again after a single upward stroke. Funny he should take a trolley, when the subway was so much more accessible to where they lived, and so much faster. She picked it up again from where she had discarded it, and straightened out the creases so that it expanded to twice its length.

Why, this wasn't even a downtown line, she could tell by the list of transfer points running down one side of it, under the heading "Not Good if Detached."

> "Canton Boulevard, South.
> Macomber Avenue, South.
> Fillmore Avenue, South."

The coat fell off her lap and she stepped over it in moving across the room, forgetful of the fact that she had just been about to brush it. The newspaper was on the table where he'd thrown it when he finished with it, but she didn't want that one, she wanted the previous night's. She found it thrust away in a receptacle with paper bags and things.

Two words out of all the hundreds it contained were all she wanted, and she found them quickly, for she knew which text they were imbedded in. ". . . Garrett Parker, of 25 Fillmore Avenue, South . . ."

The ticket's date, printed in red, was that of two nights ago, the night he had been out drinking. It had a double row of little boxes, each with a numeral in it, to mark the exact hour of issuance. The upper ones were for A. M., the lower for P.M. The "10" of the bottom row had been neatly punched through with a little round hole. She wouldn't have known which it was, only the "9" was still there on one side of it, the "11" on the other. The time of Parker's death had been between ten and half-past.

A blind interval, during which movement became automatic, unrecorded, followed. She was standing before the stove, holding the pilot key out so that the light flared wide, thrusting the pale-green ticket into it. Her face was that of a desperately sick woman.

"Now I know," she kept saying to herself over and over. "Now I know."

She put out the lights and raised the window shade.

It was a night like any other night. There was no moon, but there were stars.

Two nights later she saw *the name* for the first time, this stranger's name that meant nothing to her. Pulled out of thin air.

"They got him," Ken said abruptly. And she thought she heard him give a long sigh.

She ran over quickly beside him, to read. They had arrested a man named Considine, on the accusation of having killed Parker. He'd worked for Parker; not in Ken's time, but more recently, a few short weeks ago. He'd been unjustly discharged. He'd borne a grudge. It was Ken's case all over again, almost terrifyingly so. Just with a change of names. He couldn't prove where he'd been that night, around ten to half-past. He said he'd gone out and had a few drinks, and couldn't remember. She was almost terrified by the similarity.

That was about all there was to it. It was only a small item at the foot of a back page. But it meant so much in someone's life. In theirs too, for that matter. Immunity from now on. She could see him go out on the streets now without that cold terror in her heart. She could hear a knock at their door, or a heavy tread coming up the stairs, without dying a little.

"He denies he did it, Ken," she said mournfully, without meeting his eyes.

"They all do," he said callousedly. "You don't expect him to admit it, do you?" He put the paper aside, stood up. "Let's go out to a movie," he said. "I—I feel a lot better tonight."

It came creeping back that night in the dark, the banished named. Considine. Just an abstract name in a newspaper. Jones, Smith, Brown, Considine. She said to herself, "I must forget this name. I must say, 'It doesn't belong to anyone real. There is no such man.'"

She tossed and turned restlessly in the bed.

There is no such man, there is no such man, there is no such—

But it kept pounding at her mercilessly, like the throbbing of a drum. "Considine. Considine. Considine."

He was working again. They'd taken him back at his old place, now that Parker was out of the way. His wages were exactly two-thirds of what they had been when he was with the concern the time before. But the world about them, beginning to struggle painfully up out of the depths, had found new standards of contentment, frugality, simplicity. Safety, security, came drifting back within sight on the troubled waters, but never again the old expansiveness.

They discontinued accepting relief almost with his first pay check. They were compelled to, under penalty of prosecution, but thousands postponed doing so as long as they could. But with him it was almost a physical restorative, an aid to convalescence. His step became firmer, quicker. The old, open untroubled width of eye returned. Slowly the soreness of spirit was eased, the bitterness was mellowed, as he basked in the renewed illusion of being of some use in the world, as under therapeutic rays.

Even heartiness, gayety, began to peer tentatively forth again at intermittent times, as when he brought her home his pay envelopes on alternate Saturdays. What they contained stood for so much more than the intrinsic value of the money they held.

"Why can't I get you to smile any more?" he asked wistfully, as she looked down at it in her lap where he'd dropped it.

"I do smile—look—I do. I smile whenever you do, like I always did."

"But it doesn't go *in*. It doesn't go inside."

("*He* had a job too, poor soul," she thought.)

The name had vanished again from the newspapers, after that first brief mention—it seemed like months ago, or was it only weeks? It was such a minor, unimportant case after all. She never went near the papers any more while he was present. But once or twice, when they were preparing for bed, she made some excuse to go back into the other room in her nightgown, stand hurriedly searching through them for a moment before putting the light out. There was never any mention of it that she could find. But still he's real, she told herself, returning wraith-like to where her own husband lay safe in the darkness; he's real, he's somewhere.

One night she asked, "Whatever became of that man they arrested—on account of Parker? Are they still holding him?"

"They must be. I haven't read of his being released."

"All this time in jail," she thought, "while we—"

And suddenly within a week, as if her question had been ill-omened, had released pent-up evil forces held in abeyance all the while, they read of his being brought to trial. It wasn't a celebrated crime, it wasn't given much space. Things like that were happening all the time in a big city such as theirs, people charged with murder being tried for their lives. In the standard-sized paper that he habitually brought home there were never any pictures, as least not of that sort of thing. But once he happened to bring a tabloid in addition; not that he had bought it, but someone had left it on the subway seat next to him and it was practically uncreased. And this was two-thirds pictures and very little text, and all of that very sort of thing.

Leafing unsuspectingly through it, she looked up, stunned.

"What's the matter?"

"He has a wife," she said aghast, as though she'd seen a ghost. "I didn't know that until now."

"Who? Oh, Considine. What made you think he hadn't?" And after a moment he added, "Even murderers have wives."

Ah yes, she agreed to herself, with poignant bitterness. Yes, Kenneth Mitchell, you're right, even murderers have wives.

That night she had a terrifying dream, in which a stranger's face hovered over her as she lay there. The face of a strange woman, stricken with grief. It bent low above her own. "You have *your* husband," it whispered balefully. "Where is mine?"

She turned her face feverishly, to try to avoid the accusing sight.

"Murderess!" hissed the phantom. "Murderess!"

"I didn't do it," she breathed tormentedly. *"He* did."

"He killed Parker. But *you* are the one who is killing my husband. By remaining silent. *You*, not he! Murderess,

murderess!"

She awoke with a stifled scream, and fled from the bed, and ran to the window and stood there looking out.

Her breast was rising and falling convulsively, and there was cold moisture on her face. She'd always had such a strongly developed feeling of sympathy for other women.

It was a night like any other night. Without a moon, and without stars.

She found herself looking at the house from the opposite side of the street. Its cracker-box outline, its canary-brick facing, dim with soot, looked so prosaic, so matter-of-fact. It was just a flat like thousands of others, all over the city. On nearly every street you could see one just like it.

She tried to tear herself away, and she couldn't. She wondered: behind which one of those windows is she sitting, agonized, stifling her pain? Waiting for the night to come. He dies tonight; tonight is his last night.

I'm the only one can save him. If I go on my way now, if I go home, nothing can save him; he'll surely die tonight. If I come back tomorrow, it'll be too late. He'll be gone, then, and nothing can bring him back.

She crossed the street, against the traffic, dazedly, like a sleepwalker. She went up to the door, pulled it open, went inside. She was in a grubby hallway that smelled of dust and stale cooking. She went over to the letter boxes and lowered her head, scanning the names.

A janitress came out from behind the stairs carrying a pail of water. "Who did you wish to see, Missus?"

"Considine. Are they—is she still living here?"

"Sure. She's up on the third. You know her?"

"No," Frances said simply. "I felt I—had to see her. I feel sorry for people in trouble."

The janitress nodded. "Yes, that's trouble, all right."

"What's she like?" Frances asked.

"Like you. About your age. Nice little body. She was so happy with him before it happened. She had another baby since they took him to jail."

"She's taking it hard, I suppose?"

Again the janitress' choice of an illustration was deadly. "Wouldn't you? He was all she had."

She had once been about Frances' own age. She was a crazed automaton now, beyond calculations of age or personality. She seemed unable to stand entirely straight, even in the narrow door opening. She stood bowed forward, as if a heavy lodestone were suspended from her neck.

"You don't know me," Frances said. "I'd like to talk to you. Please let me come in. I'd like to talk to you."

The woman in the doorway said listlessly, "Come in." Her dazed mind evidently couldn't grasp the fact that Frances was a complete stranger to her.

She began to cry again as soon as the door was closed. It had become so continuous by now there was scarcely any facial change went with it; just a renewed dimming of the puffy eyes and then a glistening track down the cheek. She said, as though she had known Frances a long time, "My sister is coming over to take the children and me back with her later, but she didn't get here yet. But *tonight!* Oh, how am I going to stand it *tonight?*"

There was a little boy standing there, staring up at Frances. The mother patted the top of his head absently. "No, you go inside. Don't come in here. Stay inside and play with the baby like I told you."

She turned to Frances when he had gone. "He doesn't know," she choked. "How can I tell him? He keeps *asking*. He keeps asking all the time where he is."

Frances kept opening and closing the frame of her handbag. Over and over, incessantly, without looking at it.

The other woman's voice rose, strangulated. "What harm has that child done? I'm not asking anything for myself, but is it right to take that child's father away from him? Is that what the Law is for, to punish innocent children?"

"Don't," Frances breathed expiringly, and covered her ears. "I can't stand it."

The woman turned toward the window. It looked out on a whitewashed brick shaft. The wall was blue with shade now nearly all the way up, only at the very top was their still a triangular wedge of crimson sunlight, shaped like a guillotine blade. She pointed to it, held her shaking arm extended full-length. "Look how fast it goes, that sun," she groaned. "Why doesn't somebody stop it? Oh, why doesn't somebody make it stay *still?"*

Frances impulsively stepped close to her, took her shoulders, gently tried to turn her away. She resisted passively. Her waist and shoulders turned under the coaxing pressure, but her face remained stubbornly fixed on the evaporating patch of sunlight out there. "That's his last sun," she whimpered. "That's the last time he'll ever see it. Don't let them take the sun away from him. Oh, miss, whoever you are, don't let them!"

Frances drew her to a chair, sat her down in it. She stroked her disheveled hair back from her brow. She brought a little water in a glass, held it for her to drink. "Sh-h-h-h," she whispered on a long-drawn breath. "Sh-h-h-h."

"I was up to see him Sunday," Mrs. Considine murmured presently, quieting a little. "I said goodbye Sunday. I don't know how I got back here. If I hadn't known my children were here waiting for me, if my brother-in-law hadn't been with me on the train—Oh, that awful train ride! The wheels kept going around in my head. They kept saying, 'Goodbye forever, goodbye, goodbye, goodbye—' "

Frances winced, and, bending down over her from behind the chair, tilted her own face for a moment, ceilingward, as if in supplication of some sort of guidance neither one of them could see.

"Did he—" She could barely make herself heard. "Did he—say it wasn't he—he didn't?"

"He told me again, like he's told me from the beginning. He swore it to me by our two children. He didn't, he didn't; he never went near that man. I *know* he's telling the truth. You'd have to know my Al like I do. He wouldn't lie to me, my Al wouldn't lie to me. It isn't in him to do that to anyone; I know him too well. He only went out for a few beers that night; is there any harm in that? Just that night he had to go. I even said to him, 'Al, don't go tonight.' Never *dreaming*, You know, just because I wanted him to stay around, I was lonely. But he went to look up his friend Nick Mano. That's a friend of his, Nick Mano. And just that night Nick had to be out. If he'd only been with him, they wouldn't have been able to say—but he waited around for him. And that's when it happened." The figure in the chair rocked desolately to and fro. "But who is there will listen? Who is there will help me? Who *can* help me?"

I can, Frances thought. I can, I alone. Only I. It was as though a bright, cold light had suddenly been turned on. Everything, the outlines of things, the room about her, the woman in the chair immediately below her, suddenly seemed so clear, crystal-clear, diamond-clear, where until now they had been hazy, blurred by her own turmoil. Everything seemed so lucid, so logical, so—inevitable.

The other woman's voice droned on, in its litany of misery. "The last words he said to me Sunday, his very last words when they were making me leave, were, 'I didn't do it, Frances. They're taking me away from you for something I didn't do.'"

"Is that your name?" Frances shuddered violently. "My God!" she moaned low.

The woman's sobbing singsong continued. Suddenly she turned her head questioningly toward the back of the chair. "Miss—?" she called out wonderingly. "Miss—?"

There was no one standing there any longer. The room was empty. The door hung cryptically open.

Suddenly she found herself in a phone booth. Somewhere, she didn't know where. It seemed so simple, so easy. A little light went on, to see by. She found a nickel and she dropped it in. Just like when you wanted to phone the grocer or the butcher. No different. So easy, so simple, so compulsory.

A voice said, "Police Department, good evening."

She said, "I want to talk to someone about that Parker case. What they're killing that man for tonight. I don't know how to go about it—"

"Just a moment." Another voice got on. It wasn't a frightening voice. It was impersonal, but it wasn't severe, or bullying, or anything. It was just like—well, once she'd had to call up one of the department stores about making an exchange; it took patience, but she'd finally succeeded in making herself understood. "Yes, ma'm. Now, what is it?"

She said, "It's about that Parker case. He didn't do it. That man they're—putting away tonight. Considine. He didn't do it. You *must* believe me—"

The voice was calmingly reasonable. First things first. "Would you give me your name please?"

You had to give your name when you were asked it by a police official, even over the telephone wire. It never occurred to you not to. The habit of being law-abiding, of never having anything to hide or fear, saw to that. "I'm Mrs. Kenneth Mitchell."

The voice showed approving consideration. "And what is your address, please, Mrs. Mitchell?"

"Forty Forthway." Then she added, gratuitously, "Apartment C." The stores always liked that, when you gave the exact flat number. It made it easier for them to deliver. It seemed to add plausibility now.

"Yes, Mrs., Mitchell. And now you say—?"

"He didn't do it. Considine. I know it, oh, I know it! You've *got* to listen to me. I wouldn't have done this, if I weren't sure—"

"What makes you think that, Mrs. Mitchell?"

"Because—because—" She floundered, helpless. "Because I *know* he didn't. I *know.*"

The voice was considerate, patient, willing to give her a fair hearing to almost any lengths. "But you must have some reason for such a belief, Mrs. Mitchell."

"I have," she protested tearfully. "I have."

"Then what is it, Mrs. Mitchell?"

Somehow she found herself in a verbal corner. She couldn't seem to extricate herself, go back along the way she'd entered and thus get out again. She hadn't thought this far ahead. There were two parts to the act of vindication. Exoneration. And then substitution. But she only realized that now. She hadn't taken the second one into her calculation, visualized it. And they were indivisible, the two.

The voice persisted, nudging her, nudging her ever so gently. Not allowing her to stand still in her cul-de-sac. "But what is your reason for thinking Considine didn't do it, Mrs. Mitchell? How can you be so sure?"

"Because—Because—" There wasn't any other way. It had to be one or the other. To be believed at all. And to be believed was uppermost in her tormented mind just then. Overshadowing every other consideration. "Because my own husband did it."

The voice showed no dramatic alteration whatever. It continued on its even tenor. It still seemed reluctant to believe her. Perhaps having found this attitude to be the most profitable up to now, it shrewdly continued with it, "Are you sure of what you're saying, Mrs. Mitchell?"

It was easier from there on. She began speaking more volubly, in the effort to convince him. "Yes! Yes! I am. Oh, I am. He worked for Parker for years. He was unjustly discharged; we've been through a lot of hardship on Parker's account. He often said he would, and I know he meant it. Oh, I can't remember every little thing now any more—I found a trolley-car ticket in his pocket that he used that night—"

"Have you kept this?"

"No, I didn't. I did away with it."

The voice said, almost skeptically, "You haven't anything more conclusive than that, then?"

"No. But I *know* he did it. I know what I'm saying. Oh, don't let them kill that man! You've got to stop them." She had to beat down his disbelief, his obtuseness; why didn't his voice change, why didn't he get excited, interested? Didn't they *care?* "Don't you believe me? I *know!"* she kept repeating.

"Yes, but how? Why?"

"Because he did it once before."

"How do you know that?"

"Because he told me!" She was almost beside herself. "He told me the night we became engaged. They never found out, but he *told* me about it. That's why I know he did it this time too."

"And how long ago was this, this first time?"

Oh, why was he so thick, so stupid? What difference did *time* make? "Ten years before we were married. In St. Louis."

"And you've been married?"

"Three years."

"Thirteen years ago, in St. Louis," the voice said with judicial impartiality. She could somehow sense that a pencil point was moving over paper; some slightly absent inflection of the voice gave her that. "But you have no way of knowing whether that's true, either; simply that he told you that. Is that right?"

"But he wouldn't have *told* me, if it weren't. Why would he have *told* me that? The man's name was Joe Bailey; I've never forgotten the name."

"Joe Bailey," the voice repeated mechanically.

"Don't you see?" she pleaded tearfully. "All I'm trying to get you to do is have them stop that thing tonight! It mustn't be carried out. Even if it's only a postponement—Oh, please; I don't know the man, I've never even seen him. But I can't sleep thinking about it—"

But to the end his voice never changed, woke up; she couldn't seem to impress it on him that she was telling him the truth. "I understand, Mrs. Mitchell, I don't know whether there's anything I can do, but I'll see. But you haven't given us very much to go by." It pondered briefly. "Perhaps it might be better if you'd come, down here. If you'd care to give us your statement personally—"

Suddenly she was frightened. In a new way. You didn't just step into a booth on your homeward way, put through a call, and secure the reprieve of a condemned man. There was more to it than that. You became involved, tangled up; your own life interfered with. Worst of all, *he'd* find out about it. It was like a dash of cold water full in the face. The clear white flame of altruism was quenched, went out with a hiss of sudden personal fear. The old blurredness came back, of before her visit to the Considine flat.

"Oh, no, I can't!" she gasped. "I can't make it. I—I have to go home and fix supper—he's waiting for me—I'm late—"

She hung up. She came out of the booth, staggering a little. Almost at once a telephone started ringing behind her, where she'd just come from. It frightened her all the more, and she started to run. She ran all the way. She ran until her hat fell off, and she left it there behind her. She ran, and a sobbing voice kept saying over and over somewhere inside her, "I didn't mean it! I didn't mean it!" She ran until the night around her had fogged with her own exhausted exertion, and she couldn't see which way she was going any more.

Then suddenly he had stopped her, on the sidewalk out in front of their home. She ran straight into his arms, without seeing him.

He said, "Frances!" and his arms were around her and the whole thing vanished. The whole thing she'd been fleeing from.

"I didn't mean it, Ken!" she panted distraught. "Ken, I didn't mean it!"

"Why, because you're late? What's so terrible, what's the difference? Don't take it like that. As long as you're here now." He took her upstairs with him, carrying her, holding her feet off the ground. "I didn't know what happened to you. I was starting to get uneasy. But it's all right now."

And there was the lamplight of home around her, and the whole thing—back there—was just like a bad dream.

"Let me fix your supper. No, I've got to fix your supper. They can't take this away from me." She went into the kitchen, and squatted on her heels before the stove, and thrust the broiler-pan with meat on it into its proper rack.

He followed her and looked at her searchingly. "Something's the matter. You're not well."

"They can't take this away from me," she kept repeating. Then she said, "She's happy now. I gave all this back to her. She'll have this again now, herself."

"Who's happy?" He put his hand across her forehead, as if to test its temperature. "Frances," he pleaded. "Don't frighten me like this. Something's happened to you. You're hysterical. Won't you tell me what it is? You saw a bad picture. You were nearly run down on the street. Won't you tell me?"

She tried to struggle to her feet, and he tried to help her. Suddenly she sagged limply backward into his arms, and he caught her and kept her from falling. "I've given it back to her," she breathed. "Oh, Ken," she whispered, "Ken, I dreamed I did a terrible thing." Her eyes dropped closed, and she lay inert, pressed against him.

He had her on the sofa when she opened them again. She was lying on the sofa, and he was crouched there beside her, holding her hand between his, his face anguished.

"Ken—"

"Shh, lie quiet now. Don't talk. The doctor'll be here soon. I phoned him to come over."

"They can't take this away from me," she breathed. She tried to turn her head a little and look out past the obtruding sofa arm. "Ken, your supper—The table, not set yet—The meat, it's been in too long—Ken, I've never been so late with you before—"

She tried to struggle upright, and he pressed her gently back. "No, never mind now. Just lie still, lie quiet—"

"Ken—"

"He'll be here soon. What is it? What hurts you?"

"The whole world, Ken," she whispered. "The whole world hurts me,"

Suddenly recollection, like a galvanic electric shock, coursed through her. He couldn't hold her prone any more. She jolted upright, fastened her hands to the revers of his coat, shook him imploringly. "Ken, it wasn't a dream—! It happened! Quick, the valise—!"

He tried to restrain her, while she struggled, strove against him.

"Our valise—the big one—where is it? Get it out. No, you've got to listen to me! Bring the valise in here. Hurry, Ken. Get out your things. And mine—"

The sudden pounding was like surf breaking against a rocky shore, and coming back again and back and back.

Her arms whipped inextricably around his neck like a knot. Like the knot of a hangman's noose.

He tried to regain his feet. "It's only the doctor. But why does he make so much noise—?"

"No!" she screamed. "Don't go! Don't go near it!"

"I've got to let him in. I sent for him."

"No," she groaned, in an access of disemboweling terror. "Don't go!" She wouldn't loosen her arms. She held him down there by her, in a headlock, with convulsive strength. "Stay here with me like this. Let me hold you tight like this. Oh, make it *last*, I want it to *last*—"

He had to exert all his strength to pry her grip loose. And then he burst the embrace and left her fallen draggingly, from sofa seat to floor, one arm still extended after him in futile desperation. And he was gone.

She couldn't call out, she couldn't speak. She couldn't even see any more. She could only listen. As to the resonance of a knell.

A door opened. "You're under arrest for the murder of Joseph Bailey, in St. Louis, Missouri, thirteen years ago." And then, "Your own wife."

She tottered to her feet, and staggered after him, arms feeling the way for her blinded eyes. She came up against the front of someone's gray suit—but Ken's was a blue one—and someone held her, propping her like a sort of spindly, life-sized doll without any bones in it.

And then that voice, tomblike, guttural with all the pain and all the dismay and all the heartbreak there have ever been in the whole world, since the first man loved the first woman. And the first woman loved the first man.

"Frances, Frances, what have you done to me?"

Calling out to her, calling, in haunting supplication, as it receded from the room, from her life, from her love, forever.

"Fran-ces, Fran-ces, what have you done to me—?"

Fading away at last into the irretrievable distance.

Somebody kept holding her up, somebody anonymous, somebody in a gray suit.

"But have they saved Considine at least? At least have I done that much?"

"Considine was executed half an hour ago. He made a full confession of guilt fifteen minutes before he went to the Chair."

She was slipping down the front of the gray suit, it seemed to go rushing up past her. Her thoughts exploded into white-hot particles of agony, that slowly cooled and went out one by one.

"I will be silent as the grave, dear heart. Silent as the grave forever. For now indeed I am one."

It was a night like any other night. There was no moon; there were no stars.

Murder at the Automat

We find quality detective work in **"Murder at the Automat"** wrapped up in a masterfully conceived mystery plot with satisfying twists and turns. The cop in this story stops at nothing to bring justice to a man found poisoned to death in an automat, even if it means the person he suspects of murder must die in order for their guilt to be proven. The bygone automat, a fast food-restaurant in which food and drinks were accessible only by vending machine, not only features in the detection elements of the plot, but conjures for the reader the squalid character of Depression-era New York. Aside from its original publication in *Dime Detective* in 1937 and subsequent inclusion in the 1971 *Nightwebs* collection, this story has not been available to readers until now.

NELSON PUSHED THROUGH THE revolving-door at twenty to one in the morning, his squadmate, Sarecky, in the compartment behind him. They stepped clear and looked around. The place looked funny. Almost all the little white tables had helpings of food on them, but no one was at them eating. There was a big black crowd ganged up over in one corner, thick as bees and sending up a buzz. One or two were standing up on chairs, trying to see over the heads of the ones in front, rubbering like a flock of cranes.

The crowd burst apart, and a cop came through. "Now, stand back. Get away from this table, all of you," he was saying. "There's nothing to see. The man's dead—that's all."

He met the two dicks halfway between the crowd and the door. "Over there in the corner," he said unnecessarily. "Indigestion, I guess." He went back with them.

They split the crowd wide open again, this time from the outside. In the middle of it was one of the little white tables, a dead man in a chair, an ambulance doctor, a pair of stretcher-bearers, and the automat manager.

"He gone?" Nelson asked the interne.

"Yep. We got here too late." He came closer so the mob wouldn't overhear. "Better send him down to the morgue and have him looked at. I think he did the Dutch. There's a white streak on his chin, and a half-eaten sandwich under his face spiked with some more of it, whatever it is. That's why I got in touch with you fellows. Good night," he wound up pleasantly and elbowed his way out of the crowd, the two stretcher-bearers tagging after him. The ambulance clanged dolorously outside, swept its fiery headlights around the corner, and whined off.

Nelson said to the cop: "Go over to the door and keep everyone in here, until we get the three others that were sitting at

205

this table with him."

The manager said: "There's a little balcony upstairs. Couldn't he be taken up there, instead of being left down here in full sight like this?"

"Yeah, pretty soon," Nelson agreed, "but not just yet."

He looked down at the table. There were four servings of food on it, one on each side. Two had barely been touched. One had been finished and only the soiled plates remained. One was hidden by the prone figure sprawled across it, one arm out, the other hanging limply down toward the floor.

"Who was sitting here?" said Nelson, pointing to one of the unconsumed portions. "Kindly step forward and identify yourself." No one made a move. "No one," said Nelson, raising his voice, "gets out of here until we have a chance to question the three people that were at this table with him when it happened."

Someone started to back out of the crowd from behind. The woman who had wanted to go home so badly a minute ago, pointed accusingly. "*He* was—that man there! I remember him distinctly. He bumped into me with his tray just before he sat down."

Sarecky went over, took him by the arm, and brought him forward again. "No one's going to hurt you," Nelson said, at sight of his pale face. "Only don't make it any tougher for yourself than you have to."

"I never even saw the guy before," wailed the man, as if he had already been accused of murder, "I just happened to park my stuff at the first vacant chair I—" Misery liking company, he broke off short and pointed in turn. "*He* was at the table, too! Why doncha hold him, if you're gonna hold me?"

"That's just what we're going to do," said Nelson dryly. "Over here, you," he ordered the new witness. "Now, who was eating spaghetti on his right here? As soon as we find that out, the rest of you can go home."

The crowd looked around indignantly in search of the recalcitrant witness that was the cause of detaining them all. But this time no one was definitely able to single him out. A white-uniformed busman finally edged forward and said to Nelson: "I think he musta got out of the place right after it happened. I looked over at this table a minute before it happened, and he was already through eating, picking his teeth and just holding down the chair."

"Well, he's not as smart as he thinks he is," said Nelson. "We'll catch up with him, whether he got out or didn't. The rest of you clear out of here now. And don't give fake names and addresses to the cop at the door, or you'll only be making trouble for yourselves."

The place emptied itself like magic, self-preservation being stronger than curiosity in most people. The two table-mates of the dead man, the manager, the staff, and the two dicks remained inside.

An assistant medical examiner arrived, followed by two men with the usual basket, and made a brief preliminary investigation. While this was going on, Nelson was questioning the two witnesses, the busman, and the manager. He got an illuminating composite picture.

The man was well known to the staff by sight, and was considered an eccentric. He always came in at the same time each night, just before closing time, and always helped himself to the same snack—coffee and a bologna sandwich. It hadn't varied for six months now. The remnants that the busman removed from where the man sat each time, were always the same. The manager was able to corroborate this. He, the dead man, had raised a kick one night about a week ago, because the bologna-sandwich slots had all been emptied before he came in. The manager had had to remind him that it's first come, first served, at an automat, and you can't reserve your food ahead of time. The man at the change-booth, questioned by Nelson, added to the old fellow's reputation for eccentricity. Other, well-dressed people came in and changed a half-dollar, or at the most a dollar bill. He, in his battered hat and derelict's overcoat, never failed to produce a ten and sometimes even a twenty.

"One of these misers, eh?" said Nelson. "They always end up

behind the eight-ball, one way or another."

The old fellow was removed, also the partly consumed sandwich. The assistant examiner let Nelson know: "I think you've got something here, brother. I may be wrong, but that sandwich was loaded with cyanide."

Sarecky, who had gone through the man's clothes, said: "The name was Leo Avram, and here's the address. Incidentally, he had seven hundred dollars, in C's, in his right shoe and three hundred in his left. Want me to go over there and nose around?"

"Suppose I go," Nelson said. "You stay here and clean up."

"My pal," murmured the other dick dryly.

The waxed paper from the sandwich had been left lying under the chair. Nelson picked it up, wrapped it in a paper-napkin, and put it in his pocket. It was only a short walk from the automat to where Avram lived, an outmoded, walk-up building, falling to pieces with neglect.

Nelson went into the hall and there was no such name listed. He thought at first Sarecky had made a mistake, or at least been misled by whatever memorandum it was he had found that purported to give the old fellow's address. He rang the bell marked *Superintendent*, and went down to the basement-entrance to make sure. A stout blond woman in an old sweater and carpet-slippers came out.

"Is there anyone named Avram living in this building?"

"That's my husband—he's the superintendent. He's out right now, I expect him back any minute."

Nelson couldn't understand, himself, why he didn't break it to her then and there. He wanted to get a line, perhaps, on the old man's surroundings while they still remained normal. "Can I come in and wait a minute?" he said.

"Why not?" she said indifferently.

She led him down a barren, unlit basement-way, stacked with empty ashcans, into a room green-yellow with a tiny bud of gaslight. Old as the building upstairs was, it had been wired for electricity, Nelson had noted. For that matter, so was this basement down here. There was a cord hanging from the ceiling ending in an empty socket. It had been looped up out of reach. "The old bird sure was a miser," thought Nelson. "Walking around on one grand and living like this!" He couldn't help feeling a little sorry for the woman.

He noted to his further surprise that a pot of coffee was boiling on a one-burner gas stove over in the corner. He wondered if she knew that he treated himself away from home each night. "Any idea where he went?" he asked, sitting down in a creaking rocker.

"He goes two blocks down to the automat for a bite to eat every night at this time," she said.

"How is it," he asked curiously, "he'll go out and spend money like that, when he could have coffee right here where he lives with you?"

A spark of resentment showed in her face, but a defeated resentment that had long turned to resignation. She shrugged. "For himself, nothing's too good. He goes there because the light's better, he says. But for me and the kids, he begrudges every penny."

"You've got kids, have you?"

"They're mine, not his," she said dully.

Nelson had already caught sight of a half-grown girl and a little boy peeping shyly out at him from another room. "Well," he said, getting up, "I'm sorry to have to tell you this, but your husband had an accident a little while ago at the automat, Mrs. Avram. He's gone."

The weary stolidity on her face changed very slowly. But it did change—to fright. "Cyanide—what's that?" she breathed, when he'd told her.

"Did he have any enemies?"

She said with utter simplicity. "Nobody loved him. Nobody hated him that much, either."

"Do you know of any reason he'd have to take his own life?"

"Him? Never! He held on tight to life, just like he did to his money."

There was some truth in that, the dick had to admit. Misers seldom commit suicide.

The little girl edged into the room fearfully, holding her hands behind her. "Is—is he dead, Mom?"

The woman just nodded, dry-eyed.

"Then, can we use this now?" She was holding a fly-blown electric bulb in her hands.

Nelson felt touched, hard-boiled dick though he was. "Come down to headquarters tomorrow, Mrs. Avram. There's some money there you can claim. G'night." He went outside and clanged the basement-gate shut after him. The windows alongside him suddenly bloomed feebly with electricity, and the silhouette of a woman standing up on a chair was outlined against them.

"It's a funny world," thought the dick with a shake of his head, as he trudged up to sidewalk-level.

It was now two in the morning. The automat was dark when Nelson returned there, so he went down to headquarters. They were questioning the branch-manager and the unseen counterman who prepared the sandwiches and filled the slots from the inside.

Nelson's captain said: "They've already telephoned from the chem lab that the sandwich is loaded with cyanide crystals. On the other hand, they give the remainder of the loaf that was used, the leftover bologna from which the sandwich was prepared, the breadknife, the cutting-board, and the scraps in the garbage-receptacle—all of which we sent over there—a clean bill of health. There was clearly no slip-up or carelessness in the automat pantry. Which means that cyanide got into that sandwich on the consumer's side of the apparatus. He committed suicide or was deliberately murdered by one of the other customers."

"I was just up there," Nelson said. "It wasn't suicide. People don't worry about keeping their light bills down when they're going to take their own lives."

"Good psychology," the captain nodded. "My experience is that miserliness is simply a perverted form of self-preservation, an exaggerated clinging to life. The choice of method wouldn't be in character, either. Cyanide's expensive, and it wouldn't be sold to a man of Avram's type, just for the asking. It's murder, then. I think it's highly important you men bring in whoever the fourth man at that table was tonight. Do it with the least possible loss of time."

A composite description of him, pieced together from the few scraps that could be obtained from the busman and the other two at the table, was available. He was a heavy-set, dark-complected man, wearing a light-tan suit. He had been the first of the four at the table, and already through eating, but had lingered on. Mannerisms—had kept looking back over his shoulder, from time to time, and picking his teeth. He had had a small black satchel, or sample-case, parked at his feet under the table. Both survivors were positive on this point. Both had stubbed their toes against it in sitting down, and both had glanced to the floor to see what it was.

Had he reached down toward it at any time, after their arrival, as if to open it or take anything out of it?

To the best of their united recollections—no.

Had Avram, *after* bringing the sandwich to the table, gotten up again and left it unguarded for a moment?

Again, no. In fact the whole thing had been over with in a flash. He had noisily unwrapped it, taken a huge bite, swallowed without chewing, heaved convulsively once or twice, and fallen prone across the tabletop.

"Then it must have happened right outside the slot—I mean the inserting of the stuff—and not at the table, at all," Sarecky told Nelson privately. "Guess he laid it down for a minute while he was drawing his coffee."

"Absolutely not!" Nelson contradicted. "You're forgetting it was all wrapped up in wax-paper. How could anyone have opened, then closed it again, without attracting his attention? And if we're going to suspect the guy with the satchel—and the cap seems to want us to—he was already *at* the table and all through eating when Avram came over. How could he know ahead of time which table the old guy was going to select?"

"Then how did the stuff get on it? Where did it come from?" the other dick asked helplessly.

"It's little things like that we're paid to find out," Nelson reminded him dryly.

"Pretty large order, isn't it?"

"You talk like a layman. You've been on the squad long enough by now to know how damnably unescapable little habits are, how impossible it is to shake them off, once formed. The public at large thinks detective work is something miraculous like pulling rabbits out of a silk-hat. They don't realize that no adult is a free agent—that they're tied hand and foot by tiny, harmless little habits, and held helpless. This man has a habit of taking a snack to eat at midnight in a public place. He has a habit of picking his teeth after he's through, of lingering on at the table, of looking back over his shoulder aimlessly from time to time. Combine that with a stocky build, a dark complexion, and you have him! What more d'ya want—a spotlight trained on him?"

It was Sarecky, himself, in spite of his misgivings, who picked him up forty-eight hours later in another automat, sample-case and all, at nearly the same hour as the first time, and brought him in for questioning! The busman from the former place, and the two customers, called in, identified him unhesitatingly, even if he was now wearing a gray suit.

His name, he said, was Alexander Hill, and he lived at 215 Such-and-such a street.

"What business are you in?" rapped out the captain.

The man's face got livid. His Adam's apple went up and down like an elevator. He could barely articulate the words. "I'm—I'm a salesman for a wholesale drug concern," he gasped terrifiedly.

"Ah!" said two of his three questioners expressively. The sample-case, opened, was found to contain only tooth-powders, aspirins, and headache remedies.

But Nelson, rummaging through it, thought: "Oh, nuts, it's too pat. And he's too scared, too defenseless, to have really done it. Came in here just now without a bit of mental build-up prepared ahead of time. The real culprit would have been all primed, all rehearsed, for just this. Watch him go all to pieces. The innocent ones always do."

The captain's voice rose to a roar. "How is it everyone else stayed in the place that night, but you got out in such a hurry?"

"I—I don't know. It happened so close to me, I guess I—I got nervous."

That wasn't necessarily a sign of guilt, Nelson was thinking. It was his duty to take part in the questioning, so he shot out at him: "You got nervous, eh? What reason d'you have for getting nervous? How'd *you* know it wasn't just a heart attack or malnutrition—unless you were the cause of it?"

He stumbled badly over that one. "No! No! I don't handle that stuff! I don't carry anything like that—"

"So you know what it was? How'd you know? We didn't tell you," Sarecky jumped on him.

"I—I read it in the papers next morning," he wailed.

Well, it had been in all of them, Nelson had to admit.

"You didn't reach out in front of you—toward him—for anything that night? You kept your hands to yourself?" Then, before he could get a word out, "*What about sugar?*"

The suspect went from bad to worse. "I don't use any!" he whimpered.

Sarecky had been just waiting for that. "Don't lie to us!" he yelled, and swung at him. "I watched you for ten full minutes tonight before I went over and tapped your shoulder. You emptied half the container into your cup!" His fist hit him a glancing blow on the side of the jaw, knocked him and the chair he was sitting on both off-balance. Fright was making the guy sew himself up twice as badly as before.

"Aw, we're just barking up the wrong tree," Nelson kept saying to himself. "It's just one of those fluke coincidences. A drug salesman happens to be sitting at the same table where a guy drops from cyanide poisoning!" Still, he knew that more than one guy had been strapped into the chair just on the strength of such a coincidence and nothing more. You couldn't expect a jury not to pounce on it for all it was worth.

The captain took Nelson out of it at this point, somewhat to his relief, took him aside and murmured: "Go over there and give his place a good cleaning while we're holding him here. If you can turn up any of that stuff hidden around there, that's all we need. He'll break down like a stack of cards." He glanced over at the cowering figure in the chair. "We'll have him before morning," he promised.

"That's what I'm afraid of," thought Nelson, easing out. "And then what'll we have? Exactly nothing." He wasn't the kind of a dick that would have rather had a wrong guy than no guy at all, like some of them. He wanted the right guy—or none at all. The last he saw of the captain, he was stripping off his coat for action, more as a moral threat than a physical one, and the unfortunate victim of circumstances was wailing, "I didn't do it, I didn't do it," like a record with a flaw in it.

Hill was a bachelor and lived in a small, one-room flat on the upper West Side. Nelson let himself in with the man's own key, put on the lights, and went to work. In half an hour, he had investigated the place upside-down. There was not a grain of cyanide to be found, nor anything beyond what had already been revealed in the sample-case. This did not mean, of course, that he couldn't have obtained some either through the firm he worked for, or some of the retail druggists whom he canvassed. Nelson found a list of the latter and took it with him to check over the following day.

Instead of returning directly to headquarters, he detoured on an impulse past the Avram house, and, seeing a light shining in the basement windows, went over and rang the bell.

The little girl came out, her brother behind her. "Mom's not in," she announced.

"She's out with Uncle Nick," the boy supplied.

His sister whirled on him. "She told us not to tell anybody that, didn't she!"

Nelson could hear the instructions as clearly as if he'd been in the room at the time, "If that same man comes around again, don't you tell him I've gone out with Uncle Nick, now!"

Children are after all very transparent. They told him most of what he wanted to know without realizing they were doing it. "He's not really your uncle, is he?"

A gasp of surprise. "How'd you know that?"

"Your ma gonna marry him?"

They both nodded approvingly. "He's gonna be our new Pop."

"What was the name of your real Pop—the one before the last?"

"Edwards," they chorused proudly.

"What happened to him?"

"He died."

"In Dee-troit," added the little boy.

He only asked them one more question. "Can you tell me his full name?"

"Albert J. Edwards," they recited.

He gave them a friendly push. "All right, kids, go back to bed."

He went back to headquarters, sent a wire to the Bureau of Vital Statistics in Detroit, on his own hook. They were still questioning Hill down to the bone, meanwhile, but he hadn't caved in yet. "Nothing," Nelson reported. "Only this accountsheet of where he places his orders."

"I'm going to try framing him with a handful of bicarb of soda, or something—pretend we got the goods on him. I'll see if that'll open him up," the captain promised wrathfully. "He's not the push-over I expected. You start in at seven this morning and work your way through this list of retail druggists. Find out if he ever tried to contract them for any of that stuff."

Meanwhile, he had Hill smuggled out the back way to an outlying precinct, to evade the statute governing the length of time a prisoner can be held before arraignment. They didn't have enough of a case against him yet to arraign him, but they weren't going to let him go.

Nelson was even more surprised than the prisoner at what he caught himself doing. As they stood Hill up next to him in the corridor, for a minute, waiting for the Black Maria, he breathed over his shoulder, "Hang on tight, or you're sunk!"

The man acted too far gone even to understand what he was driving at.

Nelson was present the next morning when Mrs. Avram showed up to claim the money, and watched her expression curiously. She had the same air of weary resignation as the night he had broken the news to her. She accepted the money from the captain, signed for it, turned apathetically away, holding it in her hand. The captain, by prearrangement, had pulled another of his little tricks—purposely withheld one of the hundred-dollar bills to see what her reaction would be.

Halfway to the door, she turned in alarm, came hurrying back. "Gentlemen, there must be a mistake! There's—there's a hundred-dollar bill here on top!" She shuffled through the roll hastily. "They're all hundred-dollar bills!" she cried out aghast. "I knew he had a little money in his shoes—he slept with them under his pillow at nights—but I thought maybe, fifty, seventy dollars—"

"There was a thousand in his shoes," said the captain, "and another thousand stitched all along the seams of his overcoat."

She let the money go, caught the edge of the desk he was sitting behind with both hands, and slumped draggingly down it to the floor in a dead faint. They had to hustle in with a pitcher of water to revive her.

Nelson impatiently wondered what the heck was the matter with him, what more he needed to be convinced she hadn't known what she was coming into? And yet, he said to himself, how are you going to tell a real faint from a fake one? They close their eyes and they flop, and which is it?

He slept three hours, and then he went down and checked at the wholesale-drug concern Hill worked for. The firm did not handle cyanide or any other poisonous substance, and the man had a very good record there. He spent the morning working his way down the list of retail druggists who had placed their orders through Hill, and again got nowhere. At noon he quit, and went back to the automat where it had happened—not to eat but to talk to the manager. He was really working on two cases simultaneously—an official one for his captain and a private one of his own. The captain would have had a fit if he'd known it.

"Will you lemme have that busman of yours, the one we had down at headquarters the other night? I want to take him out of here with me for about half an hour."

"You're the Police Department," the manager smiled acquiescently.

Nelson took him with him in his streetclothes. "You did a pretty good job of identifying Hill, the fourth man at that table," he told him. "Naturally, I don't expect you to remember every face that was in there that night. Especially with the quick turnover there is in an automat. However, here's what you do. Go down this street here to Number One-twenty-one—you can see it from here. Ring the superintendent's bell. You're looking for an apartment, see? But while you're at it, you take a good look at the woman you'll see, and then come back and tell me if you remember seeing her face in the automat that night or any other night. Don't stare now—just size her up."

It took him a little longer than Nelson had counted on. When he finally rejoined the dick around the corner, where the latter was waiting, he said: "Nope, I've never seen her in our place, that night or any other, to my knowledge. But don't forget—I'm not on the floor every minute of the time. She could have been in and out often without my spotting her."

"But not," thought Nelson, "without Avram seeing her, if she went anywhere near him at all." She hadn't been there, then. That was practically certain. "What took you so long?" he asked him.

"Funny thing. There was a guy there in the place with her that used to work for us. He remembered me right away."

"Oh, yeah?" The dick drew up short. "Was *he* in there that night?"

"Naw, he quit six months ago. I haven't seen him since."

"What was he, sandwich-maker?"

"No, busman like me. He cleaned up the tables."

Just another coincidence, then. But, Nelson reminded himself, if one coincidence was strong enough to put Hill in jeopardy, why should the other be passed over as harmless? Both cases—his and the captain's—now had their coincidences. It remained to be seen which was just that—a coincidence and nothing more—and which was the McCoy.

He went back to headquarters. No wire had yet come from Detroit in answer to his, but he hadn't expected any this soon — it took time. The captain, bulldog-like, wouldn't let Hill go. They had spirited him away to still a third place, were holding him on some technicality or other that had nothing to do with the Avram case. The bicarbonate of soda trick hadn't worked, the captain told Nelson ruefully.

"Why?" the dick wanted to know. "Because he caught on just by looking at it that it wasn't cyanide—is that it? I think that's an important point, right there."

"No, he thought it was the stuff all right. But he hollered blue murder it hadn't come out of his room."

"Then if he doesn't know the difference between cyanide and bicarb of soda at sight, doesn't that prove he didn't put any on that sandwich?"

The captain gave him a look. "Are you for us or against us?" he wanted to know acidly. "You go ahead checking that list of retail druggists until you find out where he got it. And if we can't dig up any other motive, unhealthy scientific curiosity will satisfy me. He wanted to study the effects at first hand, and picked the first stranger who came along."

"Sure, in an automat—the most conspicuous, crowded public eating-place there is. The one place where human handling of the food is reduced to a minimum."

He deliberately disobeyed orders, a thing he had never done before—or rather, postponed carrying them out. He went back and commenced a one-man watch over the basement-entrance of the Avram house.

In about an hour, a squat, foreign-looking man came up the steps and walked down the street. This was undoubtedly "Uncle Nick," Mrs. Avram's husband-to-be, and former employee of the automat. Nelson tailed him effortlessly on the opposite side, boarded the same bus he did but a block below, and got off at the same stop. "Uncle Nick" went into a bank, and Nelson into a cigar-store across the way that had transparent telephone-booths commanding the street through the glass front.

When he came out again, Nelson didn't bother following him any more. Instead, he went into the bank himself. "What'd that guy do—open an account just now? Lemme see the deposit-slip."

He had deposited a thousand dollars cash under the name of Nicholas Krassin, half of the sum Mrs. Avram had claimed at headquarters only the day before. Nelson didn't have to be told that this by no means indicated Krassin and she had had anything to do with the old man's death. The money was rightfully hers as his widow, and, if she wanted to divide it with her groom-to-be, that was no criminal offense. Still, wasn't there a stronger motive here than the "unhealthy scientific curiosity" the captain had pinned on Hill? The fact remained that she wouldn't have had possession of the money had Avram still been alive. It would have still been in his shoes and coat-seams where she couldn't get at it.

Nelson checked Krassin at the address he had given at the bank, and, somewhat to his surprise, found it to be on the level, not fictitious. Either the two of them weren't very bright, or they were innocent. He went back to headquarters at six, and the answer to his telegram to Detroit had finally come. "Exhumation order obtained as per request stop Albert J. Edwards deceased January 1936 stop death certificate gives cause fall from steel girder while at work building under construction stop—autopsy—"

Nelson read it to the end, folded it, put it in his pocket without changing his expression.

"Well, did you find out anything?" the captain wanted to know.

"No, but I'm on the way to," Nelson assured him, but he may have been thinking of that other case of his own, and not the one they were all steamed up over. He went out again without saying where.

He got to Mrs. Avram's at quarter to seven, and rang the bell. The little girl came out to the basement-entrance. At sight of him, she called out shrilly, but without humorous intent, "Ma, that man's here again."

Nelson smiled a little and walked back to the living-quarters. A sudden hush had fallen thick enough to cut with a knife. Krassin was there again, in his shirt-sleeves, having supper with Mrs. Avram and the two kids. They not only had electricity now but a midget radio as well, he noticed. You can't arrest people for buying a midget radio. It was silent as a tomb, but he let the back of his hand brush it, surreptitiously, and the front of the dial was still warm from recent use.

"I'm not butting in, am I?" he greeted them cheerfully.

"N-no, sit down," said Mrs. Avram nervously. "This is Mr. Krassin, a friend of the family. I don't know your name—"

"Nelson."

Krassin just looked at him watchfully.

The dick said: "Sorry to trouble you. I just wanted to ask you a couple questions about your husband. About what time was it he had the accident?"

"You know that better than I," she objected. "You were the one came here and told me."

"I don't mean Avram, I mean Edwards, in Detroit—the riveter that fell off the girder."

Her face went a little gray, as if the memory were painful. Krassin's face didn't change color, but only showed considerable surprise.

"About what time of day?" he repeated.

"Noon," she said almost inaudibly.

"Lunch-time," said the dick softly, as if to himself. "Most workmen carry their lunch from home in a pail—" He looked at her thoughtfully. Then he changed the subject, wrinkled up his nose appreciatively. "That coffee smells good," he remarked.

She gave him a peculiar, strained smile. "Have a cup, Mr. Detective," she offered. He saw her eyes meet Krassin's briefly.

"Thanks, don't mind if I do," drawled Nelson.

She got up. Then, on her way to the stove, she suddenly flared out at the two kids for no apparent reason: "What are you hanging around here for? Go in to bed. Get out of here now, I say!" She banged the door shut on them, stood before it with her back to the room for a minute. Nelson's sharp ears caught the faint but unmistakable click of a key.

She turned back again, purred to Krassin: "Nick, go outside and take a look at the furnace, will you, while I'm pouring Mr. Nelson's coffee? If the heat dies down, they'll all start complaining from upstairs right away. Give it a good shaking up."

The hairs at the back of Nelson's neck stood up a little as he watched the man get up and sidle out. But he'd asked for the cup of coffee, himself.

He couldn't see her pouring it—her back was turned toward him again as she stood over the stove. But he could hear the splash of the hot liquid, see her elbow-motions, hear the clink of the pot as she replaced it. She stayed that way a moment longer, after it had been poured, with her back to him—less than a moment, barely thirty seconds. One elbow moved slightly. Nelson's eyes were narrow slits. It was thirty seconds too long, one elbow-motion too many.

She turned, came back, set the cup down before him. "I'll let you put your own sugar in, yes?" she said almost playfully. "Some like a lot, some like a little." There was a disappearing

ring of froth in the middle of the black steaming liquid.

Outside somewhere, he could hear Krassin raking up the furnace.

"Drink it while it's hot," she urged.

He lifted it slowly to his lips. As the cup went up, her eyelids went down. Not all the way, not enough to completely shut out sight, though.

He blew the steam away. "Too hot—burn my mouth. Gotta give it a minute to cool," he said. "How about you—ain't you having any? I couldn't drink alone. Ain't polite."

"I had mine," she breathed heavily, opening her eyes again. "I don't think there's any left."

"Then I'll give you half of this."

Her hospitable alarm was almost overdone. She all but jumped back in protest. "No, no! Wait, I'll look. Yes, there's more, there's plenty!"

He could have had an accident with it while her back was turned a second time, upset it over the floor. Instead, he took a kitchen-match out of his pocket, broke the head off short with his thumbnail. He threw the head, not the stick, over on top of the warm stove in front of which she was standing. It fell to one side of her, without making any noise, and she didn't notice it. If he'd thrown stick and all, it would have clicked as it dropped and attracted her attention.

She came back and sat down opposite him. Krassin's footsteps could be heard shuffling back toward them along the cement corridor outside.

"Go ahead. Don't be bashful—drink up," she encouraged. There was something ghastly about her smile, like a death's-head grinning across the table from him.

The match-head on the stove, heated to the point of combustion, suddenly flared up with a little spitting sound and a momentary gleam. She jumped a little, and her head turned nervously to see what it was. When she looked back again, he already had his cup to his lips. She raised hers, too, watching him over the rim of it. Krassin's footfalls had stopped somewhere just outside the room door, and there wasn't another sound from him, as if he were standing there, waiting.

At the table, the cat-and-mouse play went on a moment longer. Nelson started swallowing with a dry constriction of the throat. The woman's eyes, watching him above her cup, were greedy half-moons of delight. Suddenly, her head and shoulders went down across the table with a bang, like her husband's had at the automat that other night, and the crash of the crushed cup sounded from underneath her.

Nelson jumped up watchfully, throwing his chair over. The door shot open, and Krassin came in, with an ax in one hand and an empty burlap-bag in the other.

"I'm not quite ready for cremation yet," the dick gritted, and threw himself at him.

Krassin dropped the superfluous burlap-bag, the ax flashed up overhead. Nelson dipped his knees, down in under it before it could fall. He caught the shaft with one hand, midway between the blade and Krassin's grip, and held the weapon teetering in mid-air. With his other fist he started imitating a hydraulic drill against his assailant's teeth. Then he lowered his barrage suddenly to solar-plexus level, sent in two bodyblows that caved his opponent in—and that about finished it.

Out in the wilds of Corona, an hour later, in a sub-basement locker-room, Alexander Hill—or at least what was left of him—was saying: "And you'll lemme sleep if I do? And you'll get it over real quick, send me up and put me out of my misery?"

"Yeah, yeah!" said the haggard captain, flicking ink out of a fountain pen and jabbing it at him. "Why dincha do this days ago, make it easier for us all?"

"Never saw such a guy," complained Sarecky, rinsing his mouth with water over in a corner.

"What's that man signing?" exploded Nelson's voice from the stairs.

"Whaddye think he's signing?" snarled the captain. "And where you been all night, incidentally?"

"Getting poisoned by the same party that croaked Avram!" He came the rest of the way down, and Krassin walked down alongside at the end of a short steel link.

"Who's this guy?" they both wanted to know.

Nelson looked at the first prisoner, in the chair. "Take him out of here a few minutes, can't you?" he requested. "He don't have to know all our business."

"Just like in the story-books," muttered Sarecky jealously. "One-Man Nelson walks in at the last minute and cops all the glory."

A cop led Hill upstairs. Another cop brought down a small brown-paper parcel at Nelson's request. Opened, it revealed a small tin that had once contained cocoa. Nelson turned it upside down and a few threads of whitish substance spilled lethargically out, filling the close air of the room with a faint odor of bitter almonds.

"There's your cyanide," he said. "It came off the shelf above Mrs. Avram's kitchen-stove. Her kids, who are being taken care of at headquarters until I can get back there, will tell you it's roach-powder and they were warned never to go near it. She probably got it in Detroit, way back last year."

"She did it?" said the captain. "How could she? It was on the automat-sandwich, not anything he ate at home. *She* wasn't at the automat that night, she was home, you told us that your-self."

"Yeah, she was home, but she poisoned him at the automat just the same. Look, it goes like this." He unlocked his manacle, refastened his prisoner temporarily to a plumbing-pipe in the corner. He took a paper-napkin out of his pocket, and, from within that, the carefully preserved waxpaper wrapper the death-sandwich had been done in.

Nelson said: "This has been folded over twice, once on one side, once on the other. You can see that, yourself. Every crease in it is double-barreled. Meaning what? The sandwich was taken out, doctored, and rewrapped. Only, in her hurry, Mrs. Avram slipped up and put the paper back the other way around.

"As I told Sarecky already, there's death in little habits.

Avram was a miser. Bologna is the cheapest sandwich that automat sells. For six months straight, he never bought any other kind. This guy here used to work there. He knew at what time the slots were refilled for the last time. He knew that that was just when Avram always showed up. And, incidentally, the old man was no fool. He didn't go there because the light was better—he went there to keep from getting poisoned at home. Ate all his meals out.

"All right, so what did they do? They got him, anyway—like this. Krassin, here, went in, bought a bologna sandwich, and took it home to her. She spiked it, rewrapped it, and, at eleven-thirty, he took it back there in his pocket. The sandwich-slots had just been refilled for the last time. They wouldn't put any more in till next morning. There are three bologna-slots. He emptied all three, to make sure the victim wouldn't get any but the lethal sandwich. After they're taken out, the glass slides remain ajar. You can lift them and reach in without inserting a coin. He put his death-sandwich in, stayed by it so no one else would get it. The old man came in. Maybe he's near sighted and didn't recognize Krassin. Maybe he didn't know him at all—I haven't cleared that point up yet. Krassin eased out of the place. The old man is a miser. He sees he can get a sandwich for nothing, thinks something went wrong with the mechanism, maybe. He grabs it up twice as quick as anyone else would have. There you are.

"What was in his shoes is this guy's motive. As for her, that was only partly her motive. She was a congenital killer, anyway, outside of that. He would have married her, and it would have happened to him in his turn some day. She got rid of her first husband, Edwards, in Detroit that way. She got a wonderful break. He ate the poisoned lunch she'd given him way up on the crossbeams of a building under construction, and it looked like he'd lost his balance and toppled to his death. They exhumed the body and performed an autopsy at my request. This telegram says they found traces of cyanide poisoning even after all this time.

"I paid out rope to her tonight, let her know I was onto her. I told her her coffee smelled good. Then I switched cups on her.

She's up there now, dead. I can't say that I wanted it that way, but it was me or her. You never would have gotten her to the chair, anyway. She was unbalanced of course, but not the kind that's easily recognizable. She'd have spent a year in an institution, been released, and gone out and done it all over again. It grows on 'em, gives 'em a feeling of power over their fellow human beings.

"This louse, however, is *not* insane. He did it for exactly one thousand dollars and no cents—and he knew what he was doing from first to last. So I think he's entitled to a chicken-and-ice-cream-dinner in the death-house, at the state's expense."

"The Sphinx," growled Sarecky under his breath, shrugging into his coat. "Sees all, knows all, keeps all to himself."

"Who stinks?" corrected the captain, misunderstanding. "If anyone does, it's you and me. He brought home the bacon!"

CRAZY HOUSE

"Crazy House" is just that—crazy, breathlessly paced, with a side of murder. When a civil engineer is framed for a woman's murder at an old house, he must prove his innocence by returning to the scene of the crime to find the real killer. But there's a catch. The house has been completely rearranged since he fled earlier that night, and he must navigate its dark, unfamiliar halls, using only his wits to outmaneuver the culprit. In "Dusk to Dawn," our falsely accused protagonist turned murderer in his desperation, but here, the main character takes a different tack. He uses his wits to outsmart the culprit. This story first appeared in *Dime Detective* in 1941, and then in the 1985 collection *Blind Date with Death,* but has not been seen since. Woolrich uses "Chinaman" and "Chinaboy" to describe the "Chinese houseboy" character, whose few lines of dialogue are written to imply a heavy accent. While these terms are no longer used in modern publishing, the story is preserved in its original form.

HE CAB INCHED ALONG through the fog in low, telegraphing blasts of its horn every thirty seconds. The tall, sun-bronzed young fellow on its rear seat peered curiously out as though he'd never seen a fog before. He never had. He'd just landed from the boat that afternoon, and if he hadn't happened to have Diana Miller's telephone number among his effects, given him by a mutual friend in the Far East with the suggestion that he look her up, he wouldn't have known a soul in town, would have been stuck in his hotel-room all evening with nothing to do.

He wasn't surprised at the wariness in her voice at first. She didn't know him from Adam and a girl as wealthy and beautiful as she probably had to be on her guard against annoyers. But then when he'd introduced himself and explained the situation, her interest had immediately quickened. "Come out by all means, Mr.—what did you say it was again?"

"Ingham," he repeated. "Bill Ingham."

She'd given him directions for reaching it, and here he was on his way, fog or no fog.

"How much farther?" he asked the driver.

"I'm just relying on memory now myself, boss," was the answer. "It *was* straight ahead somewhere, before the whole town went up in smoke." Finally, after another block or two, he veered over to the roadside and braked. "Here's where I'll have to sign off, boss. Number twenty-three is up on the top of this hill, but I got no chains. I ain't taking a chance on climbing it in this slops."

"Big help you are!" Ingham said scornfully, climbing out.

"This is a taxicab, mister, not a stratosphere." The cab-shape turned, glided off eerily into the fuming grayness.

Ingham groped his way up the incline on foot. The fog seemed even denser up here than down in the lower part of town. He could hardly see his hand before his face. There wasn't a soul to be met with on the streets around him, the white pall had clamped its deadening grip on the entire city. He supposed he should have put off his call until a later night, but once he got indoors with her it would probably be cheerful enough.

All the homes along here were imposing mansions surrounded by their own grounds and set back at a considerable distance from the roadway. That made it worse, if anything, on a night like this. He stopped short finally at one of the blurred entrance-gates and rang the bell, to find out if he was on the right track. There was a wait, then a gleam of light came toward him along the walk inside, and Ingham could make out the face of a Chinese houseboy peering through the iron bars of the gate at him.

"Yes, please, mista?"

"I'm looking for twenty-three," Ingham said.

"This nineteen. Four more house up hill. Last house, on top." Then as Ingham took a preliminary step onward, he added: "But more betta you save time, not go. Nobody there."

Ingham closed in toward the gate again. "What do you mean?"

"House all close up, nobody inside. Everybody go 'way long time."

"You must be mistaken, Charlie. I had that house on the wire only a few minutes ago. I was told to come out. Look, is this Hillcrest Road? Is the young lady in twenty-three called Miller?"

His informant nodded vigorously. "This Hillcrest Road. Miss Milla name lady live in house. But she go 'way for winta, nobody there now. Window all close, door all close."

"You're talking through your hat," Ingham grunted. "I was speaking to her on the telephone myself, just now."

The Chinaboy shrugged. "All ri', you go look, you see." He retreated along the walk again.

Ingham continued toward his destination. That guy must have been puffing opium. He'd find out in another minute if he was right or not.

This must be it now. A low brick rampart had sprung up beside him, topped by spear-tipped iron pickets. He tried to peer through them, but couldn't make out a thing in the welter of gloom and white steam. He came to an arched brick gateway. There was an iron lantern suspended over it, but it was out. He found an electric pushbutton, thumbed it. The lantern went on with flashing suddenness, glowering down at him through the mist like a malignant orange moon. A moment later there was a muffled tread along the gravel inside, and a man's voice said: "Mr. Ingham? Good evening, sir." Some kind of a butler evidently, judging by the white kid gloves that fumbled with the gate-lock. One half swung inward with a click and Ingham moved through. It closed with a dull clang behind him.

"Right this way, sir," his mist-obscured escort said. "Miss Miller is expecting you. She was worried you might not be able to find your way out."

Well the Chinaman had been wrong after all, that was one sure thing. He could smell pines somewhere close at hand as he crunched along the graveled path, but without being able to see them through the fog. What looked like a bleary sunrise ahead turned out to be the front-door of the house, left standing hospitably open.

"Watch the step, sir." Ingham crossed the threshold and the butler closed the door after the two of them. Inside, the air was much clearer. The long hallway he found himself in was expensively wainscoted, but there was something gloomy about it.

"May I take your things, sir?" Ingham shook the fog-spray off his hat and coat, handed them over. "This way, sir."

The looks of the place didn't surprise Ingham any. His friend had told him her father was not only incredibly wealthy but slightly eccentric as well. The house had more the air of a museum than of a place meant to be lived in. There was even a suit of armor standing at the foot of the grand staircase. What was the difference. As long as she wasn't too eccentric herself, it would help to kill an evening.

The butler opened both halves of a double door at the back of the hall, and a lot of wavering firelight shone out. "Mr. William

Ingham calling," he announced, bowed him through, and retired, closing the door behind him.

Ingham couldn't see anyone in the room for a minute. Then the figure of a girl stood up from a bearskin rug before the fireplace on which she had been sprawled, hidden by the intervening furniture.

"I'm so glad you made it," she welcomed him. "I would have sent the car down to pick you up, but we're between drivers right now." Her voice was husky, but that might have been due to the damp weather. "Sit down here," she invited, indicating a sofa. She sat down opposite him. There was a brief pause, as there is when two strangers first meet.

"Tell me, how is Jack?" she said mentioning their mutual friend. "It was nice of him to ask you to look me up."

It was difficult for him to see her with any degree of distinctness, since she was sitting with her back toward the fire and it was shining out blurredly from behind her. She caught him scrutinizing her. "Are you disappointed in what Jack had led you to expect?" she said playfully.

"No. Only—he had a snapshot of you that he used to carry around with him, and it's a funny thing but you don't look at all like it. I wouldn't have known you from it."

She gave a strained little laugh. "Maybe it was an old one, taken a long time ago."

It hadn't been. As a matter of fact she'd mailed it out to Jack only shortly before he'd sailed, but he didn't contradict her. She touched a handkerchief to her mouth. "Everyone says I've changed. Father's disappearance, you know. It was a great shock to me. That may have something to do with it."

He hadn't heard about that. "I'm sorry," he said sincerely. She seemed reluctant to linger on the subject, which was understandable.

"But I'm forgetting my manners. You must be chilled after being out in that fog." She rang and the butler looked in.

"Scotch and water," Ingham said. "By the way," he mentioned, when the man had left them again, "I was told down the line that you'd gone away—that I'd find the house boarded up."

"But how stupid!" She pondered a moment, then added: "It's true, I was going immediately after that happened, but then I changed my mind. Maybe that's how the impression got around."

But if boardings had actually been seen on the windows and doors as that Chinaman claimed, he didn't see how it could have been called just an impression. Instead of mentioning that, however, he began to speak of something else, slowly, as if choosing his words with care. "Jack often told me what good times the two of you had together, when he was over here."

"We did have fun," she nodded evasively.

"You used to call him Red, and what was it he called you, again?"

"Is his hair as red as ever?" she interrupted quickly.

"It hasn't changed a bit."

The butler came in with the drinks, left again. An odd silence had fallen between them. Ingham sat staring thoughtfully into the fire, with a crooked smile at the corner of his mouth.

"You haven't touched your drink, Mr. Ingham," she suggested finally.

He came to with a start, reached for it, and somehow managed clumsily to upset it. The whole thing spilled out.

"We'll have to get you another." She sounded oddly annoyed. He thought he even saw her frown. She rang again and the butler came back. "Another drink for Mr. Ingham, Hutch." Ingham thought he saw them exchange a look.

He waited until they were alone once more, then tapped his pockets aimlessly, got to his feet with studious casualness. "Excuse me a minute. I've left my cigars in my overcoat pocket."

"Here are cigarettes—won't they do?" She held a box toward him with obvious eagerness.

He was already at the door. "Those native cigars spoil you for anything else. I won't be a second." He eased the door closed behind him so that it made no sound. The hallway was empty. Across it there was a hinged pantry-door with an oval pane set into the upper half of it. He crossed noiselessly to this, looked in at an angle, keeping his face well back out of sight.

The butler was standing there with his back to him, mixing him a new drink. Ingham saw his hand go into his trouser pocket, take a small folded paper out, empty its contents in.

Ingham shifted away, with a knowing nod to himself, continued on down the hall, treading quietly. He didn't stop to get cigars out of his coat—there weren't any in there anyway. He went on past it toward the front door, softly began to undo the fastenings. He didn't take his hat and coat with him, since he intended coming right back again—with somebody in authority to investigate this.

She must have opened the other door back there on a crack without his knowing it and peered out after him to find out what he was doing. Just as he freed the outer door, he heard her shout across the hall in a strident voice: "Stop him, Hutch, quick! He's hep!"

He turned his head just in time to see the butler come flinging out of the pantry-door, drawing a gun from under the tails of his coat. "Stay where you are, or I'll drill you!" the latter barked.

Ingham flung the door wide, swerved, and punched at the lightswitch to one side of him, plunging the hallway into protective darkness. There was a bang behind him, and something went whistling over his shoulder. He dove head-first out into the feather-bolster of fog outsight, started to try for the gate.

He could hear footsteps come running along the wood flooring behind him and then the gun banged a second time from the open doorway. Something that felt like a darning-needle went into his arm and made him lurch sideways. He recovered himself, went running on, holding his hand pressed tightly to the place.

He heard the woman's voice raised a second time from within the house, in warning to her accomplice. "Not out in the open, Hutch! It'll be heard!" Ingham wisely got off the gravel path, which they expected him to take to the gate, and cut through for the wall by a short-cut, blundering in and out through a copse of dwarf fir-trees. A moment later he heard the crunch of pursuing steps go by offside behind him.

He had tackled the boundary-wall before his adversary could correct his course and come back looking for him. It wasn't an easy thing to get over with his game arm, but he pulled himself up with the good one, straddled the wicked pickets without impaling himself, and dropped down into the clear.

The gate-lantern farther down the line flashed on, then instantly blacked-out again, but no one came through.

Ingham started beating up the other way, calling out hoarsely at intervals into the white wilderness about him: "Police! Hey, there, police!"

He was all the way down at the bottom of the hill again before he finally drummed one up. The hollow pounding of a nightstick against the ground guided him over to the right place.

"What's the trouble?" the cop said.

"Come on back with me," Ingham panted. "I was shot at just now, in a house up at the top of the hill. First they tried to dope me, then they—" He showed him his arm. "There's a girl in there, I don't know what her game is, but she's trying to impersonate the person I thought I was calling on—Diana Miller. She doesn't look like the snapshot I was shown of this Miss Miller, and she thought this guy we both know had red hair, when it happens he's as black as an Indian!"

"Now wait a minute," the cop cut him off. "Number twenty-three, the Miller place, is that the one you're talking about? That house has been closed up for weeks! I ought to know, this is my prowl."

"I was just in it!" Ingham seethed. "My hat and coat are still in it. What about this arm? Maybe I imagined that too!"

The cop reached undecidedly toward his holster. "You were fired at?" he said.

"Two shots."

"Let's go," the cop said sharply.

They groped their way back up the hill side by side. They stopped before the gate. "Those sheet-iron slats hadn't been closed across the upper part the time before," Ingham said uneasily.

"That so?" the cop grunted unfriendlily. He pushed the bell-button, waited. The overhead lantern remained dark. The cop beat a tattoo on the gate with his stick. Nothing happened. He turned and looked at Ingham. "D'ye still claim it was this house?"

"You bet I do!"

The cop shifted a few steps farther over along the wall. "O.K., after you." He gave Ingham a hoist with his shoulder, and the latter jockeyed himself across, dropped down on the inside. The cop landed beside him a moment later. They traced the gravel path back to the house in smoldering silence. The cop took out a torch, shot it at the door. It revealed a protective wooden casing blocking out the latter. The cop just looked at him eloquently. "How about it now?"

"This only proves there's something phoney going on!" Ingham rasped. "This place was open ten minutes ago! You'll still find hot embers in the fireplace, even if they've lammed out themselves!"

"O.K., we're going to do it up brown." The cop took out a clasp-knife, dug it along the seam where the boarding joined the door-frame. It was just superimposed. Finally he managed to widen it enough to hook his hands in, swung the whole thing bodily outward a short distance, like a davit. He forced the inner door-latch with the blade of his knife, squeezed through the double aperture sideways.

"Come on," he said coldly.

Ingham found himself in the same wainscoted hallway he'd been in before. Dark and clammy, as though it hadn't been heated in weeks. The cop lit it up. "Where did you say your hat and coat were, now?" he said drily.

"In here, in this closet." Ingham threw it open and a lot of emptiness—and a single discarded golf-bag—met his eyes. He turned, harassed, to the cop. "My brand-new polo coat!"

"Sure," said the latter unfeelingly. "Let's go in and ask the lady you was having the drink with." He strode down the hall toward the back, threw open the double doors at Ingham's faltering gesture. Dark as a tomb, and just about the temperature of one, too. The cop's torch pointed up the light-switch and he tapped it.

He went across to the dark fireplace, knuckled the stones, then the ashes themselves. "Come here you!" he growled. "You were in here ten minutes ago, you say, and there was a blaze going in this fireplace?"

"There certainly was!"

"Stick your hand down in there!" The cop did it for him, shoving it down flat. The ashes were cold, stiff and caked with age. The cop threw his hand back at him with a fling. "Talk up and talk up fast!"

Ingham backed dazedly to his feet. "What about this arm wound? Where'd I get that then?"

"We're going to find out about that right now." His hand landed heavily on Ingham's shoulder, spun him around. "Come on—outside!"

He started him down the hall again, stiff-arming him along. The next door down was standing slightly ajar. It had been that way when they passed it the first time just now, too. They'd gone a few steps past it, when there was a dull thud, as of something sliding heavily to the floor in there.

"Wait a minute!" the cop said crisply. He backed up and swung around without letting go his prisoner. He found the switch, clicked it on.

Ingham saw the lifeless form first, gave a jolt. A couple of chairs were overturned as though there'd been a fracas. The body had toppled face forward, from the propped-up sitting position in which it had been left. The cop backed Ingham over into a corner. "If you move, you get it," he warned. He crouched down, turned the body over. It was that of an elderly white-mustached man, still attired in traveling clothes as though he'd just come in. In the corner was a pile of hand-luggage. Even a harness-cop could get the picture without any difficulty. Death had followed the owner's unexpected return within a matter of minutes.

"That's old man Miller, the girl's father, I know him by sight," he said. He palmed his forehead. "Still warm. Ten minutes, would be about right. Polo coat, did ye say now?" One of the dead man's hands was clutching a coat-belt in a vise-like grip, though he'd snagged it out of its loops in the course of a struggle. The death-wound he had received peered out on his chest like a red star.

Ingham stood there frozen stiff with incredulous horror. The cop closed in again, gun at the ready. "Wait a minute, you don't think I—" Ingham began.

"You've been insisting all along you was in here ten minutes ago. Now ye wanna change yer tune, is that it?"

"I was in here, but—"

The cop took a twist in his sleeve, led him outside into the open again, down the fog-drenched path. He got the gate open from the inside, jolted the befuddled engineer through.

"If I'd just committed a murder in there, why would I come running out looking for a cop like I did?" Ingham tried to expostulate.

The cop was through listening for the night. This was big time now. He led him partway down the hill, snagged by a sort of half-nelson around one arm. He stopped beneath where a blurred, pearly glow marked a streetlight, cracked open a call-box attached to its base.

"Dillon, Sarge. Send me some help quick, up to Hillcrest Road. I've caught a guy that just committed a murder in Number twenty-three. Better send an ambulance, too. He's wounded in the arm and bleeding a lot. Hurry it up, will you, Sarge? He's dangerous—I think he's a mental case, and I'm holding him single-handed!"

Ingham saw that the time for trying to talk his way out of this was past. The cop was hanging onto him with his left—he needed his right to open the call-box, and he'd had to sheath his gun for a minute while he was doing so. Ingham reached out with his free hand, across the width of his own body.

He never thought he could get it out without its owner feeling the loss of weight in time, but somehow he did. There's no use reasoning with a cop at gun-point ever. There'd be too many others coming up before he got through. He chopped the gun-heft down in a beautiful overhand swipe. The cop slid down the lamppost-base into a huddle, with a tired sigh, and lay there quietly.

Ingham took the cop's shoulder holster, strapped it on, streaked back for the very house they'd just come from. Sure, they'd be back there eventually as thick as bees, but for the first few minutes or so it was the last place they'd look for him. He was going to take another look at that house if it was the last thing he did. And it might very well be the last. Technically he was an armed maniac now, liable to be shot down at sight.

He got in again through the gate and the imperfectly-closed door, the way they'd come out just now. He listened carefully a minute, from there, before he went in any deeper. The place was as still and lifeless as it had fooled the cop into thinking it was. He skipped the room containing the corpse. He knew that wouldn't tell him anything. That had been purely a set up for the cop and the detectives that were to come later.

He went back into the room in which he'd originally sat with her. That ice-cold fireplace, ten minutes after it had held leaping flames, was his chief bafflement. That had him. He poised squatted on his heels there before it. The stones facing it were real stones. The ashes lying in it were real ashes—only they had no right to cool off so quickly.

The strain told on his ankles finally, they buckled, and he slapped a hand out to the stone trim along the top to keep from going over. One of the stones wobbled loosely as though it had been imperfectly imbedded. He pushed at it harder, and it went in bodily a whole half-inch or so behind its mates. Before he knew it the whole fireplace-structure had started to swing slowly around on noiseless, well-oiled hinges, leaving a shoulder-high oblong opening in the wall.

He saw what it was. It was two fireplaces, back to back, on a turntable arrangement. When one swung out, the other swung in. While one had carried the hot embers out, the other had brought in a grate full of cold ashes in its place.

There was dim light on the other side, enough to see by, anyway. He ducked his shoulders and went through. He was in a shallow, fore-shortened room, little more than an alcove. Beyond the opening facing him, which was where the light was coming down, there was a steep, almost ladderlike staircase.

He heard something. There was a faint whimpering sound coming down, almost like a kitten trapped between walls. But it was a human voice, a girl's voice. He edged out closer to the steeply-tilted stair. Another voice sounded, a man's voice, harshly threatening. "Come on, sign this—or you get the hypodermic again!"

"But what have you done with my father?" the whimpering voice went on. "And when are you going to let me out of here?"

"Your father's taken care of. He's waiting for you outside." A double-meaning chuckle sounded. "Just sign this and then you can go out and join him—"

Ingham didn't wait to hear any more. He started up the cramped stairs, gun out, to where the sounds and the light were coming from. There was only one door up there, opening almost flush with the head of the stairs, due to lack of space. As his eyes rose above floor-level, a midget room came into focus. It had no outside opening of any kind, and a strong medicinal odor, like that of the prescription-counter of a drug store, reached his nostrils. There was a cot in it, and a girl was crouched defensively on it. There was a man standing threateningly over her, his back to Ingham. A black bag such as a doctor carries stood open on the seat of a chair. The man was thrusting a fountain-pen and a sheaf of papers bound in a light-blue folder toward her.

She saw him first. She was only vaguely recognizable as the girl on the snapshot his friend had showed him. Thin hollows in her cheeks and the pallor of her face from close confinement, or maybe something worse, gave him a good idea of what she must have been through.

"This says you don't have to sign anything you don't want to," he grated unexpectedly from the entrance.

The man whirled around and his stomach grazed Ingham's outthrust gun. He wasn't the same one that had played the part of the butler before.

The engineer frisked him, found a gun, shoved it in his holster. Then he backed him around to the other side of the cot. The girl, he could see, still couldn't make up her mind whether he was friend or enemy, they had her in such a state of mental terror. "You don't know me, but I'm a friend of Jack's. What's been going on around here?"

"They deliberately moved in on us, she and two accomplices of hers," the girl began to explain in a panting voice. "Father was always so odd in his ways, living shut up in this gloomy place without any servants and discouraging friends from visiting us—that's how they were able to get away with it. You wouldn't think they could, but they did. They've been holding us prisoners in our own house for weeks past! They even boarded it up on the outside and pretended we'd gone away, so too many questions wouldn't be asked. They've mistreated us both terribly. They kept Father downstairs and me up here. I heard them take him out awhile ago and I haven't seen him since—"

He didn't tell her that they'd murdered him. "What were they after?"

"She's my half-sister, and she's always been a bad egg. Father disinherited her years ago, gave her a settlement in cash to stay away from us, and made me his sole beneficiary. Now they want me to sign a will in her favor, leaving everything to her in case—"

"I get it. And I horned in just in time to come in handy to them as a ready-made lethal weapon. Fresh off the boat and without an alibi—" A flock of black spots unexpectedly appeared before his eyes, cleared away again. His knees gave a dip, and he caught the edge of the cot to hold himself up. He felt embarrassed.

"You've been hurt!" she said anxiously. "There's blood on your arm—"

"Yeah. I've been carrying a bullet around in it half the evening now and it's starting to catch up on me."

"*He's* a doctor—make him take it out for you."

"I'll have to. I don't think I can last long enough to get out of here." He passed her the man's gun. "Hold it on him. Where'd the others go?"

"There's a tunnel leading out from here, that comes up farther over in the grounds. They've been using it to come in and out by."

He struggled out of his coat and bared his arms. "Come here you and get busy! Hold that gun on him—see that he doesn't try anything."

The doctor shrugged off his own coat, rolled up his sleeves, dipped into the bag. "This is going to hurt plenty," he said. "You better let me give you a little of this to kill it—" He brought up a plunger with a needle attached to it.

"Skip that," Ingham said. "I'll take it straight. I'm not taking any chances on dope around you."

The pain of the probing was excruciating. He had to grit his teeth and shut his eyes in spite of himself. The doctor managed to thrust himself, several times, between Ingham and the girl, so that she couldn't see what he was doing.

"I've got it," he announced finally, and held it up to show them. Ingham wiped the sweat out of his eyes. The doctor took out a small bottle, sloshed disinfectant on the wound, slapped on a gauze dressing.

"Now come on," the engineer said, "I've got to get you out of here first, and then see if I can square myself with the cops before they hold target-practice all over me—" He interrupted himself to yawn cavernously. He took the gun over from Diana, motioned the quack toward the door with it. "You first—" Then as he tried to take a step after him, his reflexes went back on him, he sat down heavily on the edge of the cot instead. The gun started to loop over in his grasp.

He heard her draw in her breath sharply. He followed the direction of her eyes. The hypodermic needle was lying out beside the bag. The plunger was down flat, not open the way it had been before. "So you slipped me a shot anyhow—" He tried to straighten up from the slumped-over position into which he'd slowly been sinking, as though his backbone was made of rubber. He brought the gun up with an effort. It felt as if it weighed two tons.

The doctor smiled, like a cat waiting to pounce.

"Give it to me, quick!" the girl exclaimed, and made a reach for it. Her momentary deflection of it, in trying to take it from his relaxing grasp, was all that the other needed. He cut in with a swift-footed lunge, swept it up, bore ceiling-ward. For a moment all three of their hands were on it, in a sort of a triple knot. Then Ingham's dropped off inertly of its own weight. His muscles seemed to have turned to water.

The doctor wrenched it out of the girl's grasp, gave her a shove that sent her floundering back against the wall. "Now we'll take up where we left off!" he promised vindictively. "And maybe this time I got a better way of persuading you than by the needle."

He jammed the gun flat against Ingham's temple. The latter promptly fell over backwards on the bed at the slight contact, but the gun followed his head down, continuing to nudge into it. He was hanging onto consciousness by the merest thread now. His eyes felt as though their pupils were contracted to pin-points.

He heard the other's voice lash out viciously at her. "Pick up that pen! Pick up the will! Now sign it where I showed you before, or I'll send your pal's brains out all over the bed!"

"Don't do it!" Ingham tried to warn her. "It's your own death-warrant. They have got to keep you alive while you still haven't signed, and the cops'll be here any minute—" But the words wouldn't come—his thickened tongue only made drowsy, mumbling sounds.

In the silence that followed he could actually hear the slight scratchy sound that a pen-point makes tracing over paper.

"Give it here!" was the next order. Something light-blue was passed across his own supine form, and disappeared into the doctor's inside pocket.

A raspy voice suddenly sounded guardedly from below, at the

foot of the secret stairs. It was that of the other woman, Diana's half-sister. "What's taking you so long up there, Hart? Didn't you get it out of her yet?"

"We had a slight interruption," the man she had called Hart jeered, "but everything's under control again."

The woman appeared in the doorway behind him. She smiled grimly at sight of Ingham. "So the dope came back, did he? That makes it all the better. Now we can leave her right here in the house with the old man, instead of dumping her outside on the grounds like we were going to. You better make it fast, though, or we'll be cut off ourselves in another minute. There's cops and dicks all around the outside of the place, closing in. They must have traced him back here and they are getting ready to rush it. I could hear them when I was waiting for you out at the tunnel-mouth just now."

"It won't take a second now," Hart answered cold-bloodedly. "Give me a hand. Carry her down as soon as I give it to her. I'll carry him. I'm going to put one into him, too. He knows too much now. He'd identify you when you step forward later to put in your claim."

"What's the angle—suicide after he's killed her?"

"Sure, he knows they've got him surrounded, he hasn't a chance of getting out—" He raised the gun, sighted it out across Ingham's prostrate body at someone beyond. "I promised you we'd let you go with your father and I'm keeping my word," he said with macabre humor. "Only, you should have taken the trouble to ask just where your father went first!"

Ingham, eyes already slits of narcotic-induced stupor, could see his hand starting to contract on the weapon, to send the death-shot on its way.

He didn't have a muscular impulse left in him, but he managed in some way to kick one leg up, almost galvanically. The point of the knee caught Hart full in the stomach. He gave a choked cough and folded sharply over, like a suddenly-closed jackknife. The gun went off downward into the cot, and Hart lay there slumped into the cot, and Hart lay there slumped inertly across him, completely knocked out for a minute by the foul.

After that everything seemed to happen at once. There was a sudden pounding of heavy feet on the run, that carried dimly through to where they were. The woman in the doorway turned and fled for the stairs, to make good her own getaway. Halfway down she stopped short and started to retreat slowly up them again. At this point the curtain finally came down on Ingham, and he went under.

When he came to he was in bed someplace. It looked like the convalescent ward in a hospital, and Diana Miller was sitting beside him, looking solicitous. All that spoiled the picture was a cop sitting watchfully on the other side of him, and not looking solicitous. The one whose gun he had snagged the night before.

"I suppose now I get a strait-jacket after all," Ingham grimaced.

"Not," she assured him, "after the way I sat up half the night giving out statements to the police."

"Did they get that devilish half-sister of yours?"

"I had the pleasure of witnessing that personally, and she made a full confession before they got through with her. Hart was the brains of the nasty little trio. He was the one who shot Father right after you left the house the first time. She gave him away to save her own skin."

"What about the third guy—Hutch, or whatever his name was?"

"They got him too. He came back through the tunnel like a fool, to see what was keeping the other two, and walked right into the middle of nearly the whole police department."

Ingham pointedly gave the cop his back. "Then why does *he* have to sit around spoiling my recovery?"

The cop got up. "I can take a hint," he said. "I can take a hint."

When he'd closed the door behind him, Ingham said: "I had a message from Jack he wanted me to deliver to you—he's sort of stuck on you, you know—but in all the excitement and everything, blamed if I haven't forgotten what it was!"

"Mr. Ingham," she let him know sweetly, "I hardly ever

swear, but the hell with Jack! Now think hard and maybe you might come across a message from yourself you'd care to deliver instead."

New York Blues

The collection closes with **"New York Blues,"** a story of pure, despairing noir. A man sits in a dark room, torturing himself over whether or not he murdered the woman he loves, waiting for "Death" to come and take him. Amnesia, paranoia, fear and anxiety plague him to his very core as he turns himself inside out with self-scrutiny. It is an examination of human nature at its darkest and most troubled. This story was published posthumously by *Ellery Queen Mystery Magazine* in 1970, two years after Woolrich's death, and may have been one of the last tales he ever wrote. At the end of his life, Woolrich was alone, suffering from alcoholism, diabetes and failing eyesight, and in a cruel twist of fate, was confined to a wheelchair like his "Rear Window" character thanks to a foot infection that led to an amputation. Is it any wonder he produced such a dark and hopeless tale during this time? After its initial publication, the story only appeared once more in the 2004 collection *Night & Fear,* and is memorialized here as a fitting finale to our murderous montage.

IT'S SIX O'CLOCK; MY drink is at the three-quarter mark—three-quarters down, not three-quarters up—and the night begins.

Across the way from me sits a little transistor radio, up on end, simmering away like a teakettle on a stove. It's been going steadily ever since I first came in here, two days, three nights ago; it chisels away the stony silence, takes the edge off the being alone. It came with the room, not with me.

Now there's a punctuation of three lush chords, and it goes into a traffic report. "Good evening. The New York Municipal Communications Service presents the 6:00 P.M. Traffic Advisory. Traffic through the Holland and Lincoln tunnels and over the George Washington Bridge, heavy westbound, light eastbound. Traffic on the crosscut between the George Washington and Queens-White-stone bridges, heavy in both directions. Traffic through the Battery Tunnel, heavy outbound, very light inbound. Traffic on the West Side Highway, bumper to bumper all the way. Radar units in operation there. Traffic over the Long Island Expressway is beginning to build, due to tonight's game at Shea Stadium. West 70th Street between Amsterdam and West End avenues is closed due to a water-main break. A power failure on the East Side I.R.T. line between Grand Central and 125th Street is causing delays of up to forty-five minutes. Otherwise all subways and buses, the Staten Island Ferry, the Jersey Central, the Delaware and Lackawanna, and the Pennsylvania railroads, and all other commuter services, are operating normally. At the three airports, planes are arriving and departing on time. The next regularly scheduled traffic advisory will be given one-half hour from now—"

The big weekend rush is on. The big city emptying itself out at once. Just a skeleton crew left to keep it going until Monday morning. Everybody getting out—everybody but me, everybody but those who are coming here for me tonight. We're going to have the whole damned town to ourselves.

I go over to the window and open up a crevice between two of the tightly flattened slats in one of the blinds, and a little parallelogram of a New York street scene, Murray Hill section, six o'clock evening hour, springs into view. Up in the sky the upper-echelon light tiers of the Pan Am Building are undulating and rippling in the humidity and carbon monoxide ("Air pollution index: normal, twelve percent; emergency level, fifty percent").

Down below, on the sidewalk, the glowing green blob of a street light, swollen to pumpkin size by foreshortened perspective, thrusts upward toward my window. And along the little slot that the parted slats make, lights keep passing along, like strung-up, shining, red and white beads. All going just one way, right to left, because 37th Street is westbound, and all going by twos, always by twos, headlights and tails, heads and tails, in a welter of slowed-down traffic and a paroxysm of vituperative horns. And directly under me I hear a taxi driver and would-be fares having an argument, the voices clearly audible, the participants unseen.

"But it's only to Fifty-ninth Street—"

"I don't *ca-a-are*, lady. Look, I already tolje. I'm not goin' up that way. Can'tje get it into your head?"

"Don't let's argue with him. Get inside. He can't put you out."

"No, but I can refuse to move. Lady, if your husband gets in here, he's gonna sit still in one place, 'cause I ain't budgin'."

New York. The world's most dramatic city. Like a permanent short circuit, sputtering and sparking up into the night sky all night long. No place like it for living. And probably no place like it for dying.

I take away the little tire jack my fingers have made, and the slats snap together again.

The first sign that the meal I phoned down for is approaching is the minor-key creak from a sharply swerved castor as the room-service waiter rounds a turn outside my door. I'm posted behind a high-backed wing chair, with my wrists crossed over the top of it and my hands dangling like loose claws, staring a little tensely at the door. Then there's the waiter's characteristically deferential knock. But I say "Who is it?" anyway, before I go over to open it.

He's an elderly man. He's been up here twice before, and by now I know the way he sounds.

"Room service," comes through in that high-pitched voice his old age has given him.

I release the double lock, then I turn the knob and open the door.

He wheels the little white-clothed dinner cart forward into the room, and as the hall perspective clears behind him I get a blurred glimpse of a figure in motion, just passing from view, then gone, too quickly to be brought into focus.

I stand there a moment, holding the door to a narrow slit, watching the hall. But it's empty now.

There's an innocuous explanation for everything. Everything is a coin that has two sides to it, and one side is innocuous but the other can be ominous. The hall makes a right-angle turn opposite my door, and to get to the elevators, those whose rooms are back of this turn have to pass the little setback that leads to my door.

On the other hand, if someone wanted to pinpoint me, to verify which room I was in, by sighting my face as I opened the door for the waiter, he would do just that: stand there an instant, then quickly step aside out of my line of vision. The optical snapshot I'd had was not of a figure in continuous motion going past my point of view, but of a figure that had first been static and then had flitted from sight.

And if it's that, now they know which room I'm in. Which room on which floor in which hotel.

"Did you notice anyone out there in the hall just now when you came along?" I ask. I try to sound casual, which only makes me not sound casual.

He answers with a question of his own. "*Was* there somebody out in the hall, sir?"

"That's what I asked you, did you see anyone?"

He explains that years of experience in trundling these foodladen carts across the halls have taught him never to look up, never to take his eyes off them, because an unexpected bump on the floor under the carpet might splash ice water out of the glass and wet the tablecloth or spill consommé into its saucer.

It sounds plausible enough. And whether it is or not, I know it's all I'm going to get.

I sign the check for the meal, add the tip, and tell him to put it on the bill. Then just as he turns to leave I remember something I want to do.

"Just a second; that reminds me." I shoot one of my cuffs forward and twist something out of it. Then the other one. And I hold out my hand to him with the two star-sapphire cuff links he admired so much last night. (Innocently, I'm sure, with no venal intent.)

He says I'm not serious, I must be joking. He says he can't take anything like that. He says all the things he's expected to say, and I override them. Then, when he can't come up with anything else, he comes up with, half-hopefully (hopeful for a yes answer): "You tired of them?"

"No," I say quite simply, "no—they're tired of me."

He thanks me over and thanks me under and thanks me over again, and then he's gone, and I'm glad he's gone.

Poor old man, wasting his life bringing people their meals up to their rooms for thirty-five, forty-odd years. He'll die in peace, though. Not in terror and in throes of resistance. I almost envy him.

I turn my head a little. The radio's caroling "Tonight," velvety smooth and young and filled with plaintive desire. Maria's song from *West Side Story*. I remember one beautiful night long ago at the Winter Garden, with a beautiful someone beside me. I tilt my nose and breathe in, and I can still smell her perfume, the ghost of her perfume from long ago. But where is she now, where did she go, and what did I *do* with her?

Our paths ran along so close together they were almost like one, the one they were eventually going to be. Then fear came along, fear entered into it somehow, and split them wide apart.

Fear bred anxiety to justify. Anxiety to justify bred anger. The phone calls that wouldn't be answered, the door rings that wouldn't be opened. Anger bred sudden calamity.

Now there aren't two paths anymore; there's only one, only mine. Running downhill into the ground, running downhill into its doom.

Tonight, tonight—there will be no morning star—Right, kid, there won't. Not for me, anyway.

There's a tap at the door, made with the tip of a key, not the tip of a finger. The voice doesn't wait, but comes right through before the signal has a chance to freeze me stiff. A woman's voice, soft-spoken, reassuring. "Night maid."

I wait a second to let a little of the white drain from my face before she sees me, and then I go over and let her in.

Her name is Ginny. She told me last night. I asked her, that's why she told me. I wanted to hear the sound of somebody's name, that's why I asked her. I was frightened and lonely, that's why I wanted to hear the sound of somebody's name.

On her face the beauty of two races blends, each contributing its individual hallmark. The golden-warm skin, the deep glowing eyes, the narrow-tipped nose, the economical underlip.

While she's turning back the bedcovers in a neat triangle over one corner, I remark, "I notice you go around the outside of the room to get to the bed, instead of cutting across the middle, which would be much shorter. Why do you?"

She answers plausibly, "People are often watching their television sets at this time, when I come in, and I don't want to block them off."

I point out, "But mine isn't on, Ginny."

I see how the pupils of her eyes try to flee, to get as far away from looking at me as possible, all the way over into their outside corners. And that gives it away. She's afraid of me. The rumors have already reached her. A hotel is like a beehive when it comes to gossip. *He never leaves his room, has all his meals sent up to him, and keeps his door locked all the time.*

"I want to give you something," I say to her. "For that little girl of yours you were telling me about."

I take a hundred-dollar bill out of the wallet on my hip. I fold the bill a few times so that the corner numerals disappear, then thrust it between two of her fingers.

She sees the "1" first as the bill slowly uncoils. Her face is politely appreciative.

She sees the first zero next—that makes it a ten. Her face is delighted, more than grateful.

She sees the last zero. Suddenly her face is fearful, stunned into stone; in her eyes I can see steel filings of mistrust glittering. Her wrist flexes to shove the bill back to me, but I ward it off with my hand upended.

I catch the swift side glance she darts at the fifth of rye on the side table.

"No, it didn't come out of that. It's just an impulse—came out of my heart, I suppose you could say. Either take it or don't take it, but don't spoil it."

"But why? What for?"

"Does there have to be a reason for everything? Sometimes there isn't."

"I'll buy her a new coat," she says huskily. "A new pink coat like little girls all seem to want. With a little baby muff of lamb's wool to go with it. And I'll say a prayer for you when I take her to church with me next Sunday."

It won't work, but— "Make it a good one."

The last part is all she hears.

Something occurs to me. "You won't have to do any explaining to her father, will you?"

"She has no father," she says quite simply. "She's never had. There's only me and her, sir."

Somehow I can tell by the quick chip-chop of her feet away

from my door that it's not lost time she's trying to make up; it's the tears starting in her eyes that she wants to hide.

I slosh a little rye into a glass—a fresh glass, not the one before; they get rancid from your downbreaths that cling like a stale mist around the inner rim. But it's no help; I know that by now, and I've been dousing myself in it for three days. It just doesn't take hold. I think fear neutralizes alcohol, weakens its anesthetic power. It's good for small fears; your boss, your wife, your bills, your dentist; all right then to take a drink. But for big ones it doesn't do any good. Like water on blazing gasoline, it will only quicken and compound it. It takes sand, in the literal and the slang sense, to smother the bonfire that is fear. And if you're out of sand, then you must burn up.

I have it out now, paying it off between my fingers like a rosary of murder. Those same fingers that did it to her. For three days now I've taken it out at intervals, looked at it, then hidden it away again. Each time wondering if it really happened, hoping that it didn't, dreading that it did.

It's a woman's scarf; that much I know about it. And that's about all. But whose? Hers? And how did I come by it? How did it get into the side pocket of my jacket, dangling on the outside, when I came in here early Wednesday morning in some sort of traumatic daze, looking for room walls to hide inside of as if they were a folding screen. (I didn't even know I had it there; the bellboy who was checking me in spotted it on the way up in the elevator, grinned, and said something about a "heavy date.")

It's flimsy stuff, but it has a great tensile strength when pulled against its grain. The strength of the garotte. It's tinted in pastel colors that blend, graduate, into one another, all except one. It goes from a flamingo pink to a peach tone and then to a still paler flesh tint—and then suddenly an angry, jagged splash of blood color comes in, not even like the others. Not smooth, not artificed by some loom or by some dye vat. Like a star, like the scattered petals of a flower. Speaking of—I don't know how to say it—speaking of violence, of struggle, of life spilled out.

The blood isn't red anymore. It's rusty brown now. But it's

still blood, all the same. Ten years from now, twenty, it'll still be blood; faded out, vanished, the pollen of, the dust of, blood. What was once warm and moving. And made blushes and rushed with anger and paled with fear. Like that night—

I can still see her eyes. They still come before me, wide and white and glistening with fright, out of the amnesiac darkness of our sudden, unpremeditated meeting.

They were like two pools of fear. She saw something that I couldn't see. And fear kindled in them. I feared and I mistrusted but I couldn't bear to see my fear reflected in her eyes. From her I wanted reassurance, consolation; only wanted to draw her close to me and hold her to me, to lean my head against her and rest and draw new belief in myself. Instead she met my fear with her fear. Eyes that should have been tender were glowing with unscreaming fear.

It wasn't an attack. We'd been together too many times before, made love together too many times before, for it to be that. It was just that fear had suddenly entered, and made us dangerous strangers.

She turned and tried to run. I caught the scarf from behind. Only in supplication, in pleading; trying to hold on to the only one who could save me. And the closer I tried to draw her to me, the less she was alive. Until finally I got her all the way back to me, where I wanted her to be, and she was dead.

I hadn't wanted that. It was only love, turned inside out. It was only loneliness, outgoing.

And now I'm alone, without any love.

And the radio, almost as if it were taking my pulse count, electro-graphing my heartbeats, echoes them back to me: *For, like caressing an empty glove, Is night without some love, The night was made for—*

The hotel room ashtrays are thick glass cubes, built to withstand cracking under heat of almost any degree. I touch my lighter to it, to the scarf compressed inside the cube. The flame points upward like a sawtoothed orange knife. There goes love. After a while it stops burning. It looks like a black cabbage, each leaf tipped by thin red lines that waver and creep back and forth like tiny red worms. Then one by one they go out.

I dump it into the bathroom bowl and flip the lever down. What a hell of a place for your love to wind up. Like something disemboweled.

I go back and pour out a little more. It's the seatbelt against the imminent smash-up, the antidote for terror, the prescription against panic. Only it doesn't work. I sit there dejectedly, wrists looping down between my legs. I'm confused; I can't think it out. Something inside my mind keeps fogging over, like mist on a windshield. I use the back of my hand for a windshield wiper and draw it slowly across my forehead a couple times, and it clears up again for a little while.

"Remember," the little radio prattles. "Simple headache, take aspirin. Nervous tension, take—"

All I can say to myself is: there *is* no fix for the fix you're in now.

Suddenly the phone peals, sharp and shattering as the smashing of glass sealing up a vacuum. I never knew a sound could be so frightening, never knew a sound could be so dire. It's like a short circuit in my nervous system. Like springing a cork in my heart with a lopsided opener. Like a shot of sodium pentathol up my arm knocking out my will power.

All I keep thinking is: this is it. Here it is. It's not a hotel-service call, it can't be, not at this hour anymore. The waiter's been and gone, the night maid's been and gone. It can't be an outside call, because nobody on the outside knows I'm here in the hotel. Not even where I work, where I used to work, they don't know. This is it; it's got to be.

How will they put it? A polite summons. "Would you mind coming down for a minute, sir?" And then if I do, a sudden preventive twisting of my arm behind my back as I step out of the elevator, an unnoticeable flurry tactfully covered up behind the backs of the bellboys—then quickly out and away.

Why don't they come right up here to my door and get me? Is it because this is a high-class hotel on a high-class street? Maybe they don't want any commotion in the hall, for the sake of the other guests. Maybe this is the way they always do it.

Meanwhile it keeps ringing and ringing and ringing.

The damp zigzag path my spilled drink made, from where I was to where I am now, is slowly soaking into the carpet and darkening it. The empty glass, dropped on the carpet, has finished rocking on its side by now and lies still. And I've fallen motionless into the grotesque posture of a badly frightened kid. Almost prone along the floor, legs sprawled out in back of me in scissors formation, just the backs of my two hands grasping the edge of the low stand the phone sits on, and the rim of it cutting across the bridge of my nose so that just two big staring, straining eyes show up over the top.

And it rings on and on and on.

Then all at once an alternative occurs to me. Maybe it's a wrong-number call, meant for somebody else. Somebody in another room, or somebody in this room who was in it before I came. Hotel switchboards are overworked places: slip-ups like that can happen now and then.

I bet I haven't said a prayer since I finished my grammar-school final-exam paper in trigonometry (and flunked it; maybe that's why I haven't said a prayer since), and that was more a crossed-fingers thing held behind my back than a genuine prayer. I say one now. What a funny thing to pray for. I bet nobody ever prayed for a wrong number before, not since telephones first began. Or since prayers first began, either.

Please, make it a mistake and not for me. Make it a mistake.

Suddenly there's open space between the cradle and the receiver, and I've done it. I've picked it up. It's just as easy as pulling out one of your own teeth by the roots.

The prayer gets scratched. The call is for me, it's not a wrong number. For me, all right, every inch of the way. I can tell from the opening words. Only—it's not the one I feared; it's friendly, a friendly call no different from what other people get.

A voice from another world, almost. Yet I know it so well. Always like this, never a cloud on it; always jovial, always noisy.

When a thing should be said softly, it says it loudly; when a thing should be said loudly, it says it louder still. He never identifies himself, never has to. Once you've heard his voice, you'll always know him.

That's Johnny for you—the pal of a hundred parties. The bar-kick of scores of binges. The captain of the second-string team in how many foursome one-night stands? Every man has had a Johnny in his life sometime or other.

He says he's been calling my apartment since Wednesday and no answer: what happened to me?

I play it by ear. "Water started to pour down through the ceiling, so I had to clear out till they get it repaired. . . . No, I'm not on a tear. . . . No, there's nobody with me, I'm by myself. . . . Do I? Sound sort of peculiar? No, I'm all right there's nothing the matter, not a thing."

I pass my free hand across the moist glisten on my forehead. It's tough enough to be in a jam, but it's tougher still to be in one and not be able to say you are.

"How did you know I was here? How did you track me to this place? . . . You went down the yellow pages, hotel by hotel, alphabetically. Since three o'clock yesterday afternoon? . . . Something to tell me?"

His new job had come through. He starts on Monday. With a direct line, and two, count 'em, two secretaries, not just one. And the old bunch is giving him a farewell party. A farewell party to end all farewell parties. Sardi's, on 44th. Then they'll move on later to some other place. But they'll wait here at Sardi's for me to catch up. Barb keeps asking, Why isn't your best-man-to-be here with us?

The noise of the party filters through into my ear. Ice clicking like dice in a fast-rolling game. Mixing sticks sounding like tiny tin flutes as they beat against glass. The laughter of girls, the laughter of men. Life is for the living, not the already dead.

"Sure, I'll be there. Sure."

If I say I won't be—and I won't, because I can't—he'll never quit pestering and calling me the rest of the night. So I say that I will, to get off the hook. But how can I go there, drag my trouble before his party, before his friends, before his girl? And if I go, it'll just happen there instead of here. Who wants a grandstand for his downfall? Who wants bleachers for his disgrace?

Johnny's gone now, and the night goes on.

Now the evening's at its noon, its meridian. The outgoing tide has simmered down, and there's a lull—like the calm in the eye of a hurricane—before the reverse tide starts to set in.

The last acts of the three-act plays are now on, and the aftertheater eating places are beginning to fill up with early comers; Danny's and Lindy's—yes, and Horn & Hardart too. Everybody has got where they wanted to go—and that was out somewhere. Now everybody will want to get back where they came from—and that's home somewhere. Or as the coffee-grinder radio, always on the beam, put it at about this point: *New York, New York, it's a helluva town, The Bronx is up, the Battery's down, And the people ride around in a hole in the ground—*

Now the incoming tide rolls in; the hours abruptly switch back to single digits again, and it's a little like the time you put your watch back on entering a different time zone. Now the buses knock off and the subway expresses turn into locals and the locals space themselves far apart; and as Johnny Carson's face hits millions of screens all at one and the same time, the incoming tide reaches its crest and pounds against the shore. There's a sudden splurge, a slew of taxis arriving at the hotel entrance one by one as regularly as though they were on a conveyor belt, emptying out and then going away again.

Then this too dies down, and a deep still sets in. It's an around-the-clock town, but this is the stretch; from now until the garbage-grinding trucks come along and tear the dawn to shreds, it gets as quiet as it's ever going to get.

This is the deep of the night, the dregs, the sediment at the bottom of the coffee cup. The blue hours; when guys' nerves get tauter and women's fears get greater. Now guys and girls make love, or kill each other or sometimes both. And as the windows on the "Late Show" title silhouette light up one by one, the real ones all around go dark. And from now on the silence is broken only by the occasional forlorn hoot of a bogged-down drunk or the gutted-cat squeal of a too sharply swerved axle coming around a turn. Or as Billy Daniels sang it in *Golden Boy: While the city sleeps, And the streets are clear, There's a life that's happening here—*

In the pin-drop silence a taxi comes up with an unaccompanied girl in it. I can tell it's a taxi, I can tell it's a girl, and I can tell she's unaccompanied; I can tell all three just by her introductory remark.

"Benny," she says. "Will you come over and pay this for me?"

Benny is the hotel night-service man. I know his name; he brought drinks up to the room last night.

As the taxi drives away paid, Benny reminds her with aloof dignity, "You didn't give me my cut last week." Nothing personal, strictly business, you understand.

"I had a virus week before last," she explains. "And it took me all last week to pay off on my doctor bills. I'll square it with you tonight." Then she adds apprehensively, "I'm afraid he'll hurt me." Not her doctor, obviously.

"Na, he won't hurt you," Benny reassures.

"How would you know?" she asks, not unreasonably.

Benny culls from his store of call-girl-sponsorship experience. "These big guys never hurt you. They're meek as mice. It's the little shrimps got the sting."

She goes ahead in. A chore is a chore, she figures.

This of course is what is known in hotel-operational jargon as a "personal call." In the earthier slang of the night bellmen and deskmen it is simply a "fix" or a "fix-up." The taxi fare, of course, will go down on the guest's bill, as "Misc." or "Sundries." Which actually is what it is. From my second-floor window I can figure it all out almost without any sound track to go with it.

So much for the recreational side of night life in the upper-bracket-income hotels of Manhattan. And in its root-origins the very word itself is implicit with implication: re-create. Analyze it and you'll see it also means to reproduce. But clever, ingenious Man has managed to sidetrack it into making life more livable.

The wafer of ice riding the surface of my drink has melted freakishly in its middle and not around its edges and now looks like an onion ring. Off in the distance an ambulance starts bansheeing with that new broken-blast siren they use, scalp-crimping as the cries of pain of a partly dismembered hog. Somebody dead in the night? Somebody sick and going to be dead soon? Or maybe somebody going to be alive soon—did she wait too long to start for the hospital?

All of a sudden, with the last sound there's been all night, I can tell they're here. Don't ask me how, I only know they're here. It's beginning at last. No way out, no way aside and no way back.

Being silent is their business, and they know their business well. They make less sound than the dinner cart crunching along the carpeted hall, than Ginny's stifled sob when I gave her that hundred-dollar bill, than the contestants bickering over the taxi. Or that girl who was down there just a little while ago on her errand of fighting loneliness for a fee.

How can I tell that they're here? By the absence of sound more than by its presence. Or I should say by the absence of a complementary sound—the sound that belongs with another sound and yet fails to accompany it.

Like:

There's no sound of arrival, but suddenly two cars are in place down there along the hotel front. They must have come up on the glide, as noiselessly as a sailboat skimming over still water. No sound of tires, no sound of brakes. But there's one sound they couldn't quite obliterate—the cushioned thump of two doors closing after them in quick succession, staccato succession, as they spilled out and siphoned into the building. You can always tell a car door, no other door sounds quite like it.

There's only one other sound, a lesser one, a sort of follow-up: the scratch of a single sole against the abrasive sidewalk as they go hustling in. He either put it down off-balance or swiveled it too acutely in treading at the heels of those in front of him.

Which is a good average, just one to sound off, considering that six or eight pairs of them must have been all going in at the same time and moving fast.

I've sprung to my feet from the very first, and I'm standing there now like an upright slab of ice carved in the outline of a man—burning-cold and slippery-wet and glassy with congealment. I've put out all the lights—they all work on one switch over by the door as you come in. They've probably already seen the lights though if they've marked the window from outside, and anyway, what difference does it make? Lighted up or dark, I'm still here inside the room. It's just some instinct as old as fear: you seek the dark when you hide, you seek the light when the need to hide is gone. All the animals have it too.

Now they're in, and it will take just a few minutes more while they make their arrangements. That's all I have left, a few minutes more. Out of a time allotment that once stretched so far and limitlessly ahead of me. Who short-changed me, I feel like crying out in protest, but I know that nobody did; I short-changed myself.

"It," the heartless little radio jeers, "takes the worry out of being close."

Why is it taking them such a long time? What do they have to do, improvise as they go along? What for? They already knew what they had to do when they set out to come here.

I'm sitting down again now, momentarily; knees too rocky for standing long. Those are the only two positions I have left; no more walking, no more running, no more anything else now. Only stand up and wait or sit down and wait. I need a cigarette terribly bad. It may be a funny time to need one, but I do. I dip my head down between my outspread legs and bring the lighter up from below, so its shine won't glow through the blind-crevices. As I said, it doesn't make sense, because they know I'm here. But I don't want to do anything to quicken them. Even two minutes of grace is better than one. Even one minute is better than none.

Then suddenly my head comes up again, alerted. I drop the

cigarette, still unlit. First I think the little radio has suddenly jumped in tone, started to come on louder and more resonant, as if it were spooked. Until it almost sounds like a car radio out in the open. Then I turn my head toward the window. It is a car radio. It's coming from outside into the room.

And even before I get up and go over to take a look, I think there's something familiar about it, I've heard it before, just like this, just the way it is now. This sounding-board effect, this walloping of the night like a drum, this ricochet of blast and din from side to side of the street, bouncing off the house fronts like a musical handball game.

Then it cuts off short, the after-silence swells up like a balloon ready to pop, and as I squint out, it's standing still down there, the little white car, and Johnny is already out of it and standing alongside.

He's come to take me to the party.

He's parked on the opposite side. He starts to cross over to the hotel. Someone posted in some doorway whistles to attract his attention. I hear it up at the window. Johnny stops, turns to look around, doesn't see anyone.

He's frozen in the position in which the whistle caught him. Head and shoulders turned inquiringly half around, hips and legs still pointed forward. Then a man, some anonymous man, glides up beside him from the street.

I told you he talks loud; on the phone, in a bar, on a street late at night. Every word he says I hear; not a word the other man says.

First, "Who is? What kind of trouble?"

Then, "You must mean somebody else."

Next, "Room 207. Yeah, that's right, 207."

That's my room number.

"How'd you know I was coming here?"

Finally, "You bugged the call I made to him before!"

Then the anonymous man goes back into the shadows, leaving Johnny in mid-street, taking it for granted he'll follow him as he was briefed to do, commanded to do.

But Johnny stands out there, alone and undecided, feet still one way, head and shoulders still the other. And I watch him from the window crevice. And the stakeout watches him from his invisible doorway.

Now a crisis arises. Not in my life, because that's nearly over; but in my illusions.

Will he go to his friend and try to stand by him, or will he let his friend go by?

He can't make it, sure I know that, he can never get in here past them; but he *can* make the try, there's just enough slack for him to do that. There's still half the width of the street ahead of him clear and untrammeled, for him to try to bolt across, before they spring after him and rough him up and fling him back. It's the token of the thing that would count, not the completion.

But it doesn't happen that way, I keep telling myself knowingly and sadly. Only in our fraternity pledges and masonic inductions, our cowboy movies and magazine stories, not in our real-life lives. For, the seventeenth-century humanist to the contrary, each man *is* an island complete unto himself, and as he sinks, the moving feet go on around him, from nowhere to nowhere and with no time to lose. The world is long past the Boy Scout stage of its development; now each man dies as he was meant to die, and as he was born, and as he lived: alone, all alone. Without any God, without any hope, without any record to show for his life.

My throat feels stiff, and I want to swallow but I can't. Watching and waiting to see what my friend will do.

He doesn't move, doesn't make up his mind, for half a minute, and that half a minute seems like an hour. He's doped by what he's been told, I guess. And I keep asking myself while the seconds are ticking off: What would *I* do? If there were me down there, and he were up here: What would *I* do? And I keep trying not to look the answer in the face, though it's staring at me the whole time.

You haven't any right to expect your friends to be larger than yourself, larger than life. Just take them as they are, cut down to average size, and be glad you have them. To drink with, laugh with, borrow money from, lend money to, stay away from their special girls as you want them to stay away from yours, and above all, never break your word to, once it's been given.

And that is all the obligation you have, all you have the right to expect.

The half-minute is up, and Johnny turns, slowly and reluctantly, but he turns, and he goes back to the opposite side of the street. The side opposite to me.

And I knew all along that's what he would do, because I knew all along that's what I would have done too.

I think I hear a voice say slurredly somewhere in the shadows, "That's the smart thing to do," but I'm not sure. Maybe I don't, maybe it's me I hear.

He gets back in the car, shoulders sagging, and keys it on. And as he glides from sight the music seems to start up almost by itself; it's such second nature for him to have it on by now. It fades around the corner building, and then a wisp of it comes back just once more, carried by some cross-current of the wind: *Fools rush in, Where wise men never dare to go*—and then it dies away for good.

I bang my crushed-up fist against the center of my forehead, bring it away, then bang it again. Slow but hard. It hurts to lose a long-term friend, almost like losing an arm. But I never lost an arm, so I really wouldn't know.

Now I can swallow, but it doesn't feel good anymore.

I hear a marginal noise outside in the hall, and I swing around in instant alert. It's easy enough to decipher it. A woman is being taken from her room nearby—in case the going gets too rough around here in my immediate vicinity, I suppose.

I hear them tap, and then she comes out and accompanies them to safety. I hear the slap-slap of her bedroom slippers, like the soft little hands of children applauding in a kindergarten, as she goes hurrying by with someone. Several someones. You can't hear them, only her, but I know they're with her. I even hear the soft *sch* of her silk wrapper or kimono as it rustles past. A noticeable whiff of sachet drifts in through the door seam. She must have taken a bath and powdered herself liberally just moments ago.

Probably a nice sort of woman, unused to violence or emergencies of this sort, unsure of what to bring along or how to comport herself.

"I left my handbag in there," I hear her remark plaintively as she goes by. "Do you think it'll be all right to leave it there?"

Somebody's wife, come to meet him in the city and waiting for him to join her. Long ago I used to like that kind of woman. Objectively, of course, not close-up.

After she's gone, another brief lull sets in. This one is probably the last. But what good is a lull? It's only a breathing spell in which to get more frightened. Because anticipatory fear is always twice as strong as present fear. Anticipatory fear has both fears in it at once—the anticipatory one and the one that comes simultaneously with the dread happening itself. Present fear only has the one, because by that time anticipation is over.

I switch on the light for a moment, to see my way to a drink. The one I had is gone—just what used to be ice is sloshing colorlessly in the bottom of the glass. Then when I put the recharged glass down again, empty, it seems to pull me after it, as if it weighed so much I couldn't let go of it from an upright position. Don't ask me why this is, I don't know. Probably simple loss of equilibrium for a second, due to the massive infusion of alcohol.

Then with no more warning, no more waiting, with no more of anything, it begins. It gets under way at last.

There is a mild-mannered knuckle rapping at the door. They use my name. A voice, mild-mannered also, says in a conciliatory way, "Come out, please. We want to talk to you." "Punctilious," I guess, would be a better word for it. The etiquette of the forcible entry, of the break-in. They're so considerate, so deferential, so attentive to all the niceties. Hold your head steady, please, we don't want to nick your chin while we're cutting your throat.

I don't answer.

I don't think they expected me to. If I had answered, it would have astonished them, thrown them off their timing for a moment.

The mild-voiced man leaves the door and somebody else takes his place. I can sense the shifting over more by intuition than by actual hearing.

A wooden toolbox or carryall of some sort settles down noisily on the floor outside the door. I can tell it's wooden, not by its floor impact but by the "settling" sound that accompanies it, as if a considerable number of loose and rolling objects in it are chinking against its insides. Nails and bolts and awls and screwdrivers and the like. That tells me that it's a kit commonly used by carpenters and locksmiths and their kind.

They're going to take the lock off bodily from the outside.

A cold surge goes through me that I can't describe. It isn't blood. It's too numbing and heavy and cold for that. And it breaks through the skin surface, which blood doesn't ordinarily do without a wound, and emerges into innumerable sting pin pricks all over me. An ice-sweat.

I can see him (not literally, but just as surely as if I could), down on one knee, and scared, probably as scared as I am myself, pressing as far back to the side out of the direct line of the door as he can, while the others, bunched together farther back, stand ready to cover him, to pile on me and bring me down if I should suddenly break out and rush him.

And the radio tells me sarcastically to "Light up, you've got a good thing going."

I start backing away, with a sleepwalker's fixity, staring at the door as I retreat, or staring at where I last saw it, for I can't see it in the dark. What good would it do to stay close to it, for I can't hold it back, I can't stop it from opening. And as I go back step after step, my tongue keeps tracking the outside outline of my lips, as if I wondered what they were and what they were there for.

A very small sound begins. I don't know how to put it. Like someone twisting a small metal cap to open a small medicine bottle, but continuously, without ever getting it off. He's started already. He's started coming in.

It's terrible to hear that little thing move. As if it were animate, had a life of its own. Terrible to hear it move and to know that a hostile agency, a hostile presence, just a few feet away from me, is what is making it move. Such a little thing, there is almost nothing smaller, only the size of a pinhead perhaps, and yet to create such terror and to be capable of bringing about such a shattering end-result: entry, capture, final loss of reason, and the darkness that is worse than death. All from a little thing like that, turning slowly, secretively, but avidly, in the lockplate on the door, on the door into my room.

I have to get out of here. Out. I have to push these walls apart, these foursquare tightly seamed walls, and make space wide enough to run in, and keep running through it, running and running through it, running and running through it, and never stopping. Until I drop. And then still running on and on, inside my head. Like a watch with its case smashed open and lying on the ground, but with the works still going inside it. Or like a cockroach when you knock it over on its back so that it can't ambulate anymore, but its legs still go spiraling around in the air.

The window. They're at the door, but the window—that way out is still open. I remember when I checked in here the small hours of Wednesday, I didn't ask to be given a room on the second floor, they just happened to give me one. Then when I saw it later that day in the light, I realized the drop to the ground from one of the little semicircular stone ledges outside the windows wouldn't be dangerous, especially if you held a pillow in front of you, and remembered to keep your chin tilted upward as you went over. Just a sprawling shake-up fall maybe, that's all.

I pull at the blind cords with both hands, and it spasms upward with a sound like a lot of little twigs being stepped on and broken. I push up the window sash and assume a sitting position on the sill, then swing my legs across and I'm out in the clear, out in the open night.

The little stone apron has this spiked iron rail guard around it, with no space left on the outer side of it to plant your feet before you go over. You have to straddle it, which makes for tricky going. Still, necessity can make you dexterous, terror can make you agile. I won't go back inside for the pillow, there isn't time. I'll take the leap neat.

The two cars that brought them here are below, and for a moment, only for a moment, they look empty, dark and still and empty, standing bumper to bumper against the curb. Someone gives a warning whistle—a lip whistle, I mean, not a metal one. I don't know who, I don't know where, somewhere around. Then an angry, ugly, smoldering, car-bound orange moon starts up, lightens to yellow, then brightens to the dazzling white of a laundry-detergent commercial. The operator guiding it slants it too high at first, and it lands over my head. Like a halo. *Some* halo and *some time* for a halo. Then he brings it down and it hits me as if someone had belted me full across the face with a talcum-powder puff. You can't see through it, you can't see around it.

Shoe leather comes padding from around the corner—maybe the guy that warded off Johnny—and stops directly under me. I sense somehow he's afraid, just as I am. That won't keep him from doing what he has to do, because he's got the backing on his side. But he doesn't like this. I shield my eyes from the light on one side, and I can see his anxious face peering up at me. All guys are scared of each other, didn't you know that? I'm not the only one. We're all born afraid.

I can't shake the light off. It's like ghostly flypaper. It's like slapstick-thrown yoghurt. It clings to me whichever way I turn.

I hear his voice talking to me from below. Very near and clear. As if we were off together by ourselves somewhere, just chatting, the two of us.

"Go back into your room. We don't want you to get hurt." And then a second time: "Go back in. You'll only get hurt if you stand out here like this."

I'm thinking, detached, as in a dream: I didn't know they were this considerate. Are they always this considerate? When I was a kid back in the forties, I used to go to those tough-guy movies a lot. Humphrey Bogart, Jimmy Cagney. And when they had a guy penned in, they used to be tough about it, snarling: "Come on out of there, yuh rat, we've got yuh covered!" I wonder what has changed them? Maybe it's just that time has moved on. This is the sixties now.

What's the good of jumping now? Where is there to run to now? And the light teases my eyes. I see all sorts of interlocked and colored soap bubbles that aren't there.

It's more awkward getting back inside than it was getting out. And with the light on me, and them watching me, there's a self-consciousness that was missing in my uninhibited outward surge. I have to straighten out one leg first and dip it into the room toes forward, the way you test the water in a pool before you jump in. Then the other leg, and then I'm in. The roundness of the light beam is broken into long thin tatters as the blind rolls down over it, but it still stays on out there.

There are only two points of light in the whole room—I mean, in addition to the indirect reflection through the blind. Which gives off a sort of phosphorescent haziness—two points so small that if you didn't know they were there and looked for them, you wouldn't see them. And small as both are, one is even smaller than the other. One is the tiny light in the radio, which, because the lens shielding the dial is convex, glows like a miniature orange scimitar. I go over to it to turn it off. It can't keep the darkness away anymore; the darkness is here.

"Here's to the losers," the radio is saying. "Here's to them all—"

The other point of light is over by the door. It's in the door itself. I go over there close to it, peering with my head bowed, as if I were mourning inconsolably. And I am. One of the four tiny screwheads set into the corners of the oblong plate that holds the lock is gone, is out now, and if you squint at an acute angle you can see a speck of orange light shining through it from the hall. Then, while I'm standing there, something falls soundlessly, glances off the top of my shoe with no more weight than a grain of gravel, and there's a second speck of orange light at the opposite upper corner of the plate. Two more to go now. Two and a half minutes of deft work left, maybe not even that much.

What careful planning, what painstaking attention to detail, goes into extinguishing a man's life! Far more than the hit-or-miss, haphazard circumstances of igniting it.

I can't get out the window, I can't go out the door. But there *is* a way out, a third way. I can escape inward. If I can't get away from them on the outside, I can get away from them on the inside.

You're not supposed to have those things. But when you have money you can get anything, in New York. They were on a prescription, but that was where the money came in—getting the prescription. I remember now. Some doctor gave it to me—sold it to me—long ago. I don't remember why or when. Maybe when fear first came between the two of us and I couldn't reach her anymore.

I came across it in my wallet on Wednesday, after I first came in here, and I sent it out to have it filled, knowing that this night would come. I remember the bellboy bringing it to the door afterward in a small bright-green paper wrapping that some pharmacists use. But where is it now?

I start a treasure hunt of terror, around the inside of the room in the dark. First into the clothes closet, wheeling and twirling among the couple of things I have hanging in there like a hopped-up discothèque dancer, dipping in and out of pockets, patting some of them between my hands to see if they're flat or hold a bulk. As if I were calling a little pet dog to me by clapping my hands to it. A little dog who is hiding away from me in there, a little dog called death.

Not in there. Then the drawers of the dresser, spading them in and out, fast as a card shuffle. A telephone directory, a complimentary shaving kit (if you're a man), a complimentary manicure kit (if you're a girl).

They must be down to the last screwhead by now.

Then around and into the bathroom, while the remorseless dismantling at the door keeps on. It's all white in there, white as my face must be. It's dark, but you can still see that it's white against the dark. Twilight-colored tiles. I don't put on the light to help me find them, because there isn't enough time left; the lights in here are fluorescent and take a few moments to come on, and by that time they'll be in here.

There's a catch phrase that you all must have heard at one time or another. You walk into a room or go over toward a group. Someone turns and says with huge emphasis: "*There* he is." As though you were the most important one of all. (And you're not.) As though you were the one they were just talking about. (And they weren't.) As though you were the only one that mattered. (And you're not.) It's a nice little tribute, and it don't cost anyone a cent.

And so I say this to them now, as I find them on the top glass slab of the shallow medicine cabinet: *There* you are. Glad to see you—you're important in my scheme of things.

As I bend for some running water, the shower curtain twines around me in descending spiral folds—don't ask me how, it must have been ballooning out. I sidestep like a drunken Roman staggering around his toga, pulling half the curtain down behind me while the pins holding it to the rod about tinkle like little finger cymbals, dragging part of it with me over one shoulder, while I bend over the basin to drink.

No time to rummage for a tumbler. It's not there anyway—I'd been using it for the rye. So I use the hollow of one hand for a scoop, pumping it up and down to my open mouth and alternating with one of the nuggets from the little plastic container I'm holding uncapped in my other hand. I've been called a fast drinker at times. Johnny used to say—never mind that now.

I only miss one—that falls down in the gap between me and the basin to the floor. That's a damned good average. There were twelve of them in there, and I remember the label read: *Not more than three to be taken during any twenty-four-hour period.* In other words, I've just killed myself three times, with a down payment on a fourth time for good measure.

I grab the sides of the basin suddenly and bend over it, on the point of getting them all out of me again in rebellious upheaval. *I* don't want to, but they do. I fold both arms around my middle, hugging myself, squeezing myself, to hold them down. They stay put. They've caught on, taken hold. Only a pump can get them out now. And after a certain point of no return (I don't know how long that is), once they start being assimilated into the bloodstream, not even a pump can get them out.

Only a little brine taste shows up in my mouth, and gagging a little, still holding my middle, I go back into the other room. Then I sit down to wait. To see which of them gets to me first.

It goes fast now, like a drumbeat quickening to a climax. An upended foot kicks at the door, and it suddenly spanks inward with a firecracker sound. The light comes fizzing through the empty oblong like gushing carbonation, too sudden against the dark to ray clearly at first.

They rush in like the splash of a wave that suddenly has splattered itself all around the room. Then the lights are on, and they're on all four sides of me, and they're holding me hard and fast, quicker than one eyelid can touch the other in a blink.

My arms go behind me into the cuffless convolutions of a strait jacket. Then as though unconvinced that this is enough precaution, someone standing back there has looped the curve of his arm around my throat and the back of the chair, and holds it there in tight restraint. Not choking-tight as in a mugging, but ready to pin me back if I should try to heave out of the chair.

Although the room is blazing-bright, several of them are holding flashlights, all lit and centered inward on my face from the perimeter around me, like the spokes of a blinding wheel. Probably to disable me still further by their dazzle. One beam, more skeptical than the others, travels slowly up and down my length, seeking out any bulges that might possibly spell a concealed offensive weapon. My only weapon is already used, and it was a defensive one.

I roll my eyes toward the ceiling to try and get away from the lights, and one by one they blink and go out.

There they stand. The assignment is over, completed. To me it's my life, to them just another incident. I don't know how many there are. The man in the coffin doesn't count the number who have come to the funeral. But as I look at them, as my eyes go from face to face, on each one I read the key to what the man is thinking.

One face, soft with compunction: Poor guy, I might have been him, he might have been me.

One, hard with contempt: Just another of those creeps something went wrong with along the way.

Another, flexing with hate: I wish he'd shown some fight; I'd like an excuse to—

Still another, rueful with impatience: I'd like to get this over so I could call her unexpectedly and catch her in a lie; I bet she never stayed home tonight like she told me she would.

And yet another, blank with indifference, its thoughts a thousand miles away: And what's a guy like Yastrzemski got, plenty of others guy haven't got too? It's just the breaks, that's all—

And I say to my own thoughts dejectedly: Why weren't you that clear, that all-seeing, the other night, that terrible other night. It might have done you more good then.

There they stand. And there I am, seemingly in their hands but slowly slipping away from them.

They don't say anything. I'm not aware of any of them saying anything. They're waiting for someone to give them further orders. Or maybe waiting for something to come and take me away.

One of them hasn't got a uniform on or plainsclothes either like the rest. He has on the white coat that is my nightmare and my horror. And in the crotch of one arm he is upending two long poles intertwined with canvas.

The long-drawn-out death within life. The burial-alive of the mind, covering it over with fresh graveyard earth each time it tries to struggle through to the light. In this kind of death you never finish dying.

In back of them, over by the door, I see the top of someone's head appear, then come forward, slowly, fearfully forward. Different from their short-clipped, starkly outlined heads, soft and rippling in contour, and gentle. And as she comes forward into full-face view, I see who she is.

She comes up close to me, stops, and looks at me.

"Then it wasn't—you?" I whisper.

She shakes her head slightly with a mournful trace of smile. "It wasn't me," she whispers back, without taking them into it, just between the two of us, as in the days before. "I didn't go there to meet you. I didn't like the way you sounded."

But someone was there, I came across someone there. Someone whose face became hers in my waking dream. The scarf, the blood on the scarf. It's not my blood, it's not my scarf. It must belong to someone else. Someone they haven't even found yet, don't know even about yet.

The preventive has come too late.

She moves a step closer and bends toward me.

"Careful—watch it," a voice warns her.

"He won't hurt me," she answers understandingly without taking her eyes from mine. "We used to be in love."

Used to? Then that's why I'm dying. Because I still am. And you aren't anymore.

She bends and kisses me, on the forehead, between the eyes. Like a sort of last rite.

And in that last moment, as I'm straining upward to find her lips, as the light is leaving my eyes, the whole night passes before my mind, the way they say your past life does when you're drowning: the waiter, the night maid, the taxi argument, the call girl, Johnny—it all meshes into start-to-finish continuity. Just like in a story. An organized, step-by-step, timetabled story.

This story.

Endnotes

1. Nevins Jr., Francis M. *Cornell Woolrich: First You Dream, Then You Die.* The Mysterious Press, 1988.

2. Ibid.

3. Ibid.

4. Diliberto, Michael R. *Looking through the Rear Window: A Review of the United States Supreme Court Decision in Stewart v. Abend.* 12 Loy. L.A. Ent. L. Rev. 299, 1992.

CORNELL WOOLRICH

George Hopley-Woolrich (4 December 1903—25 September 1968) is one of America's best crime and noir writers who sometimes wrote under the pseudonyms William Irish and George Hopley. He's often compared to other celebrated crime writers of his day, Dashiell Hammett, Erle Stanley Gardner and Raymond Chandler.

Born in New York City, his parents separated when he was young and he lived in Mexico for nearly a decade with his father before returning to New York City to live with his mother, Claire Attalie Woolrich.

He attended New York's Columbia University but left school in 1926 without graduating when his first novel, *Cover Charge*, was published. *Cover Charge* was one of six of his novels that he credits as inspired by the work of F. Scott Fitzgerald. Woolrich soon turned to pulp and detective fiction, often published under his pseudonyms. His best known story today is his 1942 *"It Had to be Murder"* for the simple reason that it was adapted into the 1954 Alfred Hitchcock movie *Rear Window* starring James Stewart and Grace Kelly. It was remade as a television film by Christopher Reeve in 1998.

Woolrich was a homosexual but in 1930, while working as a screenwriter in Los Angeles, he married Violet Virginia Blackton

(1910-65), daughter of silent film producer J. Stuart Blackton. They separated after three months and the marriage was annulled in 1933.

Woolrich returned to New York where he and his mother moved into the Hotel Marseilles (Broadway and West 102nd Street). He lived there until her death on October 6, 1957, which prompted his move to the Hotel Franconia (20 West 72nd Street). In later years he socialized on occasion in Manhattan but alcoholism and an amputated leg, caused by an infection from wearing a shoe too tight which he left untreated, turned him into a recluse. Thus, he did not attend the New York premiere of Truffaut's film based on his novel *The Bride Wore Black* in 1968 and, shortly thereafter, died weighing only 89 pounds. He is interred in the Ferncliff Cemetery in Hartsdale, New York.

Woolrich bequeathed his estate to Columbia University to endow scholarships in his mother's memory for journalism students.

Publisher's Note

The Author and Renaissance Literary & Talent have attempted to create this book with the highest quality conversion from the original edition. However, should you notice any errors within this text please e-mail corrections@renaissancemgmt.net with the title/author in the subject line and the corrections in the body of the email. Thank you for your help and patronage.